A
Child's
Goodbye

BOOKS BY ALI MERCER

Lost Daughter
His Secret Family
My Mother's Choice
The Marriage Lie
The Family I Lost

Ali Mercer

A
Child's
Goodbye

Bookouture

Published by Bookouture in 2023

An imprint of Storyfire Ltd.
Carmelite House
50 Victoria Embankment
London EC4Y 0DZ

www.bookouture.com

ISBN: 978-1-83790-159-3
eBook ISBN: 978-1-83790-158-6

For Nanu, Luli and Helen

PROLOGUE

CALLIE

Summer 2002

Finally, she'd done it. She'd confessed. Though she probably couldn't have chosen a worse time, given everything he had been through lately. Plus he was upset about his ex-girlfriend choosing to stay away, treating him like a pariah. What on earth could he possibly have done to deserve that?

Though maybe it was because his ex was still a little in love with him. Yes, that must be it. If that was the reason, then given her own feelings for Reuben, Callie could definitely understand.

In spite of the noise of the party coming from the house behind them it was very quiet. It was the kind of hush that falls when you watch a coin spinning and wait to see which way it is going to land.

At least he hadn't bolted yet. But probably he'd make his excuses any minute now, and escape back into the party, as if she'd never said anything at all...

'Look,' he said after a while. 'It's a beautiful night.'

He was looking up at the sky, and she did too and saw the stars. Many, many stars, tiny, indomitable pinpricks in the dark, and the more she looked, the more stars she could see and the brighter they seemed.

So he wasn't about to walk away. That was something. That was more than she would have dared hope for, and a lot more than she had any right to expect.

He carried on standing there, studying the stars, and so did she. Her heartbeat slowed. To her surprise, she began to feel at ease. It was as if they had magically leapfrogged the need for conversation and reached some kind of understanding.

The air was cooling fast, and as if a shutter had opened and closed and presented her with the two of them in a different scene, she pictured them together at Christmas, with more than a chill in the air – frost on the grass, perhaps, and a tree inside with presents underneath it.

'Did you know,' he said, 'that when you look at the night sky, you're looking at history? The light of the stars you see has been travelling towards the earth for millions and millions of years. Some of those stars might not even exist any more. They might have burnt away to nothingness, and be all dead and dark. But the light is still real. The light is like a time traveller.'

'The light doesn't stop just because the star has gone,' she said.

She glanced across at him and their eyes met. They were standing quite close, almost shoulder to shoulder. And then, as if it was the most natural thing in the world, he reached out and took her hand.

In the years to come, this conversation, and that touch, would make it impossible for her to blame him for what happened later.

He had told her something she'd needed to hear years before, that no one else had said – that it was OK to carry on loving someone who was no longer there, and for as long as you did, they were still with you. And whenever she let herself remember, she would feel grateful to him.

PART ONE

THE ACCIDENT

Callie, Billy and Reuben

2014

ONE

CALLIE

The email from Sonia arrived at quarter to three, which was exactly when she was due to leave to pick Billy up from school. She should have ignored it and got ready to go, but the subject line caught her eye: *Party arrangements*.

Typical of Sonia, who was married to Callie's boss, to send a personal message to her work email address.

As she scanned the message and took in what Sonia was saying, her heart began to race as if she was facing a physical attack.

I feel like maybe we've got into a rut of always doing a joint party, but as time goes on, the boys have different friendship groups and different interests, and just because we're friends it isn't fair to always expect them to do something together...

Callie felt it as Billy would feel it – as rejection, pure and simple. Nothing hurt her more than the prospect of Billy being hurt. And here was Sonia, one of her oldest friends, saying that she didn't want Billy to share his eleventh birthday party with her son, even though they'd already agreed a date, and they always did it this way. It made sense, with the boys' birthdays being so close together.

How could Sonia do this to her, and to Billy? And in this cowardly way, by email, so she wouldn't have to face Callie's reaction when she told her.

Of course it goes without saying that Billy's still invited...

Callie shut down her email and her PC with trembling hands and stooped to swap the court shoes she wore to work for the trainers she kept in her desk drawer so she could speedwalk to school.

Mustn't keep Billy waiting. She'd have to act normal, hold off saying anything till they were safely back home and away from prying eyes, then try to find a way to break it to him as gently as possible.

She was furious with Sonia. Absolutely, murderously furious. She could *kill* her.

What a way to behave, after all these years of friendship. And Sonia knew how vulnerable Billy was, and how difficult things had been... Had Callie downplayed what was going on too much? Or had Sonia just decided that none of that mattered, compared to what she wanted for her own child?

She was going to have to calm down before she spoke to Sonia, otherwise she was bound to say something she'd regret. She needed to hang on to this job, and couldn't afford to do anything to damage her relationship with Julian, who wasn't a bad boss at the end of the day.

It wasn't easy to find part-time jobs that fitted into school hours. Nothing was easy as the single parent of a vulnerable and anxious child. She was willing to put up with pretty much anything if it was for Billy's sake, and she could certainly swallow her anger, and her pride. After all, she'd had plenty of practice.

At the end of the day, Billy's happiness was all that mattered. She'd just have to find a way to make it up to him.

Resigning herself to sprinting all the way to school, she grabbed her handbag and tore through the office, attracting startled glances from her full-time colleagues who were still at their desks. She raced down the stairs and out of the building, barely pausing to say goodbye to the receptionist.

It was now five to three. She'd turn up red-faced and panting and everybody would stare at her, but she was still in with a chance of being there on time. Sometimes Billy was late coming out. She just needed a little bit of luck to come her way and then she'd make it all right...

The traffic was bad, as it always was when she finished work. Kettlebridge was prone to congestion, being a small, ancient market town with a road system that had originally been laid down in the days of horses and carts, and it was the school run rush hour. Today the main road outside the office was even worse than normal, almost at a standstill, and the faces of the drivers were gloomy and irritable. If she'd been going by car instead of on foot, she'd have had absolutely no chance at all of making it on time.

She could save herself a minute or two by nipping straight across to the road that led up to school, rather than going down to the crossing. A motorbike was moving along the middle of the road, overtaking the stationary traffic at a pace that wasn't much faster than walking. She stopped to let it pass, then struck out for the far side of the road.

But then something was racing towards her. A cyclist, a kid on a bike, and there was no time to get out of the way.

She took in the round o of his shocked face and the screeching of his brakes and the skittering sound of his tyres on the tarmac, and then everything crashed and broke and the ground flew up to hit her.

In the instant before she blacked out she pictured Billy alone in the playground, waiting helplessly for her as all the other children disappeared to go home. She just had time for one last desperate thought: *who's going to take care of him now?*

TWO

BILLY

It wasn't too bad waiting on your own at the end of the day as long as nobody noticed. The trick was to find the right spot, though all the possible options had their downsides. Standing out in the open meant you had plenty of scope to move away if necessary, but also made you an obvious target. On the other hand, if you stayed in the shadow of the school buildings, where you were less conspicuous, you were more likely to be cornered. It was a toss-up. There really was no right answer, unlike in the tests they were always having to do at school.

He was good at getting things right in the tests: everybody knew that. He was less good at getting things right in the playground. But as Mum always said, all he could do was his best.

There was still no sign of her. Perhaps she'd been held up. He decided to move away from the classroom door and wait near the wooden pagoda in the middle of the playground. It was a sunny day and the pagoda cast a bit of shade, so it seemed like an obvious choice, and one that his mum wouldn't question. That was the other problem with choosing somewhere that offered him some cover: it made it harder for Mum to see him.

'*There* you are,' she'd say. 'What are you lurking there for?

You aren't an undercover agent, you know. You don't need to hide.'

But he *did* need to hide, and there was no way he could explain that to her, although it was less important to stay out of sight now, at the end of the school day, than it was at breaktime, when there was much more chance of something nasty happening.

At going-home time the other kids tended to be in a good mood, which helped, and also, the playground was crowded with parents, mostly mums, at least some of whom would be likely to intervene if anybody picked on him. Plus the year sixes were allowed to walk home by themselves, and most of them took off as quickly as possible.

He should have been walking home by himself too, by rights. But he didn't, because Mum said there was no rush, and he could do it when he was ready. And even though it was a bit embarrassing that she still came to collect him, he was glad she did. Otherwise he'd just be a target the whole way from the school gate to his front door.

He glanced down at his watch, which Mum had got him for Christmas. He'd wanted one like Jack's, and she'd shown him this one online and had asked apologetically if it would be all right, and he'd realised immediately that she'd picked it out because it was cheaper than Jack's and they couldn't afford one the same. So of course he had said it was perfect. And he did think it was even better than Jack's, actually.

Quarter past three. *Still* no sign of Mum.

Usually she was there waiting when he came out, even if she'd had to run all the way. But there had been one time when she hadn't made it till the playground was almost empty, and he was beginning to worry about being the last child left. He really, really hoped that wasn't about to happen again. His heart was already beginning to speed up and flutter the way it did when his anxiety set in.

He breathed as slowly and deeply as he could without attracting attention to himself and willed her to appear. It didn't work. Of course it didn't, because wanting something didn't make it happen, not outside fairy stories and comic books. He was just going to have to carry on waiting.

Her boss had probably made her stay late for some stupid, pointless reason, the way teachers did sometimes. Julian was all right, but a bit... out of it. If he was a teacher he'd be vague and distracted and his class would mess around, and then he'd try to make up for it by being strict and handing out detentions, and everyone would hate him. And if Sonia, Mum's friend who Julian was married to, was a teacher, her classes would run her ragged and she'd look desperate all the time.

Julian and Sonia weren't terrible people, as far as he could tell. They just weren't the kind of people you particularly wanted in charge. The big mystery was how they could be so blind to what Jack was really like. How could they not know, when Jack was their son?

Perhaps they didn't want to see. They probably loved him, and that might be difficult to keep up if they knew him a little better.

Mum always behaved as if going to Sonia and Julian's big house and being allowed to play with Jack's toys was a treat, and it might have been if only Jack hadn't been there too. But even when they were younger, Jack had always been exactly the kind of person who would accidentally-on-purpose knock over the Lego Death Star you'd spent ages making, and then break it a little bit more as he made a show of picking it up.

Jack was standing at a safe distance, talking to a little huddle of boys and girls. Oh, no... he'd spotted Billy. Almost as if he'd been able to hear his thoughts. And now he was coming over, swaggering towards him.

This was not good. This was not good *at all*. The other kids were watching, and Jack was bound to try and act hard to show off to them.

Billy's stomach lurched. There was nowhere for him to retreat: he was for it now. He closed his eyes and wished again, as hard as he could, for Mum to appear. But when he opened his eyes again Jack was the only person he could see.

'Where's your mum?' Jack said, scuffing the toe of his shoe on the ground and then looking up at Billy with a lopsided grin. He made it sound as if having a mum was somehow ridiculous, and something that Billy should have the good grace to be embarrassed about.

'She's coming,' Billy said.

He wanted to sound defiant and cool, like Han Solo, but it was difficult to sound like that when you were in a playground talking about your mother. Problem was, someone like Jack didn't back off when he scented weakness: he closed in on it. That was what Jack was like – ruthless. That was what the world seemed to be like, apart from home, which was the only place Billy really liked to be.

'Oh,' Jack said, and pulled a face as if this was surprising to hear. He looked around and shrugged. 'Not here yet, is she?'

'Where's *your* mum?' Billy said, trying for defiance again. Even though Jack didn't live far from school he did a lot of after-school activities, and Sonia was often in her Range Rover some-where close to the school gates at the end of the day, waiting to pick him up and whisk him off to cricket practice or tennis or whatever.

'She's not getting me today,' Jack said. 'I'm going to Zeke's house for a sleepover.'

'Oh.'

'Do you want to come?'

Billy stared at him, trying to work out the right answer. Before he could figure it out, Jack said, 'Well, tough, because you aren't invited. Nobody wants *you* around.' Then he reached forward and gave Billy a good hard shove, so that he staggered back against the wooden railing around the edge of the pagoda.

'What did you do that for?' Billy said, righting himself.

'What did you do that for?' Jack echoed, in a mocking, sing-song voice.

Suddenly Billy saw himself as Jack must see him: as a loser. An idiot. Someone to be treated with disgust, the way you would a slug or a fly or some other creature you wouldn't want around.

He clenched his fists, but kept them behind his back. He wasn't frightened of Jack, not really. He was humiliated. What he was most frightened of was that he might cry. He could feel the tears looming like a threat, and he knew that if he cried right now, on top of everything else, he'd be finished. He wouldn't just be a loser. He'd be a laughing-stock.

Jack looked round again, and Billy realised with a sick feeling in the pit of his stomach that he was checking to see if any grown-ups were watching. Then Jack reached forward, grabbed Billy's glasses and pulled them right off his face, dropped them on the ground and stamped on them.

The whole thing happened so quickly that Billy barely had any time to react. His whole body had frozen. And then Jack stooped and scooped up the glasses and offered them to Billy with a leering smile.

'You want to be more careful,' he said.

Hating himself, Billy held out his hand and took the glasses. One of the lenses had popped out, and the frame was twisted. It might be possible to mend them, but he wouldn't be able to wear them in the meantime.

Suddenly Jack leaned in again, even closer this time, much too close for comfort. Billy could see his freckles, the small golden hairs of his eyebrows where they met over the bridge of his nose, and the chip on the corner of one of his teeth.

'Stay away from me, OK?' Jack said, and prodded him in the

chest. 'You and me are not friends. I don't care if our mums know each other, or if your mum works for my dad. That's got nothing to do with it. And I don't want you coming to my birthday party.'

'How can I not come? It's a joint party,' Billy said.

'Not any more, it isn't. My mum still wants me to invite you. But nobody actually wants you to come. So don't. Say you don't want to. Got it?'

'OK,' Billy said, and managed a small shrug, as if he really didn't care.

Jack spun on his heel and walked nonchalantly back to rejoin his group, his hands deep in his pockets. Technically keeping your hands in your pockets was against the school rules, for reasons that no one had ever explained – probably because it was one of those ridiculous rules that was impossible to justify. But Jack was the kind of person who could keep his hands in his pockets and get away with it, rules or no rules.

Billy shrank back into the shadow of the pagoda to make himself as close to invisible as possible, and dipped his head to examine his glasses. He heard Jack say something and laugh, and sensed that some of the people Jack was with were turning to look at him. Were they curious or hostile? Billy couldn't be sure. Anyway, he had better not look back. Sometimes that just made things worse.

A small, cowardly, terrible thought presented itself to him. Maybe, if something had happened to his mum, Jack would be nice to him again. Or at least take pity on him and leave him alone.

THREE

REUBEN

He wouldn't normally have found himself down the pub on a Wednesday afternoon, but what was the point in being self-employed if you couldn't have the occasional afternoon off? Anyway, it was Elsa's idea, and she needed cheering up. Plus it was a beautiful summer day, the kind that invites you to step out of your normal routine and sit in the sunshine.

If she hadn't started asking him uncomfortable questions about children, it might have all been fine.

Of course she was well within her rights to ask. It was inevitable that the subject was going to come up one day, if they carried on seeing each other long enough. And it was equally inevitable that she was going to find his response evasive. And that, soon after that, she'd have second thoughts about whether she wanted to be with him at all.

He didn't want to be that guy... the shady guy, the one who was less than honest. But how could he be anything else when the truth was shady too, and he still couldn't bear to think about the things that had gone on all those years ago in his own child-hood home, in the village where he had grown up, and that he'd seen with his own eyes?

But to start with, everything was fine, and there was no reason to believe it would soon be otherwise.

The pub was surprisingly full, considering the time of day, but when he brought back their drinks from the bar he saw that Elsa had managed to find a decent table, outside in the beer garden but in the shade.

'To the future,' he said as he settled down and raised his glass to her.

Elsa raised her eyebrows as if to suggest the possibility of disagreeing with him, and lifted her vodka and slimline tonic to clink with his beer.

'To being made redundant,' she said.

'There's no way you'll be out of work for long,' he said. He wanted to sound encouraging (and he happened to believe it was true – Elsa was smart, ambitious, going places.) He hoped it wouldn't come across as patronising.

Elsa shrugged.

He said, 'You know, lots of people, when they look back, say redundancy was the best thing that ever happened to them. Once they've got over the shock.'

'In your vast experience,' she said drily.

She was seven years younger than him, nearly half a generation, as she sometimes pointed out. It wasn't all that big an age gap, not really, but still, sometimes he found himself talking to her in a way that emphasised it, as if he were an older brother or even a kindly uncle.

'I just think you're going to get yourself something better,' he said. 'You wait and see.'

Elsa gave a tiny shrug. She reached for his packet of cigarettes and lighter and helped herself without asking.

'My flatmate's having a baby,' she said.

'Oh! Well, congratulations. Er... which one?'

Embarrassingly, off the top of his head, he wasn't totally sure about her flatmates' names.

'Georgia.'

At least he knew who that was. Georgia was an ex-model, frail-looking, pretty and thin. She didn't come across as obviously maternal, but what did he know? He'd learned long ago not to trust his own judgement.

'So, uh, the dad's sticking around, is he?'

Elsa exhaled irritably and tapped her cigarette in the direction of the ashtray but missed, scattering ash on the surface of the table.

'What does it matter if he does or doesn't? She can do it without him. This isn't the 1950s, you know.'

'Sure.'

'Anyway, she's probably better off without him. Nobody needs a deadbeat dad.'

'No. Guess not. So you'll be looking for a new flatmate, then.'

'Not yet. She's got another six months to go.'

Elsa stubbed out her half-smoked cigarette, then rested her hands palm down on the table and studied him as if they were at a card table and she was waiting to see what he'd turn over.

'I guess you're one of those people who never wanted kids,' she said.

Wanted. Past tense. As if the chance to become a father had already come and gone, and was behind him. As if it was something he would never have. Maybe she was right.

He could point out that he was still young, only in his thirties, and still had plenty of time for all that. On the face of it, that would be true, but it probably wouldn't satisfy her. She looked ready to accuse him of something, but of what exactly?

He could say, *I guess I never really thought about it.* But that would be an outright lie. It took effort not to think about it. And she deserved better than to be fobbed off like that.

Had he never wanted kids? And if so, did he still feel that way? He didn't know how to answer that. It was a topic he automatically shied away from. It was easier to have her think he was too selfish to become a family man, or not ready yet, or just not cut out for it at all, than for her to understand how he really felt – the mix of hurt and bitterness and regret and hatred, with a dash of self-doubt and self-loathing thrown in.

Instead he said, 'Do *you* want kids?'

She shrugged. 'Not right now.' Then: 'I guess what I'm picking up from you, Reuben, is that sure, you might want kids with someone one day, but you can't ever imagine wanting them with me.'

'Oh, Elsa, no,' he said helplessly. 'That wasn't what I was thinking at all.'

'Then what *were* you thinking?' Her face quivered as if she'd been struck by a sudden urge to cry. 'Do you even care about me at all?'

'Of course I do,' he said. But he could see she didn't believe him.

She knocked back a bit more of her vodka and tonic, as if in need of reinforcement before a challenge, then set down the glass and looked up at him. 'So who's Callie?'

He froze. 'What do you mean, who's Callie?'

'Don't pretend you don't know,' she said. 'You talk about her in your sleep.'

He stared at her with his mouth open, then closed it. 'I do?'

She nodded and studied him with the measured hostility of the detective who has been proved right. 'So who is she? Is she some other girl you're seeing?'

'No! Nothing like that. I haven't seen her for years,' he said. 'She was someone I knew when I was growing up. She was the girl across the road.'

Whoosh! Just like that, in one smooth motion, she threw what was left of her drink in his face.

'I don't believe you,' she said.

Someone somewhere applauded. He blinked and opened

his eyes and sat there looking at her with vodka and slimline tonic and little chips of melting ice dripping from his eyebrows and his chin down onto his shirt.

Faces turned towards them, speculating, enjoying a little glimpse of drama between strangers. Elsa got to her feet and shouldered her bag and flipped her hair back over her shoulder. Her hair was long and dark and it was like her armour. That little gesture was the equivalent of a knight flipping down his visor, ready to ride off and do battle elsewhere.

'Well, whoever she is, she's welcome to you,' she said. 'I've had enough. I'm tired of you shutting me out all the time, Reuben. You can't trust someone if it seems like they're hiding something. And I don't want to be in a relationship with someone I can't trust.'

'I'm sorry,' he said. 'I didn't mean to be that way.'

'Save your explanations for somebody else,' she said. 'I don't care any more.' Her lip curled in scorn. 'You're not even going to try and talk me into staying, are you?'

'Not if what you want is to go.'

She let out a loud groan. 'That is not the point. If you really cared for me at all, you'd fight for me. You could at least have made a token effort. Anyway, just for the record, I've met someone else. OK? Someone who doesn't mutter about some other woman in his sleep, and who's not terrified of talking about the future.' She stared down at him scornfully. 'I met him at work. So, you know, at least the job was good for something. Even if they did just make me redundant.'

And with that she turned and walked out. He put on his sunglasses and drank his beer, and by and by people stopped looking at him. He was just the guy whose girlfriend had thrown a drink over him and walked out. There was nothing more for them to see.

Callie. He'd had no idea he talked about her in his sleep.

It didn't seem to make any difference how much time went

by. She was still there, somewhere, in what was left of his heart, sealed off like something radioactive in a concrete chamber. Dangerous to dig up, and equally dangerous to forget.

His shirt dried quickly in the sunshine, and after he'd finished his beer he decided he might as well stay for another one. After all, there was absolutely nobody in the world who needed him right now, and nowhere he needed to be.

FOUR

CALLIE

'She shouldn't move,' someone said, sounding weirdly indignant about it. 'Everybody knows that. You don't move someone after an accident.'

'My son,' she tried to say, but all that came out was a groan.

The pain was so intense it took an effort of will to work out where it was coming from, and whether there were limits to it. Her arm was agony, but it didn't stop there – it seemed to radiate all over her body. Had giving birth hurt this much? Of course it had. She had just forgotten what real pain was like.

'It's only if they might have spinal injuries that you don't move them.' Another unfamiliar voice, also male, coming from somewhere above her. 'Even then, you should move them if it's safer. It's better to move someone than have them get hit by a car.'

'Yeah, well, no one's going to hit her now, are they? The traffic's stopped.' The first voice again.

'Yes, and it'll be backed up for miles, probably.'

'Well, who cares? She could be dead. I mean, she could still die, for all we know.'

That was the downside to still being alive. The pain in her

left side. Her arm and elbow and hand. So much pain. Maybe she would black out soon, and then she wouldn't have to feel it any more, or listen to these strangers arguing about what to do with her.

But she couldn't die. No way. How could she leave Billy? He was only ten. He was so vulnerable. And he didn't have anybody else. No grandparents. No aunt. No family to speak of. And no dad.

There was no one else to turn to. Not the way things had worked out. There were her friends, Laurel and Sonia, but they wouldn't take him in, not for long, only for a little while, at a pinch...

She'd never allowed herself to think about what would happen to him if something really bad happened to her.

'Billy...'

She tried to say his name, but it just came out as another groan.

Her eyes were closed. That was why she couldn't see. She managed to open them, and then she understood where she was.

She was lying in the road just outside her office and people were standing round arguing about what to do with her. That was why the voices were coming from up high. She could see blood on the pavement and her left arm, which looked odd and wrong and was pocked with gore where she'd grazed it. It was like something from a horror film or a medical textbook, not like part of her normal body at all. She only knew it was hers because it hurt. She couldn't see her other arm and couldn't bring herself to try to turn her neck and look.

'It's all right,' someone said in her ear. 'The ambulance will be here in a minute.'

It was a woman's voice, and the woman was kneeling just behind her. She sounded calm and like someone who could be trusted, and the gratitude Callie felt towards her was so powerful it was almost like love.

'It wasn't my fault. She walked out right in front of me,' someone else said. A boy's voice. Maybe he had been the one riding the bike. He sounded scared and defensive. She wanted to ask if he was all right but somehow couldn't form the words.

Maybe the boy on the bike had hit her arm. Or she might have fallen on it after he collided with her.

'Yeah, and look at you, hardly a scratch on you.' This was the first voice she'd heard again, the annoyed-sounding man.

'I've got a graze here, look,' the boy said. 'Still bleeding. And my bike'll never be the same again. My mum's going to kill me.'

'I saw you, you know. You were going at quite a pace,' the second man said. 'And you weren't wearing a helmet. You've had a lucky escape, young man. If you ask me, your mum ought to be counting her blessings. When you look at the state of *her*.'

There was a small, solemn pause, and she realised she was the *her* they were talking about.

Surely she could respond. Tell them it wasn't that bad. She managed to raise her head a couple of inches. Now she could see more of the pavement and her legs and the blood on the summer skirt she was wearing. It all seemed distant and disconnected, like being in a plane and looking down just after take-off.

'Easy,' said the woman who was kneeling behind her. 'You're probably in shock. Try not to move.'

'Billy,' she said again, and this time the woman heard it and said, 'Did you say Billy? Who's Billy, love?'

'Maybe it's her husband,' said the man who'd wanted to move her.

'No, she doesn't have a husband,' said the other man. 'Look, no wedding ring.'

'That doesn't mean anything,' said the woman. 'Did anyone find her phone?'

'Billy might be her son,' the boy on the bike said. 'I think he might be in my little brother's class at Meadowside. I've seen her around. I don't know what the surname is, though.'

'Billy at Meadowside. Right. That's something. We should let the school know,' the woman said.

She turned towards Callie again. Callie could feel her soft breath. 'We'll get it sorted, don't worry,' she said. 'The school will get in touch with your other half, and he'll come and get your little boy.'

'No other half,' Callie managed to say. 'His dad's not around.'

Her angle of vision lurched and shifted and someone shouted a warning. She realised she was falling again and there was nothing she could do to stop it, and before she could say anything more it was dark.

FIVE

BILLY

His glasses were in a bad state, but it wasn't the end of the world. He had a spare pair in his bag – Mum made him carry them round with him, because this wasn't the first time his glasses had ended up getting broken at school. And she would forgive him. Depending on how tired she was, she'd complain a bit about what a nuisance it was having to go back to the opticians to get them fixed, and that would be that.

Of course he wouldn't be able to explain.

She'd expect him to be cut up about the birthday party. He'd have to persuade her that he didn't mind about Jack not wanting him there, and would be quite happy with a birthday celebration at home for just the two of them. Home would be best. If they went out anywhere, they might bump into someone from school.

He put his glasses in his pocket and took his bag off his back and started rummaging for the case with his spare glasses in it. He was still looking when someone came over to him and said, 'You're Billy Swann, aren't you?'

It was Mrs Timms from the school office, a plump, kindly woman with frizzy blonde hair. She was smiling, but he thought she didn't look entirely happy. It was difficult to tell. Without his glasses, his vision was so blurry that it was as if he was looking at her through a pane of wet glass.

'I'm afraid your mum isn't going to be able to make it today,' Mrs Timms said. 'Would you mind coming with me, Billy?'

'OK. Hang on just a minute,' he said.

Finally he found his glasses case. He put on his spare glasses, stuffed the broken ones back into the case and put it back in his bag. His hands were shaking, but Mrs Timms didn't notice, or if she did, she didn't say anything. She didn't ask him what had happened to his glasses, either, which was good, because it meant he didn't have to think of a lie.

Suddenly the world was clear again. That, at least, was a relief. His heart was pounding and his breathing was fast and shallow as he followed Mrs Timms across the playground to the school reception office. He was almost sure that something really terrible had happened, and yet he couldn't help hoping that he was wrong.

His mum was always there for him. She was the one person in the world who loved him and the only person he loved himself. No one else was as nice, as funny or as kind, or as good at making his worries seem as if they didn't really matter. As long as he had her, it didn't matter so much about not having friends, or about Jack hating him.

Just the thought of her being hurt or sick made his heart feel as if it had been flung to the ground and trampled on, the way Jack had done with his glasses.

She had to be all right. She just had to be...

But there was no good reason to go to the school reception, unless you'd been chosen to collect and return the class register from its drawer in the little filing cabinet that stood in the corner. Otherwise being there always meant something bad. It was where you went if you were late, or sick, or because you were in trouble and about to see the headteacher. Or if your mum was late, because something had happened to her and she was dead, or dying, or hurt so badly she'd gone into a coma and would never speak again.

There was a row of chairs in front of the sliding glass window where Mrs Timms sat, and today it was empty. Mrs Timms gestured towards it and said, 'Take a seat, Billy,' and he did, and then she perched next to him.

'Now I don't want you to be worried, Billy,' she said, 'but your mum's been in an accident, and they've had to take her to the hospital in Oxford. She'll be in the best place there, I promise you. The doctors and nurses there are very good, and they'll take care of her. So I need you to be brave for me, OK?'

'OK,' Billy managed to say.

'Good boy,' Mrs Timms said. 'If I find out any more, I'll tell you. Now I need to ring up and get someone to come and get you. If you need anything, you just knock on the glass and let me know. OK?'

Billy nodded. His heart was pounding so hard he thought he might actually be sick. Mrs Timms nodded approvingly and retreated to her side of the glass, leaving him staring at his trembling hands and trembling legs.

He had never felt so alone.

It wasn't that long after the end of the school day, and yet already the place felt completely different: quieter, emptier. The kids who stayed late at the after-school club, waiting for working parents to come and collect them, would already be settled in their portacabin. Everyone else had gone home. All the classrooms would be empty, except for maybe a few lurking teachers, doing whatever teachers did at the end of the school day. But soon they would go home, too. And if no one came for him, what would happen to him then?

He pictured himself still sitting here in the dark, forgotten and frozen in place as the hours of the night went by. But no, they surely wouldn't leave him here. Maybe he would have to go home with Mr Felton, the headmaster. Or maybe he could go with Mrs Timms. That would be preferable, if they gave him any say over where he went, which probably they wouldn't.

On the other side of the glass reception window, Mrs Timms was phoning people up. She tried Mum's friend Sonia, left a message and then tried her again, maybe on a different number.

'Mrs Hallam? Marie from the Meadowside school office here. It's about Billy Swann... bad news, I'm afraid. Ms Swann has been in an accident, and has been taken to hospital in an ambulance...'

It would be all right if Sonia came to get him, because Jack was off having his sleepover at Zeke's and wouldn't be there. Though Jack might not be very pleased when he found out about it. And what if Billy had to stay with Sonia for a while, if Mum was in hospital? There'd be no getting away from Jack then.

No doubt Jack would find all kinds of new ways to make Billy's life a misery. But would it even be possible for Jack to make his life any worse, if he was already missing Mum? And he would miss her so much. He wouldn't even feel like he was him, without her around. He wouldn't know who he was any more.

He had far too much imagination for his own good. That was what Mum said. He tried to keep it under control, he really did. But even now, when he was meant to be so much better, pictures of what he was afraid of still sometimes came to him. They could be very vivid, like a dream or something on TV, and hard to shake off.

It was beginning to happen now. He was sitting on the end chair in the school reception area and at the same time he could see a ghostly vision of Mum in a hospital bed, her head bandaged and her arms and legs all in plaster, almost unrecognisable. And then he saw himself, very pale and thin, kneeling at her grave to put fresh white flowers there.

She wouldn't die. It wasn't possible. She was in hospital, not dead, and hospital was where people went to get better.

Mum was all that stood between him and being an orphan. But that was a bit like saying that the sky was all there was between the earth and space. You might wonder what would happen if the sky fell down one day, but you knew it would never actually happen.

He closed his eyes, clasped his hands together and squeezed, which was one of the things it was OK to do if he was feeling anxious. But it didn't help.

All this was his fault. If he was more normal, more popular, more like Jack, this wouldn't have happened. Mum had prob-ably only been in an accident because she worried about him and had been rushing to pick him up. And she only worked the hours she did so that he could come home straight after school and chill out, and not have to be around other people at the after-school club.

Another vision of Mum came to mind: her lying broken and bleeding on the road, maybe even crying. He hated to see her cry. Hated it. Would do anything to stop it. Even more than he detested PE (especially football, cricket, any games with a hard ball), even more than he loathed it when Jack was mean to him and other people joined in, he hated the idea of anything causing her pain.

If Mum is OK I promise I will learn to be braver, he told himself. He didn't really believe that a promise like that could make any difference. But it seemed to be worth a try.

He opened his eyes and found that he felt a little better. He had to be brave. That was all there was to it. That was the bargain he needed to make. If he could just manage that, his mum would be fine.

Mrs Timms was on the phone again. 'Mrs Goodyear, I'm so

sorry to bother you, but I have Billy Swann here and he needs collecting, and you're listed as one of the emergency contacts...'

Mrs Goodyear was Laurel, Mum's other friend from way back, who was like Sonia in that she treated Mum slightly pity-ingly – Billy couldn't tell if Mum noticed this, or minded it – but different in that Laurel was quite well known, locally at least, because she hosted a regular show on Vale Radio. Laurel sometimes made jokes about how her supposed fame didn't get her very far, but even though she made a show of not being big-headed, you could tell she was proud of what she did for a living, and liked being someone who people listened to.

Finally there was silence from Mrs Timms' side of the window, apart from the sound of her moving bits of paper around. Mum said that was what a lot of office jobs involved, hers included, though these days it was more emails, and then having meetings, and afterwards sending emails about the meetings. Billy knew he'd probably end up doing a job like that one day himself, but longed to do something more exciting. Like being a spy. And maybe it would happen, if he could learn to be brave.

Then the phone rang, and he nearly jumped out of his skin.

Mrs Timms snatched it up and said, 'Oh, hello, Mrs Goodyear. Thank you so much for getting back to me so quickly. I appreciate that you must be very busy, what with your show and everything.'

Mrs Timms talked to Laurel for a while longer about how awful it was about Mum's accident, then came out in a rush with a red, pleased face, and explained that Mrs Goodyear was on her way to pick Billy up.

'Isn't that nice? I'm sure she'll be here in no time, and then you'll be on your way.'

She paused as if waiting for a response and Billy said thank you, which was usually a good thing to say when you weren't sure what was expected of you.

Mrs Timms smiled benevolently at him. 'The good thing about a time like this,' she said, 'is that you really find out what the people round you are made of.'

And with that she withdrew, leaving Billy, if anything, slightly more anxious than before.

If this was, as Mrs Timms had suggested, some kind of test, he couldn't help but feel he was failing it. He should probably be taking all this in his stride, and assuming that everything was going to be fine. Instead he was a nervous wreck.

But he was excited, too. Laurel drove one of the flashiest cars he'd ever seen, an actual Porsche in an eye-catching shade of red. Whatever else was going to happen later, it looked like he was finally about to see what it was like inside.

Laurel arrived about half-an-hour later, which didn't seem *that* quick given that she drove a fast car and lived in Kettlebridge, not all that far away from school. She came into the school reception area like a special guest arriving late at a big party, as if it was only to be expected that people would be delighted she'd showed up.

She was, as usual, wearing lots of perfume – Billy had to suppress the urge to cough – red lipstick, and brightly coloured clothes. Today she had on a purple blazer with a yellow T-shirt and handbag, black trousers and purple high-heeled shoes that made a clicking sound on the linoleum floor, as if she was about to break into a dance.

'Billy! You poor thing... you must be worried sick! Let's get you out of here,' she said, coming over to where he was sitting and holding out her hands towards him, but not quite far enough to suggest that she was expecting a hug. Which was fine by him. Laurel didn't normally hug him, and it would have been embarrassing if she'd tried.

Laurel ushered him out – she always behaved as if she was

in a rush to get somewhere important – and he saw that she'd left her Porsche in the staff car park, which was usually strictly forbidden to parents. He decided not to say anything, because it might seem ungrateful, and anyway, if anybody could get away with it, Laurel could. Besides, she probably didn't even know about the rules.

'You'll be all right sitting in the front?' Laurel said, clicking her car key to open the door for him.

'Of course,' Billy said, very slightly affronted. Did she seriously think he was that much of a baby? But then, Laurel didn't have any children of her own, so she didn't know about that kind of thing.

He climbed into the passenger seat and she got in next to him, started the car and roared out of the car park.

The radio came on – it was tuned to Vale Radio, which was all breezy chat and old pop songs. Laurel's approach to driving was very different to Mum's. She was quick on the accelerator and muttered under her breath about other people's stupidity and slowness. She made Billy think of a cowboy in a film, hurrying towards a showdown of some kind and maybe over-doing it a bit with the whip and spurs.

Suddenly he noticed that they were on the outskirts of town, even though Laurel's house was close by and they should really have already arrived.

'Er, Laurel...?'

He was allowed to call her Laurel, not Mrs Goodyear. In fact, she'd expressly told him to call her Laurel ages ago, saying that if he called her anything else it would make her feel old. Laurel seemed to worry quite a bit about getting old, which, as far as he knew, was not something his mum was bothered about.

'What is it, Billy?' Laurel said this in the exact same weary tone of voice that teachers used for the kind of people who always interrupted lessons to ask to go to the toilet.

'Where are we going?'

They were driving on a lane that led out of town round the edge of a big field. They weren't that far from Kettlebridge, where he'd lived all his life, but he wasn't sure that he'd ever been here before.

'Look, Billy, I have to go to work,' Laurel said. 'Someone's gone off sick and they need me for the six to ten slot. I can't leave you sitting in Vale Radio's reception for four hours, now can I? And there's no one at home I can leave you with. Henry's in London, and anyway, he's hopeless.'

'I don't mind waiting at the radio station,' Billy said. 'I've got a book in my bag. I can just sit and read. It might even be quite fun.'

'You might be all right with the idea of being sat there waiting, but no one else will be,' Laurel said. 'Just think about it, Billy. What would it look like? There are all sorts of people in that reception area, and some of them, I'm sorry to say, are not very nice. Someone might even tip off the local paper, and then there'd be all kinds of trouble. It's really not true that all publicity is good publicity. And being accused of child neglect would definitely be bad for me. Someone's got to look after you, and it can't be your mum, and this evening it can't be me, OK?'

'But will I have to stay overnight? I haven't got my toothbrush with me,' Billy said despairingly.

'Look, just think of it as an adventure, OK?'

Billy remembered his promise to himself to be brave, and decided to say nothing. But was this really what having an adventure was like – this sickening feeling of being out of control?

The lane had turned into a road with woodland to either side, and then they were going uphill and the trees thinned out and it was just an ordinary road with houses to either side. Wherever she was planning on leaving him, it definitely wasn't the middle of nowhere. It looked like a village. There were even bus stops. That was a good sign, surely?

'I know this isn't ideal,' Laurel said. 'But there's really nothing else for it.'

Suddenly, without indicating, she turned off the road and came to a halt in the gravelled front garden of a well-kept house with a yellow front door and net curtains in the windows. There was a car parked there already. A big old estate car, very clean and shiny. The border in front of the house was filled with frilly, brightly coloured flowers that reminded him of the ones they'd made out of tissue paper for a display in the school hall at Easter.

'I did tell your mum,' Laurel said, 'that there were certain times when it was going to be very difficult for me to come and help her. But she said the school just needed to have a couple of emergency contacts for the paperwork and it would probably never happen. To be honest, I think she didn't know who else to ask.' She sniffed. 'Apart from Sonia, of course. Who would have been ideal for this, but unfortunately is unavailable.'

Laurel got out of the car and Billy followed her and stood behind her as she rang on the doorbell, waited briefly, and then impatiently rang again. His heart was still racing. He wasn't sure it would ever beat normally again.

He had absolutely no idea whose house this was. And yet it seemed crystal clear that Laurel was planning on leaving him here, regardless of how he might feel about it.

The door opened and a lady came out. She was tall and thin, with a big wild mop of greying curly hair clipped back from her face. She was wearing quite normal clothes – light blue jeans and a big pink jumper and fluffy slippers with polka dots – but she had a keyed-up, jack-in-the-box energy that made her seem as if she might be unpredictable when unleashed. Right now she looked a bit suspicious, or maybe concerned – it was hard to tell which. Also, it seemed as if she had been expecting them.

First of all she looked very hard at Billy. She had dark

brown eyes that made him think of a lively, nervous animal, like a deer, and she was gazing at him as if she wanted to see right through him and into the thoughts going round his brain. It made him feel dizzy, as if her attention was a kind of wind that had the power to knock him off balance.

Then she turned to Laurel and said, 'You did the right thing, calling me.'

'I'm just glad you're able and willing to help,' Laurel said.

'Course I am. We both are. We'll take good care of him. You don't have to worry about that. I'll let you know as soon I get any news from the hospital. You'll be doing your show, but now I've got your mobile number, I'll leave you a message so you can pick it up as soon as you've finished.'

'Thank you, Janice,' Laurel said.

'This is what family's for, times like this,' the lady who was called Janice said. Her lower lip trembled and Billy realised that she was trying very hard to be brave, the way he often had to. But even though she must have had years and years to practise, she couldn't quite do it.

Then she pulled herself together and went on, 'It shouldn't have had to come to this. But we are where we are. And now we all just have to hope and pray for the best.'

'You'll be all right here,' Laurel said, turning to Billy. 'Janice will look after you.'

Billy pressed his lips together into a tight line and forced himself to nod his head. He would not cry. He absolutely would not.

The lady who was called Janice was looking at him again. He couldn't bring himself to meet her eyes. They seemed too bright and too searching, and he felt that if he did look back at her, for some reason he didn't fully understand, he might give in and start bawling like a little tiny baby.

She said, 'You have absolutely no idea who I am, do you, Billy?'

He shook his head. He thought he could probably just about manage that without any tears leaking sideways out of his eyes.

'I'm your granny,' the woman said. 'Your mum's mum.' Her voice came out of her very forcefully, with a heat that wasn't anger, but some other emotion that she seemed to be trying to hold back.

He risked a quick, cagey glance up at her. Was she going to expect him to hug her? He didn't want to. She seemed to have come closer to him, or was it just because she was still watching him?

He said, 'Should I call you Granny?'

And then he couldn't stop himself. Reluctantly, as if mesmerised, he allowed himself to meet her eyes.

He didn't turn to stone, or any of the other awful things that could happen to people when they stared at a magical creature, but something else happened. He felt important. Like he mattered to her. He knew he mattered to Mum, but he wasn't used to being looked at that way by anybody else.

Laurel had basically treated him like a nuisance – a problem she couldn't get off her hands fast enough. But this lady, who said she was his granny – if that was true – definitely wanted him there. Yes, she wanted something from him. He just didn't know what.

Was she happy to see him, or sad? Angry, or relieved? A bit of everything? He couldn't tell. But she definitely felt *something*.

She grimaced and he wasn't sure whether she was going to laugh or cry. 'It seems a bit much to be Granny,' she said. 'Seeing as how we only just met. Are you OK with that?'

He shrugged, then wondered if that might seem rude. 'Yeah.'

'Works for me. Beats "hey you", anyway,' Granny said. 'We're not complete strangers, you know. We have met before.

When you were a baby. I last saw you just after your first birthday. But anyway, I guess that's kind of one-sided, as you obviously wouldn't remember.'

Laurel said, 'I don't know how Callie's going to react when she finds out he's been here.'

'I don't think we ought to worry about that right now,' Granny said. 'Not while we don't even know how bad things are. Once she's recovered enough to be angry, well – let her be angry. Bring it on. Don't feel bad, Laurel. You did the right thing. Now look, before you go, there's something I need to ask you.'

Laurel looked unnerved by this, and smiled brightly to try to hide it. Billy had never seen her like that before.

'Sure, Janice, what is it? Anything I can do to help.'

'I just need a number for someone,' Granny said. 'Someone who ought to know.' Then she turned and said to Billy, 'You go on inside. I just need to talk for Laurel for a moment. I'll be with you in a minute.'

She opened the front door wide and ushered him through into the hallway, and then shut the door behind him.

He could hear her voice, but he couldn't quite make out what she was saying, and he didn't dare hold the letterbox open to see if that would make it easier to eavesdrop. He was almost certain that she was talking about him, or something to do with him, and it was pretty obvious she didn't him to know.

He had always thought of Laurel as a big, powerful personality, what with her radio show and her colourful clothes and her car and her way of walking around very fast, as if her time was more valuable than other people's. But even though his granny didn't have a flashy car or any of the other things that made Laurel seem important, and had grey hair and fluffy polka dot slippers and a pink jumper, Laurel had seemed to be a little bit frightened of her. And if Laurel was scared of her, there was no way Billy was going to risk doing something that might provoke her. Not when he could so easily get caught.

Though maybe Laurel had only been scared because Granny had sounded so very determined to find out whatever it was she was going to ask her, and had looked so very upset.

At least Granny's house was fairly normal. Or what he could see of it from the hallway was. Doors leading off in different directions, stairs going up to a landing. Brown carpet, cream walls, a mirror. Hooks for coats. Too many coats for just Granny. Somebody else lived here, too. A man, by the looks of it.

He nearly jumped out of his skin when the front door opened and Granny came back in, slipping a mobile phone back into her pocket. Laurel's Porsche roared off into the distance.

Granny closed the door again. She looked at Billy, and Billy looked back up at her. Was she a safe person to be with? She had to be, didn't she, given that she was his granny? Grannies were like policemen and teachers. They were always safe.

'You'd better take your shoes off,' Granny said, in a more normal voice. 'I've only just had all the carpets cleaned.'

He did as she said, and then she led him into the kitchen. He couldn't help but feel a thrill of excitement, even though it was obviously very weird to be going, on his own, into the house of his granny who he'd never even met before. And it was pretty clear that there was another stranger, or strangers, living here too.

Given what Laurel and Granny had just said, he wasn't at all sure that this was somewhere his mum would want him to be. But what else could he do? He couldn't go back home. He didn't even have a key.

Granny told him to sit down at the kitchen table and fussed round trying to find something for him to eat and drink – she didn't have any cake or biscuits.

'I guess I'm not geared up for children to come round,' she

said rather helplessly.

It was obvious she was embarrassed, and felt awkward about not having anything to offer him, and that made her seem less frightening. She was still quite agitated and distracted, but maybe that was because she was worried about Mum.

'It's OK. I don't really need a snack. I'm not that hungry,' he said, although he was.

Granny stared at him in surprise. Then she said, 'Bless you,' and he felt even more reassured. Surely she wasn't about to do something really dreadful to him, if she could say something like that.

In the end she gave him buttered toast and a glass of apple juice on a tray and carried it through to the living room for him, where she set it down on the coffee table in front of the TV. She switched the TV on, found the remote control and changed the channel from sports to one for children. He was pretty sure she wasn't usually the person who sat here watching TV.

'Right. You should be OK here for a bit. I have to make a phone call,' she said, and withdrew.

He ate his toast and drank his juice, and put the tray down on the table. Then he felt slightly sick. But there was no reason to believe she'd poison him. That kind of thing only happened in fairy tales.

Trouble was, he couldn't quite get comfortable. The armchair he was sitting on was a well-stuffed leather one with rigid arms and a high back, and smelt very faintly of aftershave. It didn't seem like the kind of chair you could slouch or relax on. It also seemed like the kind of chair that might belong to someone who would come home and be annoyed to find you in it.

The show he was watching was about a boy in medieval times who had magical powers. Wouldn't that be brilliant? If he had magical powers he could make Mum better just like that, and have her arrive here right now to collect him. Granny might be upset about him leaving so quickly, though. But maybe they could arrange something for another time. And then she'd have the chance to get snacks in that he might like beforehand.

Then Granny stuck her head round the door to say she was going to pop out and ask someone something, and would be back in a minute. She looked even more agitated now. Once he'd heard the front door slam behind her he dared to get out of the chair, and crept across the living room to duck down and watch her from the window.

She was marching across the road towards the rundown-looking, ivy-covered house opposite, with the breeze whipping her curly grey-streaked hair to and fro. The woman who answered didn't look especially pleased to see her, but couldn't close the door on her because Granny had stepped forward quick as lightning and shoved one of her fluffy slippers in the way.

A foot in the door! Billy had never seen anyone do that before. Nor had he realised that in order to get a foot in the door, you had to be willing to risk it getting squashed.

The conversation didn't last long. Again Granny seemed to get her own way. A few minutes later she turned round and marched back towards the house with her arms folded, looking as if she'd just done something she felt she had to do.

Her expression reminded Billy of the way people looked after they'd just told the teacher on someone. As if she'd felt guilty, and now her conscience was a little clearer.

Billy scurried back to the leather armchair in front of the TV. Suddenly he was much more curious than afraid.

He was pretty sure that whatever Granny was up to, it was to do with him and Mum. She was telling people about them, or trying to. That was what it looked like. Or maybe she was warning them.

It was a mystery, and if he could stay brave, it might be one he'd be able to solve.

SIX

REUBEN

Back in the flat, he went straight to the kitchen and got a beer out of the fridge. The only thing he could think to do with the evening ahead was to get mildly drunk in front of the TV. He took the beer through to the living room. It already seemed as if Elsa had never been here at all.

Almost certainly, she would never come back.

Then he spotted the blinking light on the phone, which meant he'd missed a call.

Elsa. Maybe. But why would she be calling on the landline?

It was probably one of those spam calls. The message would start with a suspicious click and then a robotic-sounding voice would start telling him there was a problem with his internet connection or his bank, or that he'd won a prize and should call the winner's hotline immediately.

There was only one actual human he could think of who knew that number and sometimes used it, and she was just about the last person in the world he felt like talking to right now.

He put down his bottle of beer and listened to the message.

Yes – it was her. Theresa, his father's girlfriend. But what did she want?

Theresa had a breathy, rather girlish voice, the voice of someone who flirts with strangers out of habit. Right now she sounded peevish, which she usually did when she got in touch with him.

'*Hi, Reuben, it's me, Theresa. Long time since we last spoke. Can you call me when you get this? I'll be in now for the rest of the day. You can ring anytime, but between five and eight it might be tricky for me to get to the phone. Speak to you later.*'

He listened to the message again. Saved it. '*Between five and eight it might be tricky for me to get to the phone...*' Why?

He drank some more beer and looked out of the window at his downstairs neighbour playing football with his three-year-old in the tiny courtyard garden. And wondered, as he so often did, at how some men were capable of being like that with their sons. Affectionate and capable and encouraging. Showing them how to do things, and enjoying being with them at the same time.

He couldn't remember his own dad ever being like that with him. It had always seemed as if nothing about him was quite right, or quite good enough. He'd felt that he was a thorn in Dad's side, and, even worse, that his mum had to placate Dad to make up for it.

And those feelings had lingered – the sense of inadequacy, and of being resigned to falling short. His inner critic, the judgemental commentator in his head who told him he was pretty much doomed to fail, spoke with his dad's voice.

In his personal life, at least, he'd lived up – or rather, lived down – to the old man's expectations as only a dutiful son seeking approval could do. But why should he care what his dad thought of him now? Especially after everything that had happened before he moved away to live abroad. Even since he'd come back, they'd not had much to do with each other.

Last time he'd seen Dad and Theresa – on neutral territory about six months ago, out for a pub lunch in London when they'd come for a day trip and some Christmas shopping – Dad had joked about how long he and Theresa had been together, and had put it down to them never actually having officially tied the knot. It didn't seem to have occurred to either Dad or Theresa that this could be seen as an insult to the memory of Reuben's mum, who'd been married to Reuben's dad for nearly thirty years before her death. Theresa hadn't passed comment at all, and had just sat there with a forbearing smile, as if she wasn't sure whether this was a joke at her expense but was willing to be a good sport if it was.

Presumably Dad had never told Theresa the whole truth and nothing but the truth about the way he'd conducted himself during his marriage, or why Reuben was almost entirely estranged from him. Dad never did tell the truth if he could help it.

He called back, and even though it was a little past five, Theresa picked up straight away.

'Oh, hi, Reuben. Yes. Thanks for getting back to me.' She let out a long, drawn-out sigh. 'I may not be able to talk for very long. I have to make dinner, and then clear everything up. It seems to help if I stick to a schedule. Then sometimes he likes to have a bath afterwards, and I have to keep an eye on him so we don't end up with water all over the bathroom floor. I'm sorry to have to tell you this, Reuben, but your dad's been getting quite confused lately. And random. He can still play the piano beautifully, but other things can be a bit hit and miss.'

'How long has this been going on? I mean, when did you first notice?'

'A couple of months, maybe? Definitely since the spring,' Theresa said. 'It feels longer.'

Was she exaggerating? But why would she do that? There was no particular reason for her to try and guilt-trip him – no more than there had ever been. He already knew Theresa thought he was a bad son. His mum must have thought so, too. She'd tried to raise him to be generous, considerate, loyal and unselfish, and willing to put other people's needs before his own. On her deathbed she'd looked baffled, as if something had been stolen from her and she had no idea how or why.

He said, 'Do you mean you think he has some kind of dementia? But he's still young. Relatively speaking. He's only just retired. And he's always kept himself fit and healthy. I thought that kind of thing didn't happen till people were much older.'

'I don't know about that. I can only tell you what I've seen.'

'Well, have you been to the doctor? It sounds like things must have gone downhill quite fast.'

'The problem is he won't admit anything's wrong. He's oblivious. Maybe *you* could persuade him, but I definitely can't.'

'If he won't listen to you, I don't think he'll listen to me.'

'But you're his son, Reuben. You could at least try. I know it's inconvenient, and I know you have a life of your own in London, but I think the time has come when you're going to need to do a bit more. I can't cope with it all any more. It's too much. It's not just this business with your dad.' (Reuben noted that this was how she kept referring to him – 'your dad' – almost as if she was no longer anything to do with him.) 'It's the house, too.'

'Maybe you could get someone in to help,' Reuben suggested.

'He won't hear of it,' Theresa said. 'But it's in quite a state now, to be honest with you. Especially the garden. He's completely let that go. He won't even mow the lawn any more, and the ivy's growing halfway over the house, making it all dark inside. It looks as if a crazy person lives here. I mean, I do my best, obviously. I keep the inside clean and tidy as best as I can, but that isn't easy on my own. It's like he's lost his confidence, or something. I don't know. When I try to talk to him about it, he just gets angry and tells me to leave him in peace. Anyway, I'm not going to go climbing up ladders and chopping trees and all of that, risking my neck. I don't see why I should. The house isn't even mine. *And* he's planning to leave it all to you when he dies.'

She paused, seemingly waiting for him to respond. He hesitated. *I don't want it. I hate the place. If I never set foot inside it again it'll be too soon. You're welcome to it.* That was what he wanted to say. But he knew he wouldn't. He was incapable of being that open about what he felt. He would be even more incapable of explaining why.

'I didn't know that he was planning to leave me the house,' he said. 'I certainly didn't expect him to. It's not something we ever discussed.'

The idea of receiving an inheritance from his dad, hypothetical and remote as it was, made him feel sick. And for the inheritance to take the form of *that* house... that would surely be more a curse than a blessing.

He'd have to sell it, when it came to it. But first he'd have to go there and sort through it, and the idea of that filled him with dread.

Theresa made an angry scoffing noise. 'You hardly ever talk to him. And whenever we see you, you can't get away fast enough. If things end up getting really bad, and he has to go into care or something, that will probably use up the value of the house, so who knows if there'll be anything left? That's not the point. The point is, I think it's really sad that he still feels he has something to make up to you, and you don't even know or care. I know he hoped it would change when you came back from Australia. But it didn't, did it? It would have meant a lot to him if the two of you could have come to some kind of understanding. He always wanted to be on better terms with you.'

'I can try and talk to him about the will if you like,' Reuben offered.

'He won't change his mind now,' she said. 'That doesn't matter. What matters is you're his son, his own flesh and blood, and he needs your support, Reuben. You need to take responsibility for that.'

He'd always assumed that he wouldn't have to worry about Dad getting older, as looking after him would naturally fall to Theresa, who, being ten years younger than Dad, would hopefully be able to cope. Besides, the prospect of Dad being frail and elderly had seemed a very long way off. But here was Theresa telling him Dad wasn't well. That he was vulnerable, and needed Reuben's help.

When it came down to it, in spite of everything, how could he refuse?

The softening effect of the booze from earlier was wearing off, and he was beginning to feel hungover. He massaged his forehead with the fingers of his left hand: he definitely had a headache coming on.

'I'm sorry you feel I haven't been around enough,' he said. 'I didn't realise that things had got this bad.'

'Well, you might have done if you visited more often,' Theresa retorted. 'Anyway, I don't want to be a nag. I've always done my best to stay out of your relationship with your dad – I figured it was none of my business. It hasn't been easy. Sometimes, to be honest, it's been very hard, but I never felt it was my place to intervene and I've never asked for anything from you before.'

He said, 'Does Dad know you're talking to me?'

'No. He's having a nap. He sleeps quite a bit in the day now. Like I said, he doesn't think there's anything wrong with him. Or at least, he doesn't want to admit it. But if you come and spend some proper time with him, I think you'll see that we have a problem.'

Did she use that tone of voice to Dad, like a scolding mother dealing with a disappointing, burdensome child? There had been a time when she'd treated Dad like a king, just as Reuben's mum had done before her.

'OK,' he said. 'I hear you. I'll see what I can do.'

'Good,' she said. 'I think you need to. Oh, by the way, before I forget, there's something else I have to tell you. It's about Janice. You know, the woman from across the road.'

All the air seemed to rush out of Reuben's lungs. How was it that the mere mention of Callie's mother could do this to him, after all this time?

'It's all been going on over there today,' Theresa went on. 'First Laurel Goodyear pulled up in a red Porsche – you used to know her, didn't you? She does a show on Vale Radio. And she had a kid with her. A boy, skinny little thing with glasses. Handed him over to Janice and drove off. I mentioned it to your father and he just ignored me completely and carried right on playing the piano. He does that a lot these days, now, you know. Ignores me, I mean. Just doesn't seem to hear what I've been saying.'

'Do you know who the boy was? The one Laurel handed over to Janice?'

'It was Callie's son,' she said, and then added, as if he needed reminding, 'Callie Swann. Janice's daughter. Like I said, Janice from across the road. Laurel brought him round so Janice could look after him. Callie's been in an accident. Got hit by a cyclist, had quite a nasty fall. Been rushed into hospital in an ambulance. Janice was in quite a flap when she came round. Apparently she'd tried to get your number off Laurel's husband, but hadn't managed to get through... Are you even in touch with Laurel's husband? I didn't think you had anything to do with anyone from round here.'

'I see him occasionally. It's kind of a professional connection. He works in newspapers.'

'Oh.' Theresa had never been in the least interested in anything to do with his work, or indeed any aspect of his life other than his barely-there relationship with his dad. 'Well, anyway, she seemed to want to tell me all about it. She barely gives either of us the time of day normally, but there we are, they say trouble loves company.'

'That's awful about Callie,' Reuben said.

It took an effort to say her name. It had been bad enough to hear it from Elsa. He found himself holding the phone at a slight distance from his ear, as if it was toxic.

'I know,' Theresa said off-handedly. 'Anyway, Janice was very keen that you should know, so I said I'd ring you and tell you.'

There was a small, very heavy and loaded pause. Theresa said, 'Are you OK, Reuben?'

'Me? Yes, I'm fine.'

'I suppose there's no point me asking why Janice would want you in particular to know?'

'I'm not sure. I honestly don't know what's going through her head.'

Theresa sighed. 'Well, I guess it's none of my business,' she said. 'I'm just passing the message on. She asked me to give you her number. Do you want it?'

He said he did, and she read it out and he jotted it down. And then he found himself saying, 'I could come and visit right now if you want.'

There was a silence at the other end of the line. Suddenly he felt obliged to explain himself – for his own benefit, as much as Theresa's.

'I have a quiet patch over the next few days,' he said. 'Happens sometimes, when you're freelance – you can get unexpected lulls. Also, I just broke up with someone. Seems like as good a time as any to get out of town.'

'Right,' Theresa said. 'You seriously mean you're willing to come here tonight?'

'Look, I don't want to cause you any trouble. It's only if it's convenient. I could come at the weekend—'

'How soon can you get here?' Theresa interrupted him. 'It's just that it's quiz night at the local pub. Starts at eight. I love quiz night. Always used to go with your dad. Haven't been for months. He just hasn't been up for it. He can't remember the answers any more. So what do you think? Can you make it?'

He checked his watch. He wouldn't be able to drive, given that he'd spent most of the afternoon in the pub. But the train might be better anyway, given that it was still rush hour and the traffic heading out of London would probably be terrible. He could get a fast service as far as Barrowton, and then it'd be another half-hour in a taxi.

'It'd be tight, but it's worth a go,' he said. 'Won't take me long to stick a couple of things in a bag. I'll be coming by train. If I don't make it for eight, it should be soon after.'

He couldn't quite believe what he was saying. Was he seriously thinking of that house in terms of how quickly he could get there, when usually he would go out of his way to avoid the place? Just so Theresa could make it to quiz night?

But then, that wasn't really why he was going back. Or at least, it was only part of it.

'Well, I'd certainly appreciate it if you'd try,' Theresa said. 'I'm sure your dad would, too,' she added hastily. 'You'll have to take us as you find us, obviously, and I haven't got anything in. But there's plenty of food in the cupboards and a couple of places that do takeaway.'

'That's fine. I don't want to impose, or make things harder. I want to try and help.'

'Good,' Theresa said decisively, and he almost heard her think 'about time'. 'Then we'll see you later.'

She finished the call. He rang the number she'd given him

for Janice, but there was no answer. He left a message and put the receiver back in its place, then went off to his bedroom to fish out his overnight bag and start packing.

He told himself that it was crazy, to react like this. Then he told himself it wasn't crazy, and that him going was nothing to do with Callie, not really, and was only because he wanted to see for himself what kind of state his dad was in. After all, maybe it wasn't as bad as Theresa was making out. And then he realised it didn't matter what he told himself, because he would carry on getting ready to go just the same.

The boy. Callie's boy. He still couldn't think of him without feeling wounded. But now he couldn't help but feel sorry for the kid, too.

He could remember all too well what it had been like when his mum had to go into hospital. He'd been older, and the circumstances had been different. But the fear and helplessness, the sense that the steady ground he walked on had suddenly turned to quicksand – all that was as vivid to him now as if it had happened yesterday.

Was that how Callie's boy felt? He was so young still. It would be dreadful for him. And what on earth must Callie be going through right now?

SEVEN

CALLIE

Pain relief. Blessed pain relief. But now the pain had eased a little, there was more space in her head for everything else. Like worrying about Billy, who she was now speeding away from, strapped to a stretcher staring up at the ceiling of an ambulance as it wove through traffic with its siren wailing.

She was staring up at the ceiling because it was all she could see. There were soft blocks to either side of her neck and tape across her forehead and chin. Something to do with them being worried about her c-spine and neck. C-spine? What even was that? All these crucial things that you hadn't even heard of until they were in jeopardy. They would assess her in hospital, they had said. The taping was a precautionary measure. But you didn't take such precautions unless there was a chance of bad news.

What if she'd done something to her neck? How long would they keep her in? Maybe she'd have to wear a brace when she came out. Well, that wouldn't be so bad. She'd still be able to look after Billy, wouldn't she? As long as she could still move around, she'd manage.

The woman who'd helped her had stuck around right up

until the ambulance showed up. She'd told the paramedics Callie had briefly passed out a couple of times, and had even remembered to pass over Callie's handbag. It was startling how kind people could be. Callie had tried to thank her, along with the other passers-by who had stopped after the accident, but she wasn't sure she'd been able to make herself understood. She might never even know who they were.

And then there had been questions from the paramedics to answer and she'd had to stop groaning and force herself to concentrate and speak. Had she really been in so much pain that it was hard to talk? It was already difficult to remember what it had felt like.

They'd seemed less worried about her arm than about her head and neck, even though her arm was what hurt. Looks like a dislocated and fractured elbow, they'd said. An unlucky fall. They'd packaged it up in a fat padded splint that sealed with Velcro and reminded her of the water wings she'd put on Billy when she was teaching him how to swim. Then they'd stuck a cannula in her right wrist and hooked it up to the tube that was pumping the pain relief into her body. The blessed pain relief.

No wonder she felt unmoored. Ready to float away. As if everything mattered immensely and yet, at the same time, she was separate from all of it.

Anyway, she'd got through giving birth without any pain medication, and with no one there to support her. Surely she could get through this.

Laurel and Sonia had both offered to be with her during labour, and so had Mum. But she knew none of them really wanted to be there, or to see her in pain, going through something so animal and so exposing. Mum in particular had clearly felt ambivalent about it, and later on, Callie had understood why. If she'd had a daughter, would she have been able to bear watching her being torn open from the inside? It would be hard to be on the outside of a birth. For it to be something you had to witness, rather than something that only you could give.

Anyway, in the end it had all happened in the middle of the night and by the time morning came round Billy had already arrived.

It was true what they said, that you forgot how much having a baby hurt. She'd blotted out so much. She remembered the early stages of labour, arriving at hospital, Billy's face: vivid visual impressions, like fragments of a dream, and the emotions that had gone with them. But not the pain.

What she remembered most of all was the stars. After her waters broke and her contractions got going, she had gone out into the little back garden of her flat and looked up at the night sky. She had felt profoundly alone, but not lonely. Standing under the expanse of the night sky and looking up, knowing her child was on the way into the world, she had felt more connected to everything around her than ever before.

She had thought about the baby's father, but had pushed the thought aside, something she'd had plenty of practice at both before and since. Sometime around midnight she'd got a taxi to the hospital and somehow she'd made it into the maternity ward, lugging the car seat she'd need to take the baby home in afterwards and the bag she'd packed with things for both of them, stopping a few times on the way when the contractions took over. And then Billy had arrived just an hour and a half later.

It wasn't meant to happen that fast, with a first baby. But things that weren't meant to happen, that were unusual or exceptional or extraordinary, for good or ill, happened all the time.

Her baby. Her boy. Her son. In her arms for the first time, seen through a haze of love and pain. Pink-faced, squalling, not entirely clean. Not that she'd cared about the blood on him. A badge of honour.

He had latched on with remarkable, single-minded determination, and suckled as if his life depended on it. And then he had slept, and his tiny, perfect mouth drifted away from her and she'd drunk the tea the midwife had brought her and studied him as if he was a work of art.

Once she'd seen him, she had known for sure that the name she'd had in mind was right. William, the same as her dad. Billy for short.

'Billy,' she murmured, and realised she'd spoken out loud.

She'd get back to him before long. It'd take a lot more than what had just happened to keep her away.

At least she knew he was safe, and with Laurel. The woman who had helped her after the accident had rung the school twice, once to let them know what had happened and then again to check that Billy had been picked up. The news had given Callie something to hold on to while they waited for the ambulance to arrive.

Good old Laurel, coming through after all these years. Even though she had such a demanding job, she'd been there when it counted. Odd that she'd been the one to ride to the rescue, given that Sonia was the stay-at-home mum. But anyway, Laurel would take good care of Billy. She knew about his anxiety, and how sensitive he was. She'd do her best to distract him and entertain him and take his mind off things.

That was what was really important: that Billy should be protected from his fears. Not to mention the ignorance and badness of other people, including the parts of his own family that she'd decided long ago to keep him well away from.

EIGHT

BILLY

As the children's news programme started he heard the crunch of a car pulling onto the gravel in front of the house, and got up and raced into the hallway in case this was Mum come to get him. But the person who came in was a man – a tall man in a suit, with thick white eyebrows and hair and suntanned skin. Not the kind of tan people got from working outside all day, but the kind you got from holidays to nice places, or playing golf.

The man saw Billy and stopped in his tracks. He stood there looming over him as if he was used to crouching down to get to other people's levels, but wasn't yet sure whether he was going to bother in this case. He said, 'You must be Billy.'

'I am,' Billy said, and waited for the man to say who he was. But he didn't. Really, grown-ups could be very rude sometimes.

Without taking his eyes off Billy – it was almost as if he thought Billy might sneak off and try and steal something – the man called out, 'Janice?'

'Yes, yes, I'm here,' Granny called out, and came hurrying in out of the kitchen with an apron on, looking hot and bothered. She said, 'This is Billy, Callie's boy. Like I told you. Laurel brought him here because Callie's been rushed to the hospital.'

'Yes, I figured. I can't see what other strange boy we would have about the place,' the man said.

'Billy, this is Ron, my husband,' Granny explained.

'Ron Greenwood,' Ron said, as if it was important to stress that he – and Granny too, Billy guessed – had a different surname to Billy and his mum. 'Billy, it's a pleasure to make your acquaintance. I'm sorry to hear about what happened to your mother today. But I'm sure they'll be taking very good care of her.'

Ron was trying to be twinkly-eyed as he said this but didn't do a very good job of it, like a Santa in a department store who'd just about had enough and didn't want to have to see excited kids ever again. He stretched out his hand for Billy to shake and Billy wasn't surprised when he held it a bit too tight for comfort, as if to rub it in that he was big and strong and Billy was small and probably quite weak.

Granny, who had seemed so powerful and strong when she was dealing with Laurel, now didn't look powerful at all. She was clasping her hands together beseechingly, as if she expected Ron to be angry and was ready to plead for forgiveness. Billy felt sorry for her and found himself liking Ron even less than he had at first.

'So is there any news from the hospital?' Ron asked.

'Not yet.'

'I see,' Ron said, as if he didn't. 'And Callie just happened to call on you? After all this time? And you came running?'

Granny shot a warning look in Billy's direction. 'She didn't call on me. I don't suppose she was in any fit state to call on anybody. Laurel phoned me, like I told you. You know Laurel, Callie's friend, the one who has her own radio show. She called me on the landline. I guess she had the number from way back. She said she had to work and I said I was free and I'd be glad to help out. What else could I have said, Ron? Obviously I said yes.'

'I'm not saying it's a bad thing,' Ron said, holding up his hands as if to emphasise how reasonable he was willing to be. 'I mean, like I said, I'm very sorry to hear this has happened. It sounds like a horrible thing, and obviously, it's always a good thing to help people out. I'm just trying to understand, that's all. So, as far as we know, does Callie even know Billy's here?'

Granny shook her head. Ron folded his arms and sighed. 'Well, I don't know what you expect to come of this, Janice, but given the history, I wouldn't look for gratitude.' He turned to Billy. 'How are you doing, then Billy? Bearing up? Would you say you've been well treated here? Or has Janice been terribly cruel, and locked you in the basement with the spiders?'

'It's been fine,' Billy said.

'Well, you might need to make that clear to your mother by and by,' Ron said. He turned back to Granny and sniffed the air. 'How's dinner coming along? I'm starving.'

'It's on the way,' Granny said, with an attempt at a smile.

'Good,' Ron said, nodding thoughtfully. He winked at Billy, who didn't quite know how to react. 'Enough for three?'

'Oh, I should think so,' Granny said.

'Good. Well, I'll look forward to getting to know you better over dinner, Billy,' Ron said heartily. He stretched slightly, as if he'd just made a major effort and deserved to rest. 'And now I think it's time for a drink. You'll keep me posted, won't you, Janice? If there's any news from the hospital. But I wouldn't expect it to be quick. She's probably stuck on a ward somewhere waiting for someone to come and see her. Anyway, at least we know she's in the best place.'

He disappeared into the living room. Granny and Billy stayed in the hallway, looking at each other, and Billy had the odd feeling that they were a couple of kids waiting for the inevitable moment when the grown-up who'd just left them would get annoyed by something that was both their fault, and would let them know it.

Sure enough, they heard Ron exhale sharply, as if something had exasperated him, and then the voice coming from the TV in the background changed from the children's channel newsreader to someone talking about sport.

Granny said, 'Billy, do you have some homework to do?'

'A bit.'

There were some spellings to learn, and a boring punctuation worksheet. Normally he'd have put both tasks off for as long as possible, but suddenly the idea of homework seemed quite appealing. At least it might give him an excuse not to have to sit in the living room and watch sport with Ron, who obviously wouldn't want him there.

'You can do it in the spare room while I finish getting dinner ready,' Granny said. She picked up his schoolbag, which he'd left by his shoes near the front door. 'I'll show you.'

As he followed her up the stairs he tried to picture Mum living in this house, with these people. A young version of Mum, but older than he was. She'd told him once that she'd been sixteen when she first moved to this village. Only six years older than he was now. But usually she didn't want to talk about it, although Billy knew that her dad had died not long before, and then Granny had decided quite quickly to get married again.

And now he was going to spend the night here. It was shaping up to be the longest time he'd spent apart from Mum since the winter when she got a really bad dose of flu, a couple of years ago, and hadn't been able to get out of bed and he'd gone to stay with Sonia for a couple of days. He didn't really remember much about that, but his anxiety had got much worse afterwards. He hoped it wasn't going to get the better of him tonight. He felt fluttery and weird already, and it would be awful if the really bad feelings came back without Mum around to help him.

Granny showed him into the room at the end of the upstairs

corridor. It was a small box room painted a sugary shade of pink, with a net-curtained window looking out onto the ivy-covered house on the other side of the road. There was a bed with a white quilted cover on it and no bedding, a small desk and chair, a built-in wardrobe and some shelves in the corner, but mostly it looked empty and unused.

'A long, long time ago, this room was your mum's,' Granny said.

She sounded as if she was trying to be firm and bright, but Billy wasn't fooled. Maybe this was something he'd be able to tell Mum later – that Granny had been sad about showing him her old room, which she hadn't been back to visit for so many years.

But surely Mum never would have chosen that shade of pink. That looked like a colour Granny would have chosen – it wasn't all that different from the shade of her jumper. Mum didn't really go in for pastels. Their flat was mostly painted white, because Mum said otherwise they'd feel as if the walls were closing in on them, and the place was small enough as it was.

Granny noticed him checking out the few bits and pieces of clutter arranged on top of the chest of drawers and on the shelves in the corner, none of which looked as if it could ever have belonged to Mum.

'Those are Emily's things,' she said. 'You don't know who Emily is, do you? I guess your mum never mentioned her. She's my stepdaughter. Emily Greenwood, Ron's daughter from his first marriage. Your mum could have changed her surname to be the same as ours, but she didn't want to. Anyway, we all lived here together once upon a time, believe it or not.'

She picked up the framed photograph on top of the chest of drawers, examined it briefly and passed it to Billy to look at. 'That's Emily,' she said, 'on her graduation day. She's very nice. Very easy to get along with. I think you'd probably like her.'

The photo was of a woman wearing a black scholar's cap and a black cape, edged with white fur, over her summer dress. The woman looked pleased with herself but also rather hot and as if she was worried she might be about to sneeze.

Granny retrieved the photo from Billy and put it back, and Billy said, 'Do you have a picture like that of my mum?'

'Not out on display,' Granny said. 'I do have one, but it's tucked away somewhere. I know that probably seems unfair to you.'

'Not really. I mean, I guess you haven't seen my mum for a long time, so it makes sense if you like Emily better.'

'It's not really about *liking*,' Granny said. 'The way things are, between me and your mum...' She stopped. 'The other things in here are Emily's too,' she went on. 'We're storing some stuff for her until she gets a place of her own. She's getting married soon. In December, a bit before Christmas. It's going to be a beautiful winter wedding.' She smiled at him. 'Maybe you could come. Would you like to? If your mum agreed. Maybe she would want to come too. I'm sure Emily would be delighted to have you there. Both of you.'

'I'll have to see what my mum says,' Billy said firmly. It didn't seem to him like a good idea for Granny to start talking about things like weddings, not with Mum in the hospital and nobody knowing what was going to happen next. It seemed like – what did Mum call it? – tempting fate.

'You never know, maybe what's happened today will make her have a bit of a rethink,' Granny said wistfully. She reached out and put her hand lightly on Billy's shoulder, then withdrew it. 'We had a fight, a long time ago, and I said things I shouldn't have done, and she never forgave me. But you know what they say – "blood is thicker than water". You're my grandson, and now we've met, I want you to know you're always welcome here.'

'Thanks,' Billy said cautiously.

Granny hesitated. 'You and your mum are very close, I suppose,' she said.

Billy shrugged. 'She's my mum, so yeah, I guess.'

Granny moved towards the door as if to go, then turned back as if she couldn't quite bring herself to let the subject drop and said, 'I guess she's not seeing anyone at the moment?'

'Seeing someone? You mean, does she have a boyfriend?'

Billy could barely hide his distaste for the idea. It seemed such a nosey thing to ask, and anyway, why would Mum want or need a boyfriend? She had him. It wasn't as if she was lonely.

The question also touched on something to do with their living arrangements that he and Mum had an unspoken agreement to keep quiet about, as far as possible. Mum slept on the sofa bed in the living room every night so Billy could have the flat's only bedroom to himself, and this didn't seem like the kind of arrangement a boyfriend would like.

Billy had always secretly been very glad that his mum didn't want to get involved with anybody. It would be really awful to have some stranger hanging out in their little flat, so that Billy would be forced to stay in his bedroom the whole time and wouldn't be able to watch TV.

'She doesn't want a boyfriend. Ever,' Billy said firmly. 'We're happy as we are.'

Then the doorbell rang downstairs, and Granny muttered something that sounded suspiciously like a swear word under her breath and told Billy she'd call him down when dinner was ready, and hurried off to answer it.

Billy's heart was beating fast. He hadn't liked it when Granny started asking questions about Mum. It made him feel disloyal. But he wasn't trembling. Not too bad at all, really.

He breathed slowly and gently and his heartbeat slowed. He closed the bedroom door and sat down at the desk and got his homework out of his bag and spread it out so he could pretend he was doing it if she looked in on him. And then he got up and looked around the room.

Apart from the graduation photo, the stuff Emily was keeping in here all seemed very childish. There was a costume doll with a fixed, slightly creepy smile, a plastic silver trophy and some odd bits of badly painted pottery. Someone who didn't have a spare room like this, a room they didn't actually need, would probably have thrown those things away.

He felt indignant on Mum's behalf that they had Emily's old toys out on display as if they were special, but they didn't even have a proper photo of Mum. And yet Granny had obviously felt bad about this. It was all very confusing.

The wardrobe was empty and all he found in the chest of drawers was a neat little pile of perfumed soaps, probably Granny's stash of emergency presents. The scent they gave off was too strong to be pleasant, the kind of artificial sweetness that people used to hide smells they were embarrassed about. The whole house smelt a bit like that.

He stood in the doorway and scanned the room from left to right in case he'd missed anything. He wanted to loiter here as long as possible, because once he'd checked out this room he'd have to move on to exploring the rest of the upstairs. That would mean opening the bedroom door and creeping out. It might also mean being caught, and although he'd already thought of an excuse – he could say he was looking for the toilet – he was nervous that it would mess things up if Granny guessed he'd been snooping. She seemed like a nervy kind of person, and people like that could get pretty angry when they lost their tempers.

To be a proper spy, you had to live like the people you were spying on. Had he read that somewhere, or had he come up with it himself? It made sense, anyway.

He'd tried sitting at the desk. He'd opened the wardrobe

and the chest of drawers. What else would someone who lived in this room do?

He went over to the window and looked down at the street below. An old lady was walking away from the house, down the driveway toward the road – that must be the person who'd rung the doorbell. She was properly old, small and stooping with a slightly hunched back and a thin fuzz of grey hair. She went along the pavement a little way and then turned onto the path to go into the house next door. The neighbour, then. An elderly neighbour. He wondered what she had wanted.

The view was nothing special. There was the road and trees and the house opposite with all the ivy growing on it, where the woman lived who Granny had gone to speak to earlier. The ivy had reached up from ground level to cover part of the bedroom window facing him and was sending out tendrils towards the roof. There was a car parked outside, a small one that looked as if it wouldn't go very fast. It looked like an old person's car, though the woman Granny had spoken to had been quite young-looking.

He remembered a story his mum had read him a lot when he was little, about two children, a girl and a boy, who lived across the road from each other in a place where the street was so narrow that they could run a string between their bedroom windows and send notes to each other. Later on in the story, the boy had fallen into the clutches of the evil Snow Queen and the girl had braved the cave of some brigands to rescue him. But the Snow Queen had frozen the boy's heart, and by the time the girl found him, he was as good as dead. Her tears had melted the ice in his eyes and had brought him back to life, but Billy had found that part of the story silly: it seemed much more likely to him that the Snow Queen and the brigands would have won.

He decided to try out the bed. He might as well, since he was probably going to end up sleeping here. He lay down on the mattress as carefully as he could, so as not to make it creak, then stretched out flat on his back and folded his arms behind his head.

The windowsill was painted with shiny white gloss, but whoever had done the job had cut corners, or perhaps run out of paint, because they hadn't done the underside, which was a slightly unpleasant shade of pale green left over from some previous time in the life of the house. The pale green was marked by a small smudge of dirt at the far end. Was it dirt? Or something else? It looked red. Red like blood.

He swung himself round and moved closer, and the red smudge resolved itself into a small scrawl of handwriting.

Even with his glasses, he had to squint to make it out. It was Mum's handwriting, that was for sure. A bit rounder and more upright, a bit more childish. But definitely hers. She'd left a note at the far end of the windowsill, in the green paint, on the underside where nobody would notice it unless they lay down on the bed the way he had done, and took the time to look around.

It said *Callie 4 Reuben 4 ever*, and next to it was a heart.

NINE

REUBEN

Janice had sent him a brief text message in response to his call: *No news from the hospital yet. Will let you know.* He'd managed to stop himself from contacting her again. She'd said she'd tell him when she knew anything, and surely she would honour that.

And now he was almost within shouting distance of her house, and the one he had grown up in.

As they headed up the hill he warned the taxi driver to take it slowly, because they were nearly there. He still sometimes dreamed about this road. In his dreams it was usually strangely altered – very long, or very dark, or otherwise distorted. In reality it looked quite normal – pretty, even – a country road on a summer evening with trees to either side, and a few houses on the outskirts of a village. But it still felt like travelling into hostile territory.

Then, as if in a flash of light that was so bright it was almost blinding, he spotted Callie's old house, where Janice and Ron still lived: the fussy flowers, the windows with their net curtains, and the yellow front door that he'd seen every time he'd come out of his own house. And had only once gone through.

'OK, this is it,' he said. 'You can pull up anywhere along here.'

The taxi driver pulled in, and Reuben took in the sight of his father's house.

It was so changed he almost didn't recognise it. How could it have got so bad so quickly? It looked abandoned, like something from a fairy tale, and so overgrown with ivy it was as if it was being pulled down into the ground. As if the ivy wanted nothing more for it than to be forgotten and destroyed.

But it *was* the same house – and there was his dad's old Ford right in front of him, twenty years old now. Maybe Theresa took it out every now and again. He wondered if she'd ever hidden the keys from his dad. Would Dad mind not being able to drive it any more? That was probably one of many things he was going to find out.

He paid the taxi driver, headed across the road and rang the doorbell. As he waited for Theresa to come to the door he heard the sound of a piano being played inside. Unmistakeably his father's touch. Dad had always had that gift – whenever he played any instrument, Reuben could always tell it was him.

Gifted he might be, but he had not been a particularly patient teacher, at least where Reuben was concerned. Reuben's piano lessons had been pure misery from beginning to end, until he was finally allowed to give up. Would he have struggled so much with anyone else? But nobody had ever suggested trying another teacher, and Reuben would not have dared ask. Looking back, he wondered if his dad had really been as frustrated by his lack of progress as he had seemed. Had part of him wanted Reuben to fail?

The door opened and Theresa let him in. 'Great, you made good time,' she said, and he remembered the pub quiz she wanted to go to. 'Come on in.'

She was speaking in a low voice, and held her finger to her lips to warn him to be quiet. Dad had always been sensitive to background noise when he was playing the piano. Perhaps he'd got even more tyrannical about it. Reuben attempted a sympathetic smile, as if to say that it must be tough for Theresa having to humour a maestro, and stepped into the house.

The hallway seemed not to have changed since he was last here. At least it was clean, if a little dingy. He followed her through to the kitchen, which was in much the same state as the hall – in need of a lick of paint, but not quite as decrepit as the outside of the house might suggest. She scribbled a note on a piece of paper:

If we interrupt him, he'll lose his flow. We need to leave him till he's finished and then go in.

He nodded. It seemed Dad had definitely got more temperamental. Through a process of pantomime, she offered him a drink and he asked for a glass of water. As he sipped it he took in how tired and fed-up she looked. Mind you, it was possible that she might think the same of him.

She'd obviously made an attempt to get ready to go out, and was wearing big, bright earrings and eyeshadow and lipstick, and a shiny dark red blouse. He'd always thought of her as a glamorous, dressy kind of person, keen on being taken out to shiny bars and expensive new restaurants: there was something mortifying about seeing her reduced to being grateful for a couple of hours answering quiz questions in the local pub. They had never been close – he'd kept his distance from her as well as from his dad – but he couldn't help but feel sorry for her.

The music his dad was playing was measured and classic and sad. Reuben remembered the many hours of his teenage evenings that had been spent with headphones on, listening to anything that would block out the sound of his dad's pupils on the piano in the teaching room at the back of the house, the scales and arpeggios and fumbling performances of the set pieces for grade exams. Though Reuben had been in no position to criticise even the weakest, most hesitant pupils, the ones who obviously never practised and who were only taking lessons because their mothers wanted them to. As Dad had told him once, more in sorrow than in anger, Reuben had less innate musical ability than anybody else it had ever been his misfortune to teach.

Finally the music stopped and Theresa nodded at him and moved decisively through to the living room. 'Look who's here to see you,' she declared brightly.

Dad was sitting at his upright piano, the one he reserved for his own use, which was where it had always been, in pride of place next to the sofa. Reuben had never been allowed to play it, but had practised and taken his lessons on the piano in the teaching room.

'Maybe when you know what you're doing,' Dad had said to him. 'Once you've passed grade five.' But he never had.

Dad turned, caught sight of Reuben, and then swivelled round and studied him with an expression of mild disbelief.

'You haven't come to make trouble, have you? I really don't want trouble,' he said. 'It's very important that I should have peace and quiet to practise.'

'Of course he isn't here to make trouble. He's here to see you, like I explained,' Theresa said. 'Isn't that nice? I'm going to pop out for a bit.' She turned to Reuben. 'For now, he'll probably just want to keep on playing. Later on, he might want to watch some TV. If he has a bit of a snooze that's fine, leave him be. He shouldn't need the bathroom, but if he does you might want to just keep an eye on him and check he's turned the taps off. I'll be back at eleven. He usually goes to bed quite late, around midnight, so you don't have to worry about that.'

'Why are you talking about me like that?' Dad protested. 'I

am in the room, you know. I can hear every word you're saying.'
He shook his head. 'Women! You always want to reduce men to
being absolute idiots.'

Theresa moved forwards and pecked him on the cheek.
'Just trying to make sure you have a nice relaxing evening,' she
said. 'All right then, I'll say bye-bye! Why don't you play something for Reuben? I'm sure he'd love to listen to you.'

'Oh, I don't think he would,' Dad said. Then he turned to
Reuben with a sort of awful hopefulness. 'Would you?'

Reuben had to suppress a sudden, violent urge to walk
straight out again. He couldn't very well be angry with his dad
any more, no matter what had happened in the past. The only
way to behave was to be patient and kind.

'Sure, I'll listen,' he said, and forced himself to smile.

He sat down on the sofa and Dad turned back round and
spread his hands across the piano keyboard with a sigh of relief.
Theresa gave Reuben an encouraging smile and went out. Dad
began to play, and a few minutes later Reuben heard the front
door close behind Theresa.

He carried on sitting there as if marooned, listening to
Dad's playing and remembering again what he had never quite
forgotten, the intense frustration of being subjected to music
that is not what, at that particular moment, you yourself would
have chosen to hear. He would have chosen silence. He would
have chosen to be anywhere but here.

Then Dad began to rummage through the music on the
music stand, picked something out and put it at the front,
played a couple of chords and looked over his shoulder at
Reuben.

'It's a duet,' he said, and carried on playing with his left
hand. 'One of your old exam pieces. Do you remember? It's a
lovely melody. Not particularly challenging. Beyond me why
you couldn't manage it.'

His dad had never had particularly good filters, at least

when it came to Reuben and the kind of things he would say to him. If, as Theresa said, he was becoming more confused, perhaps he would be even more outspoken now.

'I guess it isn't given to all of us to have the same gifts as our parents,' Reuben said.

Dad carried on playing, and for a moment it wasn't clear whether he had heard, or even whether he was still listening. Perhaps he was reserving all his concentration and focus for the music. But then he paused and said, 'Why don't you have anyone in your life, Reuben? Woman. Man. Whatever.' Another chord, slow and rippling. 'You don't even have a cat. A pet hamster. A goldfish. I'm willing to bet you haven't got so much as a pot plant. Why is that?'

Because I'm scared of turning out to be like you. Because of the secrets I chose to keep for you. Because I still feel like I need to be able to take off if things go wrong.

'I guess it suits me to keep things easy,' Reuben said, trying to sound like the relaxed kind of person for whom this might be true. 'Uncluttered. That's how I like it.'

Another run of notes. 'Footloose and fancy-free, eh? Problem is, I don't believe a word of it. I think you'd really like to have someone. You just don't have the least idea how to go about it.'

'Having a partner isn't the be-all and end-all,' Reuben said reasonably.

Dad played another phrase, one that swelled to a crescendo and then died away. 'No. That's true. I suppose you probably blame me.'

'I'm a grown-up. My life is my own business.'

'That means yes. Well, there we are. It's useful, isn't it, to have someone else to blame.' He was working over the high notes now, his fingers moving with a speed and confidence and delicacy that Reuben found impressive in spite of himself.

'I'm not sure we should talk about this kind of thing,'
Reuben said.

Dad gave no sign as to whether he agreed with this or not.
Instead he picked out another fast, challenging phrase, playing
with a flourish that was pure showmanship. All Reuben's old,
long-buried hatred and resentment began to rise up and reassert
itself. How could Dad still know exactly how to push his
buttons? And yet he did.

'I tried playing this with your friend from across the road,'
Dad said. 'I thought she was quite promising. She definitely
could have been taught.' Another phrase, slow and languorous
this time, the build-up to some kind of climax.

Reuben said, 'Are you talking about Callie?'

'Yes, yes. Janice's daughter. Her boy is there at the moment.
Skinny-looking thing. Wouldn't say boo to a goose.' His hands
picked out the same pattern of notes that had seemed sensuous
just minutes before, but now was angry and crashing. Then he
played a final, elegant phrase that gave the melody a sense of
finality, brought down the piano lid and swung round to face
Reuben.

'I suppose you're still annoyed with me,' he said. 'It's very
easy to be judgemental when you're young. Most of us become
more reluctant to judge as we get older and make our own
mistakes. But not you.'

'Not everyone makes the kind of mistakes you made,'
Reuben said.

His dad raised his hands and then let them drop, in a
gesture that was both a shrug and a plea for forgiveness. *I
couldn't help myself*, the gesture seemed to say. *It was so long
ago, a different time. Does any of it really matter any more? Who
cares? Who even remembers? How can you possibly still hold a
grudge over every little thing that happened back then?*

'Your mother was very happy with me, you know,' he said.
'She loved me very much, right up until the end, and she

wanted me to be happy too. People outside a marriage should never expect to be able to understand how and why it works. Especially not any child of the marriage. Any marriage is a mystery, even to the two people on the inside. But ours did work. So I don't think you have any right to reproach me. She certainly didn't.'

'That's because she never knew what you were getting up to behind her back. And she didn't know because I never told her.'

Dad waved his hand in a dismissive gesture. 'She wasn't stupid. She chose not to know. Even more so once she was sick, and realised how serious it was. The proximity of death does have an effect on one's sense of perspective. Anyway, I really can't see the point in dredging up all of that now. I suppose you want to make yourself feel better by making me feel bad. But if you want to ask hard questions, maybe you should start with yourself.'

He got to his feet, and Reuben did too. His dad was still a little taller than he was, but seemed smaller than he remembered, as if he'd shrunk slightly. Throughout Reuben's childhood he'd been a giant – a giant who other people, his mum in particular, seemed to adore, and who Reuben avoided and was terrorised by. Reuben had watched the way the women around him treated him like a golden god. But he was definitely not a giant now, and Reuben knew he had never been a god. And if Theresa was right, he was facing a faster decline than any of them would have expected.

'Young people want it all their own way,' his dad said. 'They want their freedom, and then complain about the consequences. You can't be good and have what you want. That's the trouble. You have to choose, one or the other. And trying to be good is all very well, but it can really be quite lonely. As I think you know.'

He gave Reuben a sharp, almost triumphant look, then

made for the armchair he'd always favoured and eased himself down with a sigh of satisfaction.

'Would you switch the TV on for me?' he asked. 'Theresa does insist on turning it off at the plug, and I find it very awkward putting it back on again. My knees have been playing up a bit, and once I'm down there it's not that easy to get up.'

Reuben suddenly wanted nothing more than to get away from him. He knelt down to put the TV on and adjusted it to the volume Dad wanted, and then escaped out to the small, overgrown back garden to breathe the open air.

He was still out there, sitting on the edge of the patio and watching the blackbirds get bolder and move closer, when someone hammered on the glass of the patio door to the extension that Dad had used as his teaching room.

He turned round and saw Dad there, disgruntled and seemingly baffled by the patio door mechanism, which he was pulling at feebly and without effect. Reuben got up and pulled the door back without difficulty and went through.

The teaching room was tidier than the rest of the downstairs of the house, presumably because, these days, it was used less. It was all unpleasantly familiar: the piano where Reuben had once sat for his excruciating lessons, a couple of wall-mounted guitars, the music stands, the easy chairs for the parents who occasionally liked to sit in. These days, though, it felt unused and abandoned.

Reuben said, 'What's up?'

'There's someone at the door,' Dad said querulously. 'Can you see to it? Theresa normally does. It's such a nuisance, people bothering you all the time.'

He headed back to his armchair in front of the TV, and Reuben hurried out to the hall, hoping to see Janice. But instead he opened up to the elderly neighbour from across the road, who was smiling conscientiously at him.

'Reuben – how lovely to see you back,' she said, and held

out her hand for him to shake. Her grasp was surprisingly firm. 'I don't know if you remember me – Valerie Jancett?'

He looked beyond her to Callie's house and the one next to it. Yes, he did remember her – Mrs Jancett, the one who always talked to everyone, who always knew what was going on, or at least, thought she did. It had been hard to leave the house without encountering her, as she was often either working in her front garden – which she seemed to keep full of various different plants that needed a lot of attention – or striding to and fro on various errands.

'Yes, I remember you,' he said.

Mrs Jancett held on to his hand fractionally longer than he was comfortable with, then relinquished it.

'I saw you'd come back, and I thought I'd pop round and say hello,' she said. 'Are you just back for a flying visit, or are you going to be staying for a while?'

'Just a flying visit,' Reuben said. He hadn't got as far as thinking about how long he might stay.

'I see,' Mrs Jancett said, nodding wisely. 'I just wondered if you'd heard about Callie having been in an accident? Knocked down by a bike, apparently. Sounds quite nasty. I called round there earlier and Janice told me all about it.'

'I heard Callie had been rushed off to hospital. Is there any more news?'

Mrs Jancett shook her head. 'Not that I know of. Billy is here, with Janice. Callie's boy. I don't know whether you've seen him.'

'No,' Reuben said.

'He's not been round here for years. Not since he was tiny,' Mrs Jancett said. Her face twitched as if there was something more she wanted to say, but she couldn't quite bring herself to come out with it. 'Anyway, I'm sure we're all crossing our fingers that Callie makes a swift recovery,' she said finally. 'I just wanted to let you know that I'm around, in case there's anything you need. I'm usually at home, so as I say, as long as it's at a reasonable hour, don't hesitate to ask.'

'Thanks. That's good of you. But I don't think there is anything,' Reuben said.

Mrs Jancett nodded and smiled, and he realised she felt sorry for him. 'Well then, I'll leave you in peace. It's just—'

'Yes?'

She leaned forward confidingly. 'I do have some idea of what went on before you took off for Australia, you know. I saw the comings and goings. I don't miss much.'

'I don't know what you think you know, or what you saw, or what you're trying to say, exactly,' Reuben said. 'And, with respect, I don't want to know. I'm pretty sure it's none of your business.'

Mrs Jancett raised her eyebrows at that, but appeared to decide to overlook his rudeness.

'Your mother adored you,' she said. 'She was very proud of you. Always full of the news of your latest doings. You were a good son to her. You've got a good heart, Reuben, and if I can see that, I'm sure other people can too. I wouldn't like to think that anyone might take advantage. Women can be very ruthless. Especially the kind of woman who's no better than she ought to be.'

'Mrs Jancett—'

'It's all right, Reuben, I've said my piece. I didn't come over to pick a fight, and I certainly didn't want to upset you. You're right, it's none of my business. I just wanted to say that I'm there if you need me. Now I'd better let you get back to your dad. I know Theresa feels she has to keep quite a close eye on him these days.'

She turned and went off back across the road, walking with the unhurried pace of someone who feels they've done their duty, whether or not it has been appreciated.

Reuben was briefly tempted to run after her and force her

to explain exactly what she'd been getting at. But the prospect of finding out exactly what she'd seen, and the conclusions she had drawn from it, made him feel sick.

He retreated back into the house and closed the door, and decided to do his best to avoid Mrs Jancett in future.

She'd been right about one thing. He needed to keep an eye on Dad, as she'd said.

But as for the rest...

You were a good son to her. You've got a good heart.

Clearly, she didn't know nearly as much as she thought she did.

TEN

CALLIE

Strictly speaking, she wasn't alone on the ward as night fell. She could hear the other patients – someone quietly moaning in pain, and someone, inevitably, snoring. But she felt alone, and it seemed as if she probably had a long wakeful night ahead of her.

Still, hopefully Billy would be sound asleep, tucked up in the spare room at Laurel's house. One of the many spare rooms.

Thank goodness for the nurse who, though obviously harassed and overworked, had agreed to call Laurel and let her know Callie was fine, and was due to have an operation the following day. The nurse had said she hadn't been able to get through to Laurel direct, but she'd left a message, and hopefully once that was passed on to Billy it would set his mind at rest. He might even have heard already, or otherwise Laurel would tell him first thing tomorrow.

And tomorrow afternoon, all being well, she should be able to see him.

At least it was her in here, not him. Now that really would have been unbearable. Luckily he wasn't an accident-prone child, and she'd never had to dash into hospital with him after a fall or collision. But there had been the inevitable fevers, the sore throats and earaches, and every now and then, urgent appointments at the doctor's surgery. She'd felt the full weight of her responsibilities then, and it had always been awful to see Billy laid low, pale and quiet and off his food, entirely dependent on her to care for him and decide when it was time for him to see a doctor, and get him there.

Then, each time when he recovered, there had been the wonderful relief of seeing him back to his old self, back up out of bed and off the sofa and full of energy and chat...

Those situations had been frightening but at least they had come and gone and been resolved relatively quickly. His anxiety had been much harder to deal with, in a way she couldn't have imagined before it developed. There was nothing easily diagnosable to fight off, nothing concrete and physical that could be fixed. Just symptoms. Lethargy. Loss of appetite. Disrupted sleep. The sudden reluctance to go to school in the morning. Little ritual habits, undertaken to reassure himself: nail-biting, foot-jiggling, checking the gas was off and that the car and the house were locked. Checking, and then checking again. It was contagious. His anxiety had made her feel anxious, all the more so the more she worried about him, until sometimes she barely knew who it had started with.

Other people didn't understand it and didn't always even believe it was there. And it had gone on for weeks, months, and then years, becoming part of the fabric of their lives, something she took account of when planning ahead almost without thinking about it. At the same time, the professionals she had turned to – the school, the family doctor – had told her he didn't meet the thresholds that would mean he should be referred to specialist services. And even if he did, the waiting lists were long, for non-emergency referrals – years long, she had been advised. In the meantime, there were courses she could do, and websites she could turn to for information and advice.

What they were really telling her, she had realised, was that it was down to her. Just as it had always been. And so she had read the websites, and had managed to go to one course, with Sonia babysitting, and then she had come to her own conclusions about what she needed to do: to be, as far as possible, calm and kind and consistent, and to build as much stability and happiness into her life with Billy as she could.

She had schooled herself not to put pressure on him and not to expect him to be any different to how he was, and at the same time, if he ever did volunteer any information about how he was feeling, not to contradict him or belittle him or suggest he should be feeling something different, but to accept it. Which was an uncomfortable thing to do, because him being anything other than happy made her feel bad, but she knew it was necessary to help him to cope.

They had gone on in that way together, like two people walking through bad weather who encourage each other, not with words, but by continuing side by side, and gradually, things had seemed easier. Though perhaps part of that was that both of them had got used to his vulnerability, and had begun to learn to live with it.

When she got out of hospital, she would make sure she never told him about all the frightening possibilities that had been raised with her by the doctors she had seen. That was just what medical people did, right? They told you the very worst that might happen, so you'd be pleased and relieved when everything turned out OK.

And yet, when the orthopaedic doctor had run through the risks of the operation she was to have first thing in the morning, the list had ranged from frightening to outright terrifying.

Infection. Difficulty using the arm. Nerve damage. Chronic pain...

Her arm was in a cast now – they'd put that on after they'd X-rayed it, just for the night, until they operated to fix it in the morning. They were keeping her in because of the risk of nerve damage to her dislocated and fractured elbow, she'd been told, and the danger that she could lose the use of her hand. Lose the use of her hand! It didn't seem possible. Surely the worst-case scenario, and not what was actually going to happen. Because how was she going to take care of Billy then?

She could still barely believe how easily she'd managed to damage herself. That split-second decision – putting one foot in front of the other to get to the other side of the road as she rushed to collect Billy from school – had put her here, lying on her back in a hospital gown, powerless and helpless and no use to him.

She hoped he'd had a good dinner. She hoped he wouldn't have nightmares the way he sometimes did, and wake without her there to comfort him.

It had been so easy to console him, once upon a time.

He'd been such a good baby. An easy baby, though as he was her first and only child, she had no one to compare him with.

His little face, his cheeks, the absolutely perfect curve of his smile, the eyes looking up at her with their bright, mysterious intelligence, fixed on her with love. Her baby in her arms, in her own front room with the biscuit-coloured tiles round the old gas fire. Her place. A safe space where nobody could come if she didn't want them to, and where no one could attack her or wound her with words or in other ways. And as long as she could protect herself, she could protect him too.

But that had just been an illusion. She had never really been safe.

She had realised that flat on her back waiting for the CT scan of her head, the white doughnut-shaped circle of the machine like a brilliant high-neck guillotine around her neck, though thankfully no damage to her head or neck had been found.

The possibility that she'd managed to keep herself from

dwelling on, that this was not just an accident but something more profound and permanent, had receded like a turning not taken. But the road it would have led to was still visible on the horizon, gleaming in the distance like a reminder that she wasn't out of the woods yet.

Because you could never tell, you could never be sure how anything was going to turn out...

There had been a night when it had been raining and the wet roads and stone buildings of the old town glistened under the street lights, when it seemed as if everything had been rolled out in front of her like a red carpet and all she had to do to lay claim to happiness was to step out in it.

The night that had given her Billy. The morning that had cost her Reuben.

And that night too, eventually, the darkness had closed over her and she had slept.

ELEVEN

BILLY

It seemed as if he had only just managed to fall asleep when the phone rang. One of those annoying mobile phone ringtones that most people didn't have any more. Almost immediately he was fully awake and had remembered where he was, and what had happened to put him here. He lay there on the unfamiliar bed that used to be Mum's in the strange house where his granny lived and listened to the faint, almost inaudible sound of Granny talking.

It had to be something to do with Mum. Surely. There was no other reason why anyone would call so late.

He got out of bed and pushed the door open, but he still couldn't hear properly, so he crept out on the landing. Granny was standing in the hall below. She was quiet, which meant she was listening to whatever the person who had called her was saying. Then she said, 'I see. Do you know when she might be able to come home?'

Mum was all right! That must be what the phone call was about. Billy pressed his hand to his mouth to stop himself from crying out. Mum was as good as home!

Everything was going to be fine. She'd come and get him,

maybe even tonight, and he wouldn't have to stay here any longer. Everything would go back to normal, and it would just be him and Mum at home and he'd probably never see Granny and Ron or come to their house again.

Although maybe he would actually feel a little bit sad about that...? It wasn't that he actively liked it here, and he wasn't very keen on Ron, but Granny had been quite nice and funny when she was hunting through the cupboards for a snack for him and could only find the things she ate to keep the weight off, as she'd explained to him, because they weren't very tasty and therefore it was hard to eat too much of them.

And the dinner had been all right, and afterwards she had tried to teach him how to play poker. It had been very complicated and he hadn't been very good at it, so Granny had said maybe it had better keep till he was older, and they had played snap instead. He'd never played snap with a traditional deck of cards rather than the kids' cards Mum had at home, but Granny had said they should just worry about matching the numbers and not worry about the suit, and that had worked out OK. She'd offered to read him a goodnight story, too, and had said that she'd found a copy of one of the Harry Potter books that she'd had on a shelf somewhere. He'd borrowed the book – he hadn't mentioned that he'd read it already – but had told her he was a bit too old to be read to, and she'd looked disappointed.

Granny said, 'OK. Thank you for letting me know, Laurel. I appreciate it. No problem at all, it's been an absolute pleasure having him here. Yes, we'll be in touch tomorrow. Goodbye! Sleep well!'

She sounded bright and cheery, as if everything was fine. But then he heard her inhale sharply, as if she was upset and maybe about to cry. Why would she feel sad now, when everything was about to sort itself out?

He started to sneak back along the landing, but then

Granny called out his name and he nearly jumped out of his skin.

'Billy, I know you're up there,' Granny said. 'Come on down and talk to me.'

He reluctantly moved to the top of the stairs. She was at the bottom, looking up at him. Her eyes looked a bit shiny. He hadn't been wrong about her being close to tears.

'That was good news,' she said as he came down towards her. 'Your mum's doing fine. They're going to operate to fix her elbow tomorrow morning. You should be able to see her after school, and she'll be home soon. Maybe tomorrow evening, or the next day. She'll have her arm in a cast for a bit, but it won't be long till she's good as new.'

Billy reached the bottom of the stairs. 'That's good,' he said.

'It is,' Granny agreed. 'And from now on she needs to jolly well look where she's going and not rush. You remind her, Billy. You tell her she has to take care of herself before she can take care of anyone else.'

He was never quite sure, afterwards, who had made the first move: whether he had stepped towards her, or whether she'd held out her arms towards him. But suddenly he found himself being hugged. It was a bit weird – nobody hugged him apart from Mum – but not awful. She was wearing a long pink dressing gown and flowery satin pyjamas and she smelt of lemons, and he could tell she didn't want to let him go, but eventually she did. Then she sniffed and rubbed her nose with the back of her hand, which was the kind of thing grown-ups did themselves if they felt the need but scolded kids for doing.

'So there you are, you see,' she said. 'Everything's going to be fine.'

'Are you going to come and see my mum in hospital, too?' Billy said.

'I don't know. I hope so. I'd like to. But given that she hasn't seen me for so long, maybe it wouldn't be a good time.'

'I don't know when there would be a better time,' Billy said. 'Why do you never see us? I know you said you had a fight with Mum, but why did you never make up?'

She sucked at her lower lip and regarded him ruefully, and he knew she was trying to think, not what the truth was, but what would be the best thing to say.

'That's a very good question, Billy,' she said. 'I guess sometimes people say things in the heat of the moment that are hard to go back on later. And your mum and I are both very proud, stubborn people. That's how we get by. What your mum doesn't know is that I'm actually very proud of *her*. Especially now I've met you and seen for myself what a great job she's done of bringing you up.'

'You should definitely see us,' Billy said. 'It's silly that you don't. We don't live very far away. My mum could drive here in no time at all. I mean, when she's better. When she's not got her arm in a cast any more. What's it called, this place?'

'Allingham. It's between Oxford and Kettlebridge.'

'Well, I guess she knows where it is. As she lived here before.'

Granny studied him apprehensively, as if what he might be about to say was terrifically important. 'Would you like that, Billy? To come back and visit? Or if I came to see you?'

'I think it would be nice,' Billy said. 'But I suppose it's not really for me to say. We don't really have very many visitors at our flat.'

'It's still that little ground-floor place round the corner from the school, right?' Granny said. 'It's on a close, with a name that's something to do with birds? Goosegreen Close? I remember that place.'

Now it was Billy's turn to stare. 'You've been to our flat?'

'Yeah, a long time ago. Your mum probably hasn't told you this, but I helped her buy it.'

'You did?'

This was beginning to make no sense at all. If Granny had done something kind like that, and seemed to be OK generally, why on earth would Mum refuse to see her?

'Yeah,' Granny said with an apologetic shrug, as if to acknowledge that it didn't make much sense to her either.

Then Ron appeared at the top of the stairs in his pyjamas, which were quite smart blue and white striped ones. But still, it seemed a bit undignified to see him like that, especially as Billy didn't really know him and it was pretty clear that he didn't really want Billy here, and was only putting up with him for Granny's sake.

'Janice, what's going on?' he asked plaintively.

'Laurel, with an update from the hospital. I've been trying to get through, but hadn't had much luck. But someone had actually called her. I guess Callie must have asked them to,' Granny said. 'You go back to bed, hon. I'll be up in a minute.'

'Oh. Well, that's good news, I suppose,' Ron said. 'Bit late to call, though,' he grumbled as he headed back to bed.

Granny and Billy exchanged glances, and Billy saw that she was annoyed by what Ron had said and hoped that Billy didn't mind it too much, but also, that she wasn't going to say anything about it and hoped Billy wouldn't either. He attempted to give her a reassuring smile. He felt as if he'd entered into some kind of conspiratorial pact with her, and it struck him that it sometimes felt a bit like this with Mum and he had never had that kind of unspoken understanding with anybody else.

'You'd better go back to bed too, Billy,' Granny said. 'You've got school in the morning. What time do you have to be there?'

'Twenty to nine,' Billy said, thinking how strange it was that she didn't know. But then, she hadn't been around. She was a granny and not like a granny at the same time.

'OK, well, we'll have to leave at eight then. If I can drop you off at eight thirty, I might be in with a chance of making it into work on time.'

Billy said, 'What do you do?'

'I work in sales,' Granny said. 'Part-time, but I'm actually very good at it. On a good day, I reckon I could sell just about anything to anybody.'

'What do you sell?' Billy asked. Obviously Granny was exaggerating, and boasting a little, but he was willing to believe that she could be very persuasive when trying to convince people to spend their money.

'Lingerie,' Granny said, and then, on seeing his puzzled expression, 'underwear. Ladies' underwear. Now I've embarrassed you. But, you know, it's not really embarrassing. It's just something people need, like... like pots and pans, or socks and shirts.'

'I'm not embarrassed,' Billy said staunchly. 'I'm going to go back to bed now.' And he hurried off back to his room, and lay down in the dark again and told himself to sleep.

But he couldn't. He heard the stairs creak as Granny came up to bed, and then the house was quiet, and all he could hear was the gentle hiss of rain falling outside and his heartbeat, which was still faster than it ought to have been.

He tried telling himself that everything was going to be all right now, but his heart didn't seem to believe him.

What if Mum was weird about him having got to know Granny? If she was OK with the idea of him and Granny spending time together, surely it would have happened before. And if Mum didn't like it, it might be something that wouldn't happen again.

All of which made him wonder what Mum had against Granny, exactly, and what Granny had said or done to make Mum so keen to keep them apart.

TWELVE

REUBEN

Theresa still wasn't back from her quiz night and his dad was snoring in front of the TV when a message finally came through from Janice.

> *Callie to have operation on fractured elbow tomorrow a.m. All well apart from that and she'll be home soon. Billy fine. So no need for panic. Didn't mean for you to dash over here. Just thought you would want to know, as you used to be friends. Maybe I overreacted. It's been a long day. But it seems everything is going to be OK.*

It was a huge relief. The best news he could have hoped for. And yet... *Used to be friends.* That was true, and it made him sad.

It sounded as if Janice was already regretting having got in touch with him, now the worst of the crisis had passed. Why had she, anyway? She had obviously felt that he ought to know. But had it been him she wanted to tell? Or had she thought it would be a way of reaching his dad without Theresa hearing everything that might need to be said?

Who knew what Callie had told her about what had gone on? That was a can of worms he really didn't want to open.

He replied, after some thought, *That's great news. Thanks for letting me know.* She didn't respond. Well, maybe she had gone off to have a well-earned sleep. What did she think of him? He had no idea. Probably not much. And probably, right now, she didn't care.

Theresa got back soon after, glowing and happy after her night out, and he retreated to bed himself.

Theresa had put him in his old bedroom, the small one at the front of the house – the exact equivalent of the room Callie had once slept in on the other side of the road. He listened to Theresa cajoling Dad into bed and then coming out and going into the next room along to sleep. Then, when the house was all dark and quiet, there was nothing to distract him from remembering what he had seen the morning he'd left this place for good.

Or so he had thought at the time. He had promised himself he'd never come back, and he'd gone on to leave the country, not expecting to return. And yet here he was, right back where he'd started.

At some point his dark thoughts must have given way to sleep, because he surfaced eventually to dim morning light, and found Callie sleeping soundly next to him.

Callie. Of course it was a dream. He decided not to move, not to disturb her. A dream was a bubble that you could only stay in for so long, but maybe if he was careful he could stay a little longer. In the world of the dream he was filled with tenderness towards her, as if there was no reason for them not to be together, and neither of them had ever let the other down. And there had been no lies, and no betrayal and no abandonment.

And then he woke for real, but not in the same room as the dream – he didn't know where that had been, some ideal, quiet, private space – and there was no one with him. Instead he was back in his dusty old bedroom, which hadn't been redecorated since he'd left it. It was still the same old magnolia, with a slightly faded square where one of his old posters had been taken down. What had it been? The Velvet Underground, perhaps. His dad had disapproved vigorously of his music taste. That had been part of the point.

And it was light. Seven thirty. In the hospital, five miles away, they would soon be preparing Callie for the operation. And in the house across the road, a young boy would be getting up and ready for school.

As he got dressed all he could think about was that this was his chance, and if he didn't act on it, he might not ever get another opportunity.

Maybe it was wrong, and maybe it was selfish, but he was going to try and see Billy anyway.

And that was when he let himself see it: that was why he had come. He had to see this boy, Billy, with his own eyes. This legendary boy. Callie's son. The child she'd devoted her life to. He'd heard about Billy, from time to time, but all he knew was that he was a bit shy and quiet. Reuben had no idea what he looked like, and Billy had always seemed unreal somehow, the way a child does if you still dream about their mother, but are unlikely ever to meet.

Billy was a character in someone else's story, a story Reuben had been forced out of. It was a shock to conceive of Callie's son as a living, flesh-and-blood person with hopes and thoughts and needs of his own.

Maybe it didn't make sense to feel this sense of urgency about it now, as if it was suddenly a matter of life and death, but there it was. It seemed the only way he'd ever be able to put his mind at rest.

He put his head round the kitchen door and saw that Theresa was there, watching his dad eat toast with folded arms and an expression of mild impatience. He said, 'I'm just popping out for a minute,' and hurried outside into the promising brightness of a clear summer morning after a night of rain.

Back when they were younger, he and Callie had never gone to each other's houses or called round for each other, but they had caught the same bus to school and back pretty much every day. Sometimes they had talked, but mostly they just sat near each other on the top deck. Maybe with one of them in front, or on the next seat across. In time, he'd known just by looking at her whether it had been a bad morning, which it often was. And then he had left it up to her as to whether she wanted to start chatting or not. She'd seemingly been able to read him just as easily. He'd never met anyone since who was as good at knowing when to not say anything.

In spite of what had happened, and whatever his life had turned into in the years since he'd walked away from her, he needed to be able to think that she and Billy were happy. And she had no way at all of knowing that was how he felt.

What a terrible waste it had been. But that was just the way he saw it. She'd probably never looked back.

He stepped forward and rang the doorbell, then forced himself to stand patiently and wait for a response.

He was excruciatingly nervous. He shouldn't really be here at all. He was bothering a family at a time of stress, when the last thing they needed was a long-lost neighbour calling round first thing in the morning. Janice would regret ever having reached out to him. She'd warn him off, tell him to get lost, and who could blame her...

And yet he had to try.

If there was one thing he'd learned, it was that not asking a question because you were afraid of the answer was even worse for you, in the long run, than the shock of finding out something you didn't want to know. Unasked questions were like secrets. They grew in the spaces between the things you were willing to talk about and admit. Knowing they were invisible to everybody else made them impossible to forget.

The door gave way abruptly, and he found himself face to face with a rather urchin-like boy with sticking-up hair and round glasses, wearing a slightly grubby school uniform polo shirt and grey shorts that exposed skinny legs.

'Billy,' he said.

But the first thing he thought was, *it's me*.

At that age, that was exactly what he'd been like. Small, shy, skinny, though without the glasses, and with freckles and lighter hair. Later on, around thirteen, he'd had a sudden growth spurt, and around the same time he'd got into long-distance running. He'd never been bulky or heavy, but being fitter and stronger had given him a physical confidence he'd lacked when he was younger.

He told himself the resemblance didn't mean anything. There were lots of shy skinny boys around, probably. Whole armies of them. And now that he was looking at him more closely, the boy had a look of Callie too. Something about the chin, the cheekbones. The bones. The freckles. Maybe even something of Janice there, as well. The brown eyes.

A boy with spiky dark hair that looked as if it resisted being tidy, and glasses, and brown eyes, and a delicately drawn face that suggested both defensive watchfulness and a sweetness of temperament that he was probably at pains to hide.

It was too much. He had no way of rationalising it. Reuben felt as if he'd been struck by lightning, or picked up by a tornado and deposited somewhere else, or bowled off his feet by an enormous, unstoppable wave.

But he couldn't show it. Billy was already looking at him suspiciously. Of course, he would have been taught to be wary of strangers. Kids today were probably even bigger on that kind of thing than they had been when he was young.

Billy said, 'Who are you?'

'I'm Reuben. I used to live in that house across the road,' Reuben said, gesturing towards the ivy-covered nightmare behind him. 'My dad still lives there. I'm just visiting at the moment.'

Billy screwed up his face. 'You lived in that house?'

Reuben glanced back over his shoulder at it. 'Yeah. It's kind of gone downhill since then.' He turned back to Billy and stretched out his hand. The occasion seemed to demand some kind of formality. 'Pleased to meet you.'

Billy looked up at him dubiously, then down at his hand, then back up at him again. He seemed to decide that it couldn't do too much harm, and reluctantly held out his own hand for Reuben to shake.

'I heard your mum had an accident,' Reuben said. 'I just wanted to find out how she is.'

'Oh, she's going to be OK,' Billy said. 'We're going to see her later. She might even be coming home today. That means I'll be going home too. I don't know when I'll be back.'

'That's good news. You must all be very relieved. So you're going to have to help her a lot, right?'

Billy shrugged. 'I help her a lot anyway. But yeah, I guess.'

There was a thundering on the stairs as Janice came down. 'Billy, who are you talking to? I thought it was the postman,' she said.

'It's someone from across the road,' Billy said.

'OK, well, you'd better go and finish getting ready for school.'

'I'm ready.'

'Well, go and get a bit more ready.'

Billy took the hint and retreated inside, and Janice took his place. She was fully made up with her hair pinned up, and was wearing a department store uniform. Inevitably, she'd aged since he'd seen her last, but it was obvious that she was no more willing to be a pushover now than she had been back then. She raised her chin and put her hands on her hips and eyed him defiantly.

'Reuben.'

'Janice.'

She was looking at him as if his presence could only mean trouble. As he'd feared, it seemed as if having got over the initial shock of Callie's accident, she was regretting having reached out to him.

'I know I asked Theresa to tell you about my daughter's accident,' Janice said, 'but I wasn't expecting you to show up on my doorstep. And I'm sure there's no harm done, but with all respect, Reuben, given how things are, I don't really like you talking to my little grandson without me there.'

'Sure. OK. I just thought, you know, given that you'd asked Theresa to pass on your number, and then you replied to my message about Callie last night—'

'Yes, well, when I popped over to speak to Theresa yesterday I probably wasn't thinking straight,' Janice said. 'I mean, I'd had a call out of the blue about my daughter, and I didn't know what state she was in, or how bad it was going to turn out to be, and I was out of my mind with worry. And then there was Billy. But anyway, you weren't talking to me just now. You were talking to Billy, and that's a whole different ball game.'

'OK. I'm sorry. Will you... would you give Callie my best wishes?'

Janice sniffed as if she thought this was a particularly inadequate offering, which of course it was.

'I will. But I have to tell you, Reuben, I am going to be treading very, very gently when I see my daughter. I don't know if she's even going to want to see me. I haven't seen her for ten

years. Not properly. Not to talk to. And I've missed out on
seeing my grandson for almost his whole life. Those are years
I'm not going to get back, but I have to look to the future. Now
I'm not going to jeopardise any of that to go giving Callie some
kind of polite, nice-to-know-you kind of message from you.'

Reuben blinked at her. He'd forgotten what Janice could be
like when she got her teeth into something.

'Now I know that you and Callie may have things to talk
about,' Janice went on, lowering her voice. 'But it seems pretty
obvious to me, and it should be obvious to you, that now is not
the time.' She dropped her voice lower still. 'I am not going to
have anybody come between me and my daughter and my
grandson again. Do you understand? So you better leave this
with me. I have your number. I'll let you know when I hear
about the operation, but that's it. If Callie wants to call you,
she'll call you. If she doesn't, she won't. I'm not going to try and
push her to do anything. I just want her to get well. And I don't
want you coming round here again any time soon. Especially
not uninvited, first thing in the morning. All right?'

'All right,' Reuben said.

'Good,' Janice said, nodding. 'Now if you'll excuse me, I
need to get Billy to school. You can give my best wishes to your
father and Theresa. We don't have much to do with each other,
but I know Theresa's been having a hard time. She'll probably
appreciate your support. Seems to me you've got enough going
on your side of the road to keep you busy, for now. Let's wait till
Callie's out of the woods, and then we'll see.'

And with that she withdrew and closed the door firmly in
his face.

He made his way back to his dad's house. Suddenly the
blue of the sky seemed brighter, the birdsong louder. Even
though Janice had just effectively told him to get lost, he was
elated.

He'd had the chance to shake Billy by the hand. That boy!

He was amazing. Incredible. He clearly had absolutely no idea how amazing and incredible he was. But Callie must see it, though he probably seemed slightly less miraculous to her, given that she was around him all the time.

He had to ring the doorbell to get back in, and it took a while for Theresa to come to the door, which made him feel slightly stupid. She raised her eyebrows at him, and stood back to let him in.

'Everything all right?'

'Oh... yeah. Just thought I'd pop over, you know. Callie's having an operation this morning.'

'Yes, you told me last night. Will you go and see her?'

'I don't know. Not today, I don't think. Maybe some other time. We'll see.'

'Right,' Theresa said, and then reached out to close the door to the living room, which was slightly ajar. The sound of the TV was instantly muffled. Reuben supposed his dad must be in there, and that Theresa didn't want him to overhear what she was about to say.

'Can I have a word with you? Maybe in your dad's old teaching room.'

'Sure.'

'It won't take a minute.'

He followed her, and she closed the music room door behind them.

'So,' she began, 'you coming here has made me think maybe there's a chance for us to do things a little bit differently in future.'

She talked a little about how much she'd enjoyed going out the night before, and how worried she'd been about his dad. She needed a break from time to time, she told him, and it was great that he was willing and able to come and stay, which he'd seemingly been so reluctant to do before.

'I think you can see how he is,' she said. 'He's not his old self. I would really appreciate your help, Reuben. I think you owe it to both of us. So I hope this won't be a one-off. We need to be in much more regular contact. And if you could persuade him to see a doctor, that would be a huge weight off my mind.'

Just twenty-four hours earlier he would have resisted. But as it was, he felt separated from his own normal point of view, as if he'd become a different person to that other self who had wanted to keep his distance.

'OK. I'll try,' he heard himself saying. 'And you're right. I should come back more often.'

'Great,' Theresa said, and treated him to her best smile, the one she must have used often with his dad in the early days. But maybe he was too cynical about her? Maybe she really loved his dad. After all, she'd stuck around. And Reuben was hardly in any position to be down on someone who had managed that.

THIRTEEN

CALLIE

The light in the small room outside the operating theatre seemed very bright, almost dazzling. She closed her eyes and tried not to think of all the things she'd been told could go wrong because of the general anaesthetic, a list of possible horrors to add to the list she'd already been presented with as risks of the operation itself.

People had general anaesthetic all the time with no ill effects. Most people probably didn't even want to know about the risks. When else in life were you presented with that kind of information before going ahead with something? Sometimes tunnel vision was no bad thing.

It had been like that when she decided to have Billy. She had wanted him so much, and she'd believed that wanting him, and loving him, would be enough to make everything else fall into place. She'd been sure that she could love him enough for two, that she could be there for him and protect him, and that it didn't matter about anybody else.

And she'd been right, and it had worked, more or less. Until now.

She opened her eyes and saw the anaesthetist leaning over her with a clear rubbery oxygen mask.

'If anything happens to me, tell Billy I love him,' she said.

He nodded. His face seemed very large and clear and it occurred to her that it might be the last face she would ever see. Then he fitted the mask over her nose and mouth and started counting backwards from ten.

'Nine... eight...'

It wasn't working. She was still fully conscious, and couldn't tell him, and couldn't move. She began to panic. Then she heard, as if from a dream, very faint chords of piano music, and everything disappeared.

It seemed a long time later – it could have been days or weeks – when she surfaced as if from deep underwater and found herself lying in another white room under bright lights, with a different kindly, questioning stranger looming over her.

Where had she just been? There had been apples in a tree in the front garden, and in the grass on the lawn... forgotten windfalls... and another garden, under the stars. And Christmas. Tearing wrapping paper off the most enormous, magical Christmas present imaginable. A piano. Her dad looking on, his face creased with delight when he saw how thrilled she was.

A dream. Just a dream.

But those things had all really happened. That was her life. It had been so good, so rich, and so full of wonderful, precious things. She was so lucky to still be here, and to have the chance to put things right.

Reuben. Her mum.

What had she done?

She tried to speak, but could only groan. The pain in her arm was brutally jarring. It felt as if her bones had been put on an anvil and hammered back into shape. If only she could just slip back down into the darkness that had been even deeper than sleep...

'On a scale of nought to ten, how bad is the pain?'

Eight, she managed to say. She'd said that before, hadn't she? Not so long ago, in the ambulance. How could it be as bad as that, all over again?

'OK. We can help you with that,' the nurse said, and then he was gone and there was nothing but the bright lights to look at.

She was dimly aware of someone else lying on their back on a trolley near to her, another shrouded body of someone coming round from anaesthesia, but she didn't want to look. It seemed intrusive, and also, she didn't want to risk moving anything, not yet. She didn't trust her body any more, not if it could hurt so much.

Then gradually she realised that the pain had ebbed away. She was like something dumped on the shoreline when the tide goes out: incapable of moving, but no longer at the mercy of a force that was so much bigger and stronger than she was.

The nurse came back to check on her. 'How's the pain, on a scale of nought to ten?'

'Four. Better than it was. Do you know how my son is? Billy. He's ten years old. I just wondered if my friend might have called.'

'I don't know, I'm afraid. The nurses on the ward might be able to tell you more. But I'm sure there's no reason for you to be concerned,' he said.

Then he started explaining to her what had been done to fix her arm, and she took in just enough of what he was saying to understand that it had been complicated and she'd been lucky.

'Thank you,' she told him.

'It'll take time, but you have the potential to make something close to a full recovery,' he said. 'It's going to mean a bit of work, physio and so on, but there is no reason why you shouldn't get there.'

She thanked him again and a porter came to wheel her out of recovery and back onto the ward she'd been admitted to the previous night. A nurse allowed her a little water and promised to try to get hold of her friend again, and told her not to worry about Billy and to rest, then slipped away.

If only Callie'd had the presence of mind to ask her a few more questions... Where was her handbag? It ought to be in the cabinet beside the bed. If she could find her phone, maybe she could try to call Laurel herself. Or the school office, so she could leave a message for Billy. As long as her phone, which was pretty ancient, still had some charge left.

Were you allowed to use your phone on the ward? She couldn't remember seeing a sign saying it was forbidden. Maybe it was different during the day? She wasn't really up to making it to the reception desk to call from there, or finding her way to some other part of the hospital. And besides, all she had on was a hospital gown...

Where were her clothes? No, she wouldn't want to put back on what she'd been wearing yesterday. Her skirt had been covered with blood.

She looked reproachfully at the tips of her fingers sticking out at the plaster cast. When she got home, how was she going to cook, and wash up, and do the laundry, and vacuum, and make Billy's lunchboxes? It would be tricky. She'd have to lean heavily on Billy, a thought that made her heart sink.

What about work? It was going to be a while before she could type two-handed again, and would Julian even want her there, looking like a casualty? But if she was off sick for more than a couple of days, it would hit her pay packet. And then how would they manage? She had some annual leave left, but it wouldn't be enough.

And there was still the business of Billy's birthday to sort out...

She'd waved goodbye to him so casually at the school gate the morning before, taking it completely for granted that it would be just another ordinary day. He'd gone in without looking back at her, which always made her feel hopeful and forlorn at the same time. Hopeful because it was a sign of his independence and growing ability to cope with the world without her, and that was a good thing. Forlorn because there was something so defenceless about the sight of the back of his head, moving away from her and then disappearing out of sight round the corner.

Of course he would be willing to help her, but was it fair on him to ask?

What else was she going to do, given that there was no one else?

A great wave of weariness washed over her and she allowed herself to close her eyes. The nurse was right – she had to let herself rest. To focus on getting better, so she could get back to Billy. And then she'd be able to figure out everything else.

She felt as if she was sinking. She didn't have the energy for anything any more, not even for worrying. The unfamiliar sounds around her curtained-off cubicle, of medical equipment and other people's breathing, faded into the comfort of nothingness.

Billy was running dangerously close to the edge of a cliff, crying out *Look at me!* But there were rocks just below, and the sea was crashing against them. She could taste the salt in her mouth as she gasped for air. She was running as fast as she could, but she couldn't reach him and she couldn't scream – she couldn't warn him. She had no voice. It was as if she was a ghost, racing towards him but powerless to save him...

She surfaced with her heart hammering and remembered where she was. The hospital. It had just been a dream. Thank goodness. She breathed deeply and told herself to get a grip.

One of the nurses had pulled aside the curtain that separated her cubicle from the rest of the ward and was saying brightly, 'There's someone here to see you.'

But it wasn't Laurel and Billy. Instead Sonia came in, carrying a glossy magazine and a punnet of grapes, and the nurse withdrew.

'Oh my word, Callie! Look at you! Goodness, you have been in the wars. You poor thing! However are you going to manage? Are you in very much pain?'

'It's not too bad,' Callie said. 'Do you know where Billy is? I was hoping Laurel might bring him—'

'You must be desperate to see him. Of course you are,' Sonia said. 'But look, I promise you, it won't be long, and he's absolutely fine, OK?' She checked her watch. 'Give it half an hour. The parking situation is absolutely crazy out there. There's a huge queue all along the main road.'

She came closer and stood looking down at Callie as if she didn't know whether to embrace her or not. 'I'm so, so sorry I missed the message from school yesterday,' she said. 'I was off visiting my aunt, you know, the one who lives out in the Cotswolds, and it's a bit of a mobile blackspot where she is. Too many big hills. I didn't have a clue what had happened until I got back. Julian feels terrible, too. Especially as he was in the office just across the road the whole time. He had absolutely no idea what had happened till Laurel called him and told him. Julian says you mustn't worry about work, by the way.'

She darted forward to kiss Callie on the cheek and then backed off and put the magazine and the grapes on the cabinet next to the bed. 'I thought you might want something to read,' she said.

'Thank you,' Callie said. 'It's really good to see you.'

Even though she hadn't been in hospital for long, seeing Sonia was like having a visitor from another world. Sonia was wearing a rust-coloured linen dress, miraculously uncreased, and sandals that showed her pale, soft little feet, and had her long red hair casually pinned up. Anybody who didn't know her would probably have thought that she looked elegant and composed, but Callie could tell she was a bit nervous, maybe because of the party thing.

Well – there was no point in falling out over that. After what had just happened, she wasn't going to get worked up about a party. She would just have to make sure she sorted out something that would make Billy happy.

Sonia settled down on the chair next to Callie's bed, primly crossing her legs and clasping her hands on her uppermost knee.

'It's good to see you, too,' she said. 'So what actually happened?'

'Oh... I was rushing. I was crossing the road and it was full of traffic, and I stepped out without looking properly and a cyclist hit me. It was a kid. I mean, a teenager. You know what they're like – they go at quite a pace.'

'You have to take more care of yourself, Callie,' Sonia said. 'You're always stressed out, and you never have any time for yourself. Maybe you should take this as a wake-up call.'

'I guess you're right,' Callie said ruefully. 'At the very least I need to try and remember to look where I'm going.' Then, because it seemed like she might as well address it: 'I got your email about the party, by the way.'

'Ah.' Sonia blinked at her. 'So... what did you think?'

'Well – I guess if you don't want to go ahead, or Jack doesn't want to go ahead, that's it, isn't it? I guess Billy and I will just have to make other plans.'

She couldn't help but notice that Sonia looked relieved.

'I'm glad you see it that way,' Sonia said. 'Things change, don't they? It's all part of growing up. Kids get independent.

They get minds of their own. They don't always want to do things the way their mums want them to. You know, it wasn't that easy for Jack to tell me how he felt.'

'No, I suppose not,' Callie said.

Suddenly, painfully, she saw Billy – her prize, her reason for continuing to exist – as Sonia might see him: a small, skinny kid with glasses, insecure, anxious, and unpopular.

Billy was watchful, the kind of child who noticed people, and things, and who didn't necessarily tell you what was on his mind. He'd never been like Jack, and never would be – why had she assumed they would always be friends? Perhaps it had just been wishful thinking.

There had been times when it had occurred to her to be grateful that Billy was so quiet and thoughtful, and to be proud of his good behaviour. Weren't all mothers proud of their children? Sonia was certainly proud of Jack. He'd rampaged around creating mayhem when he was younger, and Sonia had often said, with that little edge to her voice that meant she actually thought it was something to celebrate, 'They've got so much energy, haven't they?' As if the way Jack behaved was only to be expected, and was what all boys were, or should be, like. And yet it seemed to Callie that being Jack's mum would be as different to her own experience as parenting an alien from the moon.

But maybe that was how Sonia felt about Billy.

'Anyway, this is all really bad timing,' Sonia said. 'What matters now is you getting better. And like I said, I feel awful.'

'It's OK, really,' Callie said. 'You're right. They're getting older. Things are changing. And that's inevitable, isn't it? And healthy.'

Poor Billy. She felt as if she'd been forced to glimpse his future – one in which he would be lonely and isolated because he didn't give off whatever it was, the brash, male, sporty, club-bable vibe, that made a boy popular.

What did she know about friendships between men, or about becoming a man? But if she couldn't launch him into adulthood as someone who could deal confidently with his peers, then she would have failed him.

'Callie,' Sonia said carefully, 'there's something you ought to know about Billy.' She cleared her throat. 'Billy didn't spend last night at Laurel's house.'

A shiver of fear ran all the way up Callie's spine to the top of her head and spread along both her good arm and the bad one before fizzling out in her painkiller-numbed fingertips.

'Laurel did her best,' Sonia went on. 'It was an emergency situation, after all.'

'Sonia... what's happened? What's Laurel done?'

Sonia pursed her lips and her mouth twitched. She reminded Callie of a rabbit trying to decide whether or not to venture out into an exposed part of the pen.

'They wanted her to do the evening show at work, and Henry wasn't around,' she said. 'She had to make a quick decision, and she did what she thought was the best thing at the time.'

Callie stared at her in horror as it dawned on her what Sonia was trying to tell her, but was too nervous of her reaction to say outright.

'Oh, no. No, no, no, no, no. You don't mean this. You cannot seriously be telling me that Laurel decided to dump Billy on my *mother*?'

'Callie, come on, there's no need to shoot the messenger.'

'I don't believe this,' Callie said. 'He went to that house? That should never have happened. She is the absolute last person Laurel should have left him with.'

'You shouldn't upset yourself,' Sonia said stiffly. 'Your mum's bringing Billy to see you. That's what you wanted, isn't it? To see Billy?'

'Of course it is, but... you mean Mum's coming here?'

She felt sick. Actually physically sick. She'd seen Mum, once or twice, down the years, leaving the supermarket or crossing the road, always at a safe distance. But she'd never had to talk to her. For it to happen now, like this... while she was effectively a captive, stuck in bed on a public ward in a hospital gown, unwashed, drowsy from the drugs they'd given her...

And she was in Mum's debt. If Mum had taken Billy in at short notice, the least she owed her was a polite thank you.

'We've all been doing our best to help you, Callie,' Sonia said. 'Your mum came through for you. After the way things have been, I think that was pretty amazing of her.' She checked her watch and got to her feet. 'I'm going to have to go. The traffic's awful, and I need to get back and pick Jack up. He's gone home with Zeke, but Zeke's got something on later and I promised I wouldn't be late to collect him.'

'But Sonia, of all the people... I just never would have thought that Laurel would take it on herself to go and do something like that.'

'I think she didn't know what else to do. And Callie, I promise you, Billy's fine. That's the main thing, isn't it? Try not to get yourself worked up about it. After all, you can't do anything about it now. I'm sure you'll feel better about everything when you've seen him.' She stooped and kissed Callie lightly on the cheek, and then went out.

Callie gloomily ate a couple of grapes – oddly, she wasn't really hungry – and tried to talk herself into staying calm. Sonia was right. The only thing that mattered was that Billy was OK. Nothing else. And he would be here soon, and the more relaxed she was, the more she behaved as if everything was fine, the better it would be for him. She'd just have to take Mum showing up on the chin.

It wasn't good for Billy when she got wound up: he always picked up on it. He was like a canary in the mine, and the mine was her. If she suffered, he did too. She'd been the same with

Mum, in a way: she'd always known what Mum was feeling, even if she hadn't always known what she was thinking or planning.

Perhaps that was part of what had led to their estrangement. After Callie's dad died, her mum's grief had added to the burden of Callie's own sadness. But when Mum had married Ron, Callie had found she couldn't share in her newfound happiness, or welcome it or even accept it, without it feeling like a betrayal.

Was it any easier for her to understand now why Mum had behaved as she had? Mum had lost her husband. After that close brush with death, wasn't it understandable that Mum had chosen to make the most of life, and to do that quickly – violently, even – by falling into the arms of somebody else?

In the end, who was Callie to judge?

But Mum had judged her. Certain things had been said, harsh words that couldn't be unsaid, and couldn't be unheard either. Those words came back to her now, and made her want nothing more than to run away and hide...

Then the nurse pulled the curtain next to her bed aside and said, 'Someone else to see you,' and Billy walked in.

The dejection she'd felt after Sonia left was instantly replaced by a flood tide of something quite different, a wave of intense tenderness that slowed her pulse and made nothing matter but him. There he was, her sweet, thin boy in his shorts with his bony legs and wrinkled socks and glasses and hair that never quite lay flat, looking down at her.

'Billy!'

What did it matter if she made a fuss, if she showed how she felt? There was no one here to see who might tease him. Mum was standing behind him, wringing her hands and looking over-

wrought. As well she might. But for now she didn't matter
either. Callie only had eyes for Billy.

Billy's face was very serious. It was as if they were both new
to each other and she was there to rescue him, or perhaps, he
was there to rescue her, and they were both taking each other in
and hoping that they would be able to trust and care for each
other.

She noticed how tired he looked, and how much like the
kind of child who would always be aware of what was going on
around him, and be cautious about getting involved, rather than
the rough-and-tumble type who could enjoy their childhood
unreflectingly, without ever pausing to look before they leaped.
And she also saw that his legs looked a little more coltish than
she would have pictured them from memory, as if he might be at
the beginning of a growth spurt. Even such a short separation as
this last twenty-four hours was enough for her to see the
changes in him more clearly, whereas the busy but steady pace
of their day-to-day lives made the speed of his race towards
adulthood somehow invisible.

Her sweet son. Her boy. He was growing up, getting older,
and that meant one day he would be an adult and he would
leave her. And that was what she had to want for him. The
thought of it filled her with anticipated sorrow and pride and
regret, almost as if that greater separation had already happened
and he was now poised to move on through life without her.

But he was here now. And so happy and pleased to see her!
His face brightened and he moved towards her, and the faint
shadow of his future adult self vanished, along with the threat
of the distance his independence would put between them.

He leaned forward and carefully embraced her, and she
reached up with her good arm and put it round him. She was
conscious still of the nagging pain in her bad arm, and of Mum
who was standing there looking down at them, and of Laurel
having done this awful thing of leaving Billy with Mum, so

close to the scene of the old disaster. But none of that seemed to matter. All of it was swept away by the comfort of being reunited with her son.

It was always like this: things fell into place and were simple and made sense when Billy was with her. She knew what she was *for* when he was there. She had never really known what her purpose in life might be before Billy, or even if she had one. But as soon as she'd known he was on the way, even before she first saw his face, it had become clear to her. People talked about that moment of overwhelming love when you first held your child in your arms. She hadn't experienced it in that way, but more as a quiet and certain knowledge that there was no longer any room for doubt that she was needed.

As if by unspoken mutual agreement, and perhaps in acknowledgement of Mum standing there watching them, they moved gently apart.

Callie said, 'Are you OK? How are you?'

'I'm fine,' Billy said earnestly. 'How are you?' He looked down at her arm in its cast. 'Does it hurt very much?'

'Hardly at all,' Callie said, not entirely truthfully. 'It was very silly of me. That's what comes of not taking care when you cross a busy road.' She glanced at Mum, then returned to Billy. 'So were you OK at Granny's house? Did you have a nice dinner?'

Billy nodded. Mum, somewhere behind them, said, 'Pork chop, new potatoes, carrots and gravy, plus treacle pudding and custard, all eaten without complaint. He is my grandson, after all. I wasn't about to let him starve. Then off to bed at a reasonable hour and a good night's sleep, and in school in good time this morning.'

'Thank you,' Callie said.

Their eyes met. Mum's were full of distress and wounded pride. And longing. That was what surprised Callie most. That Mum had missed her enough to look at her almost hungrily, as if she was a precious prize who'd been lost long ago and had come by chance into touching distance again.

But then, there was that stubborn, defensive self-righteousness. Of course Mum would never apologise. She wasn't one for backing down, and anyway, she probably felt, to this day, that Callie was the one who was in the wrong. Maybe Callie didn't want her to say sorry, anyway. Even an apology would be painful. She didn't want to have to think about what had passed between them at all.

Callie was the first to look away.

'I brought you some clothes,' Mum said, setting down the holdall she was carrying. 'Hopefully there'll be something there that'll fit.'

Would they be old things of Emily's? Or Mum's? But what did it matter? She could hardly leave here in her hospital gown. She was beholden to her mother now, and that was that. She thanked her again and then turned back to Billy and said, 'I hope you weren't too worried.'

He looked at her steadily, as if pondering what might count as being too worried, and considering the most honest reply. His eyes were dark brown flecked with gold, and looking into them now she was reminded of the startling moment when he was a baby and she had first realised that she was looking at him and he was looking right back at her – not just as a collection of interesting shapes and shadows, nor as an automatic giver of milk and comfort, but as a person.

Billy's first word had been, not 'Mum' or 'milk' or any of the words she might have expected to emerge from his cheerful but imprecise babbling, but 'eye'. She had always connected this to that first moment when they had really looked at each other and seen each other, as if that moment had made a powerful impression on him too, had maybe even become a kind of foundation memory, and he had waited to speak until he could find a word for it.

'I broke my glasses,' Billy said. 'I have my spare pair on now.'

'Oh well, that doesn't matter,' she told him. 'Just as well you had the spare pair with you. We can sort that out later, when we're home.'

Billy looked sideways at Mum as if trying to decide whether or not what he was about to say would be a bad thing to admit in front of her, and then fixed his gaze on his shoes and said in a very small, shamefaced voice, 'Also, Jack doesn't want to do the birthday party with me.'

Poor Billy – he had expected Callie to be angry, and make a scene, and that was what had prompted him to tell her right now, like getting out news of a failure at a time when a parent is too distracted for the reaction that might otherwise be expected.

'I know about the party,' she said. 'Sonia already told me. Before the accident, actually. We'll talk about it later, Billy, but don't you worry, we are going to make sure your birthday is the biggest and best and most fun celebration that any eleven-year-old ever had.'

Billy smiled in relief, although she thought he still looked a little worried. 'We don't really need to do anything special,' he muttered.

'Of course we do,' she said. 'Here, why don't you sit down next to me? Mum, I'm sure they'd try to find a chair for you too if you asked.'

'I'll stand,' Mum said. 'I'm used to being on my feet. Billy, you sit down like your mum said.'

Billy pulled the chair closer to Callie and sat down. He glanced anxiously at her mum and then back at Callie, and that, more than anything else, helped her make up her mind what to do next.

She was proud, too. But if it was for Billy's sake, she could force herself to swallow her pride. She looked up at Mum and said, 'Thank you for looking after him. I really appreciate it.'

Mum's face twitched. Her nose had turned pink and her eyes were glistening, and Callie realised she wasn't far off bursting into tears.

She'd changed. Of course she had. Her hair was streaked with grey, her skin was lined and she looked tired. Old. And yet she'd always seemed so formidable. Like someone who would never age.

'It's a pleasure to look after my grandson,' Mum said. 'I was happy to do it. I said to Laurel I was glad she'd phoned me. What else is family for, if it's not for a time like this?' She sniffed and rummaged in her pocket for a tissue and loudly blew her nose, then put the tissue away. 'I'm sorry,' she said. 'I've been all over the place today. They actually told me to go home from work. Then Sonia had to get Billy from school because I wasn't on their approved list. It's been pretty complicated, I can tell you. The bureaucracy they have nowadays! I mean, I'm Billy's grandmother. You'd think they'd trust me. But look, I was glad to help, Callie.' She paused as if gathering up her strength for a final effort. 'Ron sends his best, by the way. He drove us here. He's sitting in the café outside, because they don't like to let too many visitors up onto the ward at the same time. I want you to know that we've talked it over, and we're both agreed. We'd love to see more of Billy. That is, if he'd like to see more of us.'

She glanced across at Billy as if hoping for backup, but he kept his head down and his eyes fixed on Callie's cast, as if this would enable him to shelter from the possibility of conflict.

'Maybe we can talk about this another time, Mum,' Callie said. It made her feel mean and ungenerous to say it. But Mum had set her off in spite of herself. She could feel herself building up to crying, too, and if she let go now she had no idea how long it would take to put herself back together again.

'I think this is a second chance,' Mum said. 'Can't we just let bygones be bygones? I want to be able to help you. And I have to say, Callie, I think what happened yesterday shows you need all the help you can get.' She hesitated. 'I do know what it's like to have to try and manage on your own, you know.'

And with that she folded her arms and looked down at Callie with a desperation that Callie had never seen on her face before.

Callie felt herself softening further still, remembering the awful days after Dad dying but before Ron appeared on the scene, when the two of them had been united in grief.

'I know you had a hard time, Mum,' she said.

She turned to Billy and willed him to look back at her so she could give him her most reassuring smile, but he just carried on staring down at the hospital bed. She reached out and took his hand and gave it a small, tight squeeze, then released it.

'What all this has shown is that you can't cope on your own. Nobody can. And it is not the best thing for Billy or you to try,' Mum said. She was talking in that tone of voice, familiar despite all the years in which Callie hadn't seen her, which meant she had something to say and was going to say it, and nobody had better interrupt her. 'Single mothers need their mothers – they need someone, anyway,' she went on. 'I'm just up the road. It obviously makes sense for me to lend a hand every now and again. And I'm sure Emily would make the most brilliant babysitter, when she has time.'

'I'm sure she would,' Callie said. 'But Mum—'

'You need us, Callie,' Mum said. Either she was oblivious to the fact that Billy was right there in front of her taking every-thing in, or she didn't care – or maybe she actually wanted him to hear. 'We need to sort things out, get onto a better footing. All of us,' she went on. 'I refuse to lose you and Billy. I just won't have it. It can't go on and on, this distance between you and me. I don't think it matters any more whose fault it was. We have to look to the future now and try and take care of each other and make the most of what we've got. It's not a weakness to need help from time to time. It doesn't mean you've failed. Of course it doesn't. You've done a brilliant job of being Billy's mum. Anyone can see that. I certainly can. He's a delight.'

Callie was stunned. That was a line she never would have seen coming. *You've done a brilliant job of being Billy's mum. He's a delight.* She'd been praised. By her mother, for her mothering. Two impossibly rare events in one.

It was as if a huge wall had been shattered and was gradually collapsing into an enormous pile of tiny, dust-like shards. Somewhere in the remote distance she could almost make out the faint sound of tinkling glass.

And then she betrayed all the promises she'd made to herself about protecting Billy from stress-inducing emotions by bursting into tears.

FOURTEEN

BILLY

It was very strange to see his mum getting told off by her mum. It was something he could never have imagined. But it wasn't really an angry telling-off, so he didn't totally understand why his mum had started crying, unless it was because her arm hurt. He hated to see her cry. But then she pulled herself together and blew her nose and he realised that they'd come to an agreement, which probably meant he'd be seeing Granny again. Which was all right by him. She was quite a dramatic kind of person, and he wasn't sure he liked her quite as much when Ron was around, but she was someone he wouldn't mind spending a bit more time with.

After that his mum wanted to know all about his day at school, about which, as usual, there was not much to say, because there was no way he was going to start telling her that he'd got in trouble for not having an eraser and he was pretty sure Jack had stolen it. Or that nobody had wanted to sit next to him at lunchtime. Then Mum and Granny started chatting and he decided it was safe to stop paying attention and let his mind wander. Even spies had to be allowed some time off.

Then Granny suddenly remembered she'd left Ron outside

and rushed off to check up on him, and Mum turned to him and said, 'So it really was OK at her house?'

He nodded. It was on the tip of his tongue to mention Reuben – the writing on the underside of the windowsill, and the visit the next morning. It would be interesting to ask Mum about Reuben. That would be the kind of thing a spy would do. And now was a good chance, while Granny wasn't around.

Granny hadn't seemed very keen on Reuben. She'd wanted to know exactly what he'd said to Billy, which was strange in itself, and Billy had struggled to remember because really, Reuben hadn't said anything much. Then Granny seemed to have decided that it wasn't something they should talk about any more, and had started fussing about getting him into school on time instead.

On the other hand, though, mentioning Reuben might make Mum upset again, and he wasn't sure he could cope with any more crying.

'It was fine,' he said.

Mum looked at him sharply but let it pass. She said, 'Did Granny find something for you to read?'

That was fine, because then they could talk about Harry Potter. After a while Granny came back, looking slightly flushed as if she and Ron had had an argument. She said Ron was going to wait until the end of visiting time and then take them home, and if Callie was discharged later that evening one or other of them would turn out to pick her up.

'Maybe you could give me a key to your place and we could swing by there and pick up some clean clothes for Billy, in case he ends up spending tonight at ours again,' she said.

Mum stiffened, and Billy knew she hated the idea of Granny going into their flat, especially without her there. She could be quite fierce about who she was willing to let in and who she wasn't. Billy had learned that he always had to check with her first if he wanted someone to come round, but it wasn't much of an issue because he didn't have any friends who wanted to come and play anyway.

But then Mum agreed, and asked Billy to get her handbag, which was in the little cabinet by the bed, and find her front door key to give to Granny.

'There is one thing I need to tell you about, Callie,' Granny said, pocketing the key. 'If we could just have five minutes on our own? Perhaps Billy could have a cake in the café with Ron?'

Mum exhaled noisily. 'OK. But it had better be quick. Is that OK with you, Billy?'

'It's all right,' Billy said, and allowed Granny to lead him out of the ward to the café area looking out over the escalators and the central hall of the hospital, with patients and visitors and doctors and nurses coming and going.

Granny got him a drink and a cake with pink icing and bought another cup of tea for Ron, who didn't look very excited about having Billy's company. When Granny had gone, Ron put sugar in his tea, stirred it thoughtfully and said, 'You'd have thought they'd have talked enough, for now. I hope this isn't going to end in tears.'

'Why would it end in tears?' Billy said. He wanted to make out that this was a ridiculous suggestion, although given that there had already been some crying that day, perhaps it wasn't.

'Well, don't say I said this, but there's a reason why those two didn't talk to each other for a decade,' Ron said. 'In my book, just ignoring a problem is no way to fix it. Still, who am I to express an opinion? I'm just Janice's husband, and Callie's stepfather, and the closest thing you have to a grandfather. Doesn't seem like anyone's in a rush to include me in their conversation, though.'

'Do you want to be included in their conversation?' Billy asked. He was beginning to worry that things might be going wrong inside the ward. Maybe it would help if Ron went and joined them.

'No,' Ron said. 'I do not. The older I get, the more I think what I really want is a peaceful life.' He glanced across at the doors to the ward as if he, too, was concerned about what might be happening there. 'But there we are, you pay your money and you take your choice,' he went on. 'If I wanted an easy life, I guess I married the wrong woman.'

Billy had no idea what to say to this, because it seemed to him that Ron was probably right, and at the same time, he could see how hard Granny normally tried to please him.

'Maybe she's warning your mum that Reuben's been sniffing round,' Ron said. 'You met him, didn't you? When he came round this morning?'

'You mean the man from across the road? He seemed OK. Do you think he's bad?'

'Well, let's just say I wouldn't have wanted him hanging round *my* daughter,' Ron said. 'Emily, I mean.'

'Why not?'

Ron shrugged. 'Like I said, I'm staying out of it. Sometimes it's the best way.' He sighed. 'Sometimes it's the *only* way.'

Billy gave up and concentrated on eating his cake. By and by Granny came back out and said, 'You should come and say goodbye to your mum, Billy, and then we need to leave her to rest.'

Ron said, 'How'd it go?'

Granny shot him a look that seemed like a warning. 'How did what go?'

'I guessed you were telling her Reuben had been round,' Ron said. 'What? What's wrong with saying that? I mean, Billy met him.'

Billy said, 'Does Reuben know that the operation went all right? He wanted to know how Mum was doing.'

'I told him,' Granny said. 'Don't you worry about that. Come on, Billy.'

He went back to the ward to say goodbye and it was a shock

all over again seeing Mum in a hospital gown in a hospital bed with her arm in a cast, in that weird fluorescent lighting, with equipment all around her and other people's conversations going on in the other cubicles on the ward. He hugged her very carefully and she said she hoped that by the next evening they'd both be home, and then Granny steered him away and he felt awful, but pleased that at least he'd managed not to cry.

Ron drove them through awful traffic and sudden rain back to Kettlebridge so he could pick up some of his stuff, as Mum and Granny had agreed, and Granny gave him the key to use to get back into their flat. It was good to see Goosegreen Close again, and his bedroom, which smelt very faintly of himself asleep, and all his precious, familiar things, even if only briefly – his Lego Death Star, his R2D2, the papier mâché volcano that Mum had helped him make for his geography project one wet weekend, now gathering a little dust in its crinkled folds. But the flat didn't quite feel like theirs, not the way it normally did, not without Mum there. He was almost glad to leave.

The next day Sonia picked him up from school in her car, along with Jack, and dropped him off at Goosegreen Close, and Mum was there. She seemed tired and drowsy and went right back to sitting on the sofa in front of the telly after she'd hugged him and said how pleased she was to be home, rather than rushing around tackling chores, the way she would normally do. He resolved to look after her as best as he could, like a doctor and a nurse and a butler combined.

That night, for the first time, he was the one who made the dinner. Mum reminded him to put an apron on and watched anxiously from the kitchen table, where she was sitting, as he fiddled round tying the bow at the back. He could feel her itching to intervene, to take over and do everything for him, but of course she couldn't, because of her bad arm.

'Mum, I can do it,' he told her sternly.

She gave a little sigh and smiled at him, but her eyes were still worried. 'I know you can, Billy. I just feel bad about you having to, that's all.'

'Well, you shouldn't. That's just silly,' he said.

He set out everything he needed on the worktop and got out a frying pan and a pot.

'Mum...?'

'Yes?'

It was embarrassing to have to ask, but there was no other way. 'How do I turn the oven on?'

'You have to switch it on at the wall socket first,' she said. 'That's it – that's the switch. Then you just turn the dial and press the button to light the gas. They're all slightly different, but this one is pretty straightforward once you get used to it.'

He knew she'd said the last bit just to make him feel better. Once again, he could feel her wanting to intervene. But once he'd got started, the cooking was easy. All he had to do was turn the sausages from time to time, and then, when they were nearly ready, warm up the baked beans and remember to stir them. It was even quite fun, though it was slightly annoying that Mum kept saying how good he was being, as if it was something he shouldn't be expected to do, or, even worse, might be expected to find difficult.

He liked her being relieved and grateful, though. It made him feel helpful and important, and there was nobody else in the world who made him feel that way. He decided to turn what he was doing into a performance. If he could make her laugh she would relax, and that would be a triumph for both of them.

'And now ze famous chef Billy le Swann will prepare for you ze famous English feast of sausage and beans,' he said, wiggling his eyebrows furiously as he imagined a proper temperamental French chef might do, and was rewarded with a smile.

She didn't offer any further comments on his progress as he laid the table, and he was grateful for that. He needed her to believe he was capable of doing at least this much for her.

He put out glasses of water for them both – nice cold water, he let the tap run for a little bit first – and served up their food. He took care to cut up her sausages without her having to ask, and made sure they were nice small pieces, each one a perfect forkful.

Mum said, 'I bet Granny's food wasn't as good as this,' and started eating. He was pleased to see that she seemed to have a decent appetite.

'Mind you, I don't want you thinking that you have to do this every night,' she went on. 'I'm sure I'll be able to figure out how to make dinner one-handed.'

'It's fine,' Billy said. 'I mean, I don't mind doing it. I quite like it. People who do Scouts do this kind of thing for fun.'

'Hm,' Mum said.

She'd wanted him to do Scouts at one time, and he had refused point blank because Jack Hallam did it, along with various cronies of his, so obviously it would have been awful. Billy knew Mum still felt slightly bad about this, as if it was her fault that he wasn't a Scout, but there was no way he could explain whose fault it really was.

'So did you sleep OK at Granny's?' Mum said, and suddenly she was watching him very closely, even more so than she had done when he'd been frying the sausages.

He set down his knife and fork. Suddenly he had completely lost his appetite. He felt like someone who has finished a particularly exhausting performance and is now called upon to come and do an encore.

'I guess,' he said.

'Where did she put you?'

'In the little bedroom upstairs. Granny said it had been yours when you were young. I don't think there was any of your stuff there, but there were some of Emily's things.' He said Emily's name a bit uncertainly, but Mum just nodded as if the presence of Emily's things in her old room was no big deal. It was so weird that all these people Billy hardly knew had once been part of her life.

Mum swallowed her last piece of sausage, then put down her fork. She said, 'You've coped so brilliantly with it all, Billy. I take my hat off to you, I really do. It must have been such a shock when I didn't come to get you and you heard about the accident, and then Laurel left you with Granny. I'm sorry that happened. I mean, I know it turned out all right, but if you were going to meet Granny after all these years, I should have been there. So I was just wondering, is there anything you wanted to ask me about it?'

He didn't even mean to come out with it. He just thought it, and suddenly the words were in the air between them: 'Who's Reuben?' And he realised it was his desire to know – even stronger, just for that moment, than his desire to protect his mother from having to tell him – that had put them out there.

Mum froze. Then she began to move again, but as if her mind was not at all on what she was doing. She spooned up some baked beans and he could see that it was hard for her, with just one hand, but hesitated to help, because what boy fed his mother with a spoon as if she was a baby? She seemed to decide it wasn't worth the effort and let her spoon drop back onto her plate, then moved her good arm across to cradle her bad arm, as if to protect it.

She said, 'You met him, didn't you? Mum said he came round. What did you think of him?'

'He seemed OK,' Billy said cautiously.

'Well, he's just an old friend of mine. I haven't seen him for a long time. He used to live across the road.'

'Yeah, I know that,' Billy said.

He couldn't bring himself to look at her. She was lying. Or not telling the whole truth. He knew that, because of what he'd seen written on the underside of the windowsill. Maybe she was embarrassed?

Anyway, he probably shouldn't mention it. But he could still picture it as clearly as if he'd just taken a photo of it. *Callie 4 Reuben 4 ever*. A little piece of the past that had been waiting all this time, for years and years, for him to see it and touch it and read it.

'I saw what you wrote about him,' he heard himself saying.

He looked up then. She was waiting for him to explain himself. It struck him how dangerous it was, being able to read, especially when you read things that other people might not want you to see.

'It was underneath the windowsill,' he said. 'You put his name. I could see it every time I lay down on the bed. If it wasn't dark, I mean.'

She froze again, but in a different way. Not angry. More shocked, as if she might be about to cry again. He suddenly wished he'd never mentioned it, or even better had never looked, and had never wanted to practise being a spy. But it was too late now.

'I used to love him,' she said, and then looked surprised at herself for having said it.

He saw the shadows under her eyes, and the worry lines on her forehead, and the cast on her arm, and he was afraid. He liked to think of her as invincible. But he knew she was not.

He said, 'What happened? Did you have a big argument?'

'We did,' she said. 'Except I don't think he understood what the argument was about.'

And then, to his horror, she started crying. Big splashy drops of tears fell on her good hand, and he watched helplessly as she angrily wiped her eyes. Then he got up and fetched her a tissue and gave her a very careful hug.

'It doesn't matter, Mum. Not any more. We're home now,' he said. Then, in an attempt to cheer her up again, 'The dinner I made wasn't that bad, was it?'

She laughed a bit at that, and stopped crying, and then she said that he should probably go off and have his bath and she was going to try clearing up one-handed.

He knew this was an attempt to make things normal between them again, and he tried to go along with it. But it didn't really work. There was no way of flying back to the life they had been living before the accident, when her arm had been unbroken and he had never heard of Reuben.

Part of him wanted to ask her more, and part of him thought that would be wrong and would probably make her cry again. And another part was scared, but didn't know what of.

FIFTEEN

REUBEN

'Anyway, that's enough about me,' Henry said after Reuben had asked for the bill. 'How about you?'

They were sitting in the slightly gloomy interior of an east London Docklands pub, once the haunt of boatmen and crooks, now favoured by finance workers from the tall glass office blocks that had sprung up when the area was redeveloped. Henry had nothing to do with either finance or the docks, but he did have an air of being someone who banked other people's secrets. He reminded Reuben of a lizard that bides its time, preserving its energy and keeping a lookout, but moves with stunning speed when an opportunity presents itself.

The two of them had been introduced years ago by Laurel, who had then been Henry's girlfriend, and was now his wife. These days, they met once or twice a year for lunch, which usually involved Henry playing the part of raconteur and Reuben taking on the role of appreciative audience. Henry was the editor of part of the glossy weekend supplement of a national newspaper (with most of the thankless checking and chasing done by a succession of conscientious and overworked deputies) and Reuben was a free-lancer whose work seemed to have become drier and more corporate as the years went by (his last assignment had been polishing up a tech company's annual report), so professionally they didn't have that much in common, but still, they had kept up the connection.

After that awful final phone conversation with Callie years before, when he'd just gone out to Australia, Reuben had been wary of asking after her or her son. But when he came back to London and looked Henry up again, Henry had mentioned Callie quite casually, as if there was no particular reason why Reuben should be interested, other than that Callie was a mutual acquaintance and a friend of Henry's wife.

Henry's occasional little updates about Callie and Billy had always been more important to Reuben than he would have cared to admit. He didn't know whether Henry realised this, but if he did, Reuben was grateful to him for not making it obvious.

But he was going to have to be more direct today. He had something in particular to ask Henry for. Still, he couldn't quite bring himself to do it.

'I think you know all my news,' Reuben said. 'What there is, anyway.'

Henry had been lolling in his chair, finishing his coffee and watching the waitress, who was young and pretty, out of the corner of his eye as she weaved her way around the room. When the waitress went out he leaned forward to give Reuben his full attention.

'You haven't really told me about this business of going back home,' Henry said. He nibbled at the little biscuit that had been provided with his coffee, then dabbed his mouth primly with his napkin to brush away the crumbs. 'I always thought you'd shaken the dust of the place off your feet and wild horses wouldn't drag you back. You always seemed so... I don't mean this to sound like a criticism... You always seemed so *detached*. And yet here you are, all set to go to and fro and take care of your aged parent, at the request of his girlfriend who you don't even like.'

Reuben shrugged. It struck him that his dad would hate to hear himself described that way, even as a joke. Especially as a joke.

'Duty calls, I guess,' he said.

The waitress reappeared and presented them with the bill, and they peered at it and held their cards out in turn for her to take payment. When she had gone Henry said, 'Did you hear about the drama with Callie having an accident?'

'I did. And I have a favour to ask you.'

Henry raised his eyebrows, which were abundant and straggly and gave him the appearance of a slightly malevolent and eccentric professor. 'Fire away,' he said.

'I need Callie's address,' Reuben said. 'That flat in Kettle-bridge where she's lived all these years. I want to write to her there, and I don't want to try and go through her mum. Could you ask Laurel for me?'

'Right,' Henry said, and frowned. 'Why do you want to write to her? I mean, won't it seem a bit odd?'

'Don't look at me like that. I'm not a stalker. I just want to drop her a line, that's all.'

Henry shook his head. 'My, my,' he said. 'You have got it bad, haven't you?'

'Got what?'

'The might-have-beens. I mean, I guess that at this stage in life, it doesn't seem such a big deal her having a kid by some mystery man as it did at the time.'

They stared at each other. Henry said, 'Sorry. Maybe I spoke out of turn. I always assumed that was why the two of you fell out, and next thing any of us knew you were living in Australia.'

'Henry, are you going to help me or not?'

'Of course. Look, write whatever it is you want to write, and send it to Laurel to pass on. How about that?'

'OK. Thank you.'

'Do you think there's a feature in it?' Henry asked. 'You know, something personal, something confessional, for my magazine. Something about going back to the fork in the road? A little glimpse of the path not taken?'

'No,' Reuben said. 'Though thanks for asking,' he added hurriedly.

'Well, don't go too far down memory lane, is my advice.' Henry got to his feet. 'Unless it's for professional purposes, of course, in which case you can play fast and loose with the truth and the lane can be completely imaginary. Otherwise, there's a reason why we all have the gift of forgetting.'

With that he ambled out of the pub, with Reuben following behind. When Reuben emerged onto the street outside Henry had just hailed a passing cab. They just had time to say a perfunctory goodbye before Henry climbed into the cab and was whisked off back to his office.

Reuben strolled on alone. Instead of making his way to the nearest Underground station he found himself circling aimlessly through the mazy Victorian streets. Some still had their old rows of narrow terraced housing intact, while others had new, pristine, curiously characterless blocks of flats. It was all very clean and very quiet, and somehow seemed completely unreal.

Or perhaps that was just his mood. It was as if he was wandering in a dream, as if time and the obligations that came with it had lost all meaning. *Don't go too far down memory lane*, Henry had said. But it seemed to him that he was already there, and had been ever since Theresa had called him and mentioned Callie. And at the same time, he knew he had not gone nearly far enough.

SIXTEEN

CALLIE

When Laurel handed over the envelope with Reuben's writing on it, what surprised her most of all was that part of her was not surprised, as if she'd always known that he would contact her one day.

But still, the sight of that almost-forgotten, immediately familiar, carefully legible handwriting was a shock. If only Mum hadn't taken it upon herself to get in touch with him... perhaps there was never going to be a good time... but did he really have to choose to start asking questions now?

'Henry said he seemed quite worried about the accident,' Laurel said. She was watching Callie closely, and was obviously curious about the contents of the envelope, but doing her best to restrain herself. 'Also, apparently his dad's beginning to get a bit confused and forgetful, and he's going to be coming back to visit a bit more often. So perhaps he just wanted to smooth things over a bit so that it's not too awkward if the two of you bump into each other.'

'Maybe,' Callie said, and put the envelope aside. She couldn't bring herself to open it in front of Laurel. Laurel must

have realised this, because she didn't mention it again, and
headed off soon afterwards.

But once she was alone in the flat again Callie still couldn't
bring herself to open the letter. Instead she tucked it in a corner
cupboard in the living room, where she kept folders of important documents – car insurance, mortgage statements and the
rest. It was somewhere she knew Billy would never look.

In a couple of hours' time she'd be due to pick him up from
school. Better settle down in front of her laptop on the kitchen
table and try to get on with some work.

She'd arranged with Julian to take some days off while she
was recovering, and also to do a few days a week from home,
which basically meant tapping out emails and slowly editing
documents on a laptop borrowed from the office – at least she
was right-handed and it was her left hand that was out of action
– plus occasionally fielding panicked queries from her
colleagues about the filing system, the milk delivery or other
aspects of office life. This was turning out to be just about
manageable, but she was surprised by how tired she felt.

There was also Billy's birthday to sort out. She'd more or
less given up on the idea of a party for him – he just didn't seem
to want one – but wasn't sure what to do in its place. Billy was
being so protective of her, and so insistent that she shouldn't put
herself to any trouble, that it was proving difficult to work out
what he might actually want.

When the doorbell rang a little later, her first thought was
that it would be Reuben. But why would he have gone to the
trouble of sending a letter via Laurel if he already knew where
she lived?

She put the chain across – she usually didn't bother with
it, but for some reason she felt like being extra cautious,
maybe because she had one arm out of action. When she
opened the door she was confronted by an eager and slightly
wet-looking young man in a suit, holding a limp bunch of red

carnations and grinning at her as if anticipating a warm welcome.

'Callie, how are you?' he said, and thrust the carnations towards her without waiting for her to reply. 'These are for you. Was talking to my sis the other day, and she told me all about the trouble you've had. So I saw these, and thought of you, and thought they might cheer you up a bit, and I just happened to be passing and figured you'd be in, so... here I am.'

And then she recognised him – it was Laurel's younger brother Gus, who she'd seen sometimes when she and Sonia used to go round to Laurel's house as teenagers, and who Laurel had always treated with brisk sisterly contempt.

She moved to take the chain off the door and accepted the carnations. 'Thank you, Gus. That was very kind of you.'

'Well, you know, I work just round the corner from you now. I don't know if Laurel told you? I'm an estate agent at Kettlebridge Estates, just opposite the sports shop in town? Doing all right, actually. I'm one of the best performers in the team.' He checked his watch. 'Anyway, don't be freaked out if you look out and see me sitting outside your house.' He gestured towards a small hatchback covered with the Kettlebridge Estates logo, neatly parked outside Callie's flat. 'Got five minutes to kill till I need to hit the road for my next appointment. It doesn't do to arrive too early, sometimes.'

'Come in and have a cup of tea if you like,' Callie said, though she didn't much like people coming into the flat unless she knew them really well, sometimes not even then, and Gus didn't qualify. But then, he had brought her flowers.

'Glass of water would be nice. Thanks,' Gus said, and showed him into the kitchen.

She decided against asking him into the living room – it would be awkward if he realised she slept there every night, usually on the sofa bed, though with her arm in a cast she'd found it was easier to doze in the armchair. Had she tidied her bedding into the storage box she kept by the sofa? She couldn't remember. Anyway, Gus was bound to realise it was a one-bedroom flat, which might well prompt him to wonder who slept where. She'd just have to trust him to be too polite to ask.

In the kitchen, she put the carnations down on the worktop and got him his glass of water, and he conscientiously drank a mouthful or two before setting it down. She felt a little uneasy – but that was probably just the old instinct to be wary of being alone with a man in an enclosed space, made worse by the state she was in. There was nothing to worry about. This was Gus, who was obviously harmless, and had brought her flowers, which was really rather sweet.

'I'm sorry about the weird clothes I'm wearing,' she said, and gestured towards her outfit. 'I'm not really dressed for company.' She had on slippers without socks (socks, it turned out, were tricky to put on one-handed, and she definitely wasn't going to ask Billy to help her with those), elasticated-waist jogging bottoms, a vest with particularly large armholes and a poncho, which Laurel had loaned her. And no bra.

'Oh, don't worry on my account. You look fine to me,' Gus said, flashing her a smile that exposed a lot of teeth and gums, and prompted her to think about his relationship with his orthodontist.

'Thanks. I have to say, I don't feel at my best,' she said.

'I'm sorry to hear that,' Gus said solicitously. 'Laurel told me it had all been a bit of a nightmare for you.'

'Hm,' Callie said non-committally. She was still secretly a little annoyed with Laurel for leaving Billy with her mum, but was trying not to be, especially as Laurel had been making a big effort to be kind and supportive since.

She opened one of the cupboards and reached for the vase on the top shelf, and Gus, who was a foot or so taller than her, stepped forward and reached to bring it down for her, saying, 'Here, let me.' She instinctively flinched away as he came closer, then reproached herself and hoped he hadn't noticed. There was really no reason to treat Gus, of all people, as a threat.

She asked Gus to take the cellophane off the flowers, stuck them in the vase, filled it with water and put them on the windowsill.

'Very nice,' Gus said, looking around the kitchen. 'Brightens the place up a bit.'

Callie told herself he was just trying to make conversation, not passing judgement, and she should be appreciative rather than touchy and defensive. It was just her pride getting in the way, that was all. Pride being what you held on to when you didn't have other things, like a flat with a bedroom each for you and your son.

Then Gus drew a deep breath. 'Callie, I was wondering... if you felt like it... if you'd like to get some lunch with me sometime? Or a coffee? Probably do you good to get out of the house. You know, during the day, while your son's at school. So no need to worry about a babysitter.'

Oh no. Was he asking her out? Her brain was so fuzzy with painkillers and lack of sleep, she couldn't quite figure out how to respond. He looked puzzled by her stunned silence. 'My treat, obviously,' he added.

'Gus, I'm really not sure...'

'You don't have to decide right now,' he said quickly. 'You're probably not feeling up to it at the minute. No rush.' He checked his watch again. 'I'd better be getting on, I guess. Anyway, it was nice to see you.'

They both went into the hallway. He fished a card out of his jacket pocket and passed it to her, and said, 'My number's on there. If there's anything you need, you let me know, OK?'

'Sure. Will do. Thanks for the flowers,' she said, and opened the door, but he made no immediate move to go. Instead he turned and gazed down at her. He was quite a bit taller than her, and was standing a little too close for comfort, though to be fair, the hallway was very small and cramped and there was nowhere else for him to go, except for out.

'Nobody else got you flowers,' he said.

This was true, which made it difficult to respond to. He seemed to find her silence encouraging, and nodded as if agreeing on her behalf.

'I would really like to get to know you better, Callie,' he said. 'I know you were my sister's friend in the first place, but things change, don't they? The age gap doesn't really matter so much now we're older.'

It suddenly struck her – more like a wheezing alarm from a little-used early warning system than a bolt of lightning – than he might be about to try to kiss her, and she should probably take steps to make sure that he didn't.

'Gus,' she began, but he lifted his finger and pressed it to her lips and shook his head.

'It's OK,' he said. 'You don't have to say anything. I just want you to know, Callie, that I'm not like other men you might have come across. Obviously I know all about your son, and how you've brought him up on your own the whole time, and it doesn't make the least bit of difference to me. I mean, I really don't mind.'

He took his finger away. She was momentarily speechless. Then she said, 'Gus, I'm really not looking for a relationship.'

His face fell. 'Are you seeing someone else?'

'No, I'm not. I don't want to get involved with anybody. I'm not interested in dating. I never have been. I mean, ever since I had Billy. I'm really quite happy on my own.'

He shook his head. 'I just don't believe it,' he said. 'I don't believe that you're ready to give up on yourself like that. To be on your own your whole life just because you slipped up and had a baby when you were younger.' He looked around the hallway and shook his head as if to say that the place where

Callie lived was part of the reason why she was doomed to never get another man.

'You're right, I'm not ready to give up on myself, which is why I'm not going to go out with *you*,' Callie snapped.

He recoiled and blinked at her in surprise, as if she'd just stepped on his toe or hurt him in some other clumsy, accidentally-on-purpose way, and she immediately felt bad. But it was a sore point. Laurel and Sonia had accepted a long time ago that there was no point trying to talk her into dating, but there had been a time when they'd been puzzled by her resistance. She couldn't very well explain it to them. It was a subject she just didn't care to think about – a side of her life that she had decided to give up on. Perhaps that's why Gus had annoyed her: because in a way, he was right.

'I never would have believed you had a nasty tongue on you,' Gus said with dignity. 'I always thought you had a good heart. Now I'm beginning to wonder.'

With that he turned away and went out. Her neighbour from across the road was sitting out in her front garden and smoking a cigarette, and Callie wondered how much she'd overheard. She gave her a sheepish little wave before going back in and closing the door on the outside world. It was a profound relief to be alone again.

By the time she left the flat to pick Billy up from school it had begun to rain, and before setting out she put on the yellow waterproof cape Laurel had dropped off along with Reuben's letter.

She was still fretting about Gus. How would Laurel react when she heard what had happened? Maybe he wouldn't say anything at all. That was probably her best hope.

She had to admit it – what he'd said had really stung. She really didn't want to think about it. But it was preferable to wondering what Reuben had said in his letter, or remembering what Billy had seen written underneath her old windowsill at Mum and Ron's house, and how much she had meant it at the time.

Callie 4 Reuben 4 ever.

In the playground, the parents who had arrived before her were clustered under the rain shelter that ran the length of the school buildings. She stationed herself at a slight distance, round the corner from Billy's classroom, where she'd easily be able to spot him when he came out but wouldn't have to talk to anyone while she waited.

She wasn't exactly looking her best, in her yellow rain-cape and clogs and jogging bottoms, with no make-up on (and still no bra), and with her hair dry-shampooed and roughly bundled back in an old scrunchie. She just wanted to keep her head down, and avoid small talk if at all possible.

'You're Billy Swann's mum, aren't you? I'm sorry, I don't know your first name.'

She turned and saw a woman a few years older than herself, dressed in office clothes – a sleeveless top and trousers – her blonde hair pinned up, a serious handbag hanging from her shoulder. Her arms were lean and toned. Not a playground regular, but Callie recognised her, the way she recognised most people in town even if she couldn't immediately place them, having lived around the area for so long.

'Hi, yes, that's me, Callie.'

Everything about the other woman said, quietly but distinctly, *Don't mess with me*, and Callie guessed she'd be the type to be on committees and doing good works, probably while also holding down a demanding job and running a perfect home.

Maybe this was going to be an attempt to rope Callie into something – volunteering to make costumes or man a stall, or signing a petition about dogs or traffic or children on scooters.

Was there anything going on at school that she'd missed – raffle donations, or PTA elections, or a long-standing member of staff retiring? There probably was. The life of the school, like most of the goings-on of the world outside the bubble of her life with Billy, went on like waves overhead, and most of the time she was oblivious to it.

'Well, this is awkward,' the woman said, not looking awkward at all. 'I'm Martha Byers. My son Zeke is in the same class as Billy?'

Callie nodded. She knew who Zeke was, just about – a tall, dark-haired boy who was a friend of Jack Hallam's. Looking at Martha, she thought she could make out the family resemblance – a certain restrained, slightly frustrated wilfulness.

Martha cleared her throat. 'My older son, Ethan, was the one who was riding his bike when...' She glanced at Callie's arm. 'When *that* happened. So I thought I ought to at least come and say hello.'

She held out a slim, manicured hand for Callie to shake, and Callie shook it.

'I don't normally come into school to do the pick-up any more,' Martha said, looking around them. 'Normally Zeke wouldn't be at all pleased to see me here. He's very independent. But I'm hoping that he'll make an exception for today, if only because the weather's so awful.'

'It's pretty miserable, isn't it?' Callie said, then, looking down at her rain cape, 'I hope Billy won't be embarrassed by the slightly odd mixture of clothes I'm wearing.'

'Oh, Zeke's embarrassed by me no matter what I wear,' Martha said. 'They're all like that. It starts around now, and gets worse and worse till they leave home, after which they seem to get over it. But mainly because they usually want something when they see you, whether it's Sunday lunch or clean sheets and a quiet place to sleep.'

Callie felt that Billy was not like that, and never would be.

His privacy was more important to him these days, which was only natural now he was getting older, but he still liked her – the little life they shared would be almost unbearable otherwise. It irked her that Martha was pulling rank as a more experienced mother when she knew so little about them. Still, it would probably be tactful, under the circumstances, to defer to her superior knowledge.

She said, 'Do you have older children, then? Older than Ethan, I mean.'

'Yes, another two. The oldest one's at uni now, and the next oldest is about to go. They're all quite spaced out. I kept getting to the point when the youngest one would be starting school, and freedom would beckon, and then...'

Martha shrugged to convey her bafflement at the force of nature that had resulted in her repeatedly finding herself pregnant again instead of free.

'How is Ethan?' Callie asked politely. 'I hope he's OK. I think he grazed himself when he came off the bike? And it must have been a shock.'

'Oh, he's fine. He always is, that one. The front wheel of his bike was a bit out of alignment. My other half made him pay to get it fixed himself. Said it'd teach him to slow down and be more careful.'

'Oh dear. Well, I don't think it was his fault. I mean, I stepped out in front of him. So I probably owe him an apology. I'm really sorry about the whole thing.'

'Nonsense. You were the one who got hurt. How are you getting on?'

'Not bad. There'll be physio and so on, and I'll have the cast on for a few weeks yet. But I should make a full recovery. It's just going to take time.'

Martha nodded and looked down at her feet, and there was a small, dry silence between them. Rain drummed on the transparent plastic roof of the shelter overhead. Callie wondered how much longer it would be till Billy came out and rescued her from this conversation. She still had an uncomfortable feeling that Martha wanted something from her, and she was none the wiser about what it was.

'It's Billy's birthday soon, isn't it?'

Callie nodded.

'But you're not doing the joint party with Jack any more?'

Callie shook her head.

'And you're good friends with Sonia, aren't you? It's complicated, isn't it, negotiating all this stuff? Anyway, look, you probably know that Zeke and Jack hang out a lot, but I've always thought that it's good for Zeke to have lots of different friends, and I was wondering if Billy would like to come over sometime? You'd be very welcome to come too, and have coffee and a chat. But if you wanted to get on and do other things, or just pop round and then pop off again, that's fine by me too. We live quite close to school, so I'm guessing it'd be pretty easy to get from yours to ours.'

'That sounds great, but I'd better see what Billy thinks,' Callie said. 'Just so you know, he sometimes has issues with anxiety. He's doing better now, but it's still a vulnerability. Sometimes he can find new social situations quite tricky.'

'Well, the offer still stands. You can always just bring him over and see how it goes, and if you feel it's time to go, take him home again. Maybe it would help to build his confidence. I'm sure it would be good for Zeke.' Martha got her phone out of her bag. 'Could I get your number?'

'Sure.'

Once Martha had saved Callie's number she slid her phone back into her bag and gave Callie a big, conclusive smile, as if their business was now complete.

'Great. That's settled then. I'm so glad I caught you. And look – here they come, right on cue!'

She was right: Billy's class had just begun to come out. The rain had eased off, and most of the pupils immediately made their way towards the gate so they could walk home. Callie saw Jack among them. Martha said, 'No sign of Zeke yet. Wonder where he's got to? I hope I haven't missed him.'

Billy sidled up to them and gave Martha an enquiring look. 'Hello, Mum,' he said, a bit self-conscious because Martha was there. 'How was your day?'

'Pretty good, actually,' Callie said. 'This is Martha, Zeke's mum. She just asked if we'd like to go over sometime, so she and I could have a cup of coffee and talk about mum stuff and you could hang out with Zeke.'

She had to hand it to him: Billy dealt with it well. She could tell he was both unnerved and delighted, but only because she knew him inside out. The expression she thought of as his poker face – attentive, inoffensive – was back in place almost instantly.

'Sure,' he said, 'that'd be nice.'

'Well, I'd better try and track down that son of mine,' Martha said. 'Nice talking to you, Callie! I'll be in touch!'

And with that she struck out towards the exit from the classroom so as not to miss Zeke when he finally made an appearance.

As Billy and Callie set off across the playground, picking their way around the puddles, Callie reflected that Martha's offer might just be a game-changer.

All Billy needed was a break. He just needed to feel that someone liked him. If he could be more confident, it would be much easier for him to make friends, and if the other kids could get to know him, then surely they would warm to him. Why wouldn't they? He was kind, funny, imaginative, loyal. He might even suddenly find himself popular. After all, these things could change very quickly.

Back home, he asked her where the red carnations had come from and she said Laurel's brother had dropped them round, and then changed the subject. And much later, when he was safely in bed and she had till the next morning to work on hiding her reaction from him – if she needed to, depending on what had been said – she went over to the cupboard and extracted the letter from Reuben and took it over to the kitchen table to read it.

It was very short. Barely three lines long.

Hope you are well. It looks like I'm going to be around your way more often in future and I wondered if you'd be up for meeting for coffee or a walk sometime? It would be really good to see you.

He'd jotted down an email address and a mobile phone number. There were no demands. No accusations or recriminations. None of the things he was entitled to say.

She found herself sobbing. It was relief, and at the same time it was because she was afraid. But she forced herself to stop, because the very last thing she needed was to disturb Billy and have him asking her what was wrong. And anyway, she had to pull herself together, and work out how on earth she was going to reply.

SEVENTEEN

BILLY

When Mum came up with a date and time for their visit to Zeke's house and wrote it down on the mostly blank calendar that hung in the kitchen, his first thought was that he'd had a perfectly good chance to put a stop to all of this. If it turned into a disaster, he had only himself to blame.

After all, Mum couldn't be expected to know that Zeke was a bully and often teamed up with Jack, her supposed best friend's son, to make his life a misery. She was a grown-up, and therefore clueless about children and the way they behaved towards each other. But she had been a child herself once. Maybe she didn't want to remember. Maybe it was something that happened to all parents – that they forgot, and thought children were nicer and happier than they actually were. For whatever reason she was blind to the potential pitfalls, and now Billy was going to have to stumble towards them with her.

The visit was to take place at eleven on Saturday morning – 'that's good,' Mum said, 'because it makes it very easy to leave. We'll have to go home after an hour, because it'll be time for lunch.' *A lot can go wrong in an hour*, Billy felt like saying but didn't, and approached the whole thing with a sense of impending doom.

It reminded him of what it had felt like sitting in the school reception after Mum's accident while Mrs Timms rang round to try to find someone to take him home. Except that had turned out all right in the end, whereas who knew how this was going to go? And this time there was no one in the hospital. Or at least not yet. It didn't make him feel any better that Zeke and Jack seemed to be leaving him alone at school, because that could just be the calm before the storm.

But Mum seemed determined to press ahead. 'Wouldn't it be funny,' she said, 'if one of the things that came out of the accident was you being friends with Zeke?' And he agreed that it would be, though funny wasn't the word he would have chosen. *Unlikely* or *unbelievable*, maybe.

He couldn't bring himself to express any doubts to her, though. It seemed like it really mattered to her, and that was reason enough to go along with it. She was in a strange mood, which he put down to the painkillers she was still taking, and her not sleeping well, and coping with everything with her arm still in a cast. She'd even been a little offhand with him once or twice, almost snappy, and then had apologised and said she had a really bad headache. But he felt sure that she was worrying about something – her job, maybe, or money (those were the usual things).

It wasn't totally bad, her being distracted. Sometimes it was quite overwhelming the way she questioned him and listened to him, as if everything he did and felt was of the utmost importance. But it was definitely odd, because usually, whatever else was going on, she behaved as if he mattered more.

Anyway, headache or no headache, there was no chance of her forgetting about the visit to Zeke.

As it came closer time seemed to slow down, and when Saturday morning finally came round, and they set off to walk to Zeke's house, Billy was conscious of every passing minute. He was glad that they were on foot. It would have made him uncomfortable to watch her parking their car, which was old and had been second-hand to begin with, outside Zeke's house, in front of whatever cars Zeke's family had (there would definitely be more than one). He would have felt vaguely embarrassed, and also, he would have felt ashamed of his embarrassment.

Mum was walking much more briskly than he was, and had to stop and wait once or twice for him to catch up. He wasn't deliberately hanging back. It was just that it was hard to walk briskly when your legs felt slow and heavy, as if, in your world, gravity was stronger than in everybody else's, and was overpowering you and pulling you back down to the ground.

Zeke's house was big and fancy, on a road of other similar big, fancy houses (no surprise there), and Zeke's mum, who was called Martha, was all smiles and cheekbones and bony arms. She was wearing a T-shirt and leggings that looked like gym clothes, except they were perfectly clean and appeared to be brand new and it was hard to believe she'd ever actually got sweaty in them.

There was no sign of Zeke, and Billy began to fret about the precise nature of the humiliation that might be in store. What if, now he was here, Zeke refused point blank to have anything to do with him?

They all went into the kitchen, which was stupidly big and had a weird solid fixed table in the middle, like a display stand in a clothes shop, except there were stools around it. Mum perched there and he did too. Martha put the kettle on and said to Mum, 'Ethan is out, doing his Saturday job, but if he was here I'm sure he'd be very sorry to see the damage done,' and gestured sympathetically towards Mum's arm.

'He doesn't need to feel bad about it,' Mum said. 'Like I said, it wasn't his fault.'

Billy felt this was far too generous of her, but Martha was behaving as if the whole exchange was a small, slightly tedious formality that both of them had to get through, and seemed to accept her son being let off the hook as her due.

Suddenly Zeke appeared, and Billy's heart rate sped up a notch but actually, weirdly, Zeke was perfectly friendly towards him. Martha offered them both a confusing range of drink options (at home Billy only had squash, and just one type), and Zeke came to the rescue by saying what he wanted, which meant Billy could ask for the same.

They ended up with glasses of cola and a plate of home-made biscuits between them. Billy wondered if he'd be able to get up the nerve to try to eat and drink here and, if so, if he would instantly choke and splutter and make a fool of himself. It would seem odd if he *didn't* eat and drink, but it might be slightly less noticeable than choking.

'Let's go to the games room,' Zeke said, picking up the plate of biscuits and his glass, and Billy picked up his glass too and followed him, trying to suppress the thought of how embarrassing it would be if he tripped and spilt his drink all over the carpet, or, worse, smashed it and then fell and cut himself, so there would be blood to add to the cola stains and he might need to go to hospital and have actual, real stitches put into his skin with a needle and thread to close up the gash.

The games room turned out to be a small but crowded extra living room. There was a slightly dusty-looking electronic keyboard on a stand in one corner, a guitar propped up against the wall, a squashy sofa, table football, a big TV in pride of place surrounded by various electronic boxes and gadgets, and an armchair with a footstool. A footstool! There wouldn't be room for any of this stuff in Mum and Billy's place. But anyway, stuff didn't really matter. The only thing that was really important was that he and Mum were there together.

'None of my brothers are here at the moment, so we'll have

the place to ourselves,' Zeke said. He sounded proud to have so many brothers, which made Billy fleetingly sad about not having any, although they didn't have space for even one brother, and he didn't really want one anyway.

Zeke dumped his drink and the biscuits on the low table in front of the sofa and went to turn on the TV. Billy felt suddenly hopeful because if that was all they were going to do – watch TV, maybe on one of the channels you had to pay extra for, which they didn't have at home – then this was going to be just fine, and no problem at all. He probably wouldn't even have to talk, and an hour would go by quite quickly. It would be much better than table football, which he hoped Zeke wouldn't make him play as anything connected to football made him think of public humiliation and failure.

He sat down on the sofa and put his drink down safely, and was just about to reach for a biscuit when Zeke said, 'Do you want to play *Star Wars*?'

He looked up to see that Zeke was holding a black plastic thing with weird-looking dials on it. It must be a controller for playing games on. Billy's heart flipped. Suddenly there was nothing he wanted more than to play a *Star Wars* computer game with Zeke. But also, there was nothing he wanted less than to make an idiot of himself in front of Zeke. If he did, he'd never hear the last of it.

'Maybe I could just watch you play,' he said as a compromise, 'and then have a go.' Surely Zeke wouldn't care if he played or not.

But Zeke stared at him in disbelief and said, 'Why would you want to do that?'

Billy shrugged. 'Just don't feel like playing right now.'

Zeke's face seemed to grow bigger and bigger until it was all Billy could see. He looked angry and scornful and Billy was filled with a sense of his own weakness and helplessness.

Zeke said, 'You don't know how to, do you? Don't you have a PlayStation?'

Billy was briefly tempted to lie and say that he did, but it was broken and he was so out of practice he'd forgotten how to play. But then he decided not to risk it. His one small hope, in so far as he had any, was to tell the truth.

'No,' he said.

He closed his eyes and steeled himself for the ridicule that was bound to follow. But then, to his astonishment, Zeke just said, 'Well, you'll pick it up. I'll show you. It's easy. It won't take you long to get the hang of it, and it'll be more fun if we can both play.'

Fun? It was very odd to hear Zeke use this word in connection with him. Odd, but surprisingly nice. Billy's heart seemed to settle back into place, a feeling that was the exact opposite of the fear he'd felt just a few minutes earlier, and just as big and sudden.

'OK,' he heard himself saying.

He reached out to take the controller, and Zeke showed him how to use the controls to move forward and back and jump, and helped him choose a character to play as. And then they played, and kept playing, and there they were, except it wasn't quite them but the characters they had chosen to be, together in the world of the game.

The rules weren't entirely clear to him but they were a lot easier to figure out, and a lot less crushing, than the rules of the real world. Here he was able to behave like a hero: he could fight and win and earn points and treasure. And to his astonishment, he was pretty good at it. Zeke was good too, but he'd obviously had plenty of practice, and Billy was new to it. This was another entirely new situation for Billy: he could tell that Zeke was impressed.

After a while Mum stuck her head round the door to check they were all right and then went away again, and they played a bit longer and then Zeke paused the game and asked Billy if he wanted more biscuits. Billy said he wouldn't mind and Zeke went off out to the kitchen with the empty plate, and Billy put his controller down and stretched and took stock.

So far, so good. Maybe Mum had been right – maybe he and Zeke were going to get along. Maybe, as she had said, this was something good that was going to come out of the accident.

As a potential future spy, he ought to make an effort to take note of the kind of things that Zeke had around him at home. It would help him to understand Zeke better, which would probably make it easier to be his friend.

He looked around, trying to impress everything on his memory, and then got up and went over to the keyboard. It would be so amazing to have something like that at home, to be able to pick out tunes whenever you wanted, like a real musician.

He reached out to touch one of the white keys, and was astonished when it made a sound – a low, gentle, middling note, calm and reassuring. He hadn't expected the keyboard to be plugged in, but now he could see that there was a faint green light glowing around the power on button, so it should have been obvious. He picked out a few more notes, and was delighted to find that they sounded almost like a tune. Perhaps he could become a great jazz pianist instead of a spy. Or he could do both! He could be a spy by day and play a black grand piano in the evenings.

'What are you doing that for?' Zeke asked, coming back in empty-handed.

Billy stumbled away from the keyboard back towards the TV set and the abandoned controllers lying on the footstool.

'I was just trying it out,' he said.

'Well, you shouldn't,' Zeke said. 'It's my brother's, and he doesn't like anyone messing with it. He'd kill you if he knew.'

'I didn't mean any harm,' Billy mumbled.

What on earth had got into him? It had all been going so well, and now he'd messed it up.

'You're all right, don't worry, he's not here,' Zeke said. 'I don't care if you touched his stupid keyboard. But maybe don't do it again, OK? At least not without asking first.'

'OK. Sorry,' Billy said.

'Mum wouldn't let me have any more biscuits,' Zeke said, and pulled a face. 'Too close to lunch. I guess you'll be going pretty soon, anyway.'

They both picked up their controllers and carried on with the game, though it didn't seem quite as much fun as before. About ten minutes later Mum put her head round the door and said, 'We ought to get going now, Billy. It's lunchtime.'

'OK, OK, we'll just have to lose that last little bit of progress,' Zeke grumbled. 'We can't save it unless we finish the level.'

'You can always carry on next time,' Zeke's mum said, hovering somewhere behind Billy's mum.

Zeke didn't answer but focused on the process of saving where they'd got to in the game. He stashed Billy's controller in a space in the TV unit and then came and loitered in the hall while Billy put his trainers on, almost as if he was a bit sorry to see him go. To Billy's relief, the awkwardness about the keyboard seemed to have been forgotten.

Zeke waved as Billy left with Mum, then withdrew and closed the door. Billy saw him through the glass of the door, a tall, thin, distorted figure in a bright yellow T-shirt, before he and Mum walked away.

'That wasn't so bad, was it?' Mum said. 'I'd say it was quite a success.'

'Yeah, not bad.'

'It would be nice for you to have a new friend,' she said rather plaintively, and he was immediately crushed by the weight of her longing for him to be popular. Or perhaps she just wanted him to be happy, but it felt as if he had failed her.

'Zeke's all right,' he said gruffly.

'Was that you I heard playing on the keyboard?'

'Yeah. I probably shouldn't have, though. It's Zeke's brother's.'

'Instruments should belong to anyone who wants to use them,' Mum said. Then, rather doubtfully: 'Is it something you're interested in? Learning to play the piano, I mean?'

He reassured her that it absolutely wasn't. He was pretty sure the lessons would be way too expensive for them to afford, but he didn't say that to her, because it would only make her feel bad. And there was no point both of them feeling like they'd let the other one down.

He had a deep, blissful sleep that night, as if he'd run and won a really long race. The next day he was still quietly pleased with himself, but then Monday morning and the beginning of the school week drew closer and began to cast its usual shadow.

What if Zeke just ignored him, and carried on as if nothing had changed?

And if he didn't, what would Jack have to say about it?

On the walk to school Mum was quiet and Billy was too. She had yet another headache, and he was trying to convince himself to expect as little as possible. Maybe he and Zeke could be friends out of school, but not in school. That would be OK. That would be better than nothing, and actually, it would be quite a big improvement on the way things had been before.

All these worries and possibilities must have slowed him down, because although he wasn't conscious of dawdling, by the time he walked into the playground he was running late, and had to hurry sheepishly in along with a scattering of other stragglers.

He made it into the classroom just before the teacher was about to take the register. Zeke was already there, sitting on a desk and loudly talking to Jack and some other boys about what kind of fried chicken they liked to eat when they went out, a conversation Billy would have struggled to join in with because he and Mum only ever ate at home. And Zeke turned, just for a moment, and gave him the tiniest, almost imperceptible nod before swinging back round to carry on talking.

The next minute the teacher banged the whiteboard eraser on his desk to make everyone shut up and started calling out the names in the register. Billy wasn't sure if Jack had seen Zeke greet him. (He rather hoped so.) But anyway, it was enough for him.

Over the next few days neither Zeke nor Jack singled him out for any kind of attention, whether hostile or otherwise. It was still lonely, but it was a lot better than constantly being on edge, waiting to be called out on some mistake you hadn't even realised you'd made.

He began to relax a little. The end of term was in sight, and after that there was the long bliss of the summer holidays. He'd probably have to go to a childminder now and then but he'd also get to hang out at home a lot, which he absolutely loved, though Mum worried about it – she always felt he should be off doing something. And then he'd be going to secondary school, which would be completely terrifying, but at least it would be terrifying for all of them – Zeke and Jack included.

And things might have gone on like that, if it hadn't been for his mum and the strength of her longing for him to be normal and happy and like the other boys – or, at least, like the other boys as she imagined them to be. Because a few days later, while they were eating dinner, she casually mentioned that she'd arranged for Zeke to come back with Billy after school the next day.

His face fell. He couldn't help it. She said, 'I thought you liked him. And Martha has to be somewhere, and asked me at short notice. This would be helping her out.'

'There must be lots of people who could help her,' Billy blurted out. 'Why does it have to be us?'

Mum made a small, helpless gesture with her good hand.

'These things can't be one-sided,' she said. 'If someone reaches out to you, you have to reach back out to them. Anyway, it's all arranged now. I've already said yes.' Her face clouded over. 'I'm sorry, I thought you'd be pleased. Did I make a mistake? Don't you want him to come?'

Billy thought it over. All he had to offer Zeke was Lego and a few old board games and the TV and a stack of DVDs, and his precious piles of comics. Which he definitely wasn't going to share with him, because it seemed highly, highly unlikely that Zeke would appreciate them properly.

But Mum was looking at him with almost open desperation, as if it really mattered to her that it should be possible for them to do this kind of thing – inviting other people in, helping them when they needed it – even though they had never gone in for it much before.

'Of course I want him to come. It'll be fine. I mean, it'll be fun,' he said, and she brightened up a bit, but he could tell that he'd worried her, and she wasn't going to perk up properly until the visit was over and had been judged a success.

Billy spent most of the next day at school dreading the inevitable moment when he would have to go up to Zeke, or fall in with him, so that he could bring him home. He had absolutely no idea how he was going to handle it, as Zeke was still more or less behaving as if he didn't exist.

After the buzzer went for home time he noticed that Zeke didn't hurry to pack away his things, and he didn't hurry either. The classroom had more or less emptied out by the time Zeke shouldered his bag and strolled nonchalantly into the playground, and Billy followed him.

Outside, the usual end-of-day chaos was already beginning to clear. He couldn't see Jack, or anyone else from their class. If people wanted to hang out before going home, they didn't do it here – they did it on the green outside school, or in the little playpark by the stream, where school rules didn't apply.

But there was no sign of Zeke.

Where had he gone? What was he playing at?

Billy's breath started to squeak through his lungs, and the blood in his arms and legs felt thick and congealed, like it did when he woke from a nightmare.

He forced himself to move forward, one step at a time, and turned the corner towards the school office, where Mum sometimes waited for him.

She was there! And Zeke, too! Standing together calmly waiting for him, as if this had always been the place where they had agreed to meet. Billy's fear and self-doubt melted away as he picked up his pace to join them.

For the first half hour or so it was all fine. Mum gave them a drink and a snack and then they went into the living room. He couldn't help but be conscious of her trying to stay out of their way and hide out in the kitchen.

Then Zeke stooped to look at the board games she'd got out of the cupboard and left on the coffee table, and frowned and said, 'What are these?'

'Oh... just some games.'

Zeke pulled a face and said, 'Let's go out.'

Billy couldn't bring himself to say that he wasn't usually allowed out on his own. After all, he wouldn't be on his own, he would be with Zeke. And surely Mum wouldn't insist on tailing them.

To his relief, she let them go. Zeke did a great job of talking her into it – told her that they'd just go to the corner shop and come straight back. She gave in so readily that Billy wondered if this was something Zeke's mum had discussed with her before-hand, and had already given permission for. She even gave them both some spare change to spend, and next thing he knew they were out of the flat and on the path on the way to the shop.

Zeke said, 'I told Jack I was coming to your house today.'

Billy couldn't think of anything to say other than 'Oh'. Something about the tone of Zeke's voice warned him that Zeke and Jack had already agreed on whatever Zeke was going to say next.

'Jack says he thinks you could be all right,' Zeke went on, 'but you need to show us. You're going to have to do a challenge and pass it, and then you can hang out with us. Are you going to do it or are you too scared?'

There was only one possible answer to this. Billy clenched his shoulders and then forced himself to shrug them. 'I'll do it,' he said.

Was he imagining it, or would Zeke have actually been slightly relieved if he'd refused?

'The challenge might not be all that easy,' Zeke said. 'If you don't pass, that's not our fault.'

'OK,' Billy said again.

'We'll tell you when it's going to be. It could be any time,' Zeke said. 'And if you're going to do this, you can't say a word to anyone.'

'I won't,' Billy promised.

In the shop, he hesitated briefly over what to get, worrying that if he chose something that Zeke thought was bad, he'd never hear the end of it. But then he just copied Zeke, and they came out with a can and a chocolate bar each and stopped to sit on the wall on the other side of the road to eat and drink what they'd bought. Billy thought his drink and chocolate bar didn't taste very nice, but maybe that was because he was already worrying about the challenge.

When they got back to the flat Mum let them in and gave him a questioning look that meant, *Did it go all right?* He smiled at her to let her know that it had. The last thing he wanted was for her to worry about him and Zeke. She looked reassured, but not completely. She was sometimes annoyingly good at being able to tell how he was really feeling.

He played Top Trumps with Zeke in the living room for a bit, and that was all right. Zeke didn't mention anything more about the challenge. Maybe he'd forgotten about it. Or maybe, which seemed more likely, he knew that Mum was in the kitchen and didn't want her to overhear him and find out about it.

When Zeke's mum came to pick him up, Billy mainly felt relief, along with a little bit of sadness. After all, having a friend round was supposed to be fun, and it was for other people, it seemed, but not so much for him. Though perhaps Zeke wasn't really a friend.

When Zeke had gone Mum let out a small sigh as she closed the front door and it was just them again. He realised that she was relieved, and that she, too, was pretending not to be.

She looked tired and pale, especially in comparison to Zeke's mum. It must have been a strain for her, having someone round, having to hide out in the kitchen, wondering if it was going all right.

He said, 'Would you like a cup of tea?' This usually worked to cheer her up.

'That would be lovely,' she said.

They both went into the kitchen. He put the kettle on and set about making her tea, and she sat at the table. They had a nice, comfortable silence. All the time he'd been with Zeke he'd been worrying about saying the wrong thing, or of running out of things to say full stop. But now it didn't matter whether he talked or not. He thought how good it would be if things could always be like this: just him and Mum and the kettle boiling, and the hard part of the day's work done.

'Would you like sugar?' he asked her.

'Oh... just half a spoonful. It might wake me up a bit.'

'Are you all right?'

'Yeah, I'm fine,' she said, and gave him an unconvincing smile. 'I mean, apart from this.' She gestured towards her hurt arm.

'It'll get better,' he said rather helplessly as he put her tea down in front of her.

'I know.' Another unconvincing smile. 'Now, I hate to be a nag, but don't you have some homework to do?'

He did – a worksheet about fronted adverbials, which was about as boring as anything to do with words could be. He fetched his schoolbag and sat opposite her to work through it. She sipped her tea and seemed to drift away into a daydream. Then she leaned forward and rubbed her forehead with her good hand, and he said, 'Are you sure you're OK?'

'Yes, just a bit preoccupied. Work stuff,' she said, and shrugged.

He wasn't sure whether to believe her. Her face looked shuttered, as if she was trying to fob him off. Then she went on, 'Also, I have a bit of a headache. I should probably give up and take something for it.'

Their eyes met and he saw that whatever was wrong, it was worse than a bit of a headache. And she wasn't OK.

She got up and found a packet of painkillers in the cupboard and he popped the pills out for her so she could take them. He tried not to let her see that he was upset, or that his hands were shaking slightly. But it was scary to know that she felt bad and wasn't even going to admit it to him. It was like a big black stormcloud that had appeared out of nowhere, and there they were, carrying on as if the sun was still shining brightly and there was no reason at all to start panicking.

EIGHTEEN

REUBEN

It had taken him a long time to compile his note to Callie, and in the end he was almost entirely unhappy with it. All that was left, after he'd written more and then taken it out again, was the blandest, most cautious statement he could contrive to put together. Then, his email address and mobile number. He'd signed off with best wishes, as if he was applying for a job.

The letter didn't say what he meant, and it didn't ask what he wanted to ask, but at least it made it clear that he wanted to see her, and it was as much as he could bring himself to send.

After he'd posted it off to Laurel for her to pass on, he didn't hear from Callie for a week, which crawled by as slowly as forever. Then, finally, when he'd just about persuaded himself to stop constantly checking his phone, a message appeared.

I'm up for a walk. During the school day is probably best for me. When would suit you?

Followed, quite soon after, by another message: *Please don't tell anyone else we're meeting. I don't need the grief.*

They agreed on a time and place to meet, and then he called his dad and spoke to Theresa.

She'd always been the one who answered the phone, but these days, she also seemed to be in charge of most of the conversation that followed, too. He said that he was going to be in the area and could pay a flying visit and was taken aback by her eagerness for him to come. It turned out she wanted him to stay so she could go out again. He promised to try and talk to his dad about going to see the doctor, and didn't mention Callie.

When he finished the call he told himself that it would all be fine, that he'd be able to handle it, as long as he kept the meeting with Callie and the visit to his dad entirely separate in his mind.

He met Callie by the river in the afternoon, just round the corner from where he'd left his car. He'd set out after rush hour that morning, and as soon as he'd left the outskirts of London behind, and was driving through open country, he'd felt his spirits lift. He had to admit it: in among everything else he felt at the prospect of meeting her, knowing he was about to see her made him happy.

The city seemed a very long way away. The air was clear here, and there was birdsong. It was a beautiful day: June at its best, warm but not hot, everything green and fresh and a big blue sky overhead. They were a little way out of Kettlebridge town centre but not far, and the church spire and the outline of the town hall were visible on the skyline downriver.

She was waiting for him when he arrived, sitting on the first bench you came to if you walked along the river meadow from the ice cream kiosk, by the poplars that screened the children's adventure playground. Her arm was in a sling, and she was wearing a yellow sleeveless dress and red lipstick, grey elasti-cated plimsolls and sunglasses. Her clothes suggested someone who was ready to enjoy a summer day out, but her face and posture conveyed an entirely different story. It seemed she was as nervous as he was.

He wasn't at all sure how he should greet her. But then it seemed to happen quite naturally. She stood up as he approached and they half-hugged each other in the way that people do when they both want to make it clear that neither of them intends to mix the embrace up with an actual kiss. Then they let go of each other and turned their backs on the town and started walking.

He said, 'Do you have long before you have to get back?'

She checked her watch. 'An hour.'

'OK,' he said. 'So how are you?'

'Oh, I'm fine,' she said, and it occurred to him not to believe her. Up close, she seemed tired, and her face had the slightly pinched look of someone who has been dealing with pain. But then she started talking about Billy, and he was immediately distracted.

She told him about Billy's love of *Star Wars*, his interest in being a spy, the new friend he'd just made at school. They walked on, and took a path that led alongside the river to their right but was screened from it by a bed of tall reeds and closely planted, tangled trees. To their left there was a grassy meadow. There were few passers-by, and he guessed this was part of why she'd chosen this walk for their meeting, so that they could avoid bumping into people they knew – always a hazard in a small town.

The path narrowed and they had to walk single file, and dodge the roots and overhanging branches of the trees that now lined the edge of the meadow. Butterflies darted past and dragonflies hovered, and from time to time he glimpsed the river moving between the trees to their right. When they set off they'd been overtaken by a couple of cyclists on off-road bikes, and they'd had to step aside for a jogger and a dog walker heading the other way, but here there was nobody else. The vegetation all around was thick and lush, and the town with its rules and codes and familiar faces felt an increasingly long way away.

They skirted round a wood and rejoined the river. Now they had woodland on one side and water on the other, and a clear view of the other bank and the fields and hills beyond it. He decided to just keep on walking and let the talking take care of itself. If they didn't know what to say to each other, what did it matter? The golden afternoon time seemed to have stretched out as if it might go on forever.

The path cut through a little tract of woodland, saplings and nettles and brambles and cow parsley to either side with the water close by to their right. Then they emerged into a clearing at the foot of an old iron railway bridge that spanned the river and carried the tracks across to the hills on the other side.

Callie had come to a halt in the shadow of the first arch of the bridge, which was supported by a column emerging from the middle of the river. The light was tinged with green from the surface of the water, reflected by the underside of the bridge, and ripples of brightness moved across her face and arms and yellow summer dress. She took her sunglasses off and put them in her bag and looked out at the bridge and the river as if considering what conclusion to draw.

'We should stop here,' she said as he caught up with her. 'I need to head back to get Billy from school. Though you could carry on if you wanted.'

'No, I'll come back with you,' he said.

He thought, but did not say, that it might not be a very safe place to be alone. It was surprising how remote it felt, even though it was only a half-hour walk from the town. But there was very little passing traffic – they'd seen one or two boats go by on the river, but there was hardly anybody on this section of the path. If something happened out here, some kind of ambush, nobody would hear you call for help, and by the time somebody found you, your attackers would be long gone.

She didn't make any immediate move to turn and go back, but instead looked out across the water.

'You can walk along the other side of the river this far, but no further,' she said. 'On this side, you can carry on to Allingham and then all the way to Oxford. Have you ever done it?'

He shook his head. She said, 'Me neither. I think it would be a bit far for Billy, to be honest. And probably for me as well. This is as far as we've ever come.' She gazed at the reflections of the river on the underside of the bridge. 'He likes walking,' she went on. 'There's lots of routes you can do round here, and it's beautiful, and it's calming. Also, it's cheap.'

Then she turned to him and her eyes were greener than he remembered, and there was a hint of an old sadness there but she definitely wasn't asking for sympathy. He got the feeling he was about to be put to the test.

'Billy's had problems with anxiety,' she told him. 'He's a sensitive boy, and he picks up on things, and sometimes it overwhelms him. That's why I took a job working for Julian. You remember Julian, right? Sonia's other half? It's part-time and round the corner from school, so I can easily pick Billy up and walk him home. Before that Billy went to after-school club, but it was just too much, in the end. Too busy, too stressful. He needs to have quiet time at home to be able to cope.'

'I guess we all need that,' Reuben said, then hoped Callie wouldn't take this the wrong way and think he was being dismissive. But she appeared not to have heard him.

'I don't like to rely on Mum,' she said. 'We fell out when he was a baby.'

'Yeah, I heard.'

'You did? How come?'

'I still see Henry every now and then,' he said. 'You know,

Laurel's other half, just occasionally. He sometimes mentions you. He mentioned about you working for Julian, too.'

She frowned. 'Laurel never said anything about it,' she said. 'I'm surprised you hang out with Henry. I didn't think you were ever particularly close.'

'I wouldn't say we are. I like him, though. He is what he is, and he doesn't pretend to be anything else. Like I said, I don't see him that often. He might not have mentioned it to Laurel.'

'I suppose Laurel might not have mentioned it to me.'

'It's not a big deal. He's just someone I stay in touch with.'

'Do you keep in touch with anybody else from round here?'

'No,' he admitted. 'Not really.'

Would she think of him as a sad, lonely character, if she knew what his life was like now? The girlfriends who never lasted, the former work colleagues he met up with once in a blue moon, the friends he'd left behind in Australia who emailed at Christmas and said, *If you're ever back over here, do look us up.* He wished he had a more solid kind of life – friends who came for dinner, a network he fitted into, family he could visit without dread. But how could he have had any of that, after what had happened, and the way he'd left?

He said, 'What made you stick around? I mean, you could have gone anywhere.'

She paused, considering. 'I guess I like it here,' she said finally. 'And I got my own place, and I had a job, and I had Billy, so... And the school's pretty good. No, I never really thought of moving away.' A shadow of something flitted across her face, a mixture of stubbornness and defiance. 'Also, I didn't see why I should leave.'

Then she gave a tiny, almost imperceptible shrug and checked her watch. 'Anyway, I'd better get going. I don't want to be late. After not being there because of the accident, I need to show Billy he can rely on me.'

She turned and started walking away, a little too fast to be careful. Then she stumbled and slowed, and he caught up with her. She stopped and turned to face him again.

'I nearly cancelled on you today,' she said.

'Oh. Well, I'm glad you didn't.'

'I wanted to come. But I wasn't feeling too good. I've been having quite bad headaches, on and off since the accident. I didn't feel too good this morning. But I'm a bit better now.'

She set off again, as if relieved to have got this off her chest. The path was wide enough here for him to walk alongside her, and they went along in step.

'Maybe there's something they could do,' he said. 'Have you spoken to anyone?'

'I went to the doctor yesterday,' she said. 'He's going to refer me to a specialist, just in case it's some kind of post-concussion syndrome. But it could just be stress, and of course being referred to a specialist is just making me more stressed. I could do without it, to be honest. I could do with never seeing the inside of another hospital for the rest of my life. Or for a good long while, anyway.'

His heart started to beat faster. 'But there's no reason to believe there's anything seriously wrong.'

'No. But they want to check me out, just to be on the safe side.'

The safe side. The words sounded heavy and hollow, and he suddenly had an intense and terrible feeling that she represented a chance he had already missed, and would never be able to grasp.

'You haven't asked me,' she said.

'Haven't asked what?'

'If Billy is yours. You've met him now. I know I fobbed you off before. But it must have occurred to you to ask again. Or is the reason you haven't asked because you still won't believe me, whatever I say?'

His heart beat faster still. He remembered the moment

when he'd first set eyes on Billy, outside Callie's old front door, the unlooked-for wave of feeling that had hit him, and that first thought: *It's me*. Had it just been wishful thinking? Delusion? Or had his instinct been right?

'I don't know what to say to you, Callie,' he said. 'I feel like you're playing a game with me. Or like you're putting me to the test. And I don't want to fail. But if he's mine, if he's my boy, of course I want to know.'

'Then ask me the right question,' she said. 'Ask me what happened.'

The path had narrowed again. They would have to go single file, and she took the lead.

'Ask me that,' she said, glancing back at him over her shoulder, 'and between here and Kettlebridge, I'll tell you the truth.'

PART TWO
THE BETRAYAL

Callie

1994–2004

NINETEEN

The day she first set eyes on Reuben was also the day she found out what they had done with her piano, which was when she understood that, since getting married to Ron, and becoming Mrs Greenwood rather than Mrs Swann, Mum was no longer to be trusted.

That morning started with a long drive in Ron's car, with Ron at the steering wheel and Mum sitting beside him, and her and Emily in the back. Mum and Ron were fresh back from honeymoon, tanned and in love, and she and Emily had been staying with Ron's mum somewhere in the north. Emily's mum lived and worked abroad and Emily, who was a few years younger than Callie, rarely saw her, and Callie could see that Mum felt sorry for her because of this, but she was too sad herself to have a lot of sympathy to spare.

She felt sick most of the way, and not because of being in the car. She was about to see where she was going to live now, in Ron's house in some village called Allingham in Oxfordshire, and she had a very bad feeling about it.

When they got there Mum took her upstairs and showed her into a little box room that had been painted an unpleasant shade of pink, and said, 'This is your room!'

There was just about enough space for a bed and a few bits of furniture. It was tiny, with a small window overlooking the street. Her case was already there – Ron must have brought it up when Mum was showing her round the ground floor. There were also a few boxes of stuff from her old room, waiting to be unpacked.

'Emily's room is a bit bigger,' Mum said, 'but we thought you wouldn't want to turf her out, as she's already settled. So what do you think?'

'It's fine. But where's my piano?'

Dad had got the piano for her, and encouraged her, and had listened to her with wonder, as if she was a prodigy. And she had played for him safe in the knowledge that if she made mistakes, as she often did, he would applaud her anyway. These were memories she flinched from, because it hurt too much to think that she would never play for him and never make him proud again.

When he died Mum had said she'd have to stop taking lessons because it cost too much. She had thought that perhaps now Mum was married to Ron, who was rich even if he was annoying, it might be possible to start again. She hadn't actually said she wanted to, though. She'd got out of the habit of saying what she wanted, because everything that had happened lately – Dad dying, Mum getting married to Ron, them moving here – had made it obvious that what she wanted had nothing to do with what actually happened.

'There isn't space for the piano,' Mum said. 'As you can see.'

And she was right. There wasn't.

'What about downstairs? There's lots of room down there.'

In their old house, they'd had no dining room and the piano

had been in the living room. It had been cramped, but Dad had figured it out.

'But you hadn't touched it for months. It was just gathering dust,' Mum said. 'I thought maybe it was upsetting for you.' She shuddered. 'A reminder.'

'Where is it?'

'Callie, please, don't make a fuss about this, today of all days. If you really wanted to take it up again, I'm sure we could look into getting you another one. Maybe something a bit more compact and modern, like a keyboard. But those old upright pianos really do take up an awful lot of space...'

'No. It's fine. Don't worry about it. I don't want another one. I think I'll unpack.'

Mum went back downstairs, and Callie started listlessly putting her clothes in the built-in wardrobe and the chest of drawers. She didn't cry. She was too angry and shocked for tears. A bit later Mum came up the stairs again and asked her if she wanted a doughnut – Ron had popped into town and bought a box of them, all iced. Callie said no, she didn't want anything except to be left alone. And this was true, even though it was mid-afternoon and all she'd had for lunch was half a sandwich at a motorway service station.

Once she'd unpacked everything she lay down on the bed, closed her eyes and tried to doze. She just wanted to be unconscious. But then she heard the strangest thing – the very faint, haunting sound of piano music.

Scales, then arpeggios. Slightly hesitant, as if it was a child picking out the notes and sometimes slipping up, then going back and starting over.

Was it real? It couldn't be.

Then whoever was playing launched into a piece, a little folk tune taken a little too fast and clumsily.

Definitely real, and not a recording. As if she needed

anything to add to her various torments, someone around here played the piano.

She straightened up and peered out of the window. The music definitely seemed to be coming from the house across the road. There was a small car parked in front and a dark-haired, mumsy-looking woman had just opened the boot. The piano music stopped and a tall, slightly gangly boy – a teenager, probably around Callie's age – came out of the house and took a couple of bags of shopping out of the boot of the car and carried them in, then returned for more. He said something to his mother – presumably that was who it was – and she smiled and said something in reply.

Callie was touched by the sight of them. It was such an unguarded moment, and they looked comfortable together – so different to the way she was with her mum, especially now.

Then the mum across the road gestured straight towards her, as if she was saying something about the newcomers who had just moved in, and Callie ducked down out of view before the boy could turn and see her. She had no intention of being caught watching them.

She curled up on the bed again. The boot of the car slammed shut, and so did the front door of the house across the road, and then the piano music started again, still halting and awkward. If it was that boy playing, he was nothing like as good as she had been.

And then she must have dozed off, because when she came to someone was standing in the middle of the room, next to her bed. Someone small and quiet and patient. Emily.

Emily said, 'Are you sad about your piano?'

Callie looked up into her stepsister's clear-eyed, sincere, innocuously pretty face and felt powerless to explain herself.

'Yes,' she said, sitting up. 'But really, I'm sad because my dad is dead.'

Emily ignored this, as if it was too obvious to need saying

and was old news anyway. 'My dad and your mum tried really hard to make this room nice for you,' she said. 'If you don't like it, they'll be sad too.'

'I can't help that,' Callie said, but Emily had already gone out, leaving the door open behind her.

Callie got up to shut it and took down one of the books she'd put on the shelves. It was an old hardback copy of *Great Expectations* that had belonged to her dad. There was a plate at the front dated 1960, with an inscription in copperplate handwriting giving his name and explaining that it was a school prize.

As she read, she could smell what Mum was cooking: gravy, sausages – a meaty, traditional dinner. Ron liked that kind of food. Dad had been more experimental, and liked curries and stir-fries, dishes cooked with coriander and chilli and lemongrass. He had been a good cook. Better than Mum, as Mum herself had acknowledged. But in this new marriage, it seemed Mum was going to be the one in charge in the kitchen.

Callie wanted to not want the meal. And yet her mouth watered in spite of herself. How could your mind want one thing, and your body another? How disloyal of her body this was – how treacherous. To be fed, or to want to be fed, was such obvious willingness to accept a bribe. But she did not want to go downstairs, tail between her legs, and accept defeat and eat everything up and say thank you for it.

There wasn't much she could do to show that she was mourning, and to remind them all that her dad's death was not over, and wasn't something to be tidied away like pieces of a game left out on the carpet. But not joining them for dinner was one small way she could resist.

By and by Mum called up the stairs to say the food was ready, and she ignored her. When Mum came up and knocked on her door and said it was time to come down, she said she wasn't hungry.

'But you'll be hungry later, if you don't eat now,' Mum said, looking flustered. 'Are you sick?'

Callie shrugged. 'I really don't want anything. You go ahead and start without me.'

Mum looked as if she was about to say something, then thought better of it and retreated back downstairs. Callie felt bad, because she knew Mum probably wanted this to be a happy occasion, the first meal together for them as a newly-minted family. But then she remembered her piano, and how it had felt to play it with her dad listening, and her resolve hardened.

She carried on reading, but kept half an ear open for discussion downstairs. When she heard Ron raise his voice she went over to open the door a crack, very carefully and quietly, so that she could hear him better without him realising that she was listening.

'There's no way I'm having you take her dinner up there,' he was saying. 'Janice, I've told you my view on this. Now be reasonable. Did I ever say you should throw her dinner away? Put it in the oven. It'll be there for her when she wants it. She'll come to her senses soon enough, and it'll still be warm. Look, why don't I help you tidy up a bit, and then we can sit down in front of the telly with a nice glass of wine?'

Callie thought about hunger, and how desperate it made you. Like poor Magwitch the convict in *Great Expectations*, terrifying a child he caught in the graveyard and forcing him to steal food for him. But she could rise above all of that. She could do without.

Her stomach rumbled. She kept turning the pages. Dishes clinked downstairs. The TV went on. It was very loud, the way Ron liked it. She heard Emily come upstairs and have a bath, and her mother saying goodnight to her. By then her hunger had settled into a steady discomfort that was at least not painful, and she thought she would be able to bear it a while longer.

She got into her night things and used the bathroom and brushed her teeth, because everyone knew you couldn't eat after brushing your teeth. Then she went downstairs into the living room and said, 'Can you turn the TV down?'

Mum and Ron looked up at her. Ron had his arm round Mum in that possessive way of his, and they both looked slightly pink in the face and slightly drunk. She really didn't want to think about what she might have almost interrupted.

'Sure,' Ron said, and reached for the remote control and fractionally turned the volume down.

The remote control was new, as was the TV and the three piece suite – new to Callie, at least. The armchair on which her dad had sat and dozed had gone, along with so much else.

'Your dinner's still in the oven,' Mum said.

'I'm still not really hungry,' Callie said.

'I could do you some toast and some hot chocolate instead,' Mum said. Ron looked disapproving.

'No thanks. Carry on watching your programme,' Callie said. 'If I want something, I can get it myself.'

She went upstairs again, shut her bedroom door, got into bed, turned out the light and closed her eyes. And even though she thought she would never sleep, suddenly she was somewhere else.

She was in a graveyard, and she was on her own. It was a cool grey day, more like spring than winter, but it could have been almost any time of year. She found a bench to sit on. It was very peaceful. And then a boy appeared from nowhere and came to sit next to her.

She recognised him but couldn't place him at first. Then she remembered. He was the boy from across the road. She didn't look at him: she didn't particularly want to talk to him, or to be friendly. He seemed to sense this and to respect it.

Quite suddenly, and for no reason at all that she could make out, he was holding her hand.

'Your dad really wouldn't have wanted you to go hungry,' he said. 'You need to look after yourself.'

'What does it matter? Nobody cares.'

'That's silly. Of course they do,' the boy said. 'Besides, you've got years and years of your life left. You have to make the most of it.'

He pointed towards the far side of the graveyard, which, now she looked at it properly, was a hillside on the horizon, all green and springlike. And there he was – her dad, turning to face her. He lifted his hand to wave goodbye, and then walked on and disappeared from view.

Callie cried out and tried to get to her feet to chase after him, but found she couldn't move. Then everything around her faded and she woke up in her new small pink bedroom in the dark with tears on her face.

She was absolutely ravenous, and knew she wouldn't be able to go back to sleep unless she ate. She crept downstairs as quietly as she could, not wanting to wake anybody up.

There was no need to turn the light on in the kitchen. The blind had not been drawn down and a full moon was clearly visible in the night sky, so brightly silvery it almost hurt to look at it. She could see the deep, sad lines cut in the gleaming rock of its face.

She stood in a pale pool of white light and took a loaf out of the breadbin and crammed a slice into her mouth, chewed it, swallowed, and then started on another. More tears came to her eyes. Standing there alone in her nightdress, her feet bare, she realised how terribly, painfully badly she still wanted to live. And she realised also that it was the boy from across the road who had given her permission to feel this way, and he would probably never know.

· · ·

Over the next few weeks she took to spending most of her spare time in her bedroom. It kept her out of Ron's way – she couldn't help but feel that she was a source of annoyance to him, a large, troublesome cuckoo in his otherwise comfortable nest. And also, she liked being able to listen to the music that drifted over from across the road.

Every now and then she caught sight of the boy who lived there, and felt both gratitude and a pang of the slight forlornness that is part of an unspoken crush, along with a frisson of mischievous secret pleasure. She knew what no one else knew: that on the underside of her bedroom windowsill she'd scrawled *Callie 4 Reuben 4 ever*, along with a red-ink heart. Ron would be furious if he'd found out. But he probably never would.

On her first day at her new school, she had seen the boy from across the road on the bus, but kept her distance. In the playground he was greeted by a pretty girl with long blonde hair who was obviously his girlfriend, and they disappeared into the school building through a side entrance while Callie went on to the main reception area to find out where she was meant to go next.

So far, so predictable. Anyway, it had just been a stupid dream. It didn't mean they were actually ever going to be together. Or even talk to each other, let alone like each other.

The boy from across the road wasn't in the form group she'd been assigned to. Not that it made any difference to her either way. They'd probably turn out to be studying different A level subjects, too.

The teacher asked two girls to look after her and show her round. One was called Laurel and seemed bossy and confident and head-girlish; the other, Sonia, had curly red hair and was quieter. Callie expected them both to dump her at the earliest opportunity, but to her surprise, when they were all ushered out into the cold at breaktime, they let her tag along with them to sit on a bench opposite a table tennis table that nobody was using.

'We always sit here,' Laurel said. 'Nobody ever uses the table. The net's been stolen so often they've given up replacing it.'

'Miss Caraway said you live in one of the villages outside town,' Sonia said. 'Is that right?'

'Yeah, in Allingham.'

Sonia and Laurel exchanged glances, and Callie wondered why. Was Allingham supposed to be a bad place to live? Or a good one?

'We both live right here in Kettlebridge, not far from school,' Laurel said. 'How do you get into school?'

'The bus. There's a boy who lives across the road from me who comes here, and he gets the bus, too. He's not in our class, though. I haven't actually spoken to him yet.'

Laurel and Sonia glanced at each other again and then turned in unison to face Callie.

'You mean you live across the road from Reuben Tallis,' Sonia breathed.

'Yeah,' Callie said. She felt as if she might be blushing. She hoped they wouldn't notice.

Laurel leaned forward confidingly. 'We like Reuben,' she said.

'Everyone likes Reuben,' Sonia said, throwing her hands up in a gesture that could equally have been one of worship or despair.

'He's gorgeous,' Laurel said, leaning a little closer still and speaking in a voice that she no doubt thought was quiet, but that was still much too loud for Callie's liking, given that some of the other students were lurking not all that far away. 'Don't you think?'

'Absolutely gorgeous,' Sonia said, folding her arms and shaking her head.

'So intelligent,' Laurel said, shaking her head in unison.

'Doesn't say much, but when he does, always worth listening to. So thoughtful. So sweet. So tall. And so nice-looking, too.'

'You could take him home to your mum,' Sonia said mournfully.

'You could go out for dinner with him and not be bored,' Laurel improvised. 'Or put off by the way he ate.'

Sonia perked up at the thought of this. 'You would love the way he ate! You'd barely be able to take your eyes off him!'

'You'd want to take a whole lot of things off him!' Laurel expostulated, and Sonia reached forward and rapped her on the knee as if to indicate that she had broken the rules of the game by going too far.

'Only when he was ready,' she said.

'Of course. You wouldn't want to rush him,' Laurel agreed, and then, turning back to Callie, 'Welcome to the world of our obsession.'

'So... you like him, then,' Callie said.

'Of course!' Laurel interjected. 'But he has a girlfriend. Who just happens to be the most gorgeous girl in the school!'

'Which is just as well,' Sonia said, 'because if we had to fight over him, there'd be nothing of him left.'

The two of them started laughing, and Callie held back for a minute and then started laughing too. It was all so absurd, the whole thing: the boy across the road, and his inevitable girl-friend, and him appearing in her dream and speaking to her as if he knew all about her, whereas actually, he was completely unobtainable. He was a fantasy, that was all, and the pull he'd exerted on her was no different to the draw of someone famous for a fan. Even though she had the advantage of living right across the road from him, none of them stood a chance.

And maybe that was just as well. What Sonia had said about fighting for him made her uneasy. She'd never fought for anybody in her life, but then, she'd never yet seen anybody she wanted enough for a fight to be worth it.

TWENTY

Summer 2002

The summer Callie moved home after finishing her degree she heard that Reuben's mum was sick. 'Cancer,' Mum told her. 'They've given her a couple of months. She should have had years of life ahead of her to enjoy. Her retirement. Grandchildren, if Reuben ever got round to giving her any. And instead...'

Then Mum got up from the kitchen table where they were sitting and began emptying the dishwasher with unnecessary vigour and clattering of china and cutlery, and Callie knew this was her way of fighting back tears and that both of them were thinking of Callie's dad, but that neither of them were going to say so. Ron wasn't in earshot, but still, it was a longstanding unspoken rule that Callie's dad should be mentioned as little as possible.

From Callie's perspective from across the road, Reuben's mum's illness had progressed with terrifying rapidity. At first Callie still saw her from time to time pottering in her front garden, pruning roses, weeding, and sometimes just sitting on a folding stool and looking around her as if to soak in the sunshine and everything else. She looked thinner than Callie remembered, and perhaps a little waxy, but if Callie had not known something was wrong she might not have guessed.

Then she disappeared. Mum said she had declined rapidly and was now in a hospice. One evening Callie looked out of her bedroom window and saw Reuben getting out of a taxi, stooped and weatherbeaten with the weary air of someone who spent many hours on a plane and has come back to face bad news, carrying a heavy rucksack. The next thing she heard was that Reuben's mum had passed away, and the funeral date had just been arranged.

'Will you come?' Mum asked her. 'Ron and I will be going. I'm sure Emily would if she could, but she's going to be off inter-railing. It would be nice to have you with us. And you knew Reuben quite well at school, didn't you? I remember you were friends. You used to get the bus together.'

'We were friends,' Callie said. 'Of course I'll go.'

She'd nursed her crush on Reuben throughout their time in the sixth form, and he'd carried on going out with Donna, his famously pretty girlfriend, the whole time. Thankfully, if Reuben had any idea how she'd felt, he hadn't made it obvious, so she'd been spared the worst of the humiliation of unrequited love. These days she looked back on all that with the mixture of nostalgia and slightly superior distance that she reserved for other things she'd outgrown, like the music she'd listened to at the time, the haircut she'd had, and some of the fashions that Sonia and Laurel had helped talk her into trying.

She'd barely seen or spoken to Reuben since they'd both left school. They hadn't talked that much when they were both still *at* school, but she'd seen him around all the time – at school, in the village, at the bus stop outside the school or down the road from where they lived, and, of course, on the bus itself.

They'd never actually sat next to each other – it was a quiet enough route for there always to be plenty of space – but they'd both always sat on the top deck, somewhere towards the back. He usually listened to music, and she usually read, and they'd acknowledged each other if their eyes happened to meet. They'd occasionally exchanged a few words about what she was reading, or what he was listening to – his taste seemed wilfully obscure to her and ranged from jazz to punk, and she was working her way through the classics. But she'd never really got to know him, not the way you only did if you spent time with someone in private.

It had sometimes struck her that his slightly distant friendliness wasn't just general niceness or politeness, and that he looked at her with a particular kind of energy that was neither sympathy nor interest but included a little bit of both. But then, all it had taken for her to realise this was wishful thinking was for her to see him with Donna again.

Now she wanted very badly to convey her sympathy for what he was going through, but was afraid of saying the wrong thing. She knew how easy that could be – she'd been so touchy herself when she was mourning her dad. Laurel and Sonia had quickly learned to leave the subject well enough alone, but once a girl at school who she barely knew had taken it upon herself to quiz her about when and how her dad had died, more out of curiosity than compassion it had seemed, and Callie had bitten her head off.

Well, she was paying for that now that she was afraid Reuben would react to her in the same way. It would be all the more mortifying because of how she'd felt about him when she was younger – the soft helplessness of that first crush. Still, she felt obliged to try.

She forced herself to go over the road and ring for him, only to find that he was out and his dad was about to have his hair cut by someone from the village who did hairdressing from home. She left feeling slightly foolish, as if she'd stuck her nose in where it wasn't wanted, and although she'd left her number with Reuben's dad in case Reuben wanted to go out somewhere to take his mind off things, she didn't hear anything more.

Reuben's silence wasn't entirely surprising. After all, they'd never really been that close, so why should he turn to her now? It did occur to her that his dad might have forgotten to pass the message on, but she couldn't bring herself to try again. If Reuben didn't want to see her, she'd only be putting him in an awkward position by persisting.

The funeral was well attended, and the rows of seats in the crematorium chapel were almost full. Callie recognised numerous faces from the village, many of them middle-aged women who used to bring their offspring to the house across the road for piano lessons. She wondered if it would be a comfort to Reuben and his dad that so many people had turned out, and remembered her own younger self, at her dad's funeral, dry-eyed and frozen, then dissolving into tears that had been so much a loss of control that she'd been frightened of not being able to stop.

She was shocked by how pale and gaunt Reuben looked. He was wearing a black suit, a black tie – she had never seen him so formally dressed – and she had never seen him speak in public. She felt, as he stepped up to the lectern, unreasonably nervous. When he paused and looked around at them, she willed him on – to find his voice, to say whatever it was he needed and wanted to say as a tribute, so he need have no regrets later.

He didn't falter. His voice was soft and warm – had she noticed that before? Had she ever really listened to him properly before? She kept her eyes fixed on him as if disaster might strike if she looked away, as if the pure force of her attention could keep him upright and help him through it. On he went with the account of his mother's life – her West Country childhood, her studies, her work as a primary school teacher, her marriage – and Callie absorbed it as if she had been waiting for it for a long time, as if these details might help her to know him better and to understand who he was.

The wake was crowded too. She couldn't see Reuben at all. Lionel, his dad, always seemed to be at the centre of a sympathetic circle. She approached to give her condolences and Lionel clasped her hand closely and looked at her with watery eyes, and she was taken aback by his intensity and didn't quite know what to say next. Then someone else broke in to talk to him and she turned away.

Just as she was thinking it might be time to join Mum and Ron and get ready to leave, the clusters of people in front of her parted and she found herself face to face with Reuben.

Up close, he looked almost ill. His skin was a greyish colour, yellow in places, with a very light sheen of sweat, and it was suddenly possible to imagine him as a tired old man.

And then he managed a smile and it transformed him. There he was, the gentle, kind-looking boy she'd watched from across the road when she was younger, and who'd somehow helped – without having any idea that he was helping – to make her home life with Mum and Ron and Emily feel less lonely. But now he was up close, and they were face to face.

He'd always seemed a little remote before – was that because she and her friends had regarded him as unobtainable? Or was it that he was shy, and guarded in a way that might come across as aloof? Whenever she had seen him, he had usually either been lost in his own thoughts, listening to music, or walking hand in hand with Donna, either at school, where they had favoured the far side of the playing field, or outside her bedroom window, on their way to Reuben's house. That relationship had long since bitten the dust, as teenage romances did, though she couldn't be sure who had told her that. Mum, maybe.

He was pleased to see her now. There was no doubt about that. Her heart swelled and contracted as if someone had just made an enormous, shattering revelation. Somewhere in the back of her mind a little warning voice said: *Be careful.* She heard it, but had no desire to follow its advice.

The space between them remained clear, and no one stepped into it. The people around them kept their backs turned, as if making space for the pas de deux in a carefully choreographed ballet, as they moved towards each other.

'Reuben,' she said, and then, because the occasion seemed to demand it, she leaned forward and pecked him on the cheek.

She had a fleeting impression of his warmth and height and of what he was – someone who remembered her, and was responsive to her, and who would be capable of listening to her and sympathising without pity. If that was a friend, that was what he was. She absorbed this in the small moment of their closeness and then withdrew and smiled back at him.

'I'm so sorry about your mum,' she said. Her voice trembled a little. She looked into his eyes and there he was, friendly and patient and looking back at her, and she recognised that he knew she meant it, and was reaching out to him with the fellow feeling born of her own experience.

'Thank you,' he said. 'And thank you for coming.'

'Sonia and Laurel send their best wishes. They're sorry they couldn't make it. They're both at work. Did you know Laurel's a production assistant at Vale Radio now? And Sonia's an art teacher at a school in London.'

'I didn't know that,' he said politely. 'Good for them.'

'You did your reading beautifully,' she said, though surely dozens of people had said the exact same thing before. 'The service, all of it – it was really moving.'

'Thank you.'

'This is probably a stupid question, but... how are you?'

He hesitated.

'Really?' he said. 'You honestly want to know?'

She nodded.

'Terrible,' he said. 'I wasn't a particularly good son to her, these last few years. I was never around. She deserved better.' He held up his hand as if to fend off an attack. 'And yes, I know she forgave me. Which says a lot about the kind of person she was. It's hard to forgive what you don't understand. I know she didn't understand why I didn't come back home more. But she forgave me anyway.'

'Why didn't you want to come back?'

She regretted asking as soon as she'd said it. His mouth opened to answer and she saw in his eyes that there was a reason, an actual, concrete reason as opposed to the more general falling-out that could happen between someone young and their parents, but also, that it was something he was not going to tell her. Not there, at his mother's wake, surrounded by other mothers from the village he'd grown up in.

But she never found out how he would have dodged the question, because her own mother chose that moment to come over and give Reuben her condolences.

'Reuben, we are all so sorry about your mother... Such a tragic loss. You must come to us if you need anything, anything at all. Will you be back home for long?'

'I'll be here for a little while,' Reuben said, and Callie's heart rose again.

In the days after the funeral she noticed a slow but steady trickle of women calling on the house across the road with Tupperware boxes and casserole dishes in which, presumably, were hearty meals that they had prepared. Callie wondered if Reuben was eating any of it. It was never him who came to the door.

Mum noted the extensive show of support for Reuben's dad too, and was cynical about it. 'Honestly, they couldn't be trying any harder if he was a Hollywood heart-throb who'd washed up among them as a lonely widower,' she told Callie. 'I've never quite seen the attraction myself, although he's a lovely man, of course, and he plays the piano beautifully, so there's that, plus he does have a fine head of hair. But in my opinion he's not a patch on Ron.'

Callie toyed with the idea of calling on Reuben again. Surely he should have at least one person asking after him, given the outpouring of support and sympathy for his dad. But he seemed to have gone to earth, and she didn't want to intrude. She worked most evenings in the nearby pub, and she wondered if she would see him in there, but he didn't make an appearance. Nor did she bump into him in the corner shop, or in the village post office, or in any of the other local places where a chance meeting might have taken place.

She had Friday night off, and got dressed up to meet Laurel and Sonia. At least she felt strong enough to go out now. She'd come down with glandular fever towards the end of her degree, and had ended up taking a year out to recover, then going back to finish the course. There had been months when she'd barely left the house, and just the idea of going for a night out would have exhausted her.

But here she was, touching up make-up and brushing out her hair, wearing a red dress that hopefully didn't make her look too sallow, and readying herself to meet her two oldest friends.

What had she achieved, compared to the two of them? What had she been doing all this time? Her life seemed such a flimsy thing, as if it might collapse at any minute. Things were very different for Laurel and Sonia. Somehow they had settled into proper careers and relationships while she had yet to escape the family home. It seemed like a conjuring trick – how had they done it? She couldn't begin to picture herself in their position.

She caught the bus into Kettlebridge and made her way to a pub called The Eagle, which was in a medieval timber-framed building in one of the oldest and prettiest streets in the town centre, with a courtyard garden and a wood-panelled interior with various cosy nooks next to ancient fireplaces. Laurel had organised the get-together, and was sitting at a table inside with a notebook and pencil next to her gin and tonic, as if ready to take notes.

As Callie joined her she said, 'Hope you don't mind. I'm working on a programme for Vale Radio about young women who are having their quarter-century crisis. I thought maybe I could pick your brain? And Sonia's, too, when she gets here. In the name of research.' She gesticulated vaguely but with impressive confidence. 'It would be good to talk about your dreams, frustrations, fears, that kind of thing.'

'You can't possibly be having a crisis,' Callie said. 'I mean, look at you. You have a man, a career, and soon you'll have a home of your own – what more could you want?'

Laurel was looking for somewhere to buy with her boyfriend, Henry, who she'd met through work and who was quite a bit older than her and had been married twice before. Apparently Henry had said he'd rather get a mortgage with her than tie the knot again, which Laurel was unperturbed by because she was convinced that if they lasted long enough, he'd marry her in the end anyway.

'Well, I definitely don't want a baby,' Laurel said, pulling a face. 'People keep trying to tell me I'll regret not having one, but I absolutely don't think I will. Work is what keeps me sane. I honestly cannot understand why any woman in her right mind would choose to build blocks of bricks and watch children's TV instead.'

'You can work and have a family too, you know,' Callie said.

'But children are such a hostage to fortune,' Laurel said. 'They're like the most enormous Achilles heel – that's if you can actually have them, which isn't a given. Then they get sick, and have problems, and in the end, they just grow up and leave. And that's if you're lucky.'

'Yeah, I guess my mum is probably feeling pretty unlucky in that regard,' Callie said. 'Since I haven't managed to leave yet.'

'I didn't mean you, silly,' Laurel said. 'But seriously, I can't see why anyone would consciously choose to have kids. Obviously it was different in the days when the only alternatives to being a wife were to be a nun or a prostitute. Or take in washing. But these days, when you can have the man without the child – why bother?'

She rummaged in her handbag and brought out an estate agent's property brochure. 'I saw this place today. Needs work, but I'm up for a project. What do you think?'

Callie leaned forward and admired the pictures of a Victorian house near the park in the middle of Kettlebridge, which seemed to her to be eye-wateringly expensive. Laurel put the details away and started telling her about Henry's plan to keep his flat in London so he could stay there during the week and not have a long commute to work. Laurel sounded convinced that this was a good idea, and Callie couldn't tell whether she was putting a brave face on it. It sounded like a semi-detached sort of living arrangement for a couple to her, but then, maybe there were all kinds of different ways to make a long relationship work.

Sonia appeared in a full-skirted floaty cotton dress, smelling of icing sugar and roses, said hello and then withdrew to the bar to get them all drinks.

'She's madly broody,' Laurel said confidentially, and tapped her forehead to convey how crazed she thought this was. 'She wants Julian to get a job somewhere round here so they can buy a place and start a family and she'll have her mum nearby to help. I'm not sure she's convinced him yet, though.'

Julian was the boyfriend Sonia had met during Freshers' Week at university and was now living with in London. Laurel and Callie had initially both found him a bit dry and reserved and maybe even pompous, but once it had become obvious that Sonia was serious about him, they'd accepted him as a permanent fixture.

'It all seems a bit quick,' Callie said.

'She's sick of teaching already, that's the trouble,' Laurel said. 'She went into it with lots of grand ideas of inspiring kids to love art, and of course they don't, and they don't love her either, or even pay attention to her, and she doesn't want to do it any more.'

Callie said, 'So do you think this is her quarter-century crisis?'

Laurel shrugged. 'Maybe. We're all vulnerable to it, don't you think? To the sense of time racing on.'

'Well, I definitely am,' Callie said. 'Especially in comparison to you two. You seem so...' She shrugged. 'So sorted. I feel like I haven't even begun to figure out what to do with my life yet.'

'Don't do that,' Laurel scolded her. 'Don't self-deprecate! Don't belittle what you've achieved! You've been ill and you've pulled yourself together and recovered and finished your studies. And all that after you lost your dad at a very sensitive age, then had to adjust to your mum remarrying just six months later—'

And then whatever Laurel was saying faded into the background, because Reuben walked in with Sonia.

'What were you talking about when we came in?' Reuben said to Callie as he and Sonia settled at the table with the drinks they'd brought over from the bar.

'Oh, Laurel was just giving me a pep talk because it took me so long to graduate,' Callie said. Her heart was beating very fast, but she felt she was putting on a decent show of behaving normally, as if Reuben showing up out of the blue was no big deal to her.

Reuben raised his eyebrows. 'Did it?'

'Yeah, I mean, I only just finished. I had to have some time out for health reasons.'

'Glandular fever,' Laurel interjected. 'Very unlucky.'

'Yes, glandular fever,' Callie said, trying not to feel annoyed with Laurel, who had a habit of interrupting other people's stories. 'It was a four-year course anyway – I did French, so I had a year abroad – and I spent a couple of years working and travelling before I started. What with one thing and another, it seems to have taken forever to finish.'

'I want to go travelling again,' Reuben said. 'If I can get the money together. Or sort out a job. I need to figure out where I can get a working visa.'

Sonia cleared her throat as if to make an announcement. 'So I have news, everybody,' she said. 'Julian asked me to marry him, and I said yes.'

Everybody froze. Callie's eyes met Reuben's and she was almost sure that they were thinking the same thing: is this where we are, already? The time of life when our friends and peers start getting married and settling down?

It was a shock – of course she was happy for Sonia, but it was a shock just the same. Not because it seemed sudden or unexpected – it did, but then, on reflection, Sonia and Julian were clearly happy and well suited and it made sense. But because there was a clock ticking somewhere for all of them, and Sonia's just seemed to have shifted forwards into a whole different time zone.

Then Laurel let out a dramatic shriek of excitement and everyone started talking all at once. There were hugs, and questions, and toasts, and Sonia explained that they didn't have a date fixed yet, but were planning to get married in the autumn.

'It's going to be a registry office do, with the reception somewhere in Kettlebridge,' she said. 'September sometime, hopefully, or October, so the weather shouldn't be too bad. Or not cold, at any rate. I don't see the point in hanging round. It'll only make Julian jittery. We just want to get on with things. But we are going to have an engagement party in a couple of weeks. I'm hoping I'll have my ring by then. My parents have said we can do it at their house – our flat in London's so tiny, we could hardly invite anybody if we did it there. Besides, my parents are about to have the whole place redecorated, so it doesn't matter if we wreck it. Not that we will, obviously.' She turned to Reuben. 'Do you think you'll be able to make it?'

'You mean, to the party? Sure, yeah. If I'm still here. Thanks. It sounds good.'

'Great,' Sonia said. She looked from Reuben to Callie and back again.

'You must come to the wedding, too,' she added.

It crossed Callie's mind that she might be remembering how they had all admired Reuben once. Now Callie was the only one who was free for him, was she trying to matchmake? It was a sweet thing to do, if she was. Was that what happened when you were happy in love yourself – you had the energy and will to spare to help other people find love and happiness too?

'So much for the quarter-century crisis,' Laurel said.

Sonia looked bemused. 'What did you say? Who's having a crisis?'

'Oh, no one,' Laurel said, and went off to the bar to get another round of drinks.

They spent the next hour or so talking about Sonia's wedding and honeymoon plans. Reuben's dead mother was the elephant in the room, and nobody mentioned her, but his loss affected the rest of them anyway. They all behaved like slightly exaggerated versions of themselves: Laurel was more impatient and opinionated than usual, Sonia was skittish and distracted, and Callie was quieter and more watchful. Eventually Sonia said Julian would be waiting for her back at her parents' house and might be being driven mad by her mother, and she'd better get back and rescue him, and all of them seemed collectively to decide that the evening was over.

As they were gathering up their things to go Sonia said to Reuben, 'You'd better give me your email address. I don't think I have it. So I can send you the engagement party invite.' She glanced at Callie. 'Unless Callie has it?'

'I don't,' Callie said.

'Well, you should, seeing as how he's your wedding date.'

'He is?'

She glanced at Reuben warily, expecting him to at least look uneasy, or, worse, to start making excuses and backing off, but he was smiling at her. He looked quite happy, and even slightly amused at her embarrassment.

'If you'd like me to be,' he said.

'Of course,' Callie told him, and Laurel ceremoniously tore a strip of paper off a page of her notebook and gave it to Callie, along with a pencil.

'I only have a Hotmail address,' he said.

Both Sonia and Laurel stood and looked on while Callie wrote down Reuben's email address, and then wrote down her own, along with her mobile number – 'just in case' – and handed it over to him. She felt that they were watching with approval – like witnesses to a small but important transaction that had just been concluded.

Then they all went outside, and Laurel offered Sonia a lift home and then turned to Callie, opened her mouth as if about to speak, glanced at Reuben and then turned away again. In any case, Allingham would have been well out of her way. She and Sonia went off to the car park, and Reuben said to Callie, 'Are you getting the bus?'

'I am,' Callie said, and they began to walk towards the nearest bus stop.

'Just like old times,' Callie said, and then felt foolish. It seemed like a silly thing to say. But Reuben didn't make her feel stupid. He just said, 'I suppose it is.'

Next thing she knew, the bus arrived. She'd been hoping that it would take ages, so they'd have a chance to talk. Instead they made their way up to the top deck, as they had done so many times before. She settled into a seat towards the back and he looked at her questioningly and then sat beside her.

The bus moved off. Neither of them spoke. The view of the rooftops of the old buildings in the centre of town slid away from them to either side, and she was suddenly, dizzyingly happy. She wished this bus ride could go on for ever. She'd never been on any journey before that she had wished would never end.

'I used to listen to you on the piano, you know,' she said. 'When I first moved in across the road. Do you still play?'

'Me? No,' he said shortly. 'As you'll know if you heard me playing, I was never very good.'

'Oh, I wouldn't say that.' She felt slightly crestfallen, as if she'd made a faux pas or inadvertently touched a nerve. 'Anyway, you don't have to be really brilliant at something to enjoy doing it.'

'No, but it probably makes it more fun, right? I begged to give up, in the end,' he said. 'I don't think it helped being taught by my dad.'

'Ah.'

'How about you? Did you ever play?

'Yeah. Actually, my dad encouraged me. My piano was one of the things that didn't survive the move here.'

'Ah,' he said.

They sat in silence as the bus left the houses and street lights on the outskirts of Kettlebridge and plunged into the darkness of the open countryside. Then Reuben said, 'When did he die?'

'Six months before Mum and I moved here.'

'That must have been hard for you.'

'Yeah. It was.'

It had been a long time since she'd talked to anybody about her dad. On the whole, the people around her treated his death as something that had happened long enough ago to have been effectively defused by the passage of time. But sometimes it did not feel like that at all. Sometimes it felt as if nothing would ever defuse it – as if it would always have the same devastating power, like an unexploded World War II bomb waiting for someone to stumble across it and detonate it.

'I'm still really sad about it,' she said. 'Every now and then it just hits me. But, you know...' She swallowed. 'I think there's some truth in the clichés. The things people say to you. It does get easier. It actually does. It doesn't always hurt as much. And it isn't always as much of a shock.'

She paused, and found she was holding her breath. He didn't say anything. She went on, 'I really am sorry about your mum.'

He turned away from her slightly and looked out at the darkness. 'It's all right,' he said. 'I mean, it isn't. But it is bearable, I suppose.'

He glanced at her and gave her a wry half-smile and then reached out and rang the bell, and she jumped as if he'd shaken her out of a dream.

They'd reached the village, and it was time to get off the bus. They went awkwardly down the narrow spiral stairs and out onto the pavement, and walked on together as the bus pulled past them and disappeared into the darkness.

She just had time to notice what a clear, starry night it was before they reached her house, and both came to a standstill.

'I enjoyed tonight,' he said. 'I didn't expect to. But I did.'

'I did too,' she said.

They stood there for a moment and studied each other's

shadowy faces. She felt as if she was floating up towards him. Surely they would kiss...

But something made him hesitate and freeze as if he doubted her.

'Well, so long. It was good to see you,' he said stiffly, and turned and went off across the road, leaving her not knowing whether to be downcast or elated.

TWENTY-ONE

Some weeks later, towards the end of an August day of heat and sudden showers, Callie set off to catch the bus from the village into Kettlebridge and make her way to Sonia and Julian's engagement party.

When the bus arrived she went up to the near-empty top deck and watched the familiar woods going by, fresh and green because of the recent rain, though really they were on the cusp of autumn. She knew she was about to see Reuben again. He'd been housesitting in London, and was planning to go straight to the party – she'd emailed him the day before to check. And knowing she was going to see him made the evening seem brighter and more promising than it would otherwise have done. It felt like a day when something might happen. All the same, she told herself not to get her hopes up.

When she arrived the party was already in full swing, even though it was not yet nine o'clock. There was a carnival mood that could only have been unleashed by the prospect of two people the same age as the rest of them turning their backs on the freedom of youth and taking the alarmingly grown-up step of getting married. Perhaps this was what impelled her to drink a bit more than she ought to have done.

She kept expecting to catch sight of Reuben any minute, but there was no sign of him anywhere. In the living room there was dancing, and she joined in because why not, she might as well make the most of the evening, whether or not Reuben turned up. People were smiling at her. Maybe she wasn't bad at this living in-the-moment business. She should do it more often. But then, just as suddenly, the press of people and their shining faces was too much for her and she escaped into the kitchen, where the gang seated around the breakfast bar were too absorbed in uproarious laughter to notice her. The back door was slightly ajar, and she stumbled out into the coolness of the night air.

There was no one outside, but people had obviously been here earlier – there was a full ashtray on the round table on the patio, and a couple of abandoned glasses. She kept walking, down the path to the end of the garden.

Sonia's father was a very keen and proud gardener and was known for the creatures he had cut into the hedge at the front of the house. There was a topiary archway at the back too, and as Callie approached it she noticed a faint smell of fresh cigarette smoke and realised it was coming from the other side. Someone else was already there. In the gloom ahead she could see a darker, man-shaped patch of shadow and a small, bright point of suppressed flame, which almost instantly resolved itself into the shape of Reuben smoking, something she had never known him do before.

Her heart somersaulted and then settled into place, like a figure skater taking to the ice who has no time to be frightened because, finally, this is it. She stepped through the dark greenery and joined him.

'Callie,' he said, and carefully put out his cigarette. 'So you're hiding from the party too.'

'I just wanted to get some air. Are *you* hiding?'

He shrugged. 'Maybe. A little.'

The silence seemed to thicken, the darkness to become more dark. She blinked and forced herself to focus and it was just a garden after dusk with a party going on in the house behind her and Reuben standing next to her.

He seemed upset. Not surprisingly. He was still grieving. That must be why he'd taken up smoking, which seemed quite out of character, even slightly undignified, like the kind of thing other boys did under the illusion that it made them look cool.

'Apparently Donna decided not to come,' he said. 'She was invited. One of her friends told me she stayed away because of me.'

He sounded bitter, which caught Callie by surprise. She wouldn't have expected Reuben to still be nursing sore feelings about a relationship that had finished, as far as she knew, around the time they had all left school.

'I take it you're not in touch, then,' she said.

'No,' he said shortly.

So what happened? She suddenly wanted to know – but not quite enough to ask. Anyway, he almost certainly wouldn't tell her. And besides, it was really none of her business.

There was another silence. Any minute now he'd say he was going back inside, and she'd lose him to the party and that would be that.

'I didn't know you smoked,' she said, to change the subject.

'I don't, normally.'

'You should give up.'

'Don't you ever do anything that's bad for you? Perhaps you don't.'

He turned to study her, his face illuminated by the moonlight. She felt a frisson that came and went like a little bird taking flight, seen out of the corner of her eye. Then he turned away.

She said, 'It seemed like you and Donna were really in love when we were younger.'

'"Love is not love which alters when it alteration finds,"' he said grimly. 'If that's true, it was never really love at all.'

'Do you think even Shakespeare really believed that? I know it sounds good. But it's an awful lot to live up to – the idea that if you love someone, you'll always love them, no matter what they do or how they change.'

'Why is it so hard to believe? I think it's just how it is,' he said. 'If you love someone, you don't stop just because they've done something bad. You might feel different about them. You might be angry with them. The love might be mixed up with all kinds of other feelings. But it would still be love. Love isn't a rational thing, like deciding to do more exercise or... or give up smoking. Maybe it isn't always very good for you. But when it's there, it's there, and you can't get rid of it just because it isn't convenient any more.'

'I think I love you,' she said suddenly.

He didn't reply. What could he possibly say? Why had she just come out with it like that? She'd drunk too much. That was what it was. And now she'd started talking, it was almost impossible to stop.

'I mean, I know that must sound mad,' she went on. 'I don't expect you to do anything about it. And I know we don't really know each other. It's just... there, like you said. I don't know, one day maybe it won't be any more. Maybe I'll grow out of it, or whatever. Move on. It's just... maybe you could take it as a compliment, you know? If you ever feel really alone, or sad, or as if things are pointless, it's something you could remember.'

He hesitated. 'OK,' he said. Then, 'And thank you. I'm honoured. But as you said, you don't know me. And I don't deserve it.'

'Like you said, even if that's true, it wouldn't make any difference,' she told him.

Even though what she had done was absolutely ridiculous, she did feel a sense of accomplishment. Or maybe she was primarily relieved.

Finally, she'd done it. She'd confessed. Though she probably couldn't have chosen a worse time, given everything he had been through lately. Plus he was upset about his ex-girlfriend choosing to stay away, treating him like a pariah. What on earth could he possibly have done to deserve that?

Though maybe it was because his ex was still a little in love with him. Yes, that must be it. If that was the reason, then given her own feelings for Reuben, Callie could definitely understand.

In spite of the noise of the party coming from the house behind them it was very quiet. It was the kind of hush that falls when you watch a coin spinning and wait to see which way it is going to land.

At least he hadn't bolted yet. But probably he'd make his excuses any minute now, and escape back into the party, as if she'd never said anything at all...

'Look,' he said after a while. 'It's a beautiful night.'

He was looking up at the sky, and she did too and saw the stars. Many, many stars, tiny, indomitable pinpricks in the dark, and the more she looked, the more stars she could see and the brighter they seemed.

So he wasn't about to walk away. That was something. That was more than she would have dared hope for, and a lot more than she had any right to expect.

He carried on standing there, studying the stars, and so did she. Her heartbeat slowed. To her surprise, she began to feel at ease. It was as if they had somehow magically leapfrogged the need for conversation and reached some kind of understanding.

The air was cooling fast, and as if a shutter had opened and closed and presented her with the two of them in a different scene, she pictured them together in winter, outside in the dark with more than a chill in the air – frost on the grass, perhaps, and a tree inside with presents underneath it.

'Did you know,' he said, 'that when you look at the night sky, you're looking at history? The light of the stars you see has been travelling towards the earth for millions and millions of years. Some of those stars might not even exist any more. They might have burnt away to nothingness, and be all dead and dark. But the light is still real. The light is like a time traveller.'

'The light doesn't stop just because the star has gone,' she said.

She glanced across at him and their eyes met. They were standing quite close, almost shoulder to shoulder. And then, as if it was the most natural thing in the world, he reached out and took her hand.

In the years to come, this conversation, and that touch, would make it impossible for her to blame him for what happened later.

He had told her something she'd needed to hear years before, that no one else had said – that it was OK to carry on loving someone who was no longer there, and for as long as you did, they were still with you. And whenever she let herself remember, she would feel grateful to him.

But he let go of her hand almost instantly, and she heard someone moving through the garden behind her, weaving drunkenly through the shrubbery and calling out her name. Then Laurel blundered through the topiary arch and stopped short, staring at the pair of them.

'So this is where you got to,' she said to Callie, eyebrows raised. 'I've been looking for you everywhere.'

'We should go back in,' Reuben said to Callie, and started to make his way back to the house.

'So – what happened?' Laurel demanded, as she and Callie followed him.

'Nothing,' Callie said. 'We were just talking.'

'Oh well, in that case I don't feel too bad about interrupting,' Laurel said. But she gave Callie a suspicious look, and Callie resolved to try and seem less dizzy and elated than she felt.

She was walking on air. And she carried on feeling that way even when she lost sight of Reuben, and later learned that he'd left the party without saying goodbye.

The next day she called round at Reuben's house mid-morning, having changed her outfit several times and spent much, much longer than she normally would fussing over her hair and make-up.

She figured she'd just say hello, and ask if he fancied going out for a walk or something. It wasn't such a big deal, just a way of killing time if he was still around. And after all, they'd known each other for years.

It was Reuben's dad who answered the door. He looked her up and down with a genial frown, as if he could see that she'd made an effort and thought it was amusing.

'Callie, isn't it? What can I do for you?'

'I just wondered if Reuben was in,' she said.

His smile abruptly vanished and his face turned hangdog and sad, as if he knew he was about to disappoint her and sincerely felt bad about it.

'I'm sorry, Reuben's gone back to London, I'm afraid.'

Cheeks flaming with humiliation at her own stupidity, she thanked him and said she'd better get on, and stumbled back across the road.

TWENTY-TWO

The weather in the run-up to Sonia's wedding was not promising, but when the day came, the sun shone out of a blue sky that seemed to intensify the colours of all the leaves on the trees – gold, bronze, scarlet, burgundy – as if to make a vivid final impression before the year moved on to bare branches.

As Callie got ready in her little box room she thought about the apples growing on the tree in Reuben's front garden, which were always so abundant that his mother had come over every year and offered a basket of them to Mum, who'd never known quite what to do with them. There were windfalls lying on the grass now, and Callie knew she wouldn't ask if she could collect them – it would seem too intrusive – but it made her sad to think of them being left there to rot.

She didn't look across at Reuben's window, although she knew he was there. He was living in London now, working nights writing headlines and checking punctuation on the newspaper Henry worked for – casual shifts which Henry had helped him to get. But he'd come back for the wedding, just as they'd agreed back in the summer, and this time she was determined to play it cool.

Maybe he'd forgotten what she'd said at Sonia's engagement party, or had just put it down to her having drunk too much. In any case, neither of them had referred to it.

She'd borrowed Ron's computer to email him, which was awkward because Ron wanted to know if she was sending off a job application and raised his eyebrows when she said she wasn't, then behaved as if he was doing her a big favour to let her use it anyway. But it was that or find an internet café somewhere, or book a time slot on one of the computers at the library in Kettlebridge – she hadn't managed to get the money together yet for a computer of her own.

Of course she'd spent ages trying to work out what to say. In the end she'd written, *Don't mean to hassle you... just wondered if you're still coming to Sonia and Julian's wedding?* When she pressed send her heart lurched as if even this small piece of communication was a risk.

She'd made herself wait till the next day before asking Ron if she could use his computer again to check her messages, and had been surprised and relieved to see his reply waiting for her.

Of course. Looking forward to it. I'm coming back the night before. How about we get a taxi down there? I'll book it – how about 10.30?

What was really remarkable about the message wasn't the words, or the fact that he'd replied relatively quickly, but the way he'd signed off. With a kiss.

It seemed such an un-Reubenish thing to do. He wasn't usually demonstrative like that. Though of course people signed off emails with kisses all the time, and he might have just picked up the habit. Or maybe he'd just been reciprocating, because she'd signed off that way herself.

Sounds good, she'd replied. And then another kiss: *x*

She'd printed off his message so she could keep it. Which

was ridiculous. But still, it made her happy. And wasn't it worth hanging on to anything that made you feel that way?

When the doorbell rang she was out of her room almost without thinking and flew down the stairs to answer it. And there he was, smiling and waiting for her.

He said, 'Are you ready?'

'Nearly,' she said.

She stuck her head round the kitchen door to say goodbye to Mum, who was sitting on her own with a cup of tea and that day's *Daily Mail*. Emily had left home for university in Sheffield a few weeks before, and Mum was missing her to an extent that Callie couldn't help but find slightly offensive. Ron was going to take Mum to London later for a meal out and a West End show and a stay in a hotel to cheer her up, but it didn't look like the prospect of the trip had succeeded in raising her spirits just yet.

'You're off, then,' Mum said, looking her up and down. Her mouth twitched as if she was fighting back the urge to compliment her – she never went in for flattering Callie. It was as if she was afraid of making her big-headed, though she didn't seem to feel any such reservations when it came to Emily.

'Yeah, Reuben's here and the taxi he called is waiting.'

'You look nice,' Mum said, as if making a concession. 'That colour suits you. You should wear it more often.'

Callie was wearing a coral-coloured 1950s-style dress that Laurel had encouraged her to buy. It was brighter than the clothes she usually wore, and made her feel flighty and adventurous.

'Thanks.'

'Don't forget your keys, will you? Because we're not haring back from London if you lock yourself out.'

'I won't.'

'Well, have a nice time. Give my best to the bride and

groom. I hope they have a wonderful day. Sonia's done very well for herself, hasn't she?'

'She has,' Callie agreed.

'Just as well not to leave it till all the good ones have been snapped up,' Mum said.

'I'll bear that in mind,' Callie said, and hurried out to the hall to slip her shoes on and make good her escape.

When she was in the taxi with Reuben there was a niggling sense of friction between them, of something unrelieved or unaddressed. Maybe it was because of what she'd said to him at Sonia's party. The tension made Callie more talkative than she would ordinarily have been, as if she was showing off to him, even though she knew she already had his attention.

The civic hall where the ceremony was taking place was long and narrow with panelled white walls, an ornately plastered arched ceiling painted in white and green, a polished wooden floor and high square windows giving onto a view of blue sky. It was set out with white-skirted chairs in rows of four either side of a narrow aisle, and Callie ended up sitting next to the aisle, with Reuben on her other side and Laurel and Henry in front of them.

As the music began to play for Sonia's entrance – some suitably serene piano composition – Callie turned, as everybody did, to see the bride, but she was just as conscious of Reuben as of her friend in white, advancing triumphantly towards the end of the hall where Julian was waiting with the registrar.

As Sonia and Julian began to say their vows she realised that Julian was nervous, and that made her like him more. There was something so uptight about Julian, it had been hard not to regard him as a caricature – a young-fogey lawyer, whose off-duty clothes looked as stiff and formal as a suit. But no one was a caricature to themselves. Inside Julian, as much as anybody, there was a beating heart, dreams, hopes. Maybe secrets, even.

Was there room for secrets, inside a marriage? Secrets that you didn't share with your spouse, but kept to yourself?

She supposed there must be. But would that be true even in a marriage that people regarded as a rock-like success – like Mum and Ron's, or Reuben's parents? Or even her own parents' marriage? Were the happy marriages the ones without secrets, or the ones where secrets were successfully kept?

The words were said, the vows were taken: the bride was kissed. But how could anyone do it? This huge undertaking, the promise to love someone for the rest of your life? Because if the promise was kept, that meant the marriage would be ended only by death, as it had been for her parents, and for Reuben's parents... and wouldn't that be a tragedy, one of even more devastating proportions than if the promise was broken and the marriage wound down by solicitors and a decree nisi, leaving both parties wounded but at least alive, and free to look for happiness wherever else they could find it?

Whatever you chose, whatever you promised, in the end time would come calling for you and you would be undone. No one's love could last forever, because no promise could outlive you and life was, when all was said and done, not long. Not when you looked back at it. All the sixteen years she'd had with her dad still alive seemed to her now as short as the time between the first leaf falling and the branches being bare, and she did not know what to make of that, or what to learn from it, other than to carry on living and embrace the knowledge that, sooner or later, for you or another, darkness would fall.

Then she felt Reuben's hand resting next to hers.

She did not know who moved first – whether she slipped her hand into his, or whether he took hers. His touch was warm and soft and dry. And there they were, holding hands in the hall, and the air smelt of perfume and flowers and there was nothing to see but light and a celebration of love. A triumph against the odds.

The music struck up again, and the new Mr and Mrs Hallam filed out, Sonia looking flushed and demure and triumphant, Julian dazed with relief. The congregation stirred. At the front, Sonia's mum dabbed at her eyes with a hanky and Sonia's dad briskly patted her back. He was presumably trying to be comforting, but it looked more as if he wanted to stop her choking.

Callie turned to Reuben. They were no longer holding hands, but she didn't know who'd let go first. Last time, in Sonia's garden, it had been him.

'It was a lovely service, wasn't it?' she said.

'It was,' he said, rather sadly, and she wondered what he'd been thinking.

But then he smiled and she smiled back at him, and they went out to stand on the steps in front of the Guild Hall together and wait for the bride and groom to finish signing the marriage certificate and reappear.

It was a lull in the day like a dip in a series of waves that would soon carry them effortlessly forward again. Nothing more was required from them than to be present and unresisting. The sun was so bright she had to fish in her bag for her sunglasses, and she was happy to be standing so close to him that they were jostled together by the movements of the other wedding guests who were crowded around them.

There was a hubbub of conversation going on – people greeting and complimenting each other, exclaiming about the ceremony, discussing the problems they'd had getting there, making introductions – but neither she nor Reuben made any attempt to join it. Laurel came through the crowd to join them and raked over them with a look that was both knowing and amused, as if to say, *I see you're finally getting there.* Another time Callie might have found this presumptuous, but as it was, she was too happy to mind.

'Confetti,' Laurel said, handing her a little packet. 'Make sure you get it over them.' Then she moved away from them to distribute more confetti.

By and by Sonia and Julian came out. Callie tossed her handful of confetti in the air and it glinted in the sunlight like tiny bright stars as it fell and caught on Sonia's hair and dress and brightened the steps to the registry office. Then there were photographs of the bride and groom with different groups of guests, and Reuben stood aside and waited as she and Laurel and Henry took part in one of the line-ups.

When she came back down the steps to join him, he very gently picked a heart-shaped piece of golden confetti out of her hair, and looked at her in a way that she knew she would not forget.

The day sped up and rushed on, a succession of rituals and watched moments. She drank champagne, lost sight of Reuben, had brief, scattered, warm conversations with people she knew a little or not at all, then found her place at the table for the wedding meal and found him next to her again.

On her other side, she was seated next to a cousin of Sonia's who was a musician, and who told her at length about the diffi-culties and politics of the orchestra he played in. She nodded and sympathised but her attention drifted and she thought of her dad and how proudly he'd listened to her playing her piano. What had her mum been thinking when she gave it away?

But then, Mum must have genuinely believed it was for the best. Maybe she had been trying to protect herself, too, and to draw a line between one part of her life and another.

And all the time, Callie was conscious of Reuben sitting there next to her. It was as if they'd spent years sitting by different shores, and were both finally swimming in the same water. She sensed that he was as aware of her as she was of him.

As the day of the wedding wore on the gathering grew wilder and looser, taking in newcomers and fresh energy as the hours ticked by. Time fragmented and blossomed into a succession of impressions and memories for later. Sonia's bouquet was thrown and Callie, who had always been a butterfingers and an unpopular choice for the rounders team in school, caught it as if it was meant to be hers, then passed it on to Laurel.

Laurel breathed in the scent of the flowers, white roses and freesias, then looked quizzically at Henry, as if pondering whether or not to resign herself to her lot with him. But after that Callie lost track of her, and found herself in a series of brief, intense conversations with strangers she had never met before and might never meet again – the kind of conversations you can only have when you have drunk too much champagne, and witnessed two people as young as you are make a vow of lifelong fidelity. The ceremony, and the contract with the future it represented, seemed to give extra energy to the social whirl that followed, as if the dancing and chit-chat and drinking was the relief they all needed.

Sonia cut the cake with Julian standing just behind her, his arms around her waist, and a smile captured by several cameras. It was a striking image – the bride in white with tendrils of red curls escaping from her piled-up hair, the delighted husband in the background of her big day. Callie felt as if Sonia had passed through an invisible barrier that she herself could not penetrate, and was now moving through life with her new husband in a parallel but separate world. Sonia had moved on, and her first loyalty would now officially be to Julian. She'd never been one to confide everything in her friends anyway, but surely marriage would put distance between them for good.

Later, Callie found herself standing next to Reuben in the dark as Sonia and Julian executed a well-rehearsed dance routine in the clear space in front of them. When the bride and groom had finished and had been applauded, she joined the other wedding guests – uncles, little kids – who were dancing. After a while Reuben did too, and everybody was hot and giddy in the dark and by that time nobody cared in the least about whether they looked stupid.

Laurel sought Callie out to say goodbye, looking harassed and limping slightly in her high heels. Henry had to work the next day, she said, and they'd decided it was time to call it quits.

'Couldn't you stay on a little longer?' Callie asked.

Laurel grimaced. 'It seems not,' she said.

Callie glimpsed Henry waiting somewhere up ahead, looking sozzled and rather irritable. It struck her that Laurel, who'd always been so assertive, almost domineering, did not have the upper hand in that relationship. And Callie felt almost sorry for her, as if she'd glimpsed a little piece of evidence that Laurel had settled for something that would not make her happy.

A little while after Laurel and Henry left, a ragged line of assorted wedding guests, along with the more recent arrivals who had come for the evening party, assembled at the front of the hotel to watch Julian drive Sonia away – or at least, out of sight round the corner – in a white car festooned with shaving-foam and trailing clattering cans. Callie saw Reuben was among them, and as everybody filed back inside they gravitated towards each other and he said, 'You'll come and find me when you're ready to leave?'

'Yes. Quite soon, I think,' she said.

With the bride and groom gone and the elderly and youngest guests by and large having left to find their beds, the wedding shifted into a new phase of even giddier abandon, as if everybody who was still there was determined to make the absolute most of it before finally giving up the ghost. As Callie finally left the dance floor and was about to begin to search the mayhem, Reuben approached her. Even though neither of them could quite make out what the other was saying over the music, they turned and walked as if by firm agreement towards the exit, and then strolled out into the quiet and dark of the town centre to head for the nearest taxi rank.

Callie was surprised to see that it had been raining – not heavily, but enough to wet the pavements and set up gleaming reflections of the street lights. It was cool but not cold, a mild October night. The street lights picked out in vivid detail the texture of the stones of the old church facing them, and its grinning gargoyles. They passed under the archway that had once been the gateway to the town's medieval abbey, and was now almost all of it that survived.

Ahead of them was the town hall, the market square and a wide road with shops and restaurants to either side, all dark and closed now. In the market square the leaves of the acers, flamered by daylight, were as glossy and dark as fresh blood in an old film. A solitary car swung round the bend of the road in front of them and accelerated into the distance, and then there was hush again, apart from the sound of their footsteps.

She said, 'Sonia and Julian will be well on their way to Paris by now.'

'Are they spending their whole honeymoon there?'

'I think so. They've booked quite a grand hotel. Have you been to Paris?'

'Me?' He hesitated just long enough for her to be almost certain that he'd been there with a girlfriend he'd since broken up with. Donna, maybe? 'Yeah, ages ago. Have you?'

'Yeah, on my year abroad during my degree. I loved it,' she said.

She couldn't help but think of going there with him. The Eiffel Tower at sunset, the little brasseries and cafés, the art galleries, the view across the rooftops of the city from Montmartre.

There were so many places they could go...

There was a lone taxi at the rank next to the traffic lights ahead, waiting as if it was there purposely for them. They climbed into the back together and Callie gave the taxi driver her address. Her heart was beating as if she was near the end of a race. She gazed out of the window at the quiet town at night slipping away from them, and then the fields and the climb up the hill through the trees until they arrived and pulled up outside the house she still thought of as Ron's.

Reuben insisted on paying, and as they stood on Callie's side of the road and the taxi drove away he turned to Callie and said, 'Well, I suppose this is goodbye.'

'Come in if you would like. There's no one at home,' she said.

He hesitated and frowned slightly, as if he was either trying to interpret what this might mean or worrying about where it might lead. Then he said, 'If you're sure...?'

'Of course I'm sure,' she said impatiently.

And then, as artlessly as a bird pecking at something on a lawn, she reached up to kiss him.

A moment later they were separate again as if nothing had happened, and were looking at each other in the darkness. Then something changed in his face and she saw how hungry he was and knew he'd seen the same in her. He kissed her back and she understood that he was trying to show her something, or perhaps to prove something to himself, though she couldn't tell what and only wanted him to forget it, whatever it was, and anything other than her.

He followed her to the front door. She rummaged in her bag and found her key and turned it in the lock, and led him into the house.

· · ·

She woke the next morning to cold and profound sadness, as if she had lost something or had it torn from her and was only now about to learn what it was.

Lying in the darkness, alone, she remembered the night before and Reuben, the way he had been with her and what they had done.

It was impossible that he would have abandoned her. He would not have left her. He would be downstairs, or in the bathroom: he would return in a minute, and come back to bed and lie with her, and she would know for sure that she would never feel alone again.

But everything about the silence in the house told her that there was no one else there.

TWENTY-THREE

She raised her head and realised that it ached, but that was nothing compared to the confusion of not knowing where Reuben had gone, or why. Then she saw that he had left her a note.

A note could be sweet, could be touching, but was it any way to say goodbye to a new lover the first time you left them?

She could still smell him. They had been so close and that had been real and not a dream. And yet, in spite of all of that, she had not been able to keep him with her and he had left at first light, like a thief. As if he'd taken her for a fool, and had been proved right.

Was it possible that she could have been completely and utterly wrong about him in every way?

How could she have been so stupid? Why had it seemed like the right time to be reckless? The thought of the risk they'd taken made her feel as if she'd just been poisoned.

The risk *she'd* taken. He'd left her to the memory of it on her own.

She got up and put on her old pink childish dressing gown, pulled it around her and tied the cord tight. When she pulled the curtains the light that filtered into the room was flat and grey and insubstantial. The road outside was filled with fog, a true Oxfordshire fog, so dense and sticky that for now, all she could make out of the house across the road was the faint outline of its roof.

She switched on the overhead light and picked up the note he had left her with.

Dear one, it said. *Good morning. I hope you slept well. I have to go back across the road, or my dad will wonder where I've got to. I'll speak to you soon. xxx*

Was it credible? Not really. It was an obvious, pathetic excuse. He could have just popped back across the road, said 'Hi, I'm with Callie,' or even 'I'm fine, I'll be back later,' and then returned. He was an adult. Yes, he was a guest in his dad's house, just as Callie was a guest here, but that didn't mean he owed his dad any further explanation. And if his dad was still asleep, he could just have left a note. Which was obviously something that came naturally to him. Or he could have left her sleeping while he phoned, and then come back up to be with her...

But he hadn't. Which meant that here, with her, was not where he wanted to be.

She did not rush to dress. It felt as if there was no point rushing to do anything. The pulse of her blood was lethargic and sluggish, and the pace of the day seemed to have slowed with it. She ran herself a bath, and lay in the water until it was tepid, and she allowed herself to remember the time they had spent together at the wedding – the touch of his hand, the ceremony, the spectacle of the dancing, and the sense of some kind of understanding between them.

If he had chosen to betray that, or if he had recoiled from it now, that was not her failing, it was his.

She told herself it did not mean she had cause for regret. Not yet, anyway. That was what other people would expect her to feel, because it was such a cliché, so wholly predictable, to be used and cast aside the way it seemed she had been. But she still could not quite bring herself to believe that version of events. He might have abandoned her, but if he had, it would be at a cost to himself as well as to her. She could not imagine him to be indifferent.

And then she closed her eyes and let her thoughts slow to the pace of her breathing, as if she was about to drift off into sleep.

She thought of Reuben the first time she'd seen him, dutifully lifting his mother's groceries out of the car. With Donna, walking up and down the road. Under the stars at Sonia's engagement party, hiding from everyone at the end of the garden.

Was he weak? Frightened? Was she a fool for wanting to look for excuses for him?

She got out of the bath, dressed in jeans and an old shirt and a cardigan, brushed out her hair. The girl who looked back at her from the mirror appeared to have had all the life sucked out of her. Which was how she felt. Slowly, grudgingly, she got her phone out of her bag and checked it.

Nothing from Reuben. Somehow she had known to expect that. There was, however, a message from Laurel.

How was the rest of your evening? Henry foul mood (hangover) this morning. Thank God I'm at work now. Cocktail and debrief sometime?

What would Laurel say when she heard?

Oh Callie, I'm so sorry. I really wouldn't have thought it of him. That he would treat you that way.

And Sonia?

You deserve so, so much better, Callie. I know you always

*had a crush on him, but don't you think it was all just a bit of a
fantasy?*

Though doubtless both her friends would scold her if they
knew how careless she and Reuben had been. She supposed she
ought to go out and find a pharmacy, get the morning-after pill...

Maybe later. Once she'd got her head together.

She picked up the note and put it in a drawer: her impulse
was to hide it, although it wasn't as if anybody was about to
come looking for it. She felt as if an invisible hand was pressing
down on her, and that she would have to escape it in order to
leave the house. Perhaps it was the fog, which made everything
so quiet and dull and sleepy. Perhaps it was just fear of what
there was to find.

He'd done this to her before, in a way, the morning after the
party. It seemed like every time they got close, he ran away. But
this time they'd been so much closer, about as close as it was
possible to get, and it was that much more of a shock. She still
couldn't quite believe it. But she had to admit, it did look a lot as
if Reuben had just made use of her and then given her the most
stereotypical humiliating brush-off imaginable.

Anyway, she didn't have to accept it passively.

She went round dutifully locking up the house and put on
some red lipstick, for armour. Laurel had got it for her, and she
rarely wore it. She thought of Laurel as she put it on, and what
Laurel had said about the make-up she chose to wear: 'It makes
me feel confident. It's like a mask.'

Did the lipstick make her look bold – or just pale and
hungover? At any rate, it made her look less like herself.

She fluffed out her hair, pocketed her keys and let herself
out, and saw that the morning's fog was already beginning to
lift. She didn't want or expect to talk to anybody. But there was
Mrs Jancett, the next-door neighbour, out on her kneeler,
weeding her front garden.

When she saw Callie she straightened up with a small,

weary sigh which left it unclear whether the prospect of a chat was a welcome respite or just another chore. 'Morning, Callie. You're up bright and early.'

Callie didn't feel bright, and it wasn't particularly early. 'Not a very nice morning for doing the gardening,' she said.

Mrs Jancett let out another small sigh. 'Oh, when this bit of fog lifts it'll be lovely,' she said. 'And all the rain we've had means the ground elder comes up nice and easy, and at least it's not cold. Were you off somewhere nice yesterday? I saw you as you were leaving. You looked very glam.'

The small, shrewd glimmering of expectation and curiosity in her eyes told Callie she'd not only seen her getting into a taxi with Reuben the day before but had also noted their return late at night, and might well also have observed that Reuben hadn't immediately crossed the road to go back into his own house.

'It was my friend Sonia's wedding,' Callie said.

'Ah, lovely,' Mrs Jancett said, eyebrows raised. 'I expect you're tired this morning, then. Weddings are often very lively occasions, aren't they?'

Her voice was both speculative and unmistakeably disapproving. Callie said, 'Yes, I guess they often are,' and walked away from her across the road.

The fog had lifted enough for her to be able to see Reuben's bedroom window quite clearly, and to note that the curtains were open but the room was dark. Still, at least there seemed to be a light on downstairs, in the living room, and she could hear the faint sound of piano music. At least she wasn't about to face the further humiliation of knocking only to find that nobody was home, and of having to walk right back across the road under Mrs Jancett's watchful eyes.

She had to pick her way round a couple of windfall apples lying on the path to reach the front door. When she rang the doorbell, the piano music continued to the end of the phrase and then broke off. Presumably it was Reuben's dad playing.

Then the door opened an inch or two, as wide as it could go with the security chain on, and Mr Tallis peered through.

'Oh, hello. You're looking for Reuben, I suppose?'

'I'm sorry to disturb you. Yes, I am. Is he here?'

Maybe, even if he was, he would have asked his dad to pretend that he wasn't. Maybe things were that bad.

'No... No, I'm afraid he isn't,' Reuben's dad said. 'He seems to have gone back to London.'

He paused, observed her, hesitated. When he spoke his voice was light but sympathetic, like a kindly uncle or encouraging grandpa. 'I take it that's a disappointment to you.'

'Well... it's certainly a surprise.'

He sighed, a little louder than Mrs Jancett but in much the same way, and she supposed that he, too, guessed that Reuben had spent the night with her before vanishing into thin air.

'I'm sorry to hear that,' he said, and took the chain off the door and opened it a little wider. 'Would you like to come in? There's tea in the pot. Just made it.'

'Oh, I wouldn't want to intrude.'

'You wouldn't be intruding. Honestly. You'd be doing a lonely old widower a favour. It'd be nice to have the company. Especially now Reuben's decided to disappear again.' He hesitated, and studied her sympathetically. 'I'm sorry. Was that tactless of me?'

'I guess it's the truth,' she said helplessly. 'I'm just sorry if I'm the reason he left.'

'Oh, no, you mustn't blame yourself. He's just like that, I'm afraid,' Mr Tallis said. 'He can be... unpredictable. Volatile. And not always very fair.' He sighed. 'Plus he's had a difficult time lately. Grief can make people behave in all kinds of odd ways. As I'm sure you know, having lost your dad at such a young age. I always thought that must have been very difficult for you.'

'It was,' she said. 'I'm so sorry about your wife, Mr Tallis. I didn't know her well, but she seemed lovely.'

'She was,' Mr Tallis said sadly, and then, 'I really do make a very good cup of tea, you know.'

She found both his melancholy and his kindness irresistible. She could have said no, but it would have been mean, wouldn't it? And anyway, what was the harm? And so, for the first time in all the years she'd lived across the road, she stepped forward over the threshold and right into Reuben's house.

It was all spick and span, which surprised her, under the circumstances. Maybe someone came in to help clean. The kitchen was immaculate bar a few crumbs on the worktop, and some unwashed crockery piled up on the side. The draining board was stacked with clean, empty Tupperware and a lone casserole dish.

'Some very lovely and thoughtful people have been looking after me,' Mr Tallis said, seeing that she was taking it all in. She noted that he'd said 'people', not 'women', but assumed they had been women.

She remembered the way Mum had spoken about Mr Tallis sometimes, about his popularity at the tennis club and how all the ladies fell over themselves to be the ones to fetch him refreshments. Mum had always mentioned him indulgently, with a kind of protective pride. It was as if she thought his powers of attraction were the mark of a kind of effortless, charming superiority, and it would be unreasonable to blame him for the effect of it. It went without saying that Mum would have had a different attitude entirely to a woman who attracted similar attention from all the men.

Mr Tallis was, now that she had the opportunity to look at him a little more closely, handsome – handsome in the self-conscious way of people who had been vain and gorgeous when they were young. His hair was dark gold streaked with silver and he wore it tousled and long enough to fall into his eyes, which she suspected was a deliberate choice, a kind of vanity, rather than neglect. But it was thinning at the temples and his skin was lined, and his body had the thin, sinewy look of the fit older man who has kept in shape but has lost the softness and suppleness of youth.

She felt bad for noticing these things. Then he ran his hand through his hair and she realised that he was aware of her studying him and didn't mind. Perhaps he thought that she had been looking for a resemblance to Reuben. There was certainly something of Reuben about his hands, which were soft and sensitive-looking, but otherwise Reuben looked much more like his mother, who had also been dark-haired and unshowy and thoughtful. Mr Tallis seemed like the opposite – someone who likes to perform.

He fussed around with the teapot and milk and sugar and then passed her a small mug of unappetising greyish liquid. It definitely didn't look as fresh as he'd said. Still, at least he was willing to spend half an hour in her company. Reuben hadn't been able to get away fast enough.

'I'm sorry, that's probably not very nice, is it?' he said after she'd made a show of sipping the tea.

'No, it's fine,' she insisted, but blushed a little.

'You're really very sweet, aren't you?' he said, and shook his head. 'My son's a fool. He has always been his own worst enemy. Anyway, I'm afraid I don't think he's going to be back any time soon. He took his stuff with him. Not that he had much. He was never planning to stay for long.'

'Oh.'

He looked at her with a knowing sympathy that didn't make her feel much better – as if it was only to be expected that Reuben would behave this way. As if Mr Tallis had done all this before, with other girls who'd turned up looking pitiful on his doorstep after Reuben walked out on them.

Callie remembered Reuben at Sonia's engagement party,

telling her that he'd heard Donna had stayed away because he was going to be there. He must have really hurt her for her to be so keen to avoid him, even though they'd broken up years before. Had Donna been reduced to this too, at the end – pathetically, helplessly chasing round after Reuben and trying to make sense of the way he'd behaved, before she came to her senses and, presumably, decided she never wanted to see him again? And how could someone be so gentle and tender one minute and just disappear the next?

Mr Tallis said, 'You have his number, right? And his email?'

She nodded.

'What about his London address?' She shook her head. 'Would you like it?'

What did he think she was going to do – turn into Reuben's stalker? Stand outside keeping vigil like a ghost? But then he smiled at her and said, 'You could send him a postcard. Ideally from somewhere extremely nice. *"Don't you wish you were here?"*' and she smiled and shrugged and said, 'Guess I might as well. If you don't mind.'

'Of course.' He went to a shelf above one of the worktops and took down a Post-it with an address written on it in Reuben's handwriting, copied it out onto a jotter, tore off the strip of paper and passed it to her. She pocketed it, feeling as if she'd just been given a receipt – as if her dealings with Reuben had now reached some kind of perfunctory conclusion, at least as far as Mr Tallis was concerned.

He said, 'Why don't you come on through to the living room and finish that cup of tea in a bit of comfort?'

'OK, sure. Thank you.' She picked up her tea and followed him.

Just the day before she would have felt this was an immense privilege – to see right inside Reuben's house, to move through his family home – and she would have taken in every detail, looking for evidence of who he was and what he was really like and why. But as it was, it felt oddly claustrophobic.

Anyway, there was nothing particularly revealing about the room. It was perfectly normal, tidy and comfortable, done up in tasteful pastels, with well-stuffed furniture and a beautiful upright Steinway piano in one corner.

'That's for me. It's not the one I use for teaching,' Mr Tallis said. 'There's an extension at the back that I use for private lessons. I've always tried to keep my own music and my teaching separate.'

She thought how sad it must be, to play piano alone in an empty house after years of having his wife around to hear him. And then, disconcertingly, he headed for the piano and settled down in front of it.

He played a chromatic scale, then turned to her and said, 'Why don't you sit down in the armchair there? You can put your tea on the side table. It would be nice to have an audience for once.'

She sat as he'd suggested, and he played, and she left her tea untouched, and the window onto the road brightened as the fog lifted and the sunlight made it through.

When had she last sat and listened to someone playing the piano? She couldn't remember. The music Mr Tallis was playing was much more complicated than anything she'd ever learned. It rose and fell and twisted and made her think about love, how it changed but stayed with you, like a melody you forgot most days but recognised when you heard a burst of it somewhere, or when you were alone and it came back to you.

She was close enough to be able to follow the sheet music, and got up automatically to turn the page when it was necessary. Then the piece came to an end and she wasn't quite sure what was expected of her, but brought her hands together to clap.

'Thank you,' Mr Tallis said, with a quick sideways glance at her. Then he rummaged through the books and sheets of music propped up on the piano's music stand and brought something else to the front. His left hand picked out a phrase, a sequence of notes that rose like a question, and his right answered it.

Something stirred inside her, because she recognised this too, in a different, more concrete way. She knew it. She'd played it.

He stopped and looked at her. 'Carry on,' she said.

'I wondered if you might know it,' he said, and ran through the phrases again – the left hand first, and then the right. 'It's a duet. Not too challenging. Suitable for around grade four or five.'

'Oh, I don't play.'

'Well, you used to, didn't you?'

'A long time ago.'

'I knew it! I knew it from the way you were listening.' He picked out the first phrase again, then inclined his head to indicate the piano stool next to him. 'I promise you, you never lose it. It's all still there. And once you start, it'll come back. It's like riding a bike.'

'I haven't done that for years either,' she said, but in spite of her reluctance she found herself getting up and walking across to take the seat next to him.

'I'm very rusty,' she said.

'Well, all you need is a little practice,' he said briskly.

He played the left-hand phrase. She reciprocated with the right. And then he played on, and she did too, and she realised he was right. It was still there. She could still do it. And the pleasure of it came back to her in a sweet rush, and suddenly she had no idea why she'd ever stopped and given up.

This was what she was good at. This was what she'd missed. What had she been so afraid of? Of what it might bring back – the ghost of her dad, listening, ready to applaud? Or had she been afraid because she knew it would not, could not, bring him back?

She stopped with a sudden, discordant clash.

Her fingers, which had been picking out the notes almost unconsciously, seemed to have rebelled. Her whole body seemed to be in the grip of a violent reaction that was completely out of her control. Her hands didn't look like her own. There was a cold sweat on her forehead, and a ringing in her ears, and everything seemed to be on the verge of moving out of focus completely, as if someone was turning a dial and might, at any moment, push it to max and force her to lose consciousness.

Mr Tallis had stopped playing. He began to speak to her, as slowly and reassuringly as you might to an upset horse or child.

'Take it easy, that's the ticket. Remember to breathe. That's the thing. You'll be fine. It'll pass. Just put your head down. Right down between your knees. Go on, trust me. Helps with the blood flow.'

His hand was on the back of her neck, pushing her head down, and then her face was resting on her knees and she was doubled over, which was entirely undignified but did seem to be helping. Or at least, it wasn't making things any worse.

He moved her hair away from the back of her neck and she realised it was damp with sweat.

'That's better, isn't it?' he said.

His hand moved onto her upper back and started circling. 'You poor thing. You've overheated. I really thought I was going to lose you for a minute there. I mean, I thought you were about to faint.'

'So did I,' she managed to say.

'Do you think you can sit up?' He tugged at her cardigan. 'It might be a good idea to take this off, if you can bear to.'

She sat up, and he pulled at one sleeve and then the other, and said, 'There, that should help. Do you think you can make it over to the sofa and lie down there? You're probably feeling a little disoriented. I'll fetch you a glass of water.'

She nodded, and he got up and moved away and she somehow made it to the sofa and lay on it and closed her eyes. It was a leather sofa, and she thought inconsequentially that she'd never lived in a house with a leather sofa – Mum didn't like them, and always said she thought they'd stick to you in the heat.

Then she heard Mr Tallis's footsteps returning and the gentle chink of a glass of water being placed on the side table, and the creak of the sofa underneath him as he sat down next to her.

He said, 'Do you think you could sit up and have some water now?'

She would have just liked to lie there – she could have quite easily drifted off to sleep – but felt she couldn't, really. It would be bad manners, and he was being so nice, and so gentle with her. And she'd only come over here because of Reuben, and the way he'd walked out on her...

'Nice and easy, that's the way,' he said, and she sat up and he passed her the glass of water and she obediently sipped it, and then he took it from her again and put it down.

'That's the way,' he repeated, and reached out to brush a drop of water from her lower lip. His thumb came away reddened with a small smear of her lipstick, and he rubbed it against his fingertips and looked at her.

She stared back at him. She had gone very still. It was beginning to dawn on her that something was wrong. That this might have been a mistake. A bad one. Wrong place, wrong time, wrong person to be alone with.

'You had me worried there,' he said. 'You look much, much better now.'

Something unseen in the room seemed to come sharply into

focus. His eyes were fixed on her and his gaze was hard and there was no doubt in it at all.

'You're beautiful,' he said. 'A beautiful young woman who deserves to be loved.'

And then he kissed her.

She would think about this afterwards, from time to time: at night when she couldn't sleep, in queues at supermarket checkout tills, and whenever the subject of victims and accusers came up. She would remember the sensation of his mouth on hers, and his hands wandering over her clothing, making out the shape of her body, moving to the buttons of her shirt, not expecting to be stopped. She would remember that she had not hit him, and she had not screamed at him. She had barely even recoiled from him. Instead she had frozen. And try as she might, when she put herself back into the shock of the moment, she could not imagine ever having been able to respond in any other way.

After all, this was Reuben's dad, the neighbour from across the road who'd so kindly invited her in for a cup of tea, and she'd had no idea that this was something he might do.

She hadn't seen it coming. And she would reproach herself for that later – not only for having frozen, which meant she had failed to defend herself, but for having failed to avoid the situation to begin with.

But the only way she could have foreseen it would have been if she'd known herself to be living in a world in which any woman alone in a room with any man had to be prepared to face a threat. And at the time, before that day, she had not yet been living in that world.

What would also puzzle her later was why he'd done it. Had he genuinely thought that she would respond, and that she would want him in that way? If so – why? How could he have thought that of her? Had he misread the signs – had she been signalling a willingness that she was quite unaware of? Or had it been a rogue impulse that he had given into – a kind of brain-storm, a moment of madness, something to do with having just lost his wife? You could not really be angry with someone for that. Anybody could fall victim to a moment of madness in a state of grief – couldn't they?

The worst of it was, she would feel sorry for him, and it would be easier to feel sorry for him than it was to feel sorry for herself.

And the thoughts would go round and round until she dismissed them, because she would be a mother-in-waiting or a mother by then, and her body would have work to do, and she would have devoted herself fully to the purpose in life that motherhood gave her. And remembering her purpose would make Mr Tallis and his mouth and hands seem less important, a past humiliation that it was no longer necessary or practical to think about.

But at the time he paused to say in her ear 'I know exactly what you need,' and his hand moved to her belt buckle at the precise moment that she heard Reuben's key turn in the lock of the front door.

TWENTY-FOUR

Mr Tallis moved away from her and got to his feet, tucking his shirt into his jeans. She sat up as Reuben came into the room with the strap of his bag slung across his body and his jacket still on underneath it. He was holding a bunch of red flowers and he stood there and stared at the pair of them.

Her lipstick was on Mr Tallis's mouth and she was buttoning her shirt. It was obvious what had happened. And at the same time it was not obvious at all.

She saw the shock on Reuben's face turn very quickly to fury and revulsion, and she could not defend herself against that either. The words to explain what had happened to her just weren't there and all she felt was shame and guilt and a vulnerability so intense that it was a kind of pain in itself.

Her instinctive response was not to explain herself or to accuse Mr Tallis, but to behave the way she might have done if the situation was perfectly normal – as if she'd just popped over to say hello, and found that Reuben had gone out, and nothing more intimate had happened than that.

It was as if the pretence of normality could change reality into something familiar that she would know how to deal with.

And at the same time her body had gone rigid and all she wanted was to play this down, to stop it turning into something worse, and to get away so she could be alone and safe.

'I was looking for you,' she said stupidly.

He said, 'Well, it looks like you found someone else.'

Mr Tallis said, 'Really, there's no need to get this out of proportion, Reuben. I mean, next to nothing happened, it was just one of those things, just a little kiss—'

'Save it for someone who'll believe it,' Reuben said. 'I'll never believe a word you say again.'

He looked down at Callie. 'I came back for you,' he said. 'I got cold feet and I was going to go back to London and then I saw these outside a shop and got them for you and came back. When I realised you were out I thought you might have called round for me. But anyway, it seems like it wasn't a totally wasted journey. If I hadn't come back for you, I'd have felt really bad about leaving. So thank you for saving me the effort of feeling guilty. Looks like the instinct to leave was the right one, doesn't it?'

He dropped the flowers on the carpet and turned and walked out. A minute later she heard the door slam.

Mr Tallis pressed his knuckles to his red-smudged mouth as if deep in thought, then took his hand away and examined it as if baffled by how the lipstick could possibly have got there. He took a handkerchief out of his pocket and dabbed at his mouth and wiped his hand, then carefully folded it so the stained part was on the inside and put it back in his pocket.

'I must say, I didn't know the two of you were an item,' he observed. 'I take it this is a new thing, is it? You slept with him last night?'

And again she didn't know what to say. He had spoken in the tone of voice used by a doctor who wants to know how much a patient smokes and drinks, or by a teacher trying to work out where to apportion blame. He didn't even seem flustered. He was quite calm, as if what had just happened, and what he had just done, was nothing untoward. As if that tidy, rather staid living room, with its sofa and sideboard and piano and old TV, had seen it all a thousand times before.

He seemed to take her silence as an admission. 'It wouldn't have come to anything,' he said. 'Reuben doesn't have the best track record when it comes to relationships.' Then he went over to the sideboard and pulled down a flap to reveal a selection of bottles of spirits. His hands weren't trembling: she realised hers were. 'I know it's still early, but if there was ever a morning for the hair of the dog, this is it,' he said, glancing back at her. 'Can I offer you a small whisky? Or brandy, perhaps?'

'I don't want anything,' she managed to say. 'I think I'm going to go.'

Somehow, she was on her feet. At least Reuben had broken the spell – she could move. That meant she could get away.

He said, 'Really – so soon? Please don't, Callie. Why don't you stay here with me?'

She shook her head. She couldn't look at him – she kept her eyes down, on the carpet. He didn't move to try to stop her. She stepped round the flowers on the carpet – red roses, half a dozen – and left the house and closed the door behind her and went back across the road.

The fog had disappeared and it had turned into a bright, beautiful day. Mrs Jancett was still on her knees in her front garden, weeding. Had she really been there all this time? It felt as if hours had passed, but perhaps it had not been that long.

As Callie approached Mrs Jancett straightened up and gave her a hard look, a look full of suspicion. Callie forced herself to smile at her as if nothing was wrong. Mrs Jancett did not smile back.

Callie rummaged in her pocket for her key, couldn't find it, panicked, and then there it was, in her hand, and even though she was shaking now she managed to get the door open and go inside.

The first thing she did was to find the matches Mum kept in a drawer and burn up the slip of paper with Reuben's address. She watched it curl and let the ashes drop into the sink and washed them away. Then she went upstairs to her room and found the note Reuben had left her and the printout of the email he'd sent her, and burned them over the sink and washed them away, too.

Back in her room, she drew the curtains and took off all her clothes – she didn't want to wear anything that man had touched. She'd left her cardigan behind. Well, that didn't matter. She'd left her flowers, too. And her lipstick on his handkerchief. He would probably throw all these things away. Maybe he, too, would want to forget she had ever been there.

Or maybe he would keep them, but that didn't matter either.

She put on her pyjamas and lay down in her bed and pulled the duvet over her head.

This will pass, she told herself. *I'll live.*

It was the kind of thing that happened all the time. Nothing, really. It could have been so much worse. The best thing by far would be to let it go.

But the memory of the shock of unwanted physical contact – the point at which Reuben's dad had pressed himself on her – made her feel soft and weak, and she knew that what she was trying to tell herself, that it was unimportant and trivial, was a lie.

Her body knew this. Her body remembered: she felt what had happened in her body still, as if it had left traces, like the touch of a malignant ghost. But her mind and her will recoiled from what her body knew, and insisted on telling a different story: *Don't dwell on it. Forget it. Don't make a fuss. If you do, all that will happen is that everything will get a great deal worse.*

People won't believe you. And Reuben will never forgive you, either way.

Reuben. She'd lost Reuben. Whatever happened.

If she tried to explain things to him... He'd ask questions. He'd want her to recount exactly what had happened. He'd need to hear it, one thing after another, to get it clear. To get the facts straight, so that he could be sure she was telling the truth. So that he could believe her.

She would have to tell him: the duet, the near-faint, the invitation to lie on the sofa. Each touch, the precise nature of it. The things his father had said. She would have to live through it again in the telling. That would almost be worse than knowing what he believed about her now: that after they'd slept together and he'd left her, she'd gone across the road and, voluntarily, straight into his dad's arms.

And whether he believed her a willing partner or not, he would never want to touch her again.

How could he? She was tainted. If he believed her to be innocent, and if he cared for her, how would he be able to forgive his father? She would come between them. Their relationship was bad enough as it was: this would finish it off. Was what Mr Tallis had done really so bad, that he deserved that? Was she worth Reuben hating his father for?

What chance had she ever had with Reuben anyway? There had been so much longing and yearning, but that had all been in her head, the stuff of fairy tales. In reality, they had been lovers once. There would never be another time. And you couldn't really grieve for something that only happened once ...

She would never be able to explain. And even if she did, he still wouldn't want her.

She thought of how everything had looked when they had left Sonia's wedding just the night before. The dark town all quiet and empty and glistening after the rain, the ink-black puddles gleaming with reflected light. That, and the evening when she had finally sat next to him on the bus on the way home, and the night when they had talked under the stars, would have to be enough. She'd had everything she could ever have with him. There would be nothing more.

She didn't weep. Some part of her was not surprised. She told herself she shouldn't be lying here like this, that she ought to get up and go out and find a pharmacy and take the morning-after pill. But her energy and willpower seemed to have disappeared, as if Mr Tallis had stolen it. All she wanted was to be unconscious. And then, perhaps, when she woke up, she would feel better.

She closed her eyes and curled up tight and let her mind empty out as if her thoughts were fog dissolving in sunlight, and finally she slept.

TWENTY-FIVE

By early November one of the employment agencies she'd signed up with had found her a temporary placement as an executive assistant in the IT department at the hospital in Oxford. Leaving the house early in the morning when there was frost on the ground, catching the bus, sitting at her computer doing various tasks that mainly seemed to revolve around booking, arranging and recording other people's meetings, eating her lone sandwich at lunchtime, then catching the bus home when it was already dark – all of this helped to make her feel as if she had become someone else.

She had never realised that the routines of office life, the gloom of Monday morning and the cheerful freedom of Friday afternoon, could actually be comforting.

At night she slept deeply, barely dreaming: her body seemed to want to hibernate. At work she thought about little other than the tasks she had to do, and in the evenings she was too tired to think. Reuben crossed her mind but as a closed chapter. She felt sorry for him, knowing that he would never know that she had wanted to protect him. But she could not dwell on it, any more than she could bring herself to imagine what he must think of her. Her brain slid away from the whole subject as if there was nothing there but impenetrable darkness and emptiness.

When Mum and Ron got back from their trip to London, she'd been so lethargic and sluggish Mum had been convinced she was sickening for something. But then some kind of ruthless self-protective instinct had kicked in that wasn't under her conscious control, and forced her to concentrate on the prosaic business of her own day-to-day survival.

Thankfully, she rarely saw Mr Tallis. He seemed to stay inside a lot, and to venture out only in his car. When she glimpsed him, even from a distance, her reaction was immediate and physical. She would experience it again, the sense of exposure and vulnerability which was so close to shame and grief. Her heart would pound, and she would tell herself that she was being ridiculous and there was nothing to be afraid of. And then he would go and it would pass. She was able to avoid talking to him completely, and nobody else ever noticed her response to him.

It was slightly more awkward steering clear of Mrs Jancett. She was afraid that the old lady might say something to Mum or, even worse, Ron, about her having had Reuben over while they were away. But Mum said nothing that suggested this was the case, and by and by she stopped worrying about it. Perhaps she had just imagined Mrs Jancett looking at her askance. She could be doing her an injustice – Mrs Jancett might not be the sort to go telling tales in that way. Or maybe she hadn't even noticed Reuben going into the house with her that night.

Mum had been very interested in finding out more about Sonia's wedding, but mainly she wanted to see the photos and cast an eye over everyone's outfits. Callie hadn't actually lied about what had happened – Mum just hadn't asked. Besides, she and Ron were busy with other plans to go away.

Which was just as well, because surely Mum would have

been furious if she knew Reuben had stayed the night. Ron, too. They'd always made it clear that any boyfriend she brought back should sleep separately, so as not to set a corrupting example for Emily, and even though Emily had now gone off to university, she was pretty sure the rule would still stand. She'd never clashed with them about it before, because she'd never wanted to bring anyone home.

If Mum got even a sniff of something having happened between her and Mr Tallis... If Ron found out...

That was something Callie was not sure she would be able to bear. She was afraid her mum would take Mr Tallis's side, and she was not ready for that and never would be.

She was on the bus to work, rattling along the road that led into Oxford from the village, when two words presented themselves to her like a message from the future: *You're pregnant.*

In theory, it was possible. Unlikely, but possible. She was definitely late... How late? She'd been so preoccupied with work, she hadn't thought about it.

Or hadn't been ready to think about it.

Another piece of information presented itself to her, crystal clear and undeniable: she hadn't had her period since before Sonia's wedding. And she had never got round to taking the morning-after pill.

She probably should have felt anxious, but instead she felt weirdly calm. She either was pregnant or she wasn't. If she was, she would have a choice, and in the end, the choice would be hers and hers alone.

If there was a baby on the way, no one could compel her to have it, and no one could compel her not to. Her body belonged to her and no one else, and nobody could tell her what to do. Well, they might try. But she would not have to pay them any attention.

She didn't have a man, she didn't have a home of her own, she had very little money put by and she barely had a job. But still, if she decided to – if it had happened, if she had the decision to make – she could have a baby.

And then she would belong to someone. And someone would belong to her. She would find a way to make a life for the two of them, and nobody would be able to part them.

She shoved the possibility right down to the bottom of her conscious mind, and concentrated on looking out at the view of the outskirts of Oxford.

Beyond the rooftops there was woodland, and beyond the bare trees she could see distant green hills on the horizon. A pale, rain-washed grey sky stretched over everything. She tried to breathe in the sense of space and her place in all of it, and two more words presented themselves to her: *keep faith*.

At the end of her two-week placement at the hospital she was told there was a permanent job available doing exactly the same kind of work, and was asked if she'd like to apply for it. She did, and was offered the job, and took it. She didn't tell Mum and Ron. Not yet. She would, all in good time. This was not a matter of deceit, or if it was, she told herself it was necessary.

She was merely doing what had to be done. She did not feel entirely in control of her own actions, but it was a kind of lack of control that she relished, as if an older, stronger, wiser version of herself had come back from the future to whisper little suggestions into her ear, and all she had to do in order to become that older self was to follow them.

And then she stopped off in the village store on the way home one evening to pick up some milk and bread, and saw a card on display that said, *Flat to rent. One double bedroom. North Kettlebridge. Garden. No pets. Young professional female only. Non-smoker. Bills not included.*

It was cheap. The cheapest such place she'd seen. Almost

too good to be true, though even so, the monthly rent was not far off half her new monthly take-home salary.

She found herself rummaging in her bag for a notebook and pencil. She wrote down the phone number, then went out and found a seat on the bench in the churchyard and called it.

Next thing she knew, she was ringing home – nobody picked up – and leaving a message to say she was going to be late. Then she was up on her feet and running because she'd just seen the bus to Kettlebridge heading towards the stop near the village store, and if she missed it, she'd have a twenty-minute wait for the next one.

The flat to rent turned out to be the ground floor of a yellow-brick two-storey building with a square of grass bordered by cottage flowers in front. The address was Goosegreen Close and Callie liked the idea that maybe, once upon a time, it really had been a green with geese on it. OK, so she was just looking for reasons to like the place now, but at least it wasn't number thirteen.

She was due to meet the owner, who had given her name as Mrs Sheila Castle. It seemed that Mrs Castle was not keen on cutting anyone else in on a deal she thought she could handle herself, as she had chosen to let the place herself directly, rather than going through a letting agent. Perhaps she didn't want to pay the fees they would charge her. Or maybe there was a worse reason: maybe the place wouldn't pass the checks they would undertake. Anyway, Callie hoped that Mrs Castle's desire to manage things herself would play out to her advantage.

When she rang the doorbell Mrs Castle took a little while to answer and then peered at her suspiciously, as if Callie might be up to no good.

'I've got half an hour,' she said. 'So we'd best make this quick.'

'OK. Sure. I won't keep you,' Callie said.

She followed Mrs Castle into a dingy entrance hall. But who cared if it was dingy! This could be her own place with her own front door, and nobody would be able to enter who she didn't want to let in.

There was a living room to the right with the kitchen beyond it, and a bedroom to the left. The bathroom was at the end of the hall. Someone older must have lived here, she thought. Someone who didn't have much money to spend on the place, but liked to keep the garden nice and the house clean.

Everything was old and the predominant colour was beige. There was a gas fire in the living room, surrounded by biscuit-coloured tiles, and the carpet was brown with red and blue swirls in it, and the wallpaper was beige and white stripes. The bedroom carpet was a faded pink and its wallpaper was patterned with posies of flowers. The bedroom curtains were pink to match the carpet, in a material that might have been meant to pass for velvet but more closely resembled towelling. The bathroom suite was actual avocado and looked as if it hadn't changed since the 1970s.

Everything in the kitchen looked similarly ancient, but there was a cooker, a fridge, a washing machine and a little table with chairs for two, and the window looked out onto a strip of overgrown grass with a tree at the end of it. A cat, stalking through the grass, stopped and looked at her, then turned and elegantly retreated, leaped up onto the neighbour's fence and disappeared.

'The garden's pretty,' Callie offered.

Mrs Castle sniffed as if to beg to differ. 'My mother used to grow vegetables in it. It's good soil here. They say there used to be a chimney-sweep who lived further up, and he used to give everyone the ashes, and that's why the earth's so good. Anyway, there's not a lawnmower. You'd have to get your own.'

'I see,' Callie said. 'Do you mind if I...?' She gestured towards one of the cupboards.

Mrs Castle sniffed again and checked her watch. 'No, go ahead, have a look.'

Callie's heart was singing *I want it* so loudly, Mrs Castle was surely bound to hear it. She put down her shopping and made a show of peering in the cupboards and the fridge, and asked some questions about council tax and the neighbours. A retired couple lived upstairs, she was told. They wouldn't bother her. They had their own entrance, to the side, and their own strip of back garden, running parallel to hers, but she'd have to take care of the front.

Finally, she asked when the flat was available.

'Well, I think that's negotiable,' Mrs Castle said. 'There's no one here at the moment, obviously. I've been let down, that's the trouble.' She sniffed again. 'It's not been easy, I can tell you.'

Callie sympathised, and Mrs Castle seemed to forget she was meant to be heading off shortly and started talking about her health problems. Forty-five minutes later Callie gathered up her shopping and walked out, having managed to haggle the rent down, and with a promise to drop round a deposit cheque and sign a contract the following day.

As Mrs Castle zipped past her in her little Ford Fiesta she actually waved and smiled at her, and Callie waved back. She couldn't have been any happier or more relieved if she'd already had the keys in her pocket.

There you are, you see? she thought as she made her way to the bus stop. *It's all going to work out all right.* And suddenly she had a very strong, very clear sense that there was someone else with her, and it wasn't just herself she was trying to reassure.

TWENTY-SIX

She didn't have morning sickness. The closest she came was in the hospital cafeteria, when someone near her was eating cabbage and she had to get up and change tables. What she did have was waves of intense hunger that could only be satisfied by eating very particular things – custard tarts, or yoghurt smoothies. Also, she could sleep for hours.

Those weren't the only changes. Her hair was slightly thicker and bouncier, the way it was when it had just rained, and the smell of her skin had a very faint, almost ghostly milkiness. Her body felt inconspicuously but definitively different: softer and stronger at the same time, subtly altered in every way from her head to her toes.

She felt different. She wept easily at films or books – she'd suddenly become more sentimental – but she was also calm and placid, as if an important question had been settled and her old restlessness and self-doubt had been dissolved.

But she still didn't take a pregnancy test. That really would be definitive, and she wasn't quite ready for that. Not yet.

She didn't think about Reuben, or Mr Tallis. Nor did she give a great deal of thought to the future. Instead she lived quietly and dressed conservatively and made excuses not to go out. She was tired after work. She felt under the weather. She was trying to save money. It was surprisingly easy to get away with. Nobody seemed to suspect anything. Perhaps people tended not to see what they didn't expect to see.

After all, they were all busy with their own lives, and why should they play detective? It was good for her, she thought, to learn how to live with a secret. It was practice. Practice for getting by on her own. And that was what she intended to do, as much as she could. That was the safest way and the best way.

When she told Mum she was moving out Mum looked both slightly affronted and unexpectedly upset, as if Callie's decision was a kind of rejection and her feelings were hurt. But she said only, 'Are you sure? Can you afford it?' and when Callie said yes, she shrugged and pursed her lips and looked away as if this was something she had always known was going to happen sooner or later, but didn't much like now the day had come. 'Well, it's not as if you're not going far,' she said. 'I suppose you'll be wanting some help moving?'

'I could probably get a taxi,' Callie said.

'Oh for heaven's sake, that's ridiculous,' Mum said. 'I'll give you a lift. How well equipped is this place, anyway? Are you going to need kitchen stuff? Have you budgeted for that? I hope you've thought all this through.'

Ron's reaction was, unsurprisingly, one of relative equanimity. He took the news as a prompt for a long, boring story about how he'd left home at sixteen and never looked back, all of which Callie had heard before, then checked where Callie's new place was and what the rent was, sighed and said, 'Well, everybody has to start somewhere.'

A couple of weeks later she moved in. Her mum inspected the place and rather doubtfully pronounced it satisfactory, helped her make her bed and plugged in Callie's new kettle but declined the offer of a cup of tea.

'No, I'll leave you to it. I need to get going,' she said.

'Thank you for helping me,' Callie told her.

'Of course I helped you. I'm your mum,' Mum said, and there was a slight tremble to her voice.

They hugged, standing in Callie's slightly bare new living room. She hadn't brought much – didn't have much to bring: a couple of boxes, a couple of bags, a suitcase. Mum had bought her a ficus plant as a housewarming present, which was standing on the floor by the old gas fireplace. 'They're very hard to kill,' Mum had said, and Callie had felt both fear and a rush of excitement at the thought that before long she'd have something much more demanding than a pot plant to look after.

'Well, take care of yourself,' Mum said, and the ancient central heating rumbled into action as she detached herself and determinedly made her exit.

When she'd gone, Callie allowed herself to sink down into the lone armchair in the living room, just for a minute, and to absorb the experience of being on her own, in her own place. The calm of it. She felt bad about Mum and her departure had been more of a wrench than she had anticipated but at the same time it was a relief. Although she didn't think it had occurred to Mum that she might be pregnant, she wasn't sure how much longer they could have gone on living under the same roof without Mum suspecting something. And it was a piece of news she only wanted to break once she had her own territory to retreat to.

She finally did a pregnancy test the next day, and when it showed up as vehemently, unmissably positive, the outcome was in no way a shock or a surprise.

She was going to get exactly what she wanted. Now *that* was remarkable. What did anything else matter, in comparison to that? Someone to love. Someone to look after. Someone to hold and nurture and keep. What did anything in the whole world matter, in comparison to that?

She didn't tell anybody. After all, there was no rush, was there? She hadn't quite made it through the first trimester yet, and lots of people didn't say anything before then. And she was determined not to turn to Mum. Not with this. Mum was too closely tied to Ron, and the last thing Callie needed was to have to cope with Mum trying to manage Ron's reaction, which she already knew would be a mixture of disapproval and the kind of grim satisfaction that comes with being proved right in your low expectations of someone.

They would see Emily as a success and her as the daughter who could have done better, who'd finally managed to get her degree but had only a modestly-paid job to show for it, and was now on the way to becoming a single mother. And they would disapprove all the more if she didn't tell them who her baby's father was. But how could she tell them when she hadn't actually told him? Really, he should know before anyone. And she still couldn't face him.

But of course Mum was going to want to know. Callie would have to make it clear that it wasn't a subject that was up for discussion. Same with Sonia and Laurel. Hopefully they'd soon get the message, and understand that she had decided to do this on her own, and back off and leave her to it.

The person she was going to become would not need other people. The person she was becoming knew that the only person you could rely on – the only person you could really trust – was yourself.

As for Reuben... She would have to talk to him, sooner or later. But she recoiled from the thought of it. She could only imagine him being angry, or disgusted, or walking away.

Now that she'd moved out, she didn't see all that much of Mum and Ron. They were too busy with weekend minibreaks and golf and tennis lessons and pub quizzes and being committed to village life. Sonia had gone quiet since coming back from honeymoon – wrapped up in newlywed bliss, presumably – and Laurel was always busy anyway, so Callie didn't have much contact with anybody outside work. It was easy to carry on keeping herself to herself. Most of the people she knew from going to school in Kettlebridge had moved away, though occasionally she saw a familiar face, waved, smiled, exchanged a few details about where she was living and working, and moved on.

A week or so later she registered with a doctor's surgery in Kettlebridge and booked herself an appointment. The relative anonymity of the unfamiliar waiting room made her feel safe. She could never have done this at the doctor's surgery in Allingham that Mum and Ron used, and probably Mr Tallis, too. Here, she was that much less likely to bump into someone who recognised her, and might feel entitled to ask what was wrong with her.

She was startled by how disinterested the doctor seemed to be when she said that she was pregnant – but then, of course, people had babies all the time: it was only to her that it was exceptional. She half expected to be pressed on her suitability for parenting – was she ready to cope on her own? Did she know what she was taking on? Had she calculated what her monthly income would be after childcare costs? – but all he did was note a few details, check her blood pressure, ask her about smoking and drinking and send her away again with a few leaflets and a rough idea of when to expect an appointment for her first scan.

It seemed strange to her that she was actually allowed to go ahead with this – that she could take charge of the life of another human being without having to pass some kind of test first. But then it occurred to her that perhaps the test was yet to come, and would go on for years. And that was such a daunting thought that she immediately set it aside. Denial, she was beginning to learn, was a pretty effective coping mechanism – at least for now.

Soon after the visit to the doctor, she found herself getting in touch with Reuben. Again, this did not follow a decision she was conscious of making: again, it felt as if she was doing something her older, braver self had instructed her to do, because she would regret it otherwise.

Her first move was to text him: *Can we talk? There's something I need to tell you. It won't take long.*

She felt rash as she sent it, but also fatalistic. She knew what *she* wanted. And she was steeling herself to be disappointed in him.

It seemed to her that there was only one right answer for any man to give in this situation – *I will support you whatever you choose to do.* But she was not at all sure that she trusted him to give it. Especially not given the way they'd parted. She had a dim, sneaking suspicion that he might try to pressurise her not to go ahead, and to terminate the pregnancy, and she had already mentally rehearsed her response to that, which was to tell him to stay out of it. But what if he reacted in a different way, once he'd had time to process what had happened? What if he wanted to be involved? She found it very hard to believe this would happen, but it was not impossible.

And involvement would give him rights. A small part of her longed for this, but a larger part of her remembered him leaving her, and then coming back to find her with his father, and the way he had looked at her, and that made her dread the prospect of him staking any kind of claim to her body and her child and her future. Another, coolly objective part of her questioned whether he was someone it was safe to rely on anyway. Whatever else had happened later that morning, however many excuses she made for him, it had started with him getting cold feet and walking out on her while she was still asleep.

She could still look back fondly to the Reuben she had once daydreamed about, who'd sat on the top deck of the bus with her. But the prospect of contact with him now filled her with the same awful, visceral sense of exposure and vulnerability that she had felt after his father touched her, and she could only keep these feelings at bay by thinking of the baby she was carrying as hers and hers alone.

He didn't reply to her text. Then she emailed him, and received a brief answer a day later: *If you could give me some indication of what this is about, that would be helpful.*

He had not signed it off with love, or with a kiss, or with best wishes, or with anything at all – not even his name.

In another rush of boldness, she wrote back to him: *I just wanted to let you know I'm expecting a baby, due next summer. I thought you should hear it from me.*

Then, two days silence. She imagined him writing emails and deleting them: she imagined him wrestling with his conscience, wondering about the right thing to say and do, or maybe just feeling upset and angry and out of control.

She found it almost – almost – possible to feel sorry for him.

Finally, a reply. *I'm in Australia at the moment. Can I call you on Saturday morning, ten o'clock your time?*

She agreed, and gave him her new landline number to call her on. She told herself nothing he said could make any real difference to her. Especially not given that he was on the other side of the world. He had moved just about as far away from her as it was possible to get.

TWENTY-SEVEN

'Callie?'

'Hi, Reuben. Thanks for calling.'

She was in her scantily-furnished living room, perched on the new armchair she'd bought from a charity shop in town, surrounded by the old striped wallpaper that had been chosen by Mrs Castle's dead mother, with the decades-old brown swirly carpet at her feet. It was a dim and quiet winter morning: she'd heard her upstairs neighbours moving around and listening to their radio, but outside it was quiet. None of the kids had come out to play football, and she suspected that, this close to Christmas, at least some of the adults were probably hungover.

Reuben's voice was startlingly crisp and clear, and her immediate reaction to it surprised her. *She was pleased to hear from him.* His voice had a magical effect on her, in spite of everything: she felt soothed, the same way she did when she lay in her avocado-coloured bath and contemplated her belly and allowed herself the quiet satisfaction of knowing she now had someone to love.

Then they both spoke at the same time.

'What are you doing in Australia?'

'About this baby—'

Both of them stopped. Then he took the lead: 'I got a job here. In Sydney. I'm working on a magazine. I have a visa for a couple of years, and there might be potential to stay on after that.'

'I see. So you're not planning to come back.'

'No. I didn't think there was anything much to come back for.'

Silence. She let the hurt and the coldness in his voice sink in. Then he said, 'So you're having a baby. Are you saying it's mine? Or is it my father's? Or someone else's?'

Her heart started to thud. 'I'm not sure I like your tone. I'm not asking for anything from you. I'm just ringing to tell you so that you're aware, that's all—'

'So you *are* saying it's mine. Does that mean you weren't sleeping with my father around the time we had our one-night stand? Because I have to say, Callie, the two of you looked pretty intimate when I walked in on you.'

'That's a disgusting thing to say.'

'Is it? I have to believe the evidence of my own eyes. Or are you telling me that you suddenly got together within five minutes of showing up on his doorstep? Don't get me wrong, I know he has a way with women. Obviously I would rather not know that, being his son, but it's been rather hard to miss. Look, I'm not judging you for having a relationship with him—'

'I don't *have* a relationship with him.'

'Have you had this conversation with him?'

'I don't need to have any conversation with him.'

Reuben sighed. 'This is going round in circles. I know what I saw. I just wish you could have told me before you took me to your bed. If I'd known, I would have wished you a polite good-night and gone my own way.'

Another silence. She thought she might be sick. She

gripped the phone tightly and forced herself to carry on sitting there, to hear him out. Let him do his worst. After this she would never have to hear from him again. And she would never want to, either.

'I know this is probably a stretch for you, but try putting yourself in my shoes,' Reuben said. 'Unless you know something about him that I don't know, or unless you're telling me that what I saw wasn't what it looked like, I cannot see how you can be so sure that this baby is mine and not his. I know him being older makes it a bit less likely, but it's not impossible. It happens. And as far as I know, he never had a vasectomy—'

'Reuben, for God's sake! Stop it. I don't want to hear about this.'

'Are you telling me it's not relevant? I can see that it might not be something you took the time to find out.'

He sounded so scornful she couldn't bring herself to reply. She wanted to be angry – with Reuben, and with his father too. But instead she just felt disgusted, and sad and cold and ashamed.

'Believe me, I didn't want to know that about him either,' Reuben said. 'I overheard my mum talking about it on the phone to someone. She thought he saw it as emasculating. Anyway, it shouldn't be any of my business. But you've made it my business, Callie. If there's any prospect of confusion over the paternity of this child, we need to be clear about it right from the start. I don't know how it works with genetic testing, whether it can distinguish between family members to tell who is the father, but I guess, once he's aware of the situation, we need to find out...'

'Shut up! Stop it! How can you speak to me like that? This is a baby we're talking about, my baby...'

'But you're telling me it's mine. Or are you? You're being kind of evasive. Callie, you cannot fob this baby off on me just because it's more convenient.'

'More convenient? Why on earth would it be more convenient? You're not even in the same country—'

'OK, I'm sorry, I'm just trying to digest this. To me it seems like an absolute disaster, and I don't even know if you've really thought it all through. And I can't get over what you did to me, Callie, and I never will. You're still not being honest with me, even now. You can hardly bring yourself to admit to it, can you? How long had it been going on for? Were you seeing him when my mother was still alive?'

'Why would you think that?'

'Because it happened before! You remember Donna, don't you? I broke up with her when I found out she was sleeping with him. It had been going on for months. She thought she was in love with him. I told him I wouldn't say anything to Mum as long as he finished it, and he broke it off with her. Mum never knew. Was that where you came in, Callie? Did you step in where Donna left off?'

All her fear and rage and helplessness rose up in her at once, with the violence of a suppressed force rising to the surface. But to her astonishment she didn't scream or cry. She found herself capable of speaking sternly and coldly, and saying what she needed to say to keep him away forever.

'I don't owe you any answers or explanations, Reuben. I don't owe you anything. This baby is nothing to do with you. Or your father. I'm sorry to hear about what happened with Donna. But that's nothing to do with me, either.'

A bleak, heart-sickening pause. He said falteringly, 'But if it *is* his, it could be my half-brother or half-sister.'

She put her hand on her belly to steady herself. 'Why did you leave me, Reuben? That morning. Why did you sneak off the way you did?'

He sighed. 'I was scared. And I wasn't wrong, was I? It felt much too close to home.'

'We never really knew each other at all, did we?'

He didn't answer. She drew a deep breath. 'The thing is, Reuben, there's several men out there who could have been this child's father, and none who would want to be.'

It was a necessary lie. A good lie. A way for her to stay safe, body and mind, and keep her baby safe too.

Another deep breath. Her heart was fluttering the way they said a baby did when you first felt it quicken.

'I'm going to do this on my own. There will be no paternity test and I'm not planning to make any demands on anyone. Least of all you.'

'You can't do that. You can't leave it like this—'

'Oh yes I can. How are you going to stop me?'

'What are you going to tell her? Or him? When the kid is old enough to ask?'

She hesitated. What was she going to say? She could not lie to the child. *I knew your dad just for a little while, but then he went away and I knew I could love you enough to make up for him not being there?*

'I'll figure that out when the time comes, and anyway, it's none of your business.'

'I just don't think you're being realistic about this. How are you going to cope?'

'Oh, spare me. Don't pretend to be worried about my welfare. I'm not going to contact you again, Reuben. I suggest you don't get in touch with me either.'

'But you haven't even got a job. Or a place to live. Callie, I really don't think you should be having this baby.'

'Screw you, Reuben,' she said, and hung up on him.

TWENTY-EIGHT

Laurel had organised a night out for the three of them at the pizza place in town. *If we don't,* she had written in her email, *it'll be New Year before we see each other.* The Christmas lights were illuminated in the street outside and there was tinsel around the framed pictures of Italian landscapes on the walls of the restaurant. Callie had agreed to come because she couldn't think of a good reason not to. She was hoping to get through the meal without giving anything away.

As they were looking over their menus Laurel suggested getting a bottle of wine, and Callie's heart sank. Surely the minute she said she wasn't drinking they would guess something was up, and she'd have to explain. And then they might have questions that she didn't feel ready to answer.

But then Sonia said she was going to be driving to her parents' house after the meal, so had better stick to lemonade. Callie said she was feeling a bit off colour and would go for lemonade too, and nobody looked at her sharply. Neither of them thought anything of it. There was a lot of sickness about, and no one would expect her to be about to announce that she was pregnant.

But with Sonia it was different. Sonia was recently married, and had made no secret of being broody. Callie took in the slight extra fullness of her face, and her faint, almost-bashful aura of being rather pleased with herself. Laurel was obviously making the same assessment. It seemed that it was pretty obvious to both of them what Sonia was about to tell them.

But Sonia didn't come out with it till she and Callie had their desserts in front of them and Laurel, who had passed on dessert, had finished her second glass of wine.

Then she cleared her throat and said, 'I've felt absolutely knackered ever since we got back from honeymoon. I just hope I get to do a bit of blooming in the second trimester.'

Laurel's mouth, still somehow neatly outlined with red lipstick even at the end of a meal, dropped open in perfectly-acted surprise. Then she squealed and leaped to her feet, knocking over her empty wine glass (which Callie promptly righted), and Sonia rather awkwardly stood too and Laurel leaned across the table to embrace her.

'That is absolutely wonderful news! Wonderful. Congratulations! Isn't that brilliant?' Laurel released Sonia and turned to Callie with a slightly questioning look, as if inviting her to join in the celebrations but not entirely sure as to whether she would share wholeheartedly in the excitement.

'Brilliant!'

Callie got to her feet too. She felt sheepish and a little hypocritical, and as if the whole restaurant was looking at her, or would be if they knew what they were looking at. Here she was, a pregnant woman who'd conceived her baby on her friend's wedding night, was no longer on speaking terms with the baby's father – having failed to make clear to him there was no one else it could be – and who had, so far, kept her news more or less entirely to herself. And she was congratulating that same newly-wed friend, who was also expecting a baby and had no reason at all to be anything other than open and jubilant about it.

She gave Sonia a hug and sat down. She felt slightly dizzy. She was going to *have* to tell them now. Otherwise it would only be more awkward when she did.

'So when are you due?' Laurel said to Sonia.

'June. It was a honeymoon baby,' Sonia said, looking even more pleased with herself. 'I thought it would probably take longer. We were amazed at how quickly it happened, to be honest. Anyway, there are some people I wouldn't say that to – people who are, you know, having difficulties with all that. Which must be awful.' She pulled a sympathetic face. 'But it doesn't matter with you,' she said to Laurel. 'I know it's not what you want, so it's all quite straightforward, isn't it?' Then she turned to Callie, a little less confidently. 'I mean, I feel I can speak freely with both of you. I just hope you won't get too bored if I start going on about nappies and feeding and contractions and so on.'

'Oh, I won't mind,' Callie said, and then, 'I'm due in June, too.'

Both her friends turned to stare at her. Neither of them squealed.

Laurel was the first to speak, as usual. She was never one to hold back from asking awkward questions; in fact, she was proud of it. It was a point of professional pride – she saw that as key to her success at work, and maintained that all you really needed to be able to make good radio programmes was to be shamelessly nosey.

'Callie,' she said, 'who on earth is the father?'

'It doesn't matter who he is,' Callie said evenly. 'I'm going to be doing this on my own.'

Laurel and Sonia exchanged glances. Laurel said, 'Does he even know?'

Callie shrugged. 'He's quite happy to stay out of it.'

Sonia said, 'Does your mum know?'

'Not yet, so please don't mention it to either Mum or Ron if you bump into them,' Callie said.

'OK. Sure,' Laurel said.

And then there was silence – the kind of silence you get when people are thinking things they don't want to say. Both Laurel and Sonia looked crestfallen, as if Callie's unexpected pregnancy was a collective personal defeat. Then Laurel rallied and said, 'Well... congratulations!'

'Thank you!'

'Yes, that's really exciting news!' Sonia chipped in brightly and unconvincingly.

Neither of them attempted to hug her, but Laurel reached out to give her hand a reassuring squeeze, as if she'd just shared bad news.

Sonia said, 'Well – I insist on giving you a lift home! Can't let the mother-to-be make her way home alone through the wild streets of Kettlebridge. You too, Laurel. Can't have you tripping over your high heels because you've had a few too many wines.'

'Kettlebridge is hardly wild,' Callie said. 'You'll remember that if you move back here.'

'Oh, we're definitely coming back,' Sonia said. 'We think it'll be a great place to bring up our family. Plus you get so much more for your money.' She gave Callie a determinedly reassuring smile. 'How exciting that we're going to be going through this at the same time! And our little ones both have a ready-made friend!'

Laurel caught the waitress's eye and asked for the bill, and Sonia started telling Callie about a cream she'd found that was really good at stopping you from getting stretch marks. She seemed to have instantly assumed the role of the more knowledgeable friend, and Callie decided to let her make the most of it.

Sonia dropped Laurel off first, which perhaps Callie ought

to have taken as a sign that something was coming, but she was listening to Sonia telling Laurel that she was definitely no way ever going to use disposable nappies, and forgot to be on her guard. Finally, Sonia pulled up outside her flat, killed the engine and said into the sudden night-time silence, 'Well, I take my hat off to you. It's a big deal, trying to do this on your own.'

'Thanks for the lift. And don't worry about me. I'm going to be fine. I think it's the best thing that ever happened to me.'

Sonia looked her up and down, her face half in shadow, partly illuminated by the street light in front of Callie's flat. She clearly didn't believe her.

'People are going to wonder why you don't want to say who the father is,' she said. 'They'll think you've had an affair with a married man.'

'No they won't,' Callie said. 'I don't think they'll care. They'll accept it. As long as I can cope, and the baby's doing fine, everyone will get used to the way it's going to be.' Then she said, 'Sonia, if you want to know who I've been sleeping with, you'd better come out and ask me.'

Sonia said, 'OK – who?'

'These days? Absolutely nobody,' Callie said. 'And that's the way it's going to stay for the foreseeable future.'

She opened the car door and got out. Her heart was beating very fast again, and she told herself to stay calm, because to get too agitated wouldn't be good for the baby. Then, on impulse, she stooped and leaned into the car to face Sonia again.

'Oh, and Sonia?'

'Yes?'

'If you want us to stay friends, don't ask me about this ever again.'

And with that she slammed the car door and went to let herself into her flat.

Well, she'd said her piece, and nobody could make her say any more if she chose not to.

It was a victory of sorts, but maybe it was a hollow one. She felt both vindicated and lonely, as if she'd just proved herself to someone – her mum? Reuben? Reuben's dad, even? – who had not been there to witness it.

But then she ran herself a warm bath and lay and contemplated her avocado bathroom suite and her belly just under the surface of the water and her knees and her toes, and imagined seeing her baby for the first time.

A person. A small person, ready to grow. *Her* person. Was it really possible?

All the tension left her body, and she was drowsy and content. She had to force herself to climb out of the bath and dry herself and get into her pyjamas, because otherwise she was going to fall asleep right there.

She decided to break the news to Mum, Ron and Emily all together, when she joined them for lunch on Christmas Day. It did not turn out at all the way she had expected.

She was doubly nervous – not just about how they would react, but also, she always felt anxious about going back to the village. She told herself that the only time she was likely to bump into Mr Tallis would be if they went out for a walk, and if that did happen, which it probably wouldn't, she could just more or less ignore him and keep her distance until they moved on.

As for how Mum and Ron would respond when she told them she was expecting a baby – what was the worst they could do? They couldn't throw her out – she'd already gone. She had a job. She had a roof over her head. And she wasn't a kid any more. They had no say over what she chose to do or how she chose to do it. The only thing they could hurt her with was words, and she told herself she was well past that.

The bus service didn't run on Christmas Day, so Emily

offered to borrow Mum's runaround and come over to collect her. Callie didn't particularly want to be beholden to Emily, but it beat splashing out on a taxi, which she definitely could not afford to do if she was ever going to get a car of her own.

She hoped she didn't look too obviously pregnant – she didn't want them guessing her news before she told them. She wasn't showing as such, but she'd definitely filled out a bit. She picked out a long, loose skirt to wear, and a big red jumper with a picture of a reindeer on it, which looked a lot more festive and Christmassy than she felt.

At the last minute, she put on some of the same red lipstick she'd worn the day after Sonia's wedding. It felt like a gesture of defiance. So what if Reuben's dad had ended up rubbing it off his mouth with his handkerchief? She wasn't about to let that put her off. Why should that man's behaviour have any impact on how she chose to present her body to the outside world, and how she decided to live in it?

When Emily arrived to pick her up she made sure to be resolutely cheerful. But Emily, to her surprise, looked a little tired, and said she was recovering from a stomach bug.

'You look great,' she said to Callie as she put the car into gear. 'Positively radiant.'

'Thank you,' said Callie, who couldn't remember ever being described as radiant before.

Not for the first time, she thought what a shame it was that she wasn't closer to Emily. It was, after all, not Emily's fault if her dad was annoying, or if Callie's mum found her easy to get along with. And it must have been difficult for her too, having a stepmother and a grumpy older stepsister suddenly moving into her house. Maybe it could all have been different under other circumstances, if Callie hadn't been still so grief-stricken at the time, and so angry and resentful about Mum's swift remarriage. But it was too late now. And if she planned to keep her mum and Ron at arm's length over the months and years ahead, she could hardly start cosying up to Emily.

They took the turning that led to the village and she imagined herself getting out of the car and looking at Reuben's father's house, and began to feel queasy. She found herself responding to Emily's small talk distractedly and without enthusiasm – which Emily seemed to take as par for the course.

As they drove up the hill a taxi appeared behind them, and indicated to turn right the instant after Emily indicated to turn left for Mum and Ron's house. Emily drove onto the gravel and parked, and Callie turned towards Reuben's father's house – somehow she couldn't stop herself – and saw the taxi pull up in front of it.

Somebody got out – not Reuben – a woman. A young woman, judging by her hair and clothes, which was all Callie could see of her. Or young-ish. Her hair was long and dark and swishy and she was wearing a ritzy blazer and tight-fitting jeans tucked into high-heeled boots. She sashayed towards the front door and Callie looked away.

'That's Theresa,' Emily said. 'Apparently she's been dating Mr Tallis. You've got to hand it to him, he really does seem to have something when it comes to women. She's rather glamorous. And she's not the only one, apparently. He seems to be fighting them off!'

'Is he?' Callie said, as neutrally as she could manage.

'Well, you can't really blame him, can you? I mean, why shouldn't he have a good time, poor man? Reuben won't have anything to do with him, apparently. Plus he lives in Australia now, so he couldn't really have got much further away. Mum and Dad think it's really heartless. You used to know him a bit, didn't you? Are you still in touch with him?'

'No.'

Emily sighed as if yet another attempt at small talk had just bitten the dust. 'Right then, let's go and do the Christmas thing,' she said brightly, taking the keys out of the ignition. 'Janice is in a bit of a stress about the lunch. But I'm sure it'll all work out.'

'Yeah, it always does. Thanks for the lift.'

Emily looked slightly surprised by the thank you, and flashed her a smile. 'No problem.'

They got out of the car and Mum came out to welcome them. Callie steeled herself and smiled and embraced her, and they went in.

She waited till they'd finished their turkey with all the trimmings and had cleared the table. In the fraction of a second before Mum could ask if people were ready for pudding or wanted to pause, while Ron was frowning at his cracker joke as if still trying to work it out, Callie saw her opportunity and took it: 'So, I have something to tell you, and I thought now would be as good a time as any.'

Mum's eyes widened apprehensively and Emily stared at Callie with a face full of foreboding. Ron frowned, shifted in his seat and carefully set down his joke.

Mum said, 'You're not.'

Callie said, 'Not what?'

'Oh no. You *are*.' Mum's hands went to her mouth. 'Callie, *no*.'

Emily said, 'Janice, what? What's going on?'

Mum turned to Emily. 'She's *pregnant*,' she said, and got up and rushed out.

Callie stayed where she was, looking down at the table, which Mum had laid with her special festive tablecloth. She could hear Mum crying. Then she lifted her head and said, 'Well, that went well.'

'It's the shock, that's all,' Ron said, in much the same matter-of-fact tone of voice he might have used to describe a minor problem with his car, or something in the house that needed fixing. 'She'll get over it. I have to say, I've told her many a time that something like this might happen—'

'Dad,' Emily said warningly.

Callie left the table and went out to the living room, where Mum was no longer crying but was standing with her arms folded, looking out through the net curtain at the house opposite. When Callie reached out tentatively and put a hand on her back she didn't soften or respond. Callie withdrew and her mum remained standing there, gazing out of the window.

'Mum, I'm going to be fine,' Callie said. 'I promise. They know at work, and I'll get maternity leave, and I've got a place booked in the hospital crèche. I've looked at my budget, I figure that with child benefit I'll be able to make ends meet—'

'You're going to need money,' Mum said, cutting her off.

'Well, obviously, but like I said, everything's sorted with work, and as long as I make sure my performance doesn't drop off I think I'll be all right—'

'Your father had some savings he had earmarked for you,' Mum said. 'I've never withdrawn them. They weren't officially left to you – everything came direct to me. So that money is technically part of everything that I own with Ron, now. But, if Ron's agreeable, and I think he will be, if I present it to him the right way, I'll look into transferring it to you. It's quite a substantial sum – it might be enough for a deposit. Though you won't get anything much, not round here. It's so expensive these days. Not unless you get really lucky.'

'Mum, that's incredible news,' Callie said. 'Amazing. It couldn't have been better timed. My landlady mentioned the other day that she was thinking she might put up the place I'm renting for sale. She said she'd try and make sure that if someone bought it, they'd keep me on as a tenant. But maybe, if she did go ahead and put it on the market, I might be able to buy it myself.'

She was already imagining what she might be able to do

with the flat, if she could get the money together. OK, so it only had one bedroom, but she might be able to get an extension built, and she and the baby could share for now. And it had a separate sitting room and kitchen – three rooms, plus the hallway – and a garden! And actually, she'd got quite attached to the place, avocado bathroom suite and all.

'Thank you,' Callie said. 'Seriously, it's a Christmas miracle.'

'Just try and use the money wisely,' Mum said, with a little catch in her voice. 'It was always meant for your future.' Then she turned to face Callie and said, 'Is the father of this baby going to support you at all? Or have any contact with the child?'

Callie shook her head. 'I don't want him to. He doesn't want to know. Don't ask me about him, Mum. He's nothing to do with it any more.'

'Right,' Mum said. She reached up and carefully adjusted her paper crown, which had slipped down over one eye. Her eyes were glimmering with tears again. 'Well, I suppose congratulations are in order,' she said, and reached out to take Callie in her arms.

As they stood there together Callie felt that Mum was clinging to her, rather than the other way round. Mum's face on her shoulder was damp with tears. She was reminded of other times they'd held each other for comfort and the tears they had seen each other shed, as if all of that was coded and locked away in their bodies, and all that was needed to bring it back was for them to embrace.

Then they were separate again.

'Nothing will bring you happiness like this will,' Mum told her. 'And nothing will have quite as much power to break your heart. Because it will break you, Callie. Being a parent breaks everybody. The only question is, who are you going to be when you put yourself back together again?'

With that she turned and went back into the dining room,

but Callie lingered to look at the house across the road with its leafless apple tree and rising tendrils of ivy.

'You won't break me,' she said under her breath, and put her hand on her belly. 'You're going to be the making of me.' And after another minute or two, she felt ready to go back into the dining room and face the rest of her family.

TWENTY-NINE

Summer 2004

Callie knew the minute they arrived to celebrate Billy's first birthday that something was up. Mum looked drawn and haggard, and stayed stiff and distant as Callie leaned forward to peck her on the cheek. She only softened when she gazed down at Billy, who Callie had brought in still strapped into his car seat, and who was gurgling and smiling winsomely and experimentally kicking his feet.

'Come on in, then,' Mum said, as if trying to make the best of a bad job. 'I baked a cake.'

In the hallway, as she took off her shoes, Callie wondered what she'd done wrong this time, and how long it would take Mum to tell her. It certainly wasn't that they were late – they'd showed up on the dot of four, as agreed. Perhaps it was because Mum felt Callie only ever called on her in an emergency, like when Billy was sick and couldn't go into nursery, and then neglected her in between times.

It had been a tough first year and right from the start, the tensions between her and Mum had been impossible to ignore.

Mum had come to see her in hospital straight after the birth, and had looked enchanted when she first held Billy in her arms. But then she had looked up at Callie and her first words had been, not 'How are you?' or 'Congratulations!' or 'He's gorgeous', but 'Why didn't you call me?' Callie had mumbled something about expecting the labour to take ages, but she knew Mum didn't believe her and was hurt.

Then Ron, who was lurking in the background, had said something about Billy's name. Not her decision to name him after her dad, but about his surname – that he'd have to be a Swann, the same as Callie, rather than a Greenwood like Mum and Ron and Emily. She couldn't even remember exactly what Ron had said now – it was all a blur of exhaustion and emotion and hormones – but she did remember that Billy had started crying, and she had cried too. A midwife had come to her rescue, ushered both Mum and Ron out and helped her latch Billy on so she could breastfeed him, after which she had slept. But she'd never forgotten Mum's wounded expression as she backed out of the ward that day.

After that inauspicious start, things had gone from bad to worse. Mum appeared to be incapable of keeping her opinions of Callie's parenting to herself, and they invariably seemed to be negative. As far as Callie could tell, Mum thought everything she did was wrong, from giving up on breastfeeding after she got mastitis to putting Billy in full-time nursery care and going back to work – not that she'd had much choice financially, once her maternity leave came to an end. She knew, in theory, that Mum's fault-finding came from a place of love and concern about Billy, but still, she found it both exasperating and deeply upsetting.

Anyway, they'd made it through the first year. Hopefully everything would get easier, and Mum would have fewer quibbles to raise...

Billy's actual birthday had been a few days earlier, during

the week, and Mum had dropped several hints that she would have liked to see him then, which Callie had ignored. By the time she had finished work and collected him from nursery, and driven back through the generally dreadful traffic, it was the witching hour of bath time and bed, when Billy was at his most irritable and so was she. It would obviously have been a terrible time for a visit.

It was frustrating that Mum didn't understand that. But then, since having Callie, she'd only ever worked part-time, and she'd stayed at home until Callie started school. She seemed not to understand how desperately Callie clung to Billy's routine to get her from one week to the next. But now was probably not the time to try to explain.

Callie carried Billy through to the kitchen in his car seat, then lifted him out and put him into the high chair Mum had bought for him. Ron was out, which Callie was not surprised by. Ron was not a big fan of babies, although perhaps he might have felt differently if it was Emily who had one. Callie suspected Mum tried to arrange her visits for a time when she knew Ron would not be there.

Mum made tea for her and Callie, and Callie gave Billy some rice cakes and put some milk in his favourite cup. Billy beamed at both of them and banged his cup on the high chair table as if attempting to make an important point. Mum brought the sponge cake she'd made to the table and lit the solitary candle she'd stuck on it, and Billy was entranced by the flame but failed to blow it out. Callie gave him a little piece of cake to try, but he just crumbled it in his fist and then looked at the mess he'd made in delight.

Once the little celebratory ritual of the cake was done with, Mum's mood seemed to darken. It fell to Callie to lead the conversation, and she became acutely conscious of the kitchen clock ticking overhead, the minutes crawling by, and how much time there was left get through before she could decently say it was time to get Billy back home for dinner and bedtime.

At the same time she was aware, as she always was when she came to see Mum, of Reuben's father's house just across the road. She thought of the place as like a dark wall – a wall that was in her mind all the time, whether she was close to it or not, but that she had more cause than usual to remember when she was here.

She cleaned up Billy's sticky hands and lifted him out of the high chair, and asked Mum if she'd like to hold him. As Mum held him on her lap her expression softened, but then she looked up at Callie and Callie saw only disappointment in her eyes, and her heart sank.

'So he's over that nasty cold, is he?' Mum said.

'Yes, he's absolutely fine, as you can see.'

Perhaps that was what Mum had got herself worked up about. Callie had actually already forgotten that Billy had come down with a bug just before his birthday.

Mum sniffed. 'I did wonder whether he should have had another day or two to get over it. Still, I suppose you felt you had to get back to work.'

'He didn't have a temperature any more. The nursery's pretty strict about when they can come back after being poorly, you know.'

Mum raised her eyebrows. 'Really? I bet you some of the parents don't take any notice.' She sniffed. 'That place seems to be a right germ factory.'

'I think it's normal for them to just run through everything,' Callie said. 'He's building up his immunity.'

Mum looked unconvinced. 'And he was OK when you left him there, after a couple of days at home with you? My friend said her daughter literally has to peel her child's fingers off her before she can go.'

'He's not like that. Honestly, Mum, you don't need to worry.'

'Well, of course I worry,' Mum said flatly. She planted a kiss on the top of Billy's head, which was covered now in fair, downy hair that smelt of soap and sweetness. But the look she gave Callie was both accusatory and reproachful, as if Billy was a treasure who might need protecting from her. 'Poor little mite. He's at quite a disadvantage, isn't he? I know it doesn't matter now, but it will. When he begins to talk, when he can understand, when he can ask questions... and that day isn't all that far away... what are you going to tell him, Callie? What are you going to say when he asks who his daddy is?'

'Mum, don't start this, not now.'

But Mum just shook her head. 'I have to say it, because I'm your mother and Billy's grandmother, and no one else is going to. I know you were gutted when you lost your dad. I was too. But at least you always knew who he was!'

They stared at each other. Callie was rigid with shock. She said, with some effort, 'I don't want to get into a fight, today of all days.' She stood up and reached out towards Billy, and Billy grinned at her and stretched out his arms and she scooped him up and settled him on her chest so that he could look over her shoulder. 'I think we'd better go.'

'Oh, sure. You don't want to talk about it. You never want to talk about it. And given what went on, I can't say I'm surprised!'

Mum's mouth was quivering and she was clearly on the edge of angry tears. She got to her feet, and Callie tightened her grip on Billy as if she half expected Mum to grab him.

'Don't do this, Mum,' she said. She was surprised by how calm and firm her voice was, as if she was reining in someone else's unpredictable child. Which in a way she was. 'We spoke about this already, a long time ago. This is none of your business. If you want to see Billy, you need to respect that.'

But Mum had clearly passed the point of no return. Her eyes were blazing and her face was red with anger, and the words poured out as if she was no longer capable of holding them back.

'Respect. Respect! What respect did you ever show me? Or Ron? Or Emily? All those years you treated us like dirt. As if I'd betrayed your father by getting married again. I loved your father. You know that. But he was dead! And Ron was my future, and it would have been really nice, really helpful, if you could have at least made a tiny bit of effort to get along with him. But no, you had to make it all as difficult as possible. And then you went and got yourself mixed up with Lionel Tallis after his wife died – and slept with his son as well, under our roof – you little slut!'

Billy whimpered, and Callie swayed to and fro to comfort him. Her ears were ringing as if Mum had just slapped her. She said, 'You can't talk to me like that. If you carry on I'm going to leave.'

'But it's true, isn't it? You're not denying it,' Mum said bitterly. 'I suppose I ought to be grateful that you're not *that* much of a liar. I couldn't believe it when Mrs Jancett told me. Can you imagine how humiliating that was? To find out what you'd been up to from our elderly neighbour? I was just chatting to her the other day, the way you do, telling her about how you're getting on. I was proud, more fool me. Like any grandmother would be. And then she let it slip. But she didn't want to tell me. I could see she really felt quite awkward about it. She said she'd tried to put it out of her mind, and she didn't want to make trouble. But she saw you take Reuben back to our place, and then you'd sneaked over the road the very next day when Reuben was out, and Reuben had come back with a bunch of red roses and left again straight away looking absolutely horrified. "Like he'd seen his own ghost," was what she said. And then you scurrying back here, "looking a bit the worse for wear," was the way she put it. Caught red-handed, more like.'

'Mum, please, you're upsetting Billy,' Callie said, but her mum ignored her.

'I begged her not to say anything to anybody else,' she went on. 'Heaven knows it's the last thing anyone needs, to have people gossiping about it. But I have to say, when I heard it, suddenly it all made sense. I mean, I can understand why you didn't want to tell me, that's for sure. What I can't get my head round is how you could you have been so stupid. To be carrying on with Reuben and his father at the same time – no wonder Reuben wanted to leave the country, and didn't want anything to do with poor Billy – how could you? How could any daughter of mine have ever thought that was a decent or acceptable way to behave?'

So this was it, the confrontation she had been dreading. Perhaps it was shock, or perhaps it was because part of her had always known this was going to happen one day, but she found it was possible to speak quite coldly and calmly.

'Did it never occur to you that there might be another side to the story?' she said. 'Aside from whatever Mrs Jancett has cooked up in her festering little imagination, that is?'

'There's no need to insult her just because you're ashamed,' Mum snapped back. 'I'm ashamed too. Do you even know for sure who Billy's father actually is?'

Billy was crying in earnest now. He bucked and wriggled as Callie stooped to strap him back into his car seat, arching his back to make it as difficult as possible.

'We're leaving now, and we won't be coming back,' she said over Billy's wails as she stood and picked up the car seat. 'I will never forgive you for this. Never, ever, ever.'

Mum drew herself up to her full height and said, 'Go on then, clear out. At least I still have Emily.'

'Then you'd better make the most of her,' Callie said, 'because as far as I'm concerned, she's the only daughter you have.'

She gathered up Billy's cup and shoved it into her bag and hurried out with Billy in the car seat, pausing only to slip her feet back into her shoes in the hall. Billy was screaming now but she knew he'd quieten as soon as she started driving – being in the car always calmed him down. It wasn't the smoothest of rides – it was an old banger she'd bought off a colleague – but it didn't seem to matter.

Mum came out of the house just before she pulled out onto the road, her face convulsing in a kind of agony as if she was about to plead with Callie to stay. But she accelerated away anyway.

Billy was asleep by the time she got home, and didn't wake as she brought him into the flat. She left him to doze while she microwaved some baby food for him, and a ready meal for herself. It crossed her mind that Mum would have disapproved of her not cooking from scratch, and then she dismissed the thought. After what had just happened, it didn't really matter what Mum thought about anything any more.

Billy looked so calm and so still, almost as if he'd been anaesthetised. She told herself she was lucky. She had a healthy baby. She had all the family she needed.

The phone rang once or twice, but once she'd unplugged it and turned off her mobile the rest of the evening was uneventful. She reminded herself that this was her home, and no one could come here unless she invited them. And she told herself that some kind of rupture or falling-out with her mum had been a long time coming – probably ever since her dad died and Ron arrived on the scene. She'd thought that maybe Billy would bring them closer together, but in the end her baby had turned out to be something else for them to fight about.

She was only just coping as it was – with Billy, with work, with paying the bills, with keeping her head above water. She was tired all the time, so much so that she'd accepted it as a normal state of being. She didn't need anybody in her life who was going to make it harder, and drain what energy she had left. She had to focus on Billy, and on getting through the working week, and their survival.

That was how she rationalised it to herself. It crossed her mind to wonder how different it might have been if only she had told Mum exactly what had really happened. She would have been furious, of course. Probably would have marched right across the road to have a go at Mr Tallis, and then stopped off on the way back to tell Mrs Jancett she was a nosey old gossip and should keep her nose out of other people's business...

But if she told Mum, wouldn't she owe it to Reuben to explain to him too? And even if she didn't tell him, he would probably hear about it anyway, if Mum went on the warpath. Presumably he was still in touch with his dad and Theresa. Mr Tallis was bound to deny everything. And what if Reuben didn't believe her?

No, it was impossible. She couldn't face it. Couldn't cope with all those old feelings of shame and regret resurfacing. That intense vulnerability. Easier by far just to withdraw and keep herself to herself. That was the only way she could stay in control.

But somewhere deep down she was devastated, and wanted to howl like a child. She knew she'd never forget the insults her mum had thrown at her.

When she tried to go sleep that evening she was plagued by the memory of Billy's still, sleeping face, and by the irrational, instinctive fear that something terrible was on the way. She woke up to Billy crying in the night, and to the knowledge that her mum had been right about one thing, if nothing else. Sooner or later, Billy would need to know who his father was.

But she picked him up out of his cot and held him and soothed him, and said to herself, *Not yet.*

PART THREE

THE CROSSING

Callie, Billy and Reuben

2014

THIRTY

CALLIE

2014

'Then tell me,' Reuben said. 'I'm here, and I'm ready to hear it. Now's your time.'

Her heart was beating very fast and she had the beginning of another headache, a pulsing pain kicking in somewhere above her left temple. Her left arm ached as if she'd just knocked it. But the physical discomfort was barely a distraction from her fear and self-disgust.

He had asked the question gently, but he would have every right to be angry with her for not having told him the truth before. She'd wronged him, and she'd wronged Billy, too. She'd taken away any chance they might have had to know each other, and to grow to love each other, for the first ten years of Billy's life. And whatever her reasons had been, she knew now that this had been a truly unforgivable and terrible thing to have done.

The towpath had widened enough for two of them to walk abreast, and Reuben caught up with her and was walking next to her. He said, 'Callie, what happened?'

'He assaulted me,' she said.

As soon as the words were out something inside her froze the exact same way she had frozen when Lionel Tallis touched her all those years ago. But the river kept flowing beside her and the sun was still shining, and she carried on walking.

The past was part of who she was and always would be, but the world around her was bigger and more powerful than the past. And she was, too. She wasn't that young woman any more, who had retreated into silence because she didn't know what else to do.

And Billy still needed her, and would be expecting her to collect him from school in half an hour's time. She couldn't afford to let the weight of the past crush her. She had to be able to voice it and keep going.

She drew a deep breath and went on.

'That was what you saw. But you didn't see it. You thought it was the same as what happened between your dad and Donna. A relationship, or the beginning of one. Or consensual, at any rate. But it wasn't, and I didn't know how to tell you. I couldn't bring myself to say it out loud. I didn't want you to have to lose your dad when you had just lost your mum. I thought any dad would be better than none. And I suppose I was trying to protect myself, and I got that mixed up with what I thought I had to do to protect Billy. I lied to you, Reuben, and for what it's worth, I'm sorry. It was wrong.'

They kept walking. A twig crackled underfoot, and something moved in the river, as if a wily old fish, the kind a fisherman would be proud to catch, had come close to the surface, and then swum back down again.

'I think you tried to tell me,' Reuben said. 'When you got in touch to tell me you were pregnant. When I was in Australia. I was foul to you. If I'd handled that better, if I'd been kinder, do you think you might have told me then?'

'I don't know. Maybe. But I didn't, and I don't think you

should blame yourself for that. I've had ten years to tell you. I could have done it at any point. It wouldn't have been that hard. I could have reached out and tracked you down. But I guess I'd put everything into the idea that I had to do it on my own, and then there wasn't any room for doubt. I was just so wrapped up in caring for Billy...'

She paused. Her voice had gone hoarse and tears were stinging her eyes. Why was it that she had just managed to describe what had happened with Reuben's father quite clinically and calmly, but the minute she moved on to talking about Billy, she wanted to start crying? She cleared her throat and forced herself to carry on.

'The day-to-day just took over,' she said. 'It seemed like that was as much as I could cope with. Reuben... can I ask you something? If you'd known beyond a shadow of doubt that Billy was your baby, would you have wanted him? Or would you have tried to talk me out of it? We were still so young... Really, we barely knew each other.'

He was silent for such a long time that she thought maybe he wasn't going to answer at all. Then he said, 'I don't know. I'd like to say that I would have done the right thing. Of course I would want to think that. It's easy to say now, isn't it? But at the time... I like to think I'd have got there in the end. But it might have taken a while.'

She actually felt relieved. She knew he was telling the truth, and that was why he had taken his time before speaking. If he'd said that he would have welcomed the news and would have jumped at the chance to look after them both – maybe even to live together as a family – she might have doubted whether what he was saying was really true, but she would also have felt that much more guilty.

'But I didn't give you the option,' she said. 'You should be furious with me.'

'Why? I knew Billy might be mine. Of course I did. It was

obviously a possibility. I guess I chose not to confront it. I was frightened of facing up to it, I suppose. And maybe I still am. I'm so sorry about what my dad did, Callie. And I can't help but wonder if there is anybody else who he did that to.'

'I don't suppose you'll ever know. He might not even know himself, any more. My mum said that he's beginning to get quite confused. Do you think he has dementia?'

'I managed to persuade him to see the doctor. He's been referred to a clinic. And Theresa's threatening to leave him.'

'What, now? Isn't this when he needs her most?'

'I don't think she's up for it. She says she moved in as his girlfriend, not his carer. Between you and I, I think she might have met someone else. And she's not married to Dad. As far as she's concerned, she's free to go.'

'What will you do?'

'About him? I don't know. Get carers to go in, maybe. Otherwise, the way I feel right now, I might just end up trying to wring his neck.' He hesitated. 'Will you tell Billy?'

'About you? Yes. I don't think he'll be totally surprised.'

She remembered what Billy had said about his first impression of Reuben – 'He seemed OK' – and how warily he'd said it. How keen he'd been not to say the wrong thing. He'd been trying so hard to protect her feelings, it was difficult for her to tell how he really felt. Maybe he barely knew himself.

When Billy had mentioned seeing Reuben's name written under the windowsill of her old bedroom, she'd started crying and he'd stopped asking questions. She shouldn't have done that. She shouldn't have got upset. It would only make it harder for him to find out what he wanted to know if he was afraid of her bursting into tears all the time.

She should have found some other, better, different way to handle all this years ago.

What hurt as much as anything was that now she'd met Reuben again it was easy to imagine him and Billy getting

along, given half a chance. They seemed alike, both in their
sensitivity and in a tendency to shy away from the rough-and-
tumble of other people. And there was the physical resemblance, too. She could make out the ghost of the shy, sweet-
natured teenager Reuben had once been as a kind of distilled
potential in Billy's features, and in the way Billy moved, his
mannerisms and expressions.

This thought cost her another sharp pang of regret, as
painful as the insistent throb of the headache gathering force in
her left temple.

But then, she'd finally told Reuben the truth and he was still
here with her. He had believed her, and they were still talking.
Perhaps, in spite of everything, it would be possible for them to
be friends. After all, he would have to be part of her life if he
was going to be part of Billy's.

She hadn't quite admitted to herself that this was what she
wanted, until now – it would have seemed greedy, and like
tempting fate. And acknowledging it made her feel wickedly,
giddily happy, as if someone had lit a little fire inside her.

'I think Billy will be pleased,' she said. 'I think he will want
to get to know you.'

'I hope so,' Reuben said. 'I thought he was amazing.'

He couldn't have said anything that would have touched
her more. Because of course Billy *was* amazing... but people
couldn't be relied upon to see it. Especially not Billy's peers.
And sometimes, confusingly, other adults were oblivious to
Billy's sweetness and charm and lovability, too.

'He *is* amazing,' she agreed. 'So you'll come and see him?'

'Yes. I want to see him. If that's what he wants.'

'He will.'

They'd come back to a fork in the path on the edge of the
meadow, near the outskirts of town, not far from the children's
splash park and the ice cream kiosk. She came to a standstill and
said, 'I'm sorry, Reuben, I have to go. I have to get Billy on time.

I can cut across here, and get to school quicker. If you go straight on, the path will take you back to the town centre. That's where you're parked, isn't it?'

Had he been hoping that she might ask him to walk to school with her, so they could pick up Billy together? But that would have been too much, too soon. She couldn't do that to Billy – she couldn't go from having no contact with his dad at all, never mentioning him and keeping quiet even about who he was, to showing up at the school gate with Reuben at her side.

But Reuben said, 'Yeah, OK,' and reached out and clasped her very lightly on her good shoulder, a little gesture of acknowledgement and solidarity, and gave her a weary and regretful smile.

'Anything I can do to make this easier for both of you, I will,' he said, and released her. 'You don't have to worry about me. I'm not here to make a nuisance of myself. So, no more stress. Not on my account, anyway.' He wagged his forefinger at her as if pretending to tell her off. 'And no more headaches. You have to take care of yourself.'

'I'll try,' she said.

He leaned forward to kiss her carefully and respectfully on the cheek. 'Anyway, you'd better go. I don't want to make you late.'

So he got it. He didn't expect to escort her to school and be reintroduced to Billy on the spot. He didn't want to turn anything upside down, and he wasn't going to start shouting about his rights. He recognised that her life with Billy followed certain routines that they had settled into because that was what was best for Billy, and he was willing to try and fit in where he could, to take it slowly, and to give both of them time.

If he'd been angry, insistent, demanding, she would have snapped straight into defensive mode. But as it was...

As it was, there was nothing to stop her from liking him. Again. Still. And maybe more than liking.

There was a reason they called it falling for someone. It was because there was nothing graceful about it, and it wasn't under your control, and it was likely to hurt you when you landed.

To cover her confusion she set off quickly along the short path that cut across the meadow, and connected to the network of roads between here and Billy's school. She didn't loiter to see if Reuben would turn and wave, and when she glanced back over her shoulder he was already out of sight.

And part of her was disappointed.

But if she had feelings for Reuben... some kind of unfulfilled crush, left over from when she was younger, and now stirred up again... she'd just have to keep them to herself.

She needed to focus on Billy now. She had to figure out what to say to him, and how best to handle it. But even her apprehension about how Billy might react wasn't enough to take the edge off her happiness.

Her headache had lightened. Maybe it had just been tension. The pain in her arm had gone, too. The sun was shining and she caught sight of the blue glint of a dragonfly hovering above the rushes that lined the path, and was surprised by the sudden spring in her step. Everything seemed to be coming together as if it had always been meant to turn out this way, and she felt lighter and freer than she could ever remember feeling before.

THIRTY-ONE

She brought up the subject of Reuben with Billy after dinner that evening. When it came down to it, she was terrified. She'd said to Reuben that Billy would want to see him, but what if she was wrong? And what if Billy was angry with her for not having told him before – as he might justifiably be?

Also, she couldn't help but be conscious of Reuben waiting to hear how it had gone. Was he back at his father's house? Or would he have found somewhere else to stay, or even gone back to his place in London? He hadn't got in touch since their walk by the river that afternoon, and she didn't want to make contact until she'd followed through on her promise to tell Billy who he was.

She'd made pasta for dinner, with a little bit of help from Billy, although she'd got so adept at cooking one-handed by now she probably could have managed it by herself. And finally, when they'd finished eating, she decided she couldn't put it off any longer.

'Billy, there's something I have to talk to you about.'

The words came out of her as if somebody else had taken charge, who wasn't going to worry about whether they were precisely the right words or agonise about finding better ones, but was just going to get the job done.

Billy looked at her nervously and also a little defensively, as if he expected to be told off for something he'd done wrong.

'What?'

'It's about Reuben. You asked me about him before. He came to Granny's house when you were staying there.'

Billy folded his arms and gazed at her, waiting for her to explain. His eyes were clear and trusting, and completely free of resentment or self-pity. What choice did she have but to live up to the faith he had in her, and tell him the truth she owed him?

'Reuben is your dad,' she said.

And then she couldn't bear to look at him any more. His innocence hurt her. She put her hand across her mouth as if to silence herself, but it was too late. She closed her eyes and bowed her head and steeled herself for whatever might come next.

So this was what it must have been like to be Mum. To realise that something you'd said or done could have caused so much hurt that it might lead to you being estranged from your child.

But then she heard Billy say, 'OK.'

She looked up. He was still staring at her with big, thoughtful eyes. He rubbed his nose as if troubled by a sudden itch, then said again, 'It's OK, Mum. Really it is.'

She moved her hand to cradle her broken arm. The now-familiar pain began to pulse in her left temple again, and she remembered what Reuben had said about taking care of herself. Well, she would, one day. Once she'd got through all this.

'OK?' she said.

He nodded. 'OK. I mean, that doesn't seem too bad. I thought maybe my dad was a spy or something, and that was why you didn't want to tell me. I guess I figured you had your reasons. But if it's him, that's OK by me.' He frowned. 'Do you think he's all right?'

'Yes, I do.'

Billy let out a sigh. 'Well, that's good then. I also thought maybe he was bad, and that was why you didn't want him around. I did wonder if it might be him. Though obviously I didn't know for sure until now.'

'What made you wonder?'

Billy shrugged. 'Well, I knew you liked him once. Because of what you wrote underneath the windowsill in your old room in Granny's house.' His expression turned wary. 'And you... got a bit upset when I told you I'd seen it. Also, he looked at me quite weirdly that morning when you were in hospital and he came over.'

'Like what?'

'Like...' Billy pondered. 'Like he knew me from somewhere,' he said eventually, and then, rather helplessly, 'as if I was famous or something. Which of course I'm not. So...' He hesitated. 'Am I going to meet him again?'

'Do you want to?'

He fixed his eyes on her. He looked troubled and defence-less and wide open, and she suddenly wanted nothing more than to get up and give him a big hug, but stopped herself. That could come later. Right now, she had to give him time to ask whatever he wanted to.

He said, 'Are you sure you don't mind?'

'Do you mean, do I mind if you don't want to meet him? Or if you do?'

'Either, I guess,' Billy said.

It was shattering to see how much it mattered to him what she felt. He was trying to protect her.

'Billy, it really and truly is up to you,' she said firmly. 'There's no obligation, and you can think it over for as long as you like. If you say one thing now, and feel differently later, you're allowed to change your mind. What I will do anyway – if it's all right with you – is keep in touch with your dad, so I can tell him how you're getting on.'

'He really wants to know?'

She nodded. 'He really wants to know.'

'Because it would be kind of rubbish to do all this and then he turns round and says he isn't interested any more,' Billy said, folding his arms and speaking with the special, determined emphasis he used when he was trying to be brave.

'He's not going to do that.'

'How can you be sure?'

'I can't. It's just a hunch, I guess. A feeling.' She pressed her right hand to her chest. 'Sometimes that's all you have to go on.'

Billy studied her closely, as if looking for clues. Then he permitted her a small smile. 'Of course I'll meet him,' he said matter-of-factly, as if she'd just asked him a times tables question that was so easy it almost wasn't worth answering. 'Why wouldn't I?'

'It's good you feel that way,' she said.

'I do,' he said firmly. 'It's actually quite exciting.'

'You're being very brave about it. But you don't have to be brave. It's OK to have a mixture of feelings about it. If you do.'

'I'm not being brave,' Billy said. 'It's fine.'

And with that he got up to start clearing the table, to show that as far as he was concerned, this conversation was now over. He always helped her tidy up after dinner now. As he'd said to her once, three hands were faster than one.

She got to her feet and gathered up their glasses and put them on the side, and Billy opened the dishwasher and started stacking it. The dishwasher had seemed like an indulgence at the time, given that there were only two of them, but she was glad of it now. It was easier to deal with than washing up by hand when you had one arm out of action.

Then Billy straightened up and looked her in the eye.

'Mum, stop worrying. It really will be fine,' he told her.

And then he allowed her to hug him, but she knew the hug was more for her benefit than for his, and it lasted only a brief moment before they let go of each other and set about finishing the clearing up.

Perhaps he was getting to an age where he was going to be less keen on hugs, and would think them soppy. Well – that was only normal, and natural, and part of growing up. After all, in just over two years' time he'd be a teenager, and that was probably just how teenage boys were.

After they'd finished and Billy had retreated to his room, she composed a message on her phone to send to Reuben: *I've told him. He took it very well. He'd like to meet. x*

That sense of connection she'd had with Reuben, down by the river... was it just wishful thinking? Or an echo of what she'd felt for him when she was younger? Or was it real?

Why did people say it was better to have loved and lost than never to have loved at all? It would kill her to let herself fall for Reuben – really fall for him, as the woman she was now, and as the mother of his child – and then lose him all over again.

No. She was Billy's mum, and Reuben was his dad – *that* was their connection.

She deleted the kiss from the end of the message and pressed send, and resolved to set all thoughts of Reuben and herself aside.

THIRTY-TWO

On Billy's eleventh birthday, she invited Reuben to the flat for tea.

It was Billy's idea. He didn't want to go to Jack's party, and she promised that she would say he was feeling under the weather and get him out of it. Sonia, obviously harried by the prospect of entertaining a large group of mostly eleven-year-old boys, had not questioned the excuse. It was a bit dishonest, but Callie didn't care – she was always happy to cover for Billy when needed. It was all part of it being the two of them against the world.

How was that going to change now, with Reuben coming back into their lives?

When she'd asked Billy what he wanted to do instead, he had said, 'Maybe it would be a good day for my dad to come round?' *My dad.* Well, she couldn't argue with that. She phoned Reuben to invite him, and then found herself apologising for the flat.

'It's small. There's only one bedroom, and Billy has that. It could do with a lick of paint and a new bathroom. But anyway, I was lucky to get it, and really lucky that Mum helped me buy it.'

'Callie, I'm honoured to be invited, and I'll feel lucky to be there. What do you think Billy would like for a present? You're going to have to help me out here, or I'll get it totally wrong.'

'Surely you must have some idea. You were an eleven-year-old boy yourself once.'

'Yeah... but time moves on. Besides, it's amazing how much you forget.'

She told him about a series of spy books that she thought Billy might like to try, and even though she could tell that Reuben would have quite liked to turn up with something bigger and showier than a book, he promised he'd look into it. When they said goodbye she found herself in a weird state halfway between exhilaration and fear, as if Reuben's visit was both a triumph and a threat. And this mood of nervous anticipation lingered, and made it difficult for her to sleep or to concentrate as the day of the visit drew closer.

The Friday before the visit she was working from home, and spent her lunchtime frantically trying to tidy up, and to clean things she never normally noticed – the dusty square of kitchen worktop directly underneath the boiler, the bases of the kitchen cupboards.

She'd neglected the housework since having the cast on her arm, and it took longer to do everything one-handed, but she felt she had to make the effort. After all, Reuben wasn't going to be the only visitor. Her mum was coming for lunch. Her mum, who knew that Reuben might be Billy's dad, but did not yet know for sure. And Callie wasn't planning to tell her. Not till Reuben's visit was out of the way. One thing at a time.

After all, what if Mum came out with something unforgive-able, yet again? Would the fragile peace between them survive Mum's tendency to rush to judgement, and to lash out when she was upset?

She wasn't sure she could ever face telling Mum about Mr Tallis. Maybe she wouldn't need to, and Mum wouldn't push too hard for explanations. Anyway, she wasn't going to worry about that now.

As she set about the housework she felt she was mounting a defence – that if she could make the flat look presentable, she'd be better placed to cope with whatever was coming next.

As it turned out, the lunch with Mum was easy – to start with, at least.

Mum seemed thrilled to be in Billy's company, so much so that it was as if Callie had faded into the background – which she childishly minded for a moment or two, until she reminded herself it was actually a good thing that Mum wasn't paying her too much attention.

It was wonderful to watch how Billy charmed Mum just by being himself, and how Mum treated him as if he could do no wrong. They had cheese toasties and crisps, at Billy's request (he ate most of the crisps). Mum asked Billy about school – grandmotherly questions, gentle and not too probing, designed only to elicit information about success.

'Your mum tells me you had to do some big tests at school this term, and you did very well – is that right?'

Unused to receiving attention and approval from not just one adult but two simultaneously, Billy glowed.

'I did all right,' he said.

'You did better than all right, Billy,' Callie interrupted.

Billy shrugged slightly. 'Yes,' he said. 'I was surprised, especially in maths. Since we did the tests things have got a bit more relaxed. I've been doing a big project for history, about the Tudors.'

'Oh, I did that in school, too,' Mum said. 'King Henry chopping his wives' heads off. Just goes to show, you should never give men too much power.' She gave Callie a conspiratorial smile, then added hurriedly, 'Though I'm sure you'd never do anything horrible like that to anyone, Billy.'

'I don't think I would,' Billy said thoughtfully. 'I hope I wouldn't. But it's always hard to tell what you might do in a situation until you get there, isn't it?'

'You're so right,' Mum said fondly. 'So what about your friends?'

Billy blushed again, but more unhappily this time. 'What about them?' he said.

'Well, I'm sure you've got lots of friends,' Mum said, gazing at him hopefully.

Billy squirmed in his seat and seemed at a loss as to how to respond. Callie said, 'Billy gets on pretty well with Jack, Sonia's boy, and with another boy called Zeke Byers.'

Billy smiled at her gratefully. Mum said, 'I just wondered if you might have some people coming round later. To join you for the cake.'

She looked quizzically at Callie. Of course – she wanted to be there to sing 'Happy Birthday', and watch Billy blow out the candles on the cake. She didn't understand why she hadn't been invited to stay for that part of the birthday celebration. But she'd find it easier to accept, probably, if they were expecting some of Billy's friends to join them.

Callie held her breath. Was Billy going to mention that Reuben was coming? But he didn't say anything.

'We thought we'd keep today for family only,' Callie explained.

Mum looked at her sharply, almost accusingly, and Callie held her breath, thinking of all the birthdays that Mum had missed. But then Mum just said 'That's nice,' and seemed to consider the subject closed.

'Seeing as it's a special day,' Mum went on, turning to Billy, 'I have a little something for you.'

She leaned down to pick up her handbag, rummaged

through it and pulled out an envelope which she handed over to him. Billy tore the envelope open and took out a card with a picture of a boy playing football on the front. Little did Mum know, Callie thought, that Billy hated football – playing it himself, at any rate – although at school he pretended not to. Inside the card was a handful of crisp ten-pound notes.

'For you to spend on whatever you want,' Mum said.

'Granny, this is amazing,' Billy said. 'Thank you so much.'

He shot a worried look in Callie's direction, as if he didn't quite trust her to let him keep it, but she smiled at him and he looked relieved.

'That's very generous, Mum,' Callie said.

Billy put the money down on the table, got up from his place and went round to give his granny a stiff, awkward little peck on the cheek. She looked delighted.

'I thought, why shouldn't you have a little treat? After all, we've missed out on quite a few birthdays,' she said.

Callie felt reproached, but decided not to show it. There was no way she was going to let this visit turn into another fight, or risk getting into a disagreement that would spoil it for Billy.

Mum helped them clear up, and Callie half thought she might leave after that, but instead she said to Billy, 'I saw you had some board games in the living room. How are you at Scrabble?'

'OK, I guess,' Billy said diffidently, and glanced at Callie for affirmation.

'He's brilliant,' Callie said firmly. 'The memory for words he has is just incredible. It's like he's swallowed the dictionary.'

'Well then, you should be able to give me a run for my money,' Mum said, and before Callie could think of an excuse to stop her Mum had retrieved the game from the living room and was setting it up on the kitchen table. 'Are you going to join us, Callie?'

She could hardly say no, and then she found herself

enjoying it in spite of herself. She'd forgotten how seriously Mum took all games – she was profoundly competitive, and always played to win. But Billy was actually genuinely beating her. (Callie didn't believe for one minute that Mum would let him win.) And Mum also seemed to be enjoying Billy's progress towards victory. 'That's quite a vocabulary you've got there,' she kept saying, as Billy laid down yet another winning combination of letters, or, 'Now, I would never have thought of that.'

And then suddenly it was three o'clock and she remembered she'd told Reuben to come at half-past, assuming her mum would have left by then. She should text him, ask him to come a bit later. It was short notice. He might already be on his way. But anyway, hopefully he would understand.

Her phone was on the kitchen windowsill. She muttered that she just had to check up on something and got up from the table to send him a quick message. But what should she say? How could she put it? She was conscious of both Mum and Billy waiting for her. She couldn't afford to dither. Better just keep it short...

Mum's still here. Would you mind coming at four instead? x

She pressed send. Mum was looking at her sharply. 'I hope you're not cheating,' she said in mock outrage.

'No, of course not,' Callie said. She could feel herself blushing. She pocketed her phone and rejoined the game, and Mum said, 'It's your turn.'

'Oh yes. Course it is,' she said. She stared at the row of letters in front of her, and forced herself to concentrate.

There was no reply from Reuben. She could only hope she hadn't upset him. Finally, at quarter past three, the game was done and Billy was the winner. 'It was just luck,' he said modestly, but Callie could tell he was genuinely pleased with himself.

Mum and Billy shared another brief, slightly awkward hug. Billy thanked Mum again for the money and went off to put it away safely in his room, and then, finally, it was time for Mum to leave.

But when Callie opened the front door to show her out, she saw Reuben.

He was early. Holding the book he'd got for Billy at her suggestion, which he'd wrapped up a little clumsily in brightly striped paper. And she could see exactly what he was feeling: all the power and pain of being close to something that you'd given up on forever, and which was now tantalisingly within reach.

It was a dead giveaway. Mum would know why he was here.

'Hi, Reuben,' she said. 'I guess you didn't get my message.'

He said, 'What message?', and looked from her to Mum and back again.

'It doesn't matter,' she said quickly. 'It's great you could make it. Billy's had a really good day. He just won at Scrabble. Turns out he's a bit of a Scrabble demon...'

She trailed off. What was she saying? What *could* she say, under the circumstances – short of actually telling Mum the truth? Reuben appeared to be equally at a loss. Then he seemed to make an effort to pull himself together and present a polite social mask of friendliness to them both.

'Hi, Janice,' he said.

'Hello, Reuben,' Mum said quietly.

She was taking him in appraisingly, which was somehow even more unnerving than if she'd been straightforwardly hostile or even just shocked to see him there. Reuben shot Callie a questioning look, and Callie knew straight away what it meant: *Did you tell her about me?* She answered with a tiny shake of her head.

'Sorry. I guess it's not a good time,' he said to Callie. 'Would it be better if I came back a bit later?'

'No,' Callie said, just as her mum said, 'Yes, actually, it would.'

Callie sighed. 'OK. Yes, Reuben, maybe just give us ten minutes,' she said, and Reuben nodded mutely and beat a retreat.

As soon as he had gone Mum closed the front door behind him, beckoned Callie into the empty living room and shut that door too. She said in a low voice, 'So what's going on?'

'Nothing,' Callie said. She could feel herself blushing to the roots of her hair.

Mum's eyebrows shot up. 'Nothing?'

'Reuben's a friend. You know that. I've known him for ages.'

Mum rolled her eyes. 'For heaven's sake, Callie... All right, let me put this another way. I don't want to stick my nose in where it's not wanted. But you said you were keeping today for family only. And is he family? For Billy?'

'Yes,' Callie said.

It came out not much louder than a whisper. Her heart was pounding and her head was beginning to ache too. Of all the times to have this conversation...

'Anyone could see the resemblance,' Mum said, but then a painful shadow of doubt crossed her face. She took a deep breath and pressed on.

'I can see that this is upsetting for you, and heaven knows the last thing I want is for everything to get messed up between us again,' she said. 'What's done is done, and it can't be undone, and you know I'm not one for looking back. But just tell me one thing, and then I promise I won't ask you any more questions. You wouldn't let that boy think he's Billy's father if there's a chance he might not be? If the family resemblance might be... because of someone else?'

'Reuben is Billy's father,' Callie said. 'There is no doubt about that. Billy knows, and he wants to meet him, and Reuben knows, and it is really, really important for this to go well. The absolute last thing we need right now is a scene. So Mum, please, for Billy's sake – for all our sakes – for once in your life, don't make one.'

But Mum was speechless. She had gone very pink in the face, and had the stunned look of someone who has just been given the answer to a question that has been troubling her for ages, and now has to decide where to draw the line in asking or not asking for anything more.

'All right,' she said finally. 'Well, then I'd better just wish you luck. Let me know how it goes.'

She threw her arms round Callie in a quick, tight embrace, and then withdrew just as abruptly and opened the door and went off very quickly, without looking back, almost as if she was afraid of jinxing whatever might happen next if she stuck around.

Billy was still in his bedroom, and was presumably oblivious to the meeting that had just happened. Callie started tidying up the kitchen and had just about succeeded in composing herself by the time Reuben returned.

Standing on her doorstep with Billy's gift in his hand, he looked even more nervous than before. 'Sorry about that,' he said. 'Is everything OK...?'

'Yeah. She asked the obvious question, so I told her.'

'You mean about me being Billy's dad,' Reuben said, and looked as pained and guilty as if Mum had just ambushed him and accused him of neglect.

'Yes.' She stepped out and lowered her voice. 'Obviously she already knew it was a possibility. Look, don't worry. I'm pretty sure she won't think any less of you for not having been around, or hold it against you. It'll be me she blames for that. I didn't say anything about what happened with your dad. But I don't think she'll want to spend too much time raking over the past. Look, let's not worry about her now, OK? Billy's really been looking forward to seeing you.'

Reuben brightened a little at that, and she showed him through to the kitchen and went to knock on Billy's bedroom door and said, 'Your dad's here.'

Billy was bent over a notebook on the floor, scribbling. When he looked up he appeared slightly stunned, as if he couldn't quite believe what was happening.

'I promise you, he's more nervous than you are. You've got nothing to worry about,' she said quietly, so that Reuben wouldn't hear, and went back to the kitchen.

Her legs felt weak. She hoped her hands weren't obviously shaking. She fussed round making tea and chattered brightly about nothing – the weather, the neighbours, when she was due to go to hospital and finally have the cast removed. She flicked the kettle on and got a couple of mugs out of the cupboard, then realised she'd already done that and was behaving like someone who was beginning to lose her mind.

Then Billy came shuffling in, a bit awkward, not quite able to meet Reuben's eyes. Everything else in the room seemed to fall away and all she could see was the two of them. She had a strange but powerful sensation of being separate from what was happening, as if she was there as a witness only, and even that was a privilege.

'Hello again,' Billy said, looking down at something on the floor, and then scuffing it with his toe.

'Hi,' Reuben said, and held his hand out for Billy to shake.

And that was how they greeted each other – with a handshake, like a pair of formal acquaintances or two businessmen who might or might not shake again on a deal later.

She felt as if her heart was burning. It was agonising to see how shy and at a loss Billy was, and how Reuben was looking at him, taking in the solid reality, the Billy-ness of him, and to feel the potential for something to grow between them. A kind of love that could be just as strong as the bond between her and Billy. And she had always imagined that nothing else she would ever encounter in her life could be as strong as that.

Callie had spent so long living with the emotions that went with her family being broken, and with separation and parting and loss. She knew how to survive that, and then, with Billy, she'd withdrawn into the small, safe space of this flat, and she'd been happy. Tired, stressed and preoccupied, yes, but happy. But this, the powerful, unpredictable charge that went with two people who were family being put back together – she had not known that this would feel both bright and violent, like the release of a kind of happiness that was strong enough to be dangerous.

'Happy birthday,' Reuben said, and handed over Billy's present.

Billy sat down at the table and opened it with trembling hands. It took him a couple of goes to get into it. 'Thank you,' he said in a small voice, and Callie turned away from the tea she was making just in time to catch the expression on his face, which was one of more than gratitude. She knew straight away that Billy would treasure that book forever because it was the first thing Reuben had bought for him.

She started putting candles on the cake, which she and Billy had chosen in the supermarket the day before – a huge thing smothered in chocolate, enough for a family of ten. Reuben said, 'So what have you been up to today?'

'Oh, not a whole lot. Granny came round and we played Scrabble,' Billy said. 'I won,' he added, sounding slightly pleased with himself, and also still rather surprised.

'You'd probably beat me,' Reuben said. 'I can't remember when I last played, and I think I was pretty rubbish. Are there any other games you like?'

'I'm not too bad on the PlayStation,' Billy said, and blushed again. 'We don't have one, though. I sometimes play on my friend's.'

Would Reuben think less of her for not having managed to get Billy a PlayStation of his own? But he just nodded. She set about lighting the candles and they sang 'Happy Birthday' and Billy blew all the candles out. Both of them applauded, and Billy looked so delighted that just for a moment, it was easy to forget about everything else.

Billy ate one slice of cake, then asked for another. Reuben made his way through a token sliver. She sipped her tea even though it had cooled, and he forgot his.

What do you say to your son when you sit down with him for the first time on his eleventh birthday, and want to win his approval? Reuben was doing his best, and so was Billy, but as the minutes ticked by it became clear that they were both struggling. Reuben was asking Billy questions – about his likes and dislikes, sport, TV, books, subjects at school – and Billy's answers were getting shorter and shorter. Every now and then he glanced anxiously at Callie, as if to check that what he was saying was acceptable.

Maybe knowing that she was watching and listening was making him self-conscious. Was it possible that they needed her not to be there?

'Do you fancy going out for ice cream, Billy?' she said.

He seemed surprised by the suggestion, but nodded. 'It is pretty hot.'

'Why don't you two walk into town then, and get yourselves some? There's the place by the adventure playground next to the river, or you could try that new café that does milkshakes. What do you think?'

Billy and Reuben exchanged glances. They both looked relieved at the prospect of actually having something to do, rather than having to try to find something to talk about.

'OK,' Billy said.

Reuben said, 'What time should we get back for?'

'Oh... five o'clock? Five thirty? Call me if you have any problems. I'll be here.'

'Come on, Mum. What problems would we have?' Billy
said, a level of sass that was quite unusual for him, and went out
to the hallway to put on the new trainers she'd got him for his
birthday.

'I mean it about calling me if you need to,' she said to
Reuben. 'And I'll give you some money for the ice cream.'

'Don't, Callie, honestly,' Reuben said. 'Least I can do. And I
promise you, we'll be fine.'

As she stood by the front door and watched the two of them
set off down the road together she wondered whether she might
have made a mistake. But they looked so right together, somehow, that she couldn't find it in her heart to believe that might
be the case: the tall man and the skinny boy, going along
together at a pace that was neither too fast nor too slow, talking
about something she couldn't hear.

If they hit it off, it wouldn't make the missing years matter
less – but at least it would mean there was a chance of a future
that would be quite different, in which the two of them could
have their own relationship, separate to whatever she and
Reuben might or might not have.

Nobody else was aware of the scene that was playing itself
out – no curious neighbours, no one clocking Reuben and
wondering where he fitted in – and she allowed herself to
carrying on standing there in the doorway and watching them
until they reached the end of the road and turned the corner.
Neither of them looked back.

Reuben sent her a text message at half-past four: *All good.
Eating ice cream by the river*. She was so relieved she wept, and

then felt stupid. As Billy had said, what could possibly have gone wrong?

At quarter past five there was a ring on the doorbell and she went to let them back in. They both seemed bright and fresh, as anyone might who's been out for a stroll on a summer's day. She realised that she would never know exactly what they had talked about, and that if she asked Billy later, he would not have much to say about it – a few stray details, maybe the gist. *It was good*, he might say. *I had vanilla, like always. I really don't like strawberry. I don't know why anybody has it.*

And that would have to do. At some level, Billy would assume that what he and his father had talked about was none of her business. And it had to be that way. She had to give them space. Billy was on the cusp of adolescence now, and that kind of privacy was only going to become more important to him.

If their relationship was going to have a chance to grow, she was going to have to let go. She wasn't going to be able to control it. She shouldn't try.

She could almost have felt sad about it – the prospect of there being a part of Billy's life that, by rights, she was shut out of – but any niggling reservations were swept away by pure relief at the knowledge that the time they'd spent alone together had been a success.

Billy went off into the living room to watch TV, and Reuben said, 'Is it OK if I step into the kitchen a minute? I just want to talk to you about something. It won't take long. I don't want to intrude, and I know you've got to get dinner sorted.'

'OK, sure.'

His expression was serious. It didn't look like good news, and her spirits plummeted. Was this going to be about him and her? She told herself to stay calm, to be reasonable. Like a good mother. Billy was their connection and that was what mattered. Anything else could be set aside.

She said, 'Would you like to stay for dinner? It's just going to be pasta, at Billy's request. It's his favourite. I'm sure there will be enough to go round.'

'No, no, I should get out of your hair, I just wanted to mention—'

He closed the kitchen door behind him. She said, 'What is it?'

'It's just something Billy said, about these friends of his. Jack and Zeke?'

Jack and Zeke? Surely it couldn't be so serious, after all. So why did Reuben look as if it was something he felt duty-bound to raise with her?

'Yeah, what about them? Jack is Sonia and Julian's boy. Henry might have mentioned him? Well anyway, they've spent a fair bit of time together growing up because I'm friends with Sonia, but they're not actually that close any more. Zeke is a new friend. Zeke Byers. He's in Billy's class, too—'

'Yeah, and friends with Jack, I gather,' Reuben said. Then: 'Sorry, didn't mean to interrupt.'

Suddenly she was irritated with him – not a feeling she had anticipated. But he'd just spent an hour or two in Billy's company, and already he thought he could tell her things about her son that she didn't know?

'OK, well, yes, Zeke is friends with Jack too,' she conceded. 'But just lately, he's been getting on really well with Billy. It's actually something good that came out of the accident – his older brother was the one who was riding the bike that hit me, and then Martha, his mum, obviously felt bad – she was actually really nice about it, given that that it was my fault, really. Anyway, she invited me and Billy round, and Billy and Zeke hit it off. I think it'll do wonders for Billy's confidence to have someone he can hang out with on the weekend. Also, it's great for me. Martha's only round the corner from school and she's said she's happy to help out if he needs picking up or looking after, even if it's short notice.

And, you know, that kind of thing, that kind of support, it's like gold dust.'

She stopped, aware that what she was saying might sound reproachful. As if she was complaining about being a single parent. But he didn't seem to have noticed. He said, 'Did Billy say anything to you about a challenge?'

'What do you mean, a challenge?'

'He told me that Zeke and Jack were going to set him some kind of a test to make sure he was cool enough to hang out with them. Zeke told him a bit more about it at school on Friday, apparently. Said they were going to go to the park by the river, and then take it from there. That's all Billy said. When I tried asking him a bit more about it, he clammed up.'

Callie had to suppress another flash of irritation. She reminded herself that Reuben was bound to be overzealous in worrying about Billy. He was new to all this. He had eleven years of missed parental anxiety to make up for.

'Billy's going to Zeke's house next Saturday,' she said, glancing up at the calendar hanging on the wall, where she'd noted it down: *Billy to Zeke, 2pm.* 'But Jack's not going to be there. You can't always take everything kids say literally, you know. Billy probably just meant it *felt* like he had to pass a test. And the kids round here often hang out by the park. As you know. Anyway, thanks for the heads-up, and I'll make sure I ask Billy about it, but honestly, I don't think there's anything to worry about. This friendship with Zeke is a good thing.'

'Is it?'

That was the final straw. She said, 'Reuben, thanks for the advice. I'll bear it in mind. But I honestly don't see Billy spending time with a friend as a reason to be concerned.'

'OK,' he said, holding his hands up in surrender. 'I just thought I should mention it.'

'Sure,' she said. 'I'm sorry I snapped. It's just...'

'Maybe I overstepped the mark. I'm sorry. I don't want to

seem presumptuous. I know you know Billy's friends and I
don't. And I know I have a lot to learn... like, *everything* to learn.
I'm not trying to get ahead of myself, I promise.'

He looked so crestfallen that she instantly felt guilty. 'I
shouldn't have been so touchy.'

He shrugged. 'No, it's fine. You should tell me if I say things
or do things that annoy you, or that cross the line. That way I
can try to do better.'

'OK,' she said. 'I guess we both need to give it time.' She
smiled to reassure him, but it felt stiff and fake. 'By and by I
guess you'll meet Martha, and Zeke, and then you'll see that
there's nothing to worry about. It's probably just because you
don't know them that you feel concerned.'

'You'd be happy for me to meet them?'

'Yes, of course. Why not?'

He hesitated. 'But... how would you introduce me to them?'

'As Billy's dad. Everybody might as well get used to the
idea. My mum. Sonia. Laurel. Everyone. Maybe they'll talk
about it for a week or two, and then it'll be old news. I mean... If
you're happy for me to do that. And if Billy's happy, too.'

'Yes, ask Billy.'

She pressed her hand to her heart and exhaled. 'I mean...
we got through today all right. And it was a big one. I think we
can handle telling other people. Just maybe not all at once.'

'You think it did go all right today? With Billy?'

She looked up and met his eyes, and saw how much he
needed her reassurance. Her irritation faded away.

'Yes,' she said quietly.

They were standing quite close together, and he was still
studying her seriously. Suddenly it occurred to her that he
might be about to kiss her. It felt like a dream, the kind of dream
that you hold onto when you wake up because it's given you the
chance to experience something you barely allow yourself to
imagine in day-to-day life.

But then he took a step back and said, 'Thank you for today, Callie. I mean it. It was really generous of you to invite me.'

'Thank you for coming,' she said.

He hesitated, then appeared to think better of whatever else he might have done or said. 'Well, I'd best leave you in peace.'

He put his head round the living room door to say goodbye and a final happy birthday to Billy, and then she waved him off and he trudged away out of sight and was gone.

If she hadn't spoken sharply to him, if she hadn't been antagonistic, would he...? Was it possible that something might have happened between them?

But there was no use speculating.

She went in to make dinner, and when Billy enthused about Reuben – 'he was so nice, Mum, I'm really glad he came' – she told herself that to be threatened by Reuben's new role in Billy's life would be the most stupid, the most pointlessly self-destructive thing she could do.

She wanted the change Reuben represented. She had invited him into their little family of two. But it seemed that part of her was still scared and defensive, and maybe even willing to try to sabotage whatever the three of them could have.

THIRTY-THREE

BILLY

He had sometimes thought that if he ever found out who his dad was, it would change his life overnight. How it would change would depend, of course, on who his dad was – whether he was really rich, for example, or really famous, or really evil. The only way it wouldn't change was if his dad was a spy, in which case it would probably all be a big secret and everything would carry on as before.

In the end, it turned out that his dad wasn't a spy, or evil, or rich, or famous, but seemed nervous and took him out for ice cream and was nice. And Billy was really happy then, but when he had to go back to school he realised that he was still Billy Swann with the same old problems, stuck with his anxiety and other people mostly ignoring him or sometimes being mean to him. So in a way, his dad might as well have been a spy, because everything else was still pretty much the same.

And then, on Saturday, he went to Zeke's house in the afternoon, and Zeke said it was time to go to the park, and even though Billy didn't want to and would much rather have stayed inside and played *Star Wars* on the PlayStation, he didn't say so. After all, who was he to go against what Zeke and Jack wanted?

Plus it was quite a nice day, so there was no obvious reason to refuse.

His mum had asked him about the challenge Zeke and Jack were going to set him, and he'd pretended not to know what she was talking about, and had made a note not to tell his dad anything like that again. He'd made the mistake of assuming Dad wouldn't say anything to her. Then neither Zeke nor Jack had mentioned the test during the week, and he'd allowed himself to hope that they'd both forgotten.

But then he and Zeke reached the park next to the meadows, and he saw Jack standing there by the flowerbeds, and realised this was what they'd planned all along.

He'd been here on his birthday with his dad, and they'd sat on that bench over there and eaten their ice cream and had talked about *Doctor Who*, and he'd managed to think of things to say and had felt like maybe he wasn't a complete idiot. But that seemed very distant now, as if it had happened to somebody else. Somebody who had a nicer kind of life, and who never had their packed lunch or their PE kit stolen, or their glasses broken.

Jack looked bored, waiting, and Billy's early-warning system immediately started ringing loud and clear.

Bored was dangerous. There was always something menacing about Jack when he had nothing to do, because that was when he started thinking about what he *could* do. He looked like a gangster, skulking around and brooding, dreaming up plans – or as close to it as a kid who lived in a small town like Kettlebridge, and hadn't even started secondary school yet, could get.

As he and Zeke got closer Jack looked up, and Billy said, 'Hey, Jack – what's up?'

He thought he'd said it the way you were meant to, with the right easy-going tone of voice, but Jack just sniggered and said to

Zeke, 'You took your time. We'd better get a move on. It's at least half an hour from here to the railway bridge.'

Jack turned abruptly and started walking towards the exit from the park towards the town centre, where there was a bridge across the river. That wasn't the railway bridge, though. It was a normal road bridge. The railway bridge was quite a way away, from what he could remember. He'd seen it once on a long walk with Mum, if that was the one they meant.

Zeke followed Jack, but Billy stayed where he was, unsure what to do next.

Was this the test? Had they asked him here just so they could walk off and leave him looking stupid? In which case, what was the right thing to do so he could pass?

Then Jack turned back and shouted, 'Come on, dumb-ass, what are you waiting for?'

Somehow, almost of their own accord, Billy's feet started moving. It was amazing the power other people had to make you do things you didn't want to do, and to stop you doing the things you did want to do. He would have thought the very last thing he'd have chosen to do in this situation was to follow Jack and Zeke. But here he was, trudging along behind them like a little mourner at his own funeral.

It occurred to him in a sudden flash of brilliance, as powerful and bright as a bolt of lightning, that he could just say no. But he didn't. He couldn't.

His mum, his newfound dad, his granny, the toys and games and books back home, his daydreams about what he wanted to be in the future – none of that counted for anything, not now. He was with Jack and Zeke, and they were the closest things to friends that he had, and however mean they might be to him, they were better than nothing.

. . .

Nobody took any notice of them. If they'd been hanging out in the precinct, or in one of the play parks meant for younger children, someone might have wondered if they were up to no good, and have come to Billy's rescue by saying something. *'Don't you have homes to go to? Do your mums know where you are?'* That might have been enough. But there was no obvious reason for anyone to challenge them, and nobody did.

The problem was, they didn't look suspicious. They were too young, for a start. They were old enough to be out on their own, but they weren't old enough for it to look as if they were in a gang. They weren't teenagers. They didn't seem like a threat. Zeke was tall for his age and Jack was strong and fit, but they were only in year six, so that didn't mean all that much, and they were obviously all dressed in clothes that had been chosen for them by their mums.

They looked as if they were out for a healthy walk, which was what Zeke had told his mum they were going to do. Grown-ups encouraged kids to do this all the time – to get out into the fresh air, explore the countryside. You just maybe weren't meant to do whatever Zeke and Jack had in mind for him at the end of it.

They crossed the bridge over the river in the town centre and started making their way along the riverbank on the far side. The few people they did see were all heading in the other direction, going into town: a couple of men in old anoraks who looked as if they'd come from one of the narrowboats moored next to the path and were on their way to find a pub, a breathless jogger and a dog walker or two. Nobody said anything, and it felt as if they had been going for a long time, getting deeper and deeper into the countryside.

He told himself they weren't really all that far out. The time would have probably gone by in a flash if he'd been safely back at home with his copies of 2000 *AD*, or watching old episodes of *Doctor Who*, or reading the spy book his dad had given him.

When they came to the lock, they carried on walking upstream along the river, and the fields alongside gave way to woods. The other riverbank was lined with trees too. He definitely remembered walking there with Mum, though he'd never come this far on this side of the river.

His spirits began to sink. He knew where he was and how to get back home – all you had to do was follow the river – but the woods next to them and on the other side of the water made him feel lost. Anything could happen to you in the woods, and nobody would hear or see or come to rescue you, or even find you afterwards.

The further upstream they walked, the fewer passers-by they saw. Gradually Billy's hopes faded away till he was left with nothing to hold onto other than the faint possibility that whatever they had in mind for him, it might not actually be that bad. It certainly seemed as if they were going to make sure there weren't any witnesses.

It had been ridiculous to think anybody would save him, anyway. Whatever Jack and Zeke came up with, he was just going to have to go through with it. Otherwise his life just wouldn't be worth living.

If he hadn't been with Zeke and Jack – if he'd been with his mum or dad, or maybe even both of them – he might actually have quite enjoyed the walk. It was beautiful, especially on a sunny afternoon, and he could see that and appreciate it even though he was frightened. The river was broad here, cutting through the quiet woods in big, slow curves, and it was quite high, because they'd had a fair bit of rain lately, which gave you the feeling of walking next to something big and powerful and unstoppable, like time itself.

He'd been apprehensive to start with about how Zeke and Jack weren't really talking, but now he was glad of it. Apart from the sound of rushing water and the rustling of the breeze in the leaves, it was quiet.

Then the towpath narrowed and separated out from the river, swinging out around a dense patch of woodland, which was to their left, with fields of wheat to their right. They came to a fork in the path and he saw that there was another path cutting across the fields, heading back in the direction of the town.

Was this his chance to slip away and make a run for it? He'd fallen a little way behind, and even though Zeke and Jack were both faster than him, he'd have a head start. And even if they caught him, they couldn't drag him along with them unless he actually chose to go. Could they?

Then Zeke glanced back over his shoulder and Billy knew his chance to escape had passed.

He ducked down to pretend to retie his laces to cover up his hesitation. He was wearing his good trainers, the expensive ones that Mum had got for his birthday, and it made him feel sad to see them because he'd only asked for them so that he would fit in with everybody else. But however much they'd cost, the trainers had not been enough to do the trick, because why else would this be happening to him? Jack and Zeke were suspicious of him. They thought there was something wrong with him, and that was why they wanted to put him to the test.

When he straightened up Zeke was standing close enough to reach out and grab him and was watching him like a guard. He could see that Jack had stopped up ahead and was waiting for Zeke to sort out whatever had caused the delay, as if Billy was a prisoner or captive who needed to be kept in line.

'You want to watch you don't trip,' Zeke said scornfully, and Billy remembered the various times Jack had tripped him up, all just as a joke, of course, and felt himself blushing. He wished he didn't blush so much. It was the worst habit, other than crying, which he mostly managed not to do. But at least crying could sometimes be noble. Blushing never was. A spy might cry, under really extreme, painful circumstances, but would never, ever blush.

'Guess we'd better get a move on,' Billy said, 'or your mum will wonder where we've got to.'

'She won't. Anyway, we're nearly there,' Zeke said, and started walking again.

Billy took one last look at the path back across the fields, and then resigned himself and sped up to catch up with his friends.

A few minutes later the path they were on led them right into the woods. Here there was barely space to walk single file, and the trees were all tangled up with thick, impenetrable-looking undergrowth. Nettles flicked his legs and brambles snagged on his jeans as if trying to hold him back. The silence was different here, was closed-in somehow, as if they were in a room that someone had shut the door to, and in between the crunch and rustle of their movements, the air was thick with the small sounds of other kinds of life – leaves, birds, the small anonymous movements of creatures they couldn't see.

Billy found himself thinking about his mum, who had absolutely no idea where he was right now. He knew exactly what she'd tell him to do – to stop, turn round, and walk straight home. And he knew that he couldn't do it. He pushed the thought of her right to the back of his mind, along with the dread of being lost and alone in the woods, and kept on walking.

A few minutes later they emerged from the woods and the path rejoined the river, with a field on their right rising up towards a tall hill with a ruined barn and a spooky-looking old farmhouse on top of it. There were no other houses in sight, and no people, just trees on the far side of the river, and on their side, the field and the higher ground with the farmhouse looking down from it.

The field was marshy-looking, with pools of rainwater at the foot of the hill, and he wondered if that might be the challenge, to leave the path and walk across it. Which would be unpleasant, certainly, because his jeans would get soggy and dirty and his new trainers would get wet, and they'd laugh at him for squelching on the way home. And Mum would be angry and upset. But at least it probably wouldn't be too hard. If that was all there was to it, he'd be able to pass.

Although what if the boggy field was actually quicksand? You could get stuck in quicksand, and then you had to keep very still until someone threw you a rope and pulled you out, because struggling just made it worse. He wasn't sure if they had any quicksand in Oxfordshire, but maybe marshes were a little bit the same and there wasn't any rope to hand. Also, Jack and Zeke probably wouldn't throw it to him even if there was.

They rounded a curve in the river and he saw the railway bridge ahead of him, carrying the tracks over the water to the higher ground on his right. They wouldn't be able to go much further. Whatever was going to happen, however they were going to test him, it would happen soon.

How could he, who was so interested in spying, have walked into what was obviously a trap? There was no way out ahead, just the railway line. To his left there was the deep water of the broad river, and to his right was the marsh. He was a very small fly caught in a pincer movement by two very big spiders, and even though he was still walking, he felt as paralysed as if they'd already bound him up and poisoned him.

It was down to him to save himself, and that was something he had absolutely no idea how to do. The only thing he could think of, and it still seemed to be the best plan under the circumstances, was to do exactly what they said.

Jack was still in front, and when he reached the patch of woodland next to the bridge he turned away from the river and started making his way up the hill. When Billy got there he saw there was no other choice. The path swung round sharply to the right and that was where it led, with a spiky metal fence running along one side of it. On the other side of the fence was a steep drop to the tracks, which led back to the railway bridge across the river.

He kept on going, climbing the hill. At the top of it, past the old barn and the farmhouse, the high fields continued ahead of them as far as he could see.

There were no roads, no houses, not even any cows or sheep – just an isolated cluster of trees some way to his right. To his left, the land fell away down to the tracks and then rose again on the other side. The metal fence separating the path from the drop to the tracks had come to an end, as if nobody ever came this way so there was no longer any need for it, or perhaps because the drop was more gradual here, with the tracks running along the bottom of a V-shaped valley rather than a deep cutting. If you tripped and fell here you probably wouldn't tumble right the way down onto the tracks, but might have a chance to save yourself.

Jack turned and gestured to him to hurry up, and he sped up a little although he was beginning to feel quite tired and the wind seemed to have picked up and was against them, making it difficult to hear what anybody said. Maybe the wind was stronger up here because it was so exposed.

Ahead of him, Jack and Zeke had come to a standstill and were standing together, looking down at the railway tracks. He caught up with them and then he stopped too and understood why Zeke had brought him here.

A series of steps went right down from beneath their feet to some kind of wooden walkway across the tracks. Beyond the walkway there was another series of steps climbing up the embankment on the other side. Except they weren't really steps, not as such, more a series of gravelled ledges.

There wasn't any obvious sign forbidding you from going down to the tracks. There were even steps there to help you do it, so it must be all right. But still, it looked very steep and he didn't much like heights. Especially not with the wind buffeting him like this.

He felt himself swaying slightly and felt suddenly dizzy, as if he might be about to collapse or fall. He closed his eyes and clenched his fists. When you were a spy under torture you were meant to break down time into tiny moments and not think about the future, because if the pain and suffering was just for an instant, then you would be able to tell yourself you could bear it. He tried this now. When he opened his eyes Jack was smiling at him.

'It's easy,' he said. 'I've done it before. We both have. You just go down, cross over and go up the other side.'

'OK,' Billy said.

He was cold, but he was sweating slightly in spite of the wind, and even though it wasn't especially warm that day. He hoped Jack and Zeke hadn't noticed.

'Unless you don't want to go any further,' Zeke said.

'I'm fine with it,' Billy said.

Jack's grin widened a little. 'We wouldn't want to force you. It has to be your choice, you know? You'll have to do it twice. There and back again. Otherwise you'll be stuck on the other side. But you'll be all right so long as you keep your nerve.' His grin got wider still. He was really enjoying it. 'And don't trip.'

He turned away and started going down the steps. Zeke gave Billy a hard, impersonal stare that was almost an accusation, as if to say *I have to do this because of you*. Then he, too, began making his way down.

Billy closed his eyes again. He thought of his mum and what she might be doing now – sorting out the laundry, or checking her bank statement, or vacuuming the flat. She was so far away. Well, actually it probably wasn't that far, not if you looked at it on a map, but it might as well be the other side of the world.

He thought of Reuben, too, and of something Reuben had said to him when they went out to get the ice cream: *If someone bullies you, you don't have to pretend to like them. In the end, it doesn't help.*

Easy for him to say, though, being a grown-up. He probably didn't know anything about being bullied. And Zeke and Jack weren't bullies, anyway. They were his friends.

When Billy opened his eyes again Zeke was already halfway down. He'd better get a move on. If he took it moment by moment, it would be over in no time at all.

He forced himself down onto the first of the steps. It felt like plunging forward into quicksand, or off the edge of a cliff, but his feet found solid ground and he moved down to the next step and realised that terror in itself would not be enough to stop him.

Keep your nerve, Jack had said.

What was it Mum had said about her accident? *It happened because I was rushing. Because I didn't look where I was going.* She'd said this several times, wanting him to take it in so that he could avoid getting hurt himself. But her advice was no help to him now, any more than his dad's had been. He just wanted this to be over as quickly as possible.

Somehow, he made it down to the bottom of the steps, where Zeke and Jack were waiting for him. He said, 'Are the rails live?'

Zeke said, 'What do you mean, are they alive?'

'I mean, do they have electricity in them?'

'There's steps and a way across,' Jack said. 'It's obviously safe.' He sniggered. 'Mind you though, when we did it before, I was pretty careful not to step on the rails. But if you want to try it out, be my guest.'

'I don't want to do it,' Billy said, folding his arms.

'You have to,' Jack said. 'We came all this way so you could do it. If you don't do it, you can't hang out with us.'

'I don't care. I'm not doing it.'

'It's too late to back out now,' Jack said, and darted forward and gave him a big, brutal shove.

Billy couldn't save himself. He lost his balance, pitched forward and fell. His ankle twisted under him and he smashed down onto the rubble strewn at the edge of the tracks. For a moment he was conscious only of the pain of the impact, and then he looked up and saw Zeke and Jack's shocked faces above him, and heard someone shouting. Someone else. A man.

And then he heard the whistle of a train, and managed to turn his head just in time to see it thundering towards him.

THIRTY-FOUR

REUBEN

'Get back, both of you! Get right back out of the way!'

Stupid kids! What the hell did they think they were doing? Reuben raced down the steps as fast as he could, his feet scrabbling and sliding underneath him, and shoved his way past them.

Billy was frozen as if in shock, or pain, or maybe the grip of a panic attack. Then he began feebly trying to move, but it was obvious that he'd hurt himself – a twisted ankle, maybe, or it might even be broken – and he was struggling to put distance between himself and the tracks. He was a couple of feet away, but still, much too close to be safe – and it looked like a fast train hurtling towards them. Even if the driver saw them he might not be able to stop in time. The weight and speed of the train would suck Billy right underneath it, and he'd be battered and crushed and flung aside like meat in a grinder...

'OK, Billy, I've got you.'

He got his arms hooked under Billy's armpits and half-dragged him, half-carried him backwards, further from the tracks. It was all just a question of time and distance and speed. And will. His will. He had to make this come out right, for Billy to be safe, for the train to rattle past harmlessly while they looked on from above.

One, two, three, four, five steps. Billy was bumping against the rough ground, pushing back against it, trying to help. The noise of the train was so loud now it was like an explosion waiting to happen. Reuben closed his eyes and pulled and dragged his child with all his strength. He thought, *I don't care what happens to me. But Billy has to live. He has to. I would do anything to stop him being hurt. I would a million times rather die in his place...*

And then he opened his eyes and he was at the top of the embankment with Billy in his arms. The train was below them and had passed them, and was rattling furiously and harmlessly into the distance. And then it was out of sight, and it was quiet again, apart from the sound of crying.

The taller of the two kids who had been tormenting Billy – that must be Zeke, because the other one had a bit of a look of Sonia – was staring at Reuben and Billy in astonishment. Jack – Sonia and Julian's kid – was bawling his eyes out. As well he might.

Zeke said, 'Who are you?'

Billy's glasses had gone, lost somewhere when he fell. His eyelids were fluttering. He'd turned very pale, and there was dirt and blood on his face. His skin was cool and clammy to the touch, but he was still breathing. Shock. It had to be. Reuben yanked at the buttons on the shirt he was wearing and pulled it off over his head, and wrapped it round Billy's torso and cradled him to warm him.

'I'm Billy's dad,' he said to Zeke. 'And if you do anything like that stunt you just pulled ever again, to anyone, I'm going to come and find you and make sure you regret it.'

Perhaps he was imagining it, but he thought Billy heard him. Billy's eyes widened and focused, and he looked up at Reuben and gave him just the faintest hint of a smile.

THIRTY-FIVE

CALLIE

She decided to spend the afternoon while Billy was round at the Byers' place working in the garden. It was always neglected, always last on the list – she never seemed to have time for it. As she weeded, a slow and laborious process one-handed, she remembered Mrs Jancett and the look she'd given her that foggy morning after Sonia's wedding, when she'd been out tending to her garden and had seen Callie coming back from the Tallis house.

Perhaps the old lady had watched all sorts of other comings and goings to that house over the years – maybe she'd spotted Donna visiting at times when Reuben wasn't there, and had speculated about that, too. Callie wondered what she would think as and when Mum mentioned to her that, after all this time, it turned out Reuben was Billy's father – as she almost certainly would, sooner or later.

And what about Mr Tallis? What would *he* think? He was Billy's grandfather, a reflection that had always turned her stomach. If he was becoming more confused, as Reuben had said, would he even take it in? Or would he have lost his inhibitions enough to say terrible things about her and Billy to

Reuben, and Theresa, and Mrs Jancett, and anyone else who would listen?

She shoved the thought of Mr Tallis aside and concentrated on digging up mare's tail weeds from the borders. It was only when she went inside for a glass of water and checked her phone that she realised Reuben had been trying to reach her.

He'd rung a couple of times, starting about half-an-hour ago. He'd sent her a message, too, about five minutes earlier: *Call me. It's about Billy. We're at Kettlebridge hospital. Don't panic, he's OK, but you should come ASAP.*

What on earth had Reuben done? Had he gone and collected Billy from the Byers' place, and taken him off somewhere where Billy had ended up getting hurt? But why would he have done that?

He'd certainly known where Billy was going to be that afternoon. Though how would he have known where the Byers' house was?

This was a man who'd walked out on her, who'd thought the worst of her, and who'd avoided her and Billy for years, even though he knew Billy might be his. Maybe even *because* he knew Billy might be his. So why had she thought it was safe to trust him?

Maybe the fact that she still had some kind of stupid deluded crush on Reuben had blinded her to his shortcomings, to his unreliability and unpredictability...

She called him straightaway and the call went straight through to voicemail, so she rang a taxi and went round shutting up the house. She was in a daze and had no idea whether she was remembering to do everything that was necessary. Fortunately the taxi came quickly and the traffic wasn't too bad, but the ten-minute journey across town seemed to take forever and she still couldn't get through to Reuben.

At least Billy was in the little local hospital in Kettlebridge, and hadn't been rushed to the big accident and emergency unit in Oxford. That meant it wasn't critical. And Reuben had said he was OK. Though obviously he wasn't really OK, or he wouldn't be in hospital at all.

This was the worst thing, the absolute worst thing imaginable – for something to be wrong with Billy. If Reuben had anything to do with it, if it was his fault, she would never, ever forgive him...

Finally the taxi pulled up in the crowded hospital car park and she thrust some cash at the driver and got out before he'd had a chance to offer her change. She ran into the reception area and was conscious of the gloomy faces of people who had been waiting for a long time, turning towards her with a mixture of surprise, sympathy for her obvious panic, and faint resentment at the possibility that she might expect to be seen before them.

'Excuse me,' she said to the woman behind the glass screen in front of the reception desk, 'but my son's here... Billy Swann... I got a phone call, I don't know what's happened to him... He must have come in about half an hour ago. No, a bit more.'

The woman looked at her blankly. Then she said, 'Take a seat. I'll be with you in a moment.' Painfully slowly, she got up and disappeared through a door at the back of the reception office that presumably connected through to the treatment area where Billy was.

Callie wanted to hammer on the glass, to smash it and storm through, but instead she took a seat, like everybody else. Her breathing was shallow and fast and her heartbeat was so loud she was sure everybody else must be able to hear it. All she could think was *Let him be OK. Let him be OK*, the words tumbling over each other again and again.

Then the woman who'd been behind the reception desk came out and led her through onto the ward. She had a vague impression of beds in bays and patients and busy medical people going to and fro, but there was only one person who she really saw and that was Billy, who was sitting up with one leg stretched out and propped up in front of him, and who turned as she came in and smiled at her.

He looked pale, his glasses were missing, and he had a dressing on his arm and another on his chin and a bandage on one ankle. But he was conscious. And sitting up. And he was smiling. The relief hit her like a wave and pushed her forwards towards him.

'Billy! My goodness – what on earth happened? Are you OK?'

'I'm fine, Mum. Just a few scratches and a sprained ankle. It isn't even broken.' He beamed at Reuben, who was standing just behind him. 'Thanks to Dad.'

She swung round to face Reuben. He was smiling too, but he looked anxious.

'It was just a hunch,' he said. 'After what Billy told me about them planning to go down to the park with him and set him some kind of test. I thought it wouldn't hurt to see if I could keep an eye on things, so I went down the park around the time I thought they'd be there. I mean, I kept my distance. I didn't want to intrude or anything. I know it sounds weird. I just... I guess I just felt like I ought to be there.'

'Dad, you don't need to say it like that. You don't need to apologise. You were totally right. If you hadn't been there, who knows what might have happened? I could have been totally splatted,' Billy said cheerfully.

'There's probably going to be some follow-up, I'm afraid,' Reuben said, still apologetic. 'You should talk to the police. It ought to be reported. I dialled 999 but they said it was going to be a while before they could get someone out there, and Billy could just about walk—'

'With a bit of help,' Billy said proudly. 'Dad virtually had to carry me.'

'So I got him to my car and brought him in,' Reuben went on. 'The others had scarpered by then.'

'The others?'

Reuben and Billy exchanged glances. 'Zeke and Jack,' Billy said. 'My so-called friends.' He rolled his eyes. 'Nice of them to stick around, huh.'

'You're being sarcastic,' Callie said blankly. She'd never known Billy be sarcastic before.

'Well, yeah,' Billy said. 'Don't look so worried, Mum. It's all over now. It's all OK. There's just going to be the bit with the police to sort out.' He looked appealingly up at Reuben. 'But I don't think I should be in too much trouble. I wouldn't even have been near the railway line if Jack hadn't pushed me.'

'The railway line...'

All the blood seemed to have rushed away from her brain and her head was ringing. She realised she was about to faint. Reuben was suddenly beside her, and had magicked up a chair from somewhere. 'Sit down, Callie. Here, put your head down. You'll feel better in a minute. Honestly, you'll be OK.'

She did as he said, and rested her head on her knees. The ringing began to fade. This had all happened somewhere before... this disorientation, this coming to the edge of losing consciousness...

The sofa in the Tallises' living room, with Mr Tallis looking on. The piano refrain, a tune she had tried and failed to play. She had seen too late what was about to happen. And her lipstick had smudged, and there had been flowers on the floor when she left...

But no, she was in the hospital, a public place, with her eleven-year-old son and his father and assorted medical staff and patients. She was safe from everything apart from her memories. Billy needed her, which meant she had to pull herself together. And Reuben was nothing like his dad.

Someone else came over and said to Reuben, 'Is this Mum?'

– the way medical professionals always did if she saw them for anything to do with Billy, even if they knew her first name.

'It is,' Reuben said. 'She'll be OK in a minute. It's obviously been a bit of a shock.'

'*I* nearly fainted when it happened, too,' Billy said triumphantly.

She straightened up. There was somebody in medical scrubs – the person who'd asked if she was Mum – waiting to speak to her. Billy was still smiling. She turned to Reuben, who was standing by at a respectful distance.

'You tried to warn me, and I didn't believe you,' she said. 'So you followed them.'

He nodded. She put her hand on her heart. 'Thank you,' she said.

She didn't want to cry but felt as if she was about to. There was a sudden shine in his eyes too. She realised he hadn't expected thanks, or at least not straightaway. That he'd anticipated she might be angry with him for what he'd taken it upon himself to do.

Then Billy said, 'Mum, I think the doctor wants you,' and she got to her feet and gathered up all her energy and focused it on being Mum.

THIRTY-SIX

A few days after Billy's fall by the railway line she went into the fracture clinic at the hospital in Oxford and finally had the cast removed from her arm. She wasn't worried about making it back home for school pick-up because she knew Reuben had collected Billy and taken him back to her flat – which was just as well because she ended up spending ages on the bus in dreadful traffic, and didn't get home till four.

Billy and Reuben were both on the sofa, watching TV, and they looked round at the same time as she came in. She spread out her arms and wiggled her fingers and said, 'Ta-dah! Back to normal, or as good as.'

A huge grin spread across Billy's face. 'Well, I think it's my turn to be the invalid now.'

'I guess it is,' she agreed, though actually, Billy had made a startlingly good recovery. Reuben had driven them back from Kettlebridge hospital following the incident at the tracks, and he had been quiet and pale that evening, but the next day Mum had visited with chocolates and made a fuss of him, which seemed to revive him. Callie had wondered how he would cope with school on Monday, but he'd been determined to go. 'After all, it's nearly the end of term and then we'll all be leaving,' he had told her. 'Besides, I'm OK. I really am.'

Thankfully, he'd come out in good spirits at the end of the day, and she'd noticed him attracting a few sympathetic glances from other mums in the playground. It seemed word had got round. She could only imagine that Reuben would also have attracted some friendly attention when he showed up to collect Billy while she was at the hospital having her cast removed.

She hadn't heard from Sonia, or Martha, since the accident, and hadn't crossed paths with them – perhaps they were avoiding her – but Billy had brought home apology letters from both Zeke and Jack in his schoolbag, which she'd been barely able to bring herself to read. Billy, by way of contrast, had been very laid-back: 'I think it was just something the teacher told them they had to do,' he'd said.

In the end, she'd glanced through them, barely taking in the words – *I'm sorry I pushed you,* Jack had written, and Zeke had said, *I'm sorry we were mean to you, and said you had to do a dare to be our friend.* Their childish handwriting didn't make her feel any more forgiving – it just made her feel all the more angry and frightened to realise that these kids could have got Billy killed. She had tucked the letters away somewhere deep in her filing system, and told herself to be grateful that Billy had come through his ordeal apparently psychologically unscathed.

There was to be some kind of official follow-up to what had happened at the railway tracks – a safeguarding enquiry involving different agencies, with British Transport Police involved. It was possible that some changes would be made to the crossing and the approach to it as a result – apparently it had already been flagged up as potentially risky – and she supposed that would be a good thing. Sonia and Martha were probably upset and anxious about their sons being involved in the incident and the enquiry to follow. But she couldn't bring herself to spare much sympathy for them. As long as Billy was well and in good spirits, and Zeke and Jack never put any other kid on the spot like that again, that was all she really cared about.

She flexed her healed arm, and Billy applauded. 'You can't do anything else to yourself, you know,' he told her. 'Not for years and years. That's your accident allowance all used up.'

'It definitely is,' she agreed, and suppressed the thought of the forthcoming appointment with the neurologist. She kept thinking she'd seen the back of the headaches, and then another one would kick in and she could never be sure whether it was triggered by stress or was completely random. After all, what day in her life was ever completely free of stress?

'Congratulations,' Reuben said, looking just as pleased as Billy.

'There's something for you in the kitchen,' Billy added.

'Is there?'

She went in to find a sweet-scented pink rose in a little white wicker planter standing on the kitchen table, next to a box of chocolates and a couple of envelopes. The first envelope was addressed in Billy's writing and inside it there was a card with a cartoon picture of a bandaged-up person on the front. Billy had crossed out the message 'Get Well Soon' and had written 'Stay Well' next to it. The second card was from Reuben. It had flowers on the front, and inside it just said, *Take care of yourself.* He'd signed it with a kiss.

She arranged the cards next to each other on the table and looked up as Reuben came in.

'I thought you might be able to plant the rose in the garden later,' he said.

'I'll definitely try.' She held up both her hands. 'Bit easier now.'

'I spent so long choosing it, one of the shop assistants took pity on me and came over to offer advice.'

'It's lovely.'

She looked up at him. Her fingertips tingled. It seemed natural, almost inevitable, that he might put his arms round her. But instead he said, 'I let Billy have a packet of crisps. I hope you don't mind.'

'No, that's fine.'

'Well... I should get going. I have a rental place to look at. I said I'd call round about five.'

'Oh, right.' He was still staying at his father's house. She knew that he was planning to find somewhere else, but this was the first she'd heard of him actually viewing anywhere. 'You didn't say you had an appointment.'

'I didn't want you to feel under pressure to get back from the hospital. I could have cancelled. I'm not that sure about it, to be honest. But anyway, it's worth a look.' He dived in and pecked her on the cheek, moving as awkwardly and self-consciously as if she still had her arm in a cast and he was taking pains not to knock her arm or get too close. 'I'll let you know.'

'Yes, do that. Reuben...'

He was already heading back towards the living room to say goodbye to Billy. 'Yes?'

'It doesn't matter. It'll keep,' she said. 'Yes, let me know how it goes with the flat.'

'Will do. I'll let myself out.'

After he'd gone she watered the rose and reflected that having him around was as strange as suddenly having her other arm back in use, thin and grey-looking after the weeks in the cast, familiar and unfamiliar at the same time.

The following Saturday, exactly one week after Billy's trip to the railway line, he was sitting on the sofa next to Reuben again, watching an old episode of *Doctor Who*, when the doorbell rang. Callie went to answer it, and there was Sonia.

She looked a mess. It was pouring with rain, and even the

short walk from where she'd parked to Callie's door had been enough to soak her, but it was obvious that there was more to the state she was in than the weather. Her wet hair was in disarray and her eyes were rimmed with pink as if she'd just been crying. She was clutching a large cardboard box, spattered with damp, which looked as if it had been professionally gift-wrapped in *Star Wars* paper and tied up with a silver bow.

'I'm so glad I caught you. I thought you might be out,' Sonia said. 'This is for Billy.' She thrust the present at Callie, who was so taken aback she took hold of it.

The box was on the heavy side, and it seemed like it probably contained something substantial. Callie said, 'Sonia... what is it?'

'It's a PlayStation,' Sonia said. 'And I want you to know that Jack contributed to it with his own pocket money. We insisted.'

'Oh, Sonia. You shouldn't have. I mean, it's very kind of you, but we've all clubbed together to get him one – me and Mum and Reuben – and it's meant to be arriving next week. Do you think you'll be able to return this?'

Sonia flushed and took the box back. She looked completely at a loss. 'I feel like such a fool,' she said. 'I should have checked with you. It didn't occur to me you might have got one. I just wanted to do something nice for Billy, after what happened.'

For a split second Callie imagined their roles were reversed. How would she feel in Sonia's shoes, as the friend on the doorstep in the pouring rain, holding a gift that had just been rejected?

'Look, why don't you stick it in the boot of your car and then come in and have a cup of tea? If you've got a minute.'

Sonia hesitated. 'That's nice of you,' she said. 'Yes, that would be lovely, if you're sure.'

'I'm sure. Go on, get rid of that box and then come in out of the rain.'

As Sonia came back into the flat she pushed open the living

room door and said, 'Sonia's here, by the way.' Reuben's eyebrows shot up, but he didn't say anything. Billy glanced briefly away from the screen in Callie's direction and frowned as if annoyed at the interruption, but didn't seem to be bothered otherwise. It did look as if a fairly crucial scene was under way, with Doctor Who poised to save the world yet again, so it wasn't surprising that he didn't want to be disturbed.

'Best leave them to it,' Callie said, closing the living room door. 'Come on through to the kitchen.'

Sonia followed her in and said, 'If you don't mind me asking – who was there with Billy?'

'Oh. Reuben,' Callie said, and filled the kettle.

'Nice to see you with the cast off,' Sonia commented. 'So you're all better now, then? That must be a relief.'

'Definitely,' Callie said, looking down with pleasure and flexing her hands.

'And you've been seeing a bit more of Reuben,' Sonia went on.

Callie folded her arms. She hadn't quite got used to being able to do this again yet. 'Yes.'

'And you're all getting on.'

'Mm-hm.' Was there any reason to be shy about telling Sonia more? After everything that had happened in the last few weeks, surely this should be easy. 'He's Billy's dad. As you might have guessed,' she said, and waited for Sonia to ask why she hadn't said so before, or, even worse, if she was really sure.

But Sonia just looked slightly confused and nodded.

'Right,' she said. There was a short, awkward silence, and then Sonia went on: 'Well, look, you're being very nice about what happened at the railway tracks. I'm not sure whether I'd be quite so generous in your shoes. I'm not sure that I'd even be talking to me.'

'I'm not going to hold it against you, if that's what you're worrying about,' Callie said, with a slight effort. Did she really feel so forgiving? Perhaps if she behaved as if she was, she would feel it in the end. 'Billy's OK, and that's what matters.'

'And he got the letter Jack wrote?'

'Yeah. He got the letter. I think it helped. But to be honest, I think he just wants to put it all behind him.'

'Jack does understand how much worse it could have been,' Sonia said. 'He's very lucky that he's not going to be kicked out of school.' She shuddered. 'He did a terrible, stupid thing. I still can't quite believe what he did. And it could have been so much worse. What could have happened just doesn't bear thinking about.'

Callie poured water from the kettle into a couple of mugs, added milk, fished the teabags out. All of this was magnificently easy to do. She wondered how long it would be until she took being free of the cast for granted.

'Look, at the end of the day, there's only so much time you can spend worrying about might-have-beens,' she said. 'I could have been hurt worse when I walked out in front of Ethan Byers' bicycle, and Billy could have died right there beside the tracks. But we're still here. We've been lucky. All of us. It's really made me appreciate how much of life is luck, and how often we're just a hair's breadth away from disaster. Life is a sequence of near misses, isn't it? But anyway, I'm just glad that Reuben decided to follow the boys that day. He said he was worried that I'd be absolutely furious if I found out, but when he saw which way they were going he guessed they might be heading for the railway tracks and decided to carry on.'

'Yes, thank goodness for Reuben,' Sonia said. Callie passed Sonia her tea, and Sonia blew absent-mindedly on it to cool it and set it down on the worktop. She said, 'I take it you're both going to be seeing more of him.'

'Yeah. He's moving back to the area. He's looking for a place to rent at the moment.'

Sonia frowned slightly. 'I hope this isn't out of order... obviously you don't have to say... but are you two an item? I mean, you look... I don't know... pretty happy.' Her gaze wandered across to the rose Reuben had got Callie, which was in a sunny spot on the windowsill and was already pushing out new stems and blooms.

'We're friends,' Callie said firmly. 'I think that's enough to be going on with.'

Sonia gave Callie the long, calculating look that one woman gives another when she has some idea of what she's not being told, then changed the subject. 'You know, you're less angry with me about what happened than either Julian or Martha. Both of them seem to think it's my fault.'

'Really? How on earth did they figure that out?'

'Oh, Martha thinks Jack must have been a bad influence on Zeke, because Zeke would never come up with something like that on his own, et cetera et cetera. She's actually going to try and make a last-ditch attempt to change Zeke's secondary school so they're at different places. And Julian's absolutely furious with me.'

'Why?'

Sonia's face twitched as if she was trying to keep tears at bay. '"Absent without leave"' was the phrase he used. One of them. One of the more polite phrases, actually.'

Callie was at a loss. 'But you haven't been absent, so what's he getting at?'

'Well, I suppose I have been distracted,' Sonia said. 'It's not entirely unfair, as an accusation.'

Callie stared at her friend. She was beginning to feel disorientated, as if the Sonia she knew had been stolen and replaced by a stranger who wasn't doing a great job of passing herself off as the original.

'I don't understand,' she said. 'You're a mum, and mums are always distracted, aren't they? Or some of the time, at any rate. You're no more distracted than anybody else, surely.'

'I've been having an affair with Henry,' Sonia blurted out and Callie promptly dropped her mug on the floor, splashing tea and scattering bits of broken china from one side of the kitchen to the other.

'Henry? You mean Laurel's Henry?'

She couldn't begin to imagine it. Henry the lounge lizard, with his watchful eyes and knack for making any suit look scruffy, and arty, craft-loving, cake-baking supermum Sonia, a woman who could wear linen without it creasing, and whose life seemed as immaculate as her house?

'Yes, Laurel's Henry,' Sonia said, with a grimace. 'Though sometimes he was *my* Henry.' And then she began to cry.

'Oh, Sonia...' Callie was torn between sympathy and disbelief. Could it really be possible that Sonia, who not so very long ago had been lecturing her on how to manage her life, had been having an affair with Laurel's husband? A small part of her was suddenly angry – not only because Sonia had betrayed their friend, though she was shocked by that aspect of it, but because of the hypocrisy that had enabled Sonia to behave as if her family was in perfect, superior order while carrying on such a major deception.

But then the urge to offer comfort won through. She rummaged in a cupboard for a box of tissues and handed them over, and said, 'I guess it's over?'

Sonia blew her nose and sniffled and nodded. 'It is now,' she said, and started crying again.

Any minute now Reuben was going to come in and ask what on earth was going on. Callie reached out and pulled Sonia into an awkward, tear-damp embrace. 'It'll be all right,' she said into Sonia's curly hair. 'Whatever happens, you'll come through it.'

Sonia pulled away first, and reached for the box of tissues again. 'I've often wondered how you would react if I told you,' she said. 'I have to say, Callie, there were times when I envied you. I know things have been really hard for you. But it seemed so straightforward and simple in comparison. Just having yourself and Billy to worry about, I mean. And at least you didn't have anything to feel guilty about.'

'I don't know about that,' Callie said, and fished an old newspaper out of the recycling bin to use to wrap up the pieces of the mug she'd smashed. 'But Sonia,' she went on, looking up from the floor where she was down on her knees collecting china fragments, 'maybe you shouldn't tell me any more about this. I want you to feel you can confide in me, but I wouldn't feel great about keeping something like this from Laurel.'

'Oh, she knows,' Sonia said, and then loudly blew her nose and wiped her eyes with the back of her hand. She seemed more composed now, as if it had been a relief to come out with the truth at last.

'She knows?'

'Yes. She started it,' Sonia said defiantly. 'She'd been sleeping with Julian for quite a while before Henry and I found out what was going on. And then one thing led to another. I was just so angry, and anger makes you behave in unpredictable ways, you know? I just didn't expect to actually find myself falling for him. And I guess... you know... it made me feel special again. And I needed that.' She looked crestfallen suddenly. 'I know that must sound silly to you, given how you've coped on your own all this time. I really admire you, the way you decided you were just going to focus on Billy and whatever you had to do to get by. You didn't ever seem to feel like you needed a relationship with a man to feel good about yourself. But I'm just not like that, I guess.'

Callie found herself struggling to think of the right thing to say. Henry seemed like the precise opposite of Sonia's rather stuffy, upright husband. Had that been the attraction? And yet Julian had been seeing Laurel in secret, so he obviously wasn't quite what he seemed either.

She never would have imagined that Julian would be drawn to someone who was as big and brash a personality as Laurel, who was so unapologetically extrovert and sure of herself, but perhaps it made sense, if what had drawn them together was how different they were... She was beginning to wonder if she'd ever really known any of these people at all.

She put the packaged-up broken china in the non-recycling bin and found a cloth to mop up the puddle of cold tea on the floor. When she'd finished clearing up she said, 'So is it really over between the two of you? Between you and Henry, I mean?'

Sonia gave a tiny shrug, then looked up and met Callie's eyes. 'It is. I finished it the day you got hit by that bike. What I said to you about visiting my aunt, that was just a lie. I mean, I do have an aunt, but I haven't seen her for years. I was in London, at Henry's flat, breaking up with him. Julian knew that was what I was doing. Laurel didn't, but she did know who I was with, and where. I guess she felt she had to cover for me. She really doesn't want any of this coming out.' Sonia sniffed again. 'I don't think it'd do much for her public profile. It's pretty important for her to seem wholesome and above board. Anyway, I'm sorry I wasn't there for you when you needed me.' Her face quivered again, and she wiped away a tear with the back of her hand. 'I really have felt bad about it, believe me.'

'So... you're staying with Julian?'

'Trying to. He wanted me to stop seeing Henry, so in the end I did. I mean, he begged me. But now I feel like he's punishing me. He's being so harsh, and so distant, and he keeps insinuating that the awful thing Jack did was somehow *my* fault, because I was distracted with everything else going on...'

'Have Laurel and Julian stopped seeing each other?'

'Julian told me they had. I'm not a hundred per cent convinced though. I guess you could say we have trust issues. Anyway, what with one thing or another, it's been a really terrible couple of weeks.' Her gaze slid to the arm Callie had broken. 'But I suppose I shouldn't say that to you.'

From the living room came the sound of the *Doctor Who* theme tune, followed by Billy and Reuben's voices discussing the episode. It wasn't possible to make out what they were actually saying, but the way they were talking told its own story. Billy was explaining his point of view, sounding more than usually confident, and Reuben was paying attention, the surest sign of love, and encouraging him.

'It hasn't been all bad,' Callie said.

'No,' Sonia agreed, with a weak smile.

They heard Billy laughing in the other room. Sonia said, 'It's good to hear him sounding so happy,' and drank the last of her tea.

'I know. It is for me too. He likes hanging out with Reuben, but it's not just that. It's like he was always afraid that something bad was going to happen to him, and then it did, and he got through it, and now he isn't worried any more. So you see, you really don't need to beat yourself up about what's happened. It's OK.'

Sonia shook her head. 'I'm glad you feel that. But I can't see it that way. I mean, look how Jack behaved. I feel like I must have done something really wrong as a parent for him to bully another child like that.'

'Maybe he'll change.'

'He better had. Anyway, I don't know how you can be so forgiving,' Sonia said, and this time she was the one who embraced Callie. 'Thank you. And I'm glad you and Reuben have figured things out after all this time.'

'So far so good,' Callie said, and the two of them let each other go.

Sonia glanced at the pink rose again. 'I guess it's none of my business, but... I can see why you might have your doubts. Why you might want to take things slowly,' she added hastily, in response to whatever she'd seen in Callie's face. 'After all that's happened lately.'

'Doubt's not the problem. I know I want Reuben to be part of Billy's life,' Callie said. 'The two of them lost so much time. Eleven years. It's gone by in a flash, but when I stop and think about it, it was filled with so much. All the school assemblies, the day trips, the sports days. Reuben is Billy's dad. He should have had the chance to be there. And I didn't tell him. I... it sounds really dreadful, I can't even begin to explain, but I thought it was for the best... I thought he wouldn't want to know... and I took the chance right out of his hands.'

'Perhaps it just wasn't the right time,' Sonia said. 'But it sounds like it is now.' She hesitated. 'This is none of my business, so do tell me if you don't want to say. But I can't help wondering... You said you and Reuben are friends. Do you *want* to be more?'

'Right now I just want to get through to next week without any more disasters happening,' Callie said. Which was true, but not the whole truth.

Sonia looked at her sceptically but didn't press the point. They hugged again, and then Sonia said she'd better go and Callie came with her to the front door.

As Sonia made her way out into the rain she turned back and waved at her, and Callie waved back. For a split second she was in Sonia's shoes again, walking away from someone else's happiness and back to a house full of recriminations and blame. And then she closed the door on the outside world and its rotten weather and went into the living room, where Reuben had turned the TV off and had just started dealing out cards ready to play a game.

It was one of those rare, privileged moments when she was able to see Billy completely absorbed in something without him even being aware that she was watching him and willing him on. And then Reuben looked up and smiled at her, and she smiled back.

Do you want *to be more?* Sonia had said. The answer that came back, with the clear and undeniable ring of truth, was *Yes.* But also, *Only when I can be sure he wants me too. Not just as a friend, or as Billy's mum, but as me.*

THIRTY-SEVEN

The consultant was called Mr Styles, which was distracting because she couldn't help but think of the pop star with whom he shared a surname. But this Mr Styles was balding with a little fluff of greying hair, probably nearing retirement, and wore little metal-framed glasses with round lenses. Also, he was about to tell her what, if anything, was wrong with her brain.

It was also distracting that he was called Mr, not Dr, but she gathered that this was actually some kind of badge of seniority, or, at least, did not mean any lack of expertise. Which was just as well. Depending on how this turned out, her life might end up being in his hands. Literally. She thought how strange it must be, to be someone for whom that level of responsibility was normal. She preferred thinking about this to dwelling on what he might be about to tell her.

She understood that Mr Styles was important, and well-regarded, from the atmosphere in the waiting room she'd just come from – the mix of despair and hope on the other patients' faces, the sense of waiting for magic to happen. Or perhaps a miracle. Also, there was the respectful way the man behind the reception desk had said his name – 'I'm afraid Mr Styles is running half an hour late at the moment, but take a seat and he'll see you as soon as he can.'

Also, there was something about Mr Styles himself that inspired confidence. He had an air of quiet authority, as if he would always be calm, even in the midst of chaos. As if his hands would never shake, which she supposed was probably a prerequisite for a neurosurgeon. Or did she just think that because she needed to believe that he knew what he was doing?

It had taken him a while to locate the latest scans of her brain on the system – some kind of tech hiccup – and she could tell that he was annoyed by this, and frustrated, and embarrassed, and felt bad for her, even though she had said that it was fine. It should have made the experience of being here seem more familiar and therefore more real. It was the kind of thing that happened in her own job, after all. Computer systems could play up anywhere. But today, it just made everything feel even more like a dream.

It was one of those dreams that could go either way. Either she could find herself trapped in a steadily intensifying nightmare, or she could walk out of the hospital freed of all her worries and wake up to her life, her actual, real, day-to-day life, which was not one of fear and pain and anaesthesia and surgery, but was about Billy, her home and her job. And Reuben, too, now, though he'd also always had a place in the world of her dreams.

It all turned out to be a false alarm, she might say to Reuben when she got back to the flat. *The headaches are nothing to do with anything. Just one of those things. The consultant said I should try and learn some relaxation techniques. It doesn't sound very relaxing, having to learn how to relax.*

Surely, by and by, the headaches really would stop. Maybe it would be gradual, the way the days lengthened in spring without you really noticing it, until one day it was still light at dinnertime and you felt your spirits lift because you knew then that winter was really over. Yes, that was how it would be. One day she'd realise she hadn't had a headache for a while, and then she'd be able to forget about the whole thing and put it behind her.

'So... here we are,' Mr Styles said. 'Apologies for the delay. Never used to happen in the old days. Anyway, I have your scans here. Would you like to see?'

'I don't think they would mean very much to me,' she said, recoiling from the idea of seeing an image of the inside of her brain. 'Can't you just tell me what's going on?'

Mr Styles didn't sigh or steeple his fingers. He looked her straight in the eyes. He did her that courtesy, and that was when she knew it was serious, and the nightmare was real and she wasn't going to get out of it yet.

'You have an aneurysm. I would strongly recommend that we operate on it as swiftly as is practically feasible. Ideally within the next few weeks,' he said.

He said a lot more after that, and she asked questions, but mainly because she felt she ought to, and without really taking in the answers. What it boiled down to was this: it had to be done. He explained that her headaches were almost certainly to do with the aneurysm, rather than the fall when she'd been hit by a bike. That the scan she'd had after the accident had not picked up any issues, which was why he had ordered a different type of scan, which had revealed the aneurysm straightaway. And he told her that while the operation would not be without risk, if she did not go ahead with it, sooner or later the aneurysm would kill her anyway.

He didn't use quite those words – he said something like, 'a bleed would be more or less inevitable eventually, and that could have very serious or indeed fatal consequences,' but she knew what he meant.

She said, 'How much sooner? Or later? If I don't have the operation, how long would it be until something happened?'

Again he looked her straight in the eyes. His gaze felt like an attempt to reach out and take her by the hand. *Trust me*, it seemed to say. *I will do my best for you. I'm your only hope.*

'I can only talk about probabilities,' he said. 'But my very strong recommendation would be that you should have this operation as soon as possible, as I said. That way, the balance of probabilities remains firmly in your favour.'

She nodded. Her head was filled with a rushing sound that could have been her own blood, or was maybe the sound of impending doom. And she had a very strong sense of impending doom at that moment, even though she did trust Mr Styles and was going to do what he said, and even though, just then, she had no headache at all.

She rang Reuben and told him, very briefly, before setting off home, having first made him go into the kitchen and shut the door to make it harder for Billy to overhear and figure out what they were talking about. She was bluff and breezy about it, as if the operation was just a chore that would have to be got through, like going to the tip or sorting out Billy's uniform for the secondary school he'd be starting at in September. But she felt Reuben flinch with the shock of it, and go quiet as he tried to take it in, and then tried to work out if she felt worse about it than she was letting on.

'I don't want to tell Billy just yet, though,' she said. 'You won't say anything, will you?'

'But he knows where you are today. He's going to want to know.'

'I know. But I just want him to enjoy the end of term, and leaving primary school. After that, I'll tell him. The operation's probably not going to be for another couple of weeks, anyway, by the time they've fitted me in.'

'They can't slot you in any faster than that?'

'The consultant's secretary is going to give me a call and let me know when he can do it. Like I said, it should be pretty soon.'

He sighed. 'OK. I won't say anything to Billy. Will you tell your mum?'

'Yeah, of course. I might just give myself a day or two first, though. But I should probably ask her if she'd look after Billy while I'm in hospital. I mean... that's probably the best thing, don't you think? Given that you haven't got your new place sorted yet.'

There was a pause. 'Yeah,' Reuben said. 'I guess that would be the best thing.'

When she got home she invited Reuben to stay for dinner and afterwards, when Billy went off to have a bath, Reuben said he'd better be going. She went into the hallway with him to see him out, then, on impulse, told him to wait a minute and rushed back to knock on the bathroom door.

'I'm just popping out to say goodbye to your dad,' she called out. 'I'll be back in a minute.'

'OK,' Billy yelled back over the sound of the running taps.

She just remembered to grab her keys before she went out and closed the front door behind her, and then followed Reuben to his car and got into the passenger seat next to him.

For a minute or two, though it felt as if it was longer, they both sat there and didn't say anything. It was a fine summer's evening, the best kind, with the bright blue of the sky beginning to fade and a few clouds at the horizon to catch the colours of sunset when it came. There was no one else around. A ginger cat strolled out in front of them and disappeared into someone's front garden. She thought how lovely such an evening could be, if you didn't know you had something wrong with you that might kill you, and were facing the possibility of never seeing another summer. And then she thought that perhaps fear made the evening even lovelier.

He said, 'You know, Billy probably could come and stay with me, if he wanted. I should be getting keys to the flat next week.' This was the new place he'd found, which was on the north side of Kettlebridge, within walking distance of her and Billy. 'I'd have to crack on with sorting the place out. But it shouldn't be impossible.'

'I think it's probably best if we stick to him going to Mum's this time. Since he's been there before. And she'll want to have him there.'

'OK,' he said. 'Whatever you think. Just so you know the offer's there.'

'Maybe you could go and see him.' Then: 'Is it difficult for you, going back there? I don't know if you've been to see your dad lately?'

Reuben swallowed. 'I've been,' he said. 'I'd like to go round to your mum's. As long as she doesn't mind.'

'She won't,' Callie said.

There was another silence. Then Reuben said, 'I should have been with you, at that appointment today. Or someone should have been. You shouldn't have to go through something like that on your own.'

She shrugged. 'I didn't mind. I'd rather be sure that Billy's OK.'

'You should be able to have both. To know Billy's OK *and* to have someone with you.'

'Like I told you, I'm not bothered,' she said impatiently. 'It doesn't matter.'

'Well, I think it does,' he said gently. 'Not just because you're Billy's mum. But because you're you, and you matter too.'

She turned to face him and then it happened, the thing she hadn't quite let herself realise she'd been waiting for all this time. He kissed her. And it felt just right. Even if it should not have done. She was sitting outside her flat in a car with the man who'd got her pregnant and then disappeared to the other side of the world. She'd lied to him and he had believed that she'd betrayed him. And there was something wrong with her, with her brain, that could kill her, and she was kissing him. It was reckless. But also, it was sweet and easy and comforting, and it felt safe and right because it was him.

They stopped and looked at each other. Suddenly she felt like crying. She said, 'This is a ridiculous time to be doing this.'

He looked alarmed. He said, 'I'm sorry. I shouldn't have... Are you OK?'

'Don't be silly,' she said. 'It's not you that's ridiculous, it's this thing in my head that's going to finish me off unless I let someone dig around in there and sort it out.' She tapped her forehead. '*That's* what's ridiculous. But I don't mean that it's a bad time. I think it's a good time. As good as any.'

And then they were kissing again. She didn't say what was on her mind, which was that this might be all the time they had left. It was a possibility, that was all. On the balance of probabilities, they had all the time in the world.

The next day at work, she got a call from the consultant's secretary to book her in for the operation. Afterwards she got up and went straight into Julian's office and explained what had happened and asked if she could take the rest of the day off.

He looked at her with the kind of wary fear with which people respond to other people who they see as being in the middle of a run of bad luck. 'Of course,' he said. 'You should go. Take all the time you need.'

She thanked him and went off to gather up her things and leave, and it struck her that he'd actually been almost too keen for her to go, which wasn't very flattering – surely he needed her there? But maybe her presence made him uncomfortable. It could be that he knew she knew about Sonia's affair with Henry and his affair with Laurel. Maybe he was thinking that, however complicated and unpleasant his private life might be, at least he wasn't facing an operation on his brain to tackle a potentially fatal condition.

Everything paled in comparison to the threat of death. Even infidelity and betrayal, the possibility of a messy and expensive divorce, the end of a love affair and the fading of youthful hopes and dreams. It was odd to realise that other people might use her situation to keep their own problems in proportion, but she supposed she couldn't really object. At least her aneurysm was of use to somebody.

She had told Julian she was going to go home. But instead she walked straight to Reuben's new flat and turned up uninvited.

When he opened the door she said, 'I know this will seem crazy. But I wanted to see you. And I had a feeling that you wouldn't mind. But if I'm wrong, just tell me and I'll walk away.'

He looked her up and down. 'You're not wrong,' he said at last. 'But Callie... if you mean that you want something to happen between us... *that* kind of something... I think *that* would be wrong. Under the circumstances.'

'How could it possibly be wrong,' Callie said, 'if it's what both of us want?'

She stepped inside and pushed the door shut behind her.

Something in the air changed, as if a switch had been pressed on or off, and the way he was looking at her changed too. He was desperately worried, she could see that, but also, he wanted her. He really did. And the only thing that was stopping him was fear.

He moved forwards and put his arms around her. Once again she could hear the sound of blood rushing in her ears, but it was the absolute opposite of the moment in the consultant's office when she'd been waiting for the diagnosis. Then she'd had a very strong sense of impending doom. Now she knew there was happiness just around the corner. She had no idea how both of them had resisted it for so long.

Later that afternoon she rushed back from Reuben's flat just in time to pick Billy up from school. She tried to behave as normally as possible, but the problem was, she couldn't quite remember what her normal self was. From time to time she caught Billy giving her little sharp or anxious looks, but he didn't say anything and she was grateful for that.

She waited until after dinner, when he was in the bath, to pick up the phone to her mother and tell her about the operation.

Part of her couldn't help but hope that Mum would be going out, so she wouldn't have to do this. But Mum was there, and she forced herself to break it to her. *'They say I have an aneurysm... They have to operate as soon as possible...'*

She only just stopped herself from saying sorry. Why should she feel bad for having something wrong with her? But she did feel bad. She knew how she would have worried if it was a grown-up Billy ringing her to tell her something like that. She wouldn't have wished that on anyone.

After she'd finished Mum went very quiet on the other end of the line. Then she said, 'I see. Well, of course Billy is welcome here any time, you know that. But what about you? Someone should be with you.'

'I don't need that, Mum,' she said. 'I don't need anyone there to hold my hand. I'd rather go in on my own.'

'This is not a time to be proud, Callie,' Mum told her. 'You must ask for help when you need it.'

'But everything is going to be absolutely fine. I'm in good hands. The surgeon is very experienced. And this kind of thing happens all the time.'

'Not to my daughter, it doesn't,' Mum said fiercely.

'Well... OK. Maybe if Billy is with you, I could ask Reuben to come with me.'

'Really? I mean, I know you're getting on now... and you want him to have a good relationship with Billy... and I don't mean to pry, but after everything that's happened, Callie, is that really wise?'

'Well, I don't think it would exactly be leading him on, to ask him to accompany me to hospital to have my brain fixed,' Callie said. Then, faced with silence from the other end of the line, 'I'm joking, Mum. That's still allowed, right? Look, here's the thing about Reuben. I love him. There it is. There's nothing I can do about it. I always did. I know it probably sounds stupid, but it's true. And I want to be with him. I'm not saying there's any rush. I know we ought to take our time to get to know each other, and for Billy to have time to get to know him, too. Though you could say we've already taken enough time. But there it is. I want to be with him for the rest of my life, for as long as I can be.'

Mum went very quiet at the other end of the line. Then she said, 'Well, maybe just get through this operation and then see how you feel. Everything's bound to be a bit heightened at the moment.'

'I love you too, Mum,' Callie said, surprising herself.

'And I love you,' Mum said, a little huskily. 'Anyway, Callie, I have to go. I'll speak to you soon, OK?'

Callie realised that Mum was about to start bawling her eyes out and didn't want Callie to hear. 'OK,' she said. 'Speak soon.'

Her mum rang off. Callie put the phone down, then felt a little jolt of shock and fear as it struck her that one day, sooner or later, she and Mum would speak for the very last time. And that was inevitable. It was only on the balance of probabilities that it hadn't already happened.

THIRTY-EIGHT

BILLY

When he looked back later and tried to piece together how it had all gone so catastrophically wrong, just when it had looked as if it was finally all going right, he found that what he remembered most clearly was his last day at primary school, when his mum and dad had come to the leavers' service at church together. That had turned out to be the day when the disaster began to strike, and then there had been barely more than a week left for the three of them to be together. But at the time, all he was aware of was that he was finally leaving Meadowside school, and that he had something to read out to everyone during the service.

Already, in the run-up to the last day of school, there had been various other last things – the year six disco, the leavers' performance – and he had noticed other people getting quite upset about all this, both the parents and the other year sixes (in particular the girls, who seemed to go in for a lot of crying and group hugs.) He did not expect to be affected himself. He was actually quite glad to be leaving, and to have a chance to start over. But the emotions of the day were contagious. Also, he knew he was going to have to stand in front of everybody in the church, including both his parents, and give his reading, so to start with he was mainly worried about that.

It was a beautiful day. When he remembered it later, it was tinged with the special brightness of a time that you know, with hindsight, was already a countdown to the end. In the morning his whole school trooped down to the big church in the town centre, as they did year in, year out, and at Christmas and Easter too. The school was connected to the church in some vague way he didn't fully understand, to do with the olden times, and the main upshot of this was that they all walked down there three times a year and sat through a service.

For him and his classmates this would be the last time, and he found himself taking in everything about the walk with extra clarity – each root of a front-garden tree that buckled the pavement, the thickly clustered weeds growing by the crumbling old remnant of drystone wall by the green – because he knew that he wouldn't be walking this way with these people again.

Was that something to be sad about? Surely it wasn't, but he did find himself feeling touched by it all anyway, as if he was already looking back on it with nostalgia. Jack and Zeke kept their distance, of course – they could barely bring themselves to look at him these days, let alone dare to come near him – and that was fine. It was quite something to have the power to scare them into looking down or away if he so much as glanced at them. Neither of them could meet his eyes.

Mum had pointed out to him that he had got through as many of his schooldays as he had left in front of him. He was at the halfway mark, she'd said, but to him that wasn't much of a cause for emotion either. It wasn't as if he'd had a great time at school so far, and he was trying not to expect too much from the years ahead.

Of course home life was different now Dad and Granny were both part of it, and that was amazing. It was like having a big back-up team at HQ. But he wasn't sure yet whether it would mean he'd be better able to protect himself from the nasty side of being around other people. Which, if anything, seemed only likely to get worse at secondary school, which was huge and had loads of older and bigger students who might decide to pick on him.

One thing that was quite good was that his dad was going to pay for him to have karate lessons, so if anybody did anything horrible to him in future, at least he'd be able to karate-chop them back. At the taster session Dad had taken them to, the sensei had been very emphatic about how students should not use their karate skills on other people unless it was in self-defence or there was a suitably trained adult around. Billy had taken this on board, while secretly hoping that the karate-chopping bit would be covered later in the session. It had not been, but he was still hopeful that they'd come to it if he kept going back.

He couldn't see his parents at first when he filed into the church for the leavers' service along with his class. Usually he thought of going to church as quite boring, something it was necessary to get through at the end of term before the holidays could begin, but that day, for the first time, he appreciated the beauty of the golden stone and high arches, the way the sunlight looked as it streamed through the windows and bounced off the brass pendant lights, the stillness and relative calm of the air, and the smell of dusty old spice that was perhaps incense, or maybe left behind by old flowers.

Then, after he'd settled into place on a pew between two classmates he thought of as harmless, maybe even friendly, he looked round and caught sight of his mum and dad sitting next to each other in the section of the church reserved for parents. They were sitting very close, and Mum looked as if she was already getting ready to cry.

That was when he began to feel it. It was almost like the fluttering of his anxiety in the old days, the beginnings of a sense of something strange or unsettling that would have the power to grow until it crowded everything else out.

The service began. The church was packed – with children of all ages between four and eleven, and the parents of the older children – and the large congregation rustled restlessly in between the Bible readings, the prayers, the songs and the sermon. Then, finally, it was his moment, the part of the service when he, along with other pre-selected year sixes, would go up in turn and stand at the front of the church and read out an account of their favourite memory of school.

He had to force himself to walk up the aisle. As he held up the piece of paper he was going to read from it struck him both how messy and bad his handwriting was, and also, how embarrassing it would be if anyone could see his hands shaking or his legs trembling in his shorts. Also, no one would really want to hear what he had to say anyway. His teacher had probably only asked him to read because she felt bad about what had happened near the railway line.

Someone coughed. The congregation stirred. His mouth was dry. He could not, must not, look up at all those people who were watching him and waiting for him to fail. It would paralyse him. His mum was among them, and would be bitterly disappointed, and make excuses for him later. *You did very well, considering how nervous you were.* And his dad...

He heard someone snicker, but perhaps he was only imagining it.

Then he looked very hard at what he had written and somehow, he had begun to read out loud, and the words were carrying him through.

'I haven't always had a very good time at school, but I was happy at the year six leavers' disco we had a few weeks ago. We were in the school hall with lights making patterns across all of us in the dark, all listening to the same music, and I felt part of something with everybody. Some of us won't see much of each other any more, but I think we'll all remember that we were there together then, and I think we will all feel the same about today.'

He looked up. Nobody was laughing. A few people looked unsure, as if they would have liked to applaud but thought it wasn't the right thing to do. Somehow his gaze settled on his mum. She was watching him with a really intense mix of love and forlornness, as if she would have liked nothing more than to scoop him up and hug him but knew she couldn't.

The girl next to him started reading from her piece of paper, and then there was one more reading and the group of them made their way back to their seats to wait for the next thing they would have to do, which was the final ritual of the whole service.

He'd seen this before plenty of times, at the end of other years. Now it was his turn to participate. Each of the year sixes, the children who were leaving, had to get up in turn and queue in the aisle to collect a candle from the headteacher and hold it carefully while it was lit, then carry it back to their pews.

And then he was on his feet again, and waiting, and looking down at the small glowing point of light rising from the candle in his hands. As he walked carefully back he dared to glance quickly up at Mum and saw that she was crying openly now, and that Dad had his arm round her.

He immediately looked away again because he didn't want them to know he'd seen, but he couldn't help but get his hopes up that it meant they were going to get together again. They ought to just get together and get on with it. He couldn't see any point in them waiting, because what would they be waiting for? To get really old, so their marriage would just be them sitting in armchairs next to each other? It was pretty obvious that they liked each other, and they had missed out on enough time already – almost his whole life. But he had yet to share this opinion with Mum. Sometimes you just had to leave people to figure things out for themselves.

He saw Mum and Dad after the service, but only briefly. By then they both looked as if they'd been crying, but so did almost everybody. He couldn't hang round to talk to them, but was swept up in the procession of children making their way back to school.

There was a special lunch party out in the playground, with streamers strung from the corners of the buildings and long tables covered with paper cloths, and paper plates and cups for the food they had all brought in. All the girls seemed to be crying, wherever he looked. Crying, and hugging each other. He still didn't cry. He began to feel like it, a bit, but managed to hold back. He didn't want to cry in front of everyone there. After all, most of his classmates had either ignored him or been actively mean to him, at least until fairly recently when they had begun to be a little bit nicer.

Parents began to turn up towards the end of the lunch party to listen to the headmaster's farewell speech and collect younger children. He saw Mum among them, and when the headteacher was done talking, he gratefully broke free from the hugging and goodbyes going on around him and went to join her, and walk with her across the green to home.

Neither of them said anything until they got to the flat, and Mum rummaged in her pocket and brought out her keys to let them in.

'I can't quite believe we've just done that walk for the very last time,' she said.

'Me neither,' Billy said, because she sounded just a little bit sad about it, so the best thing seemed to be to agree. Actually, he felt quite pleased. When he started at his new secondary school, which wasn't very much further away, he was going to walk home by himself, which was what pretty much everybody else did already. After all, he knew the way. And people would probably find it odd if his mum turned up to wait for him outside the school, although Mum had said that on the first day she might lurk round the corner somewhere, just so she could meet him halfway and check he got home all right.

Back in his bedroom, he took off his old school uniform for the last time, and put it in the laundry bag for Mum to wash and then donate to the school second-hand shop. The rest of the afternoon passed pleasantly and uneventfully, filled with nice, normal after-school summery things: an ice cream from the van when it came down the close, some time on his PlayStation, which he still thought of as new, and a bit more of one of those spy books. Dad came to join them for dinner and afterwards they all played poker for jelly beans, and Billy went off to bed feeling that he'd done rather well.

He'd got through the Meadowside years, he'd vanquished Zeke and Jack (with some help from Dad) so that they would never make his life miserable again, and in future he was going to walk home from school by himself. He just needed to find a way to get Mum and Dad properly back together, and then everything would be all right. Better than all right. It would be a happy ending, except it wouldn't be the end, and they would all get to carry on being happy. Then what Mum had written on the underside of her windowsill when she was a kid would turn out to be true: *Callie 4 Reuben 4 ever.*

But then he woke up with his heart pounding because of a really terrible, alarming noise. A noise he in no way should have been hearing, not that night, and not ever again.

It was Mum crying.

He got up and went closer to his bedroom door and listened. Surely she couldn't be that sad about him leaving primary school? He would have to go and tell her it was fine, and if he wasn't upset about it then she shouldn't be either.

But what if she wasn't crying about that at all? What if she was sad about something else?

Was Dad still there? What if they'd had a fight? Were they breaking up? But how could they break up when they weren't even properly together?

It was probably possible. Grown-ups had all sorts of complicated ways of falling out with each other and hurting each other. And Mum and Dad seemed to have messed things up completely once before. Not that it was any of his business. Though it kind of was his business.

Then he heard the low murmur of Dad's voice.

So Dad was still there. He didn't sound angry, more as if he was trying to be reassuring. Would he be like that if they had broken up? Maybe he would.

He put his hand on the door handle and very gently and carefully turned it and went into the hall. The living room door was slightly ajar, which made it quite easy to lurk outside and eavesdrop.

'We're going to have to tell him sooner or later,' he heard Dad say.

That did it. There was a limit to how long he was willing to be a spy for. Sometimes, you just needed to step into the room and make them explain.

He pushed open the living room door and said, 'Tell who what? What's wrong? Mum, why are you crying?'

Their two startled faces turned round towards him. Dad had his arm round Mum and her face was wet with tears. She dried it quickly with the back of her hand and said, 'I'm fine, Billy. It's just been a long day. You should go back to bed.'

He folded his arms and stood his ground. 'No. Something's going on, and you have to tell me.'

'Billy,' his dad said, 'I think you should go to bed, like your mum said.'

'No, it's all right,' Mum said. 'He's right. We should explain. Come here, Billy.'

She pulled away from Dad so that there was a space on the

sofa between them, and patted it to show that Billy should sit down there. He did, although it was a bit of a squash. But then, it was quite cosy being there between the two of them like that.

'I'm going to have to go back into hospital soon, and have another operation,' she said. 'It's all going to be fine, and the doctors know what they're doing, and there won't be any problems. I was just crying because I'm a bit sick of hospitals, and I was feeling sorry for myself. But really, I should feel pleased and happy because the operation is going to make me better.'

'But your arm is better already,' Billy protested. 'Why do you have to go back?'

She touched her head. 'I have something called an aneurysm. It's a kind of weird bubble of blood in my brain. It's quite big, and the problem with aneurysms is that sometimes they burst, which can be very dangerous. So what they are going to do is a very special, very clever operation which will fix it so that it won't burst, and I'll be safe. They found it because of those headaches I'd been having, which I thought was something to do with the accident. But they were nothing to do with the accident. It was probably because of the aneurysm pressing on some of the nerves in my brain. So they sent me to a brain doctor. They knew I'd had a brain scan after the accident and it didn't show anything was wrong, so they did a special kind of scan that's very good at picking up aneurysms, and then they found it. So really I'm very lucky, because now they know it's there, they can treat it. If they hadn't found it, it might have carried on getting bigger until it burst.'

Billy looked carefully at Mum's face, and the shape of her head. It looked quite normal, and he found it very hard to believe that there could be something inside her brain that could be so dangerous.

'So they can fix it?'

'They certainly can. They fix these things all the time. The surgeon who is going to do it has done so many of them he's probably lost count.'

'So why didn't you want to tell me?'

Mum and Dad exchanged glances. 'I was being silly,' Mum said. 'But I was going to tell you. And now I think you should go to bed, because in the morning something special is going to happen.'

'What something special?' Billy knew she was just trying to take his mind off the whole blood bubble thing, but he had to admit it, this was a good tactic.

She gave Dad another little sideways look, but she was smiling this time. 'We're going to go with your dad to the beach.'

The beach! Soon after that she said that he should go to bed because they had an early start the next day, and he went off quite happily and sank into a deep sleep. From time to time he surfaced to what sounded almost like his parents whispering, but it was in the middle of the night so surely his dad would have gone by now and they wouldn't still be talking. He decided it must just be the sound of the wind in the elder trees further down the close.

The next day was magical right from the start. He woke at seven as usual, and Mum was already up and dressed and Dad had arrived and had parked outside. The sun was shining and it was going to be warm and dry but not too hot, and everything was set to be perfect.

Dad drove them south on the busy dual carriageway – it occurred to him later that maybe Mum didn't drive because she wasn't feeling well, or had one of her headaches, but she didn't complain. Instead she sang along to the music, which she only ever did when she was feeling happy. The drive took an hour and a half. And then, finally, in the distance, he caught sight of the sea, a very thin patch of watery blue between buildings and hills. It was still only nine o'clock, and back home in Kettle-bridge, the neighbours were probably only just finishing their breakfasts.

The day stretched ahead, waiting to be filled with pleasures. They walked on the beach, paddled, sat on the sand, watched the waves going in and coming out, built a sandcastle, ate a picnic lunch of sandwiches that tasted better than any sandwiches ever normally did, had ice cream. He found a favourite stone and a favourite shell. The sweet smell of suntan lotion, which always made him think of holidays even though holidays were something he and Mum had never had money for, clung to his skin, mixed with salt from the sea and the air.

Eventually the heat went out of the day and the blue of the sky began to fade. They ate fish and chips outside at a little café on the edge of the beach, and when they'd finished Dad looked at Mum and said regretfully, 'I suppose we ought to be getting back.'

'I suppose,' she said, and it was the first time he'd seen her look sad all day. But the sadness seemed to pass very quickly, and the next minute she was smiling. 'Never mind, we're going to do lots of other fun things. After all, it's only the first day of the holidays, right? Plenty more to come.'

'Will we come back to the beach?' Billy asked.

Mum glanced at Dad, who said, 'Sure we will. I don't know when, but we will.' And then they stood up and made their way back to the car. His shadow was long but theirs were even longer, and he liked seeing their shadows all moving along together. On the way back he slept, even though it wasn't quite dark yet, and when he woke up Mum was sleeping, too. And he thought how strange and ordinary this was at the same time, that both he and Mum should be dozing while Dad drove them all the way back home to Goosegreen Close.

Over the days that followed, it seemed as if everybody was trying to be especially nice to each other. He figured that maybe it was because it was the first summer holiday when his dad had been around to spend time with them. Mum had taken the week off work and they went on several more outings, which were all especially good. It was as if Mum and Dad felt they were running out of time to take him places and wanted to pack in as many trips as possible.

They visited some hills with big views of the countryside and a castle and a museum where you could pretend to drive a train, and another one with dinosaur bones. They went bowling and to the cinema and out for pizza at a restaurant. The days went by slowly, because they were so full and he was doing so many interesting things, but eventually they passed by and came to an end. And then it was the day before his mum's operation and he was packing a bag ready to go to Granny's the following morning.

His dad wasn't there. He'd gone back to the flat he was renting, and when Billy said goodnight to his mum he wished Dad was still around. He felt suddenly guilty about leaving her all alone on the sofa, but then he told himself that was ridiculous and went off to bed.

But he couldn't sleep.

His heart began to pound and he thought perhaps he couldn't breathe. He hadn't felt like this for ages but it was all very familiar and it was horrible to know that he could feel like this again. And then, because it was all so hopeless and the night was so long and so lonely and he knew he would never, ever sleep, he began to cry.

He heard a knocking on the door and froze in despair and humiliation. Now he'd stopped Mum from sleeping, just when she needed her rest. That was how helpless and babyish he still was. He couldn't even be brave when she was only going away for a little while, to have an operation that was going to keep her alive.

He just about managed to raise his head off his damp pillow

enough to say 'Come in', and Mum did come in, but she didn't sit down on the bed next to him. Instead she went over to the window and drew the curtains, and said, 'Billy, come and see.'

He got out of the window and looked out, but their garden looked exactly the same as it always did, just dark, with the houses of the next road at the end.

Then Mum said, 'Look up.'

And he did, and he saw that the night sky was full of stars, with a very fine, delicate crescent moon floating among them.

'Did you know,' Mum said, 'that when you look at stars, what you're seeing is time travel? That light has been falling towards us for so long that the stars it came from might not even be there any more. But you don't think of that when you're looking at the night sky. All that really matters is the light. The light is what you see. It doesn't matter where it came from, or even if the source of it is still there.'

He didn't quite understand what she was getting at, but decided not to say anything. She put her arm around him. They stood together like that for a little while and looked up at the stars, and the more he looked at them the more he saw.

He said, 'Do you know what any of them are called?'

'I don't. Not for sure.' She pointed at one particularly bright one. 'See that one? I think that's the Evening Star, which actually isn't a star at all, but a planet. It's Venus, and it shines so brightly because of the light from our sun. But I might be wrong. Do you think you might be ready to go back to bed now?'

'I guess,' he said with a small sigh.

'After all, the stars will still be there for you to look at tomorrow evening.'

He got back under the covers, and she smoothed them over him.

'Night night, Billy. Sleep well,' she said, then, 'Do you remember the day we went to the beach?'

'Of course I do,' he said, slightly affronted by the idea that he might have forgotten. 'I want to go there again.'

'Well, if you dream about it, it'll be the next best thing. And if you think about it, maybe you'll dream about it. So you might want to try that,' she said. 'See you in the morning.'

After she'd gone and closed his bedroom door behind her, he did what she'd suggested and thought about the beach, and it seemed to help, because soon after that he dropped off. Though it could equally well have been looking at the stars together that did the trick, or the gentleness of her voice and the reassurance that came from realising that she wasn't angry with him for still being awake, and didn't think he was too old to need to be comforted.

The next morning he hugged her to say goodbye and she held him very tightly.

'It's all going to be fine, you'll see,' she said. 'And I promise you this is going to be the last time, OK? After this, no more invalids and no more hospitals. Not for a good long while, anyway. Be good for Granny, OK? You might want to let her win at Scrabble. I don't know if you've realised this yet, but she's *very* competitive.'

'He certainly will not let me win,' Granny said, pretending to be outraged, but her voice sounded thick and strange and she didn't look her normal self at all. She looked pale and tired, as if she hadn't slept, and worried and very upset. He wanted to tell her that Mum was telling the truth and everything was going to be all right, but he decided against it because he was only a child still, and so she probably wouldn't believe him.

Mum and Dad came out and stood in front of Mum's flat as he got into Granny's car. Granny said, 'OK, are you ready then, kiddo?' And that was strange too, because she'd never called him 'kiddo' before, but he understood that she was trying to sound encouraging, as if they were about to set off on a zany adventure.

'I am,' he said.

Granny started the car and determinedly forced it into gear, and then they were off. He waved vigorously at Mum and Dad and they smiled and waved back, and then he couldn't see them any more and he turned round to face forwards again.

'Well done,' Granny said.

He didn't reply. He didn't quite know what to say. He supposed she was congratulating him because he'd been brave and hadn't made a fuss, even though what had just happened was no big deal, because it was all going to be fine anyway. But even though he truly believed that, he couldn't help but feel that Granny was right, and he had been at least a little bit brave. It felt very odd, as if he had left part of his younger self behind.

Granny must have realised he didn't much feel like talking, because she didn't say anything either. She'd taken a day off work specially, and Ron wasn't there, so they had the house to themselves. They watched *The Phantom Menace* together, which he had seen before but she hadn't, and he explained a bit about *Star Wars* to her. After lunch, which neither of them much felt like eating, she got out her old board games. They were playing Monopoly when Granny's landline phone rang. She went out to answer it, and he sat and stared at the names of the streets on the board, which were names of real London streets, and his heart beat as fast as the feet of someone sprinting away from danger.

Then Granny came back and she was smiling, so he knew straight away that everything was all right.

'Good news. It's all gone well, and she's come round from the anaesthetic and is doing fine. She's not ready to have visitors just yet, but you should be able to see her tomorrow or the day after that.'

He didn't know quite how it happened, but somehow he

found himself hugging her. Then they broke apart and Granny said, 'I'm going to phone your dad now. He's at his place – he went back there after they took your mum off to get her ready for the operation. No point him sitting in the hospital for hours on end when there's nothing he can do to help, so he decided he might as well wait at home. Would you like to speak to him?'

Billy nodded. She went back out to the hallway and he could just make out the tone of her voice, which was different to the way she spoke to him, or to Mum, and definitely different to the way she spoke to Ron.

She was proud of Ron, and wanted to please him. That was obvious. His mum was more difficult for her. Granny sounded both warm and slightly prickly when she talked to Mum, as if she loved Mum much too much to be cool with her, but was always half-expecting to be pushed away and readying herself to take offence first. And with Billy, she was just warm, with a kind of fierce attention that Billy relished because it reminded him so much of Mum, and because it was good to have people around who treated you as if you were special and important even if you knew you weren't.

But to his dad she was both encouraging and slightly distant. Billy was aware that Mum felt Granny was quite hard on her, or had been in the past, and it seemed to him that in a polite way, she was being hard on Dad too. At least, it didn't sound as if he'd entirely won her over yet, although she was clearly making an effort to be nice.

Then she beckoned Billy into the hallway and handed the phone over to him. 'All yours,' she said, and retreated back to the living room.

'Billy?'

'Dad? Granny said you're at your flat. Are you all right, Dad?' Now he came to think about it, it bothered him that Dad had been waiting on his own.

'I'm OK,' Dad said, then sighed, which made it difficult to

believe him. 'I've been trying to do a bit of work, not very well. It's been quite hard to concentrate. How are you getting on?'

'Playing Monopoly. It's been OK. Dad, I think I can concentrate OK.'

'That's good. Very good. You keep on concentrating, Billy. And try not to worry, OK?'

'OK,' Billy said, and wished everybody would stop behaving as if he had something big to worry about.

'OK, good. Would you hand me over to your Granny again? There's something I want to ask her.'

It turned out that what Dad wanted to ask was whether it would be OK for him to take Billy out somewhere for dinner, and Granny said yes, so after Billy had won the game of Monopoly Dad picked him up and drove him to the Chinese place in Kettlebridge. Billy ate with chopsticks for the first time and had fortune cookies, and he was happy. He allowed himself to be happy. Then Dad took him back to Granny's and he went to bed in Mum's old room. Just before he switched off the light he looked again at what she'd written on the underside of the windowsill all those years ago – *Callie 4 Reuben 4 ever* – and thought that life was amazing and full of surprises, and sometimes promises came true.

Then, in the dark, he held the curtain aside and looked out at the stars, and even though it was a cloudy night he could still see some of them, though he wasn't sure which of the bright ones was the Evening Star. He remembered what Mum had said the night before and went to sleep thinking about the beach.

It was all fine that evening. It was still fine the next morning when he woke up. But sometime before elevenses, he knew it wasn't fine any more.

One minute he was choosing between ordinary holiday ways of passing the time like watching TV or playing patience or reading his book, and the next he was curled up on his bed in his room sobbing as if a bomb of sadness had just exploded and there was nowhere to take shelter.

He knew, but he didn't know what he knew. So when Granny came to talk to him later and her face was close to his and was very serious, and the words coming out of it were words that were heavy and dark, he couldn't make sense of it. He couldn't understand it. Mum had gone into hospital to be fixed, so she had to be fixed. It made no sense at all, and yet it was impossible and also true, for the fixing of the dangerous bubble of blood in her brain had somehow set off a reaction that no one could control or stop, not even the wisest and most experienced of doctors.

A stroke, Granny said. A stroke sounded like a kind, gentle thing. But it had killed his kind, gentle mother, and now she was dead.

Mum had been looking at the stars with him just the night before and trying to comfort him by helping him to think of them, not as stars, but as light travelling through time. He thought of that now, and wished that the light could be sent back and go into reverse, and that he could be standing next to her again. He wished it with all his heart, but he knew that his wishes were not strong enough to change the direction of time. Try as he might, he would never be able to bring her back.

THIRTY-NINE

REUBEN

It was Janice who told him Callie had gone. He heard the words – *a stroke this morning, an after-effect of the surgery. She lost consciousness and never came back round* – and suddenly he was far, far away, and his hand holding the phone was someone else's hand, part of a body that did not belong to him in a world that was totally unfamiliar to him.

It was a world he did not know how to live in. He could barely remember how to breathe or speak. He could just about manage to carry on standing there, holding the phone.

He found some questions to ask. He didn't really know what he was saying, or what there was to say. He would have liked to be able to argue with someone, to remonstrate and to question, to demand a second opinion, to insist that all possible options should be explored. But there was nobody to argue with, and no argument to be had. Callie was already dead. All he had left was shock and the possibility of blame.

Somewhere in the back of his mind, a small, self-pitying voice said: *You see? You were never meant to be happy with her. It was always going to be this way. The time between that acci-*

dent and her passing away. That's all you had, and all you were
ever going to have. And that's already more than you deserved.

But then he thought of Billy. Delicate, sensitive Billy, who
had been the focus of Callie's life and her love, and had lost her.
If his world had changed into one he barely recognised, how
much worse was it for his son?

'Does Billy know?' How could it not have been the first
thing he asked?

'I've told him,' Janice said grimly. 'He was already really
upset. It was like he knew.'

Somewhere else in the back of his mind, another small voice
raised the possibility of conflict. He had been so close to Callie
these last few weeks, and she had let him into Billy's life, too.
Would Janice now move to cut him out?

And yet Janice knew Callie trusted him. She knew that
Callie had chosen him to accompany her to the hospital on that
last morning. Not Callie's last morning of life, but the last
morning when any of them had been able to see her and talk to
her. Janice had not been there with them, but perhaps she
would be able to imagine how they had sat, side by side, among
the others in the waiting room, not speaking, Callie pale and
composed, but no doubt feeling weak from lack of food and
drink – she'd had to starve herself in preparation for the anaesthetic. And the sense of something enormous and terrible
hurtling towards them.

He had been able to pull Billy from the side of the railway
line. But there was nothing he could have done to rescue Callie.
No one could. It would have come sooner or later, and it had
come sooner. The rescue attempt in itself had doomed her.

Had she known the end was on the way – had she sensed it?
She had turned to him after they called her in from the waiting
room because it was time to go and prepare for the operation.
She had said, *'Take care of Billy'*. And she had looked at him

with those green eyes, bright and shining with tears, and he'd felt as close to her then as he had ever been.

And then she had gone. He'd been left alone in the waiting room to collect himself and make his way out and pay for his parking at the exit from the hospital and find his car, and to get on with the mundane ongoing business of living while, back in the hospital, Callie was anaesthetised, and the surgeon started on the procedure that had been meant to save her.

Reuben said, 'Where is Billy now?'

Janice didn't answer at first. Then she said, 'He's in his bedroom. The one that used to be hers. He's gone very quiet. I think he's in shock.'

He remembered that bedroom, and the autumn night after Sonia's wedding and the gentle sound of the rain falling again in the darkness, and how, when he woke up the next morning, Callie had been deeply asleep beside him, as pale and still as stone. He'd been filled with a fear he couldn't explain, and that made it impossible to stay. As if there was something terrifying to face that he was kidding himself he could run away from.

Well, he had to face it now. There could be no more running away. He had to stand firm, even if his feet were planted in quicksand.

He said, 'Can I come over? I want to see Billy.'

She hesitated. He knew she was weighing up, as he had done earlier, how much of a place she believed he deserved to have in Billy's life, and how much of a place she was willing to let him have.

Then she said, 'Come for dinner. We'll eat at six. We're all going to need to pull together now, for Billy's sake. Otherwise we're never going to make it through this. Oh, and Reuben...'

'What?'

'I am sorry. I do know what it is to lose the person you had hoped to spend the rest of your life with. But I had years with my husband and you and Callie were not so lucky. She told me how she felt about you, you know. When she rang up to tell me about the operation. I think maybe everything that had happened brought it into focus, the way these times of crisis do. It's what everybody does when they think their time might be up, isn't it? They call the people they love and tell them that they love them. She did that with me. Out of the blue. And she said that about you. That she loved you, and wanted to be with you for as long as she could.'

He couldn't speak. A sound like a sob came out of him, but that was all. Janice said, 'Don't be late. If there's one thing I am going to hang onto, it's putting food on the table at regular times.' She finished the call, and he put his phone down and stared at the text on his computer screen as if he'd never laid eyes on either screen or text before.

The work he had been doing suddenly seemed nonsensical and pointless, although of course it wasn't because the work meant money and he still needed that, and so would Billy. He got up from the kitchen table where he had been working – on hot days, it was the coolest place in the flat he was renting – and went out through the French windows in the living room to the small patio that was the flat's only outdoor space, and gave onto a grass verge leading to the road that curved round the building. The road was quiet, and the sky overhead was still blue. He looked up at the shapes of the clouds and reminded himself to breathe.

But it seemed so unfair that he still could, when Callie could not.

How was it possible that all this was still going on – the green trees in other gardens, the blackbird that was eyeing him and coming closer to him now because he was so still, the big bumblebee circling with mysterious purpose, not alighting anywhere but following a path that no doubt made perfect sense? How could the world still be there, still filled with life, and yet Callie would never see any of it again?

And how could he have been cheated of so much time, only to find her at the end and then lose her again?

Had he cheated himself? The brutality of it twisted his heart as if it was being squeezed dry by an iron fist. How had he drifted through so many days and weeks without fighting his way back to the woman and child he should have been with all along?

Somehow he stumbled through those first, nightmarish days, when they were all still in shock but there were practical decisions that had to be made, and work to be done. There was the outside world of formalities and choices and arrangements, which Janice took on the brunt of, though she increasingly turned to him for help. And then there was the inner world of what he supposed was grief, although the word didn't seem to do justice to the anguish and the remorse he felt.

He chose not to see Callie's body. He wanted to remember her as she had been, right up until that last goodbye. Janice told him that she looked calm and peaceful. He wasn't sure whether she was saying that to be kind to him because she already knew that he couldn't face seeing the woman he had loved in death. But he made an effort to believe her.

The summer days went by, each one, if anything, brighter and more beautiful than the next, and he felt guilty for being able to witness them. He came to think of grief as the grey thief – it had stolen his happiness, and had left him unable to find joy in the colours he knew he was blessed to still be able to see.

He spent the night before the funeral alone in his flat in Kettlebridge, and tried to comfort himself with the knowledge that Billy would be well looked after with Janice and Ron. He still could not quite believe what he was going to have to go through the following day, and yet he also knew he would get through it somehow, and it would pass and it was all inexorable.

In just a few weeks, they'd all moved so far from the world as it had been when Callie was still in it. How remorseless time was, and how quickly it opened up distance between you and the person you had loved and lost, who was now rooted in the past and could not reach you.

He thought of the old legends of the Greeks, of the dark river of the underworld and the ferryman who took the dead to the other side. It seemed to him that was how it was, and that the story was as true as anything else as a way of conveying the helplessness and sorrow of it.

That night he dreamed he was standing with Callie next to a river, their river, where they had gone the day she told him Billy was his son, in the watery shadow under the bridge. It was twilight, and she was looking up at him with those green eyes that had always seemed to want to tell him something. Maybe that was how the dead always appeared in dreams. As if they wanted to speak, but no longer could.

At the funeral he sat with Billy next to him and Janice on Billy's other side, with Ron sitting next to her. Billy was very still. All through the time since Callie's death he had reminded Reuben of some frail little creature frozen by the sudden onset of winter, like a tiny bird found on the ground with its wings and talons rigid with frost. Reuben was glad of Janice being close by, and grateful for her energy and stubbornness. Janice would never accept that everything was over, and that misery and defeat had won.

He imagined Billy being drawn towards her by her warmth, leaning against her, and how she would thaw him. And he thought it was right that Billy should stay with Janice and Ron, as long as he could see him often and be part of his life. Surely between them they would be able to give Billy what he needed: a home, a family, knowing who he was and where he came from. A background and an upbringing that one day, in seven years or ten or more, Billy would be ready to leave behind him, and that would give him enough strength and self-belief to be able to do that, and to step out into the unknown.

Reuben had not had a hand in choosing any of the funeral music. He had left all of that to Janice. The service finished with a piano piece which had a sort of ruthless orderly poignancy that was tragic in its way, and rose and fell and ended as if it had always been heading towards that particular conclusion. Something in it touched him so that he couldn't hold back any longer. Not that he had even realised he'd been holding back. And then he was completely lost. He cried in a way that men are not supposed to, messily and without control or dignity.

Gradually he became aware of Billy's small thin hand reaching across and resting very lightly on his back, and Billy's small voice saying, 'It'll be all right, Dad. Don't worry.' And this astonished him almost more than anything else, that the child he'd conceived and then abandoned and neglected for more than a decade, because of cowardliness and a lie and a mistake, was here beside him and trying to comfort him.

Janice reached out with a tissue and he took it, and their eyes met briefly and he saw in her face the urgency of her concern for him and that she didn't blame him. Something left him then that he hadn't realised he had been carrying, a deep disgust and contempt for himself and a sense of his own failure, and passed away from him like an exorcism. He took a deep breath and told himself that he was allowed to live, and was meant to.

When they stood to file out Ron reached out to shake his hand and tell him how sorry he was, and he saw that he'd been crying. Emily, Callie's stepsister who he hadn't seen for years, was red-eyed too, and startled him by reaching out to embrace him. Then she walked ahead with Ron, and he paused in front of Callie's coffin and Janice stood beside him with Billy.

Janice reached out and touched his arm and he saw how

hard she'd been crying, and that her make-up had blurred and
smudged around her eyes and she'd barely bothered to wipe it.
Her mouth quivered and he knew she wanted to say something
comforting but couldn't bring herself to speak because if she
did, she was going to burst into tears again. So the three of them
stood there in silence, and he closed his eyes and conjured up
the memory of Callie as she'd appeared to him in his dream of
her at twilight by the bridge over the river, her green eyes fixed
on his face as if she wanted to tell him something.

What would he say if he could speak to her now?

I love you, he thought. *I always did and I always will. I'm
sorry I let you down. I promise I will do everything in my power
to do right by our son.*

He opened his eyes and the vision of her vanished and he
was in front of her coffin again. He turned and looked down at
Billy and said quietly, 'Ready?'

Billy nodded. 'Ready.'

Billy reached out to touch the coffin, just lightly and glanc-
ingly, as if maybe it had some kind of magical power, or as if
touch might be able to connect him to his mother in a way that
words would not. And then, unthinkingly, Reuben took Billy's
hand. They'd never held hands before. They walked slowly on
together, while Janice lingered behind for a moment. He
thought he heard her say goodbye, and then she followed them
out to the small courtyard where the flowers from him and Billy
and Janice and Ron had been set out for people to look at before
going on to the wake. White roses, pink roses, red roses. The red
from him.

At Janice's suggestion, they'd invited other mourners to
make a donation to charity rather than send flowers. Billy had
chosen the charity, which supported music education for children and young people: 'Because she sometimes said she'd like
to get me lessons,' he had explained. 'But it would have been
very expensive.' And Reuben had felt bad about that – because

he could have helped to pay for lessons, if he'd known – and then worse, because it made him think of his dad, and what his dad had done. But his heart was so heavy that a fresh dose of remorse barely registered.

At the wake people came up to him and spoke to him and none of them seemed quite real and he couldn't quite take in what they were saying, but he understood and accepted the kindness of their intentions. There was Laurel, red-lipsticked in a black suit, and Henry, slightly scruffy as ever. *Sincere condolences. Best wishes. Anything we can do to help.* Sonia, anxious and nervy and sincere, and Julian, standing at a slightly formal distance. Emily, who was sweet, open-faced, straightforward-seeming, someone who it was hard to imagine ever harbouring secrets. The sort of person you would be happy to have as a babysitter for your child. *I'm so sorry. I never knew her well.* 'I think she was sorry about that too,' he said, and Emily looked startled and then shaken and then relieved, and he realised that comfort was something he had to give as well as something he was in desperate need of.

The day after the funeral he took Billy walking, all the way from the centre of the town past the bridge where he had walked with Callie, with the scene of Billy's fall near the tracks on the far side, and on towards the village upriver where he had grown up and where Billy now lived with Janice and Ron. The walk took them a couple of hours and for most of it they didn't see anybody. The river moved in long, lazy, indirect curves, taking its time, weaving through woods and fields, lined here and there with beds of reeds where dragonflies darted and startling white flowers grew. They didn't talk at all. They just trudged on. And the act of putting one foot in front of the other, and keeping going, was another kind of exorcism.

He felt Callie's presence then, not as a remembered personality but as something benign and mysterious that it wasn't possible to grasp or identify, but that could be absorbed like sunlight and remembered like the sound of rain falling at night. He still felt the loss of her like something that had been taken out of him that could never be replaced, and as the bitterest of all regrets: a path he'd taken too late. But he began to see that it really might be possible to survive her, and to learn to live with the years of his mistake.

There had been so much waste, and yet here he was, with Billy, when he might not have been here at all. He'd had so little time with Callie, and yet perhaps it had just been enough.

He tried to conjure up the precise memory of her face and voice, as if she was there with him, and he couldn't. Not exactly. He had the essence of her, the way she would appear to him in a dream, but there was a slight fogginess there already, as if she was beginning to dissolve. And then he felt a different kind of grief: the grief of forgetting, which is a kind of letting go.

That night he dreamed that he was sitting alone on a bench in a graveyard, and she came to him and sat quietly next to him. He had no idea how long she would remain with him and started talking very quickly, afraid that she would vanish.

He said, 'I wish you could have stayed. I wish it with all my heart. I wish we could have spent more time together. There were so many conversations we could have had. So many places to go. So many meals we should have eaten together. And all the nights we should have slept through. Billy misses you terribly. So does Janice. We all love you so much.'

She inclined her head and he took it as a sign that she had heard. He turned to look at her and she faced him and he saw that she felt sorry for him, but not for herself. Then she reached out with a warm hand and squeezed his, and he heard from somewhere a faint refrain, a falling sequence of piano notes played over and over again, and then she was gone.

FORTY

The day after Callie's funeral he had looked online and ordered a keyboard and a stand for it. When it arrived it took him a day or two to get round to unpacking it. Finally, he set it up and plugged it in, brought over a chair and sat down in front of it.

A sequence of notes. Scales. The building blocks of every melody. Could he still remember them? He wasn't sure. He wouldn't know until he allowed himself to begin.

He let his fingers rest on the keys and began to play. Stopped. Started again. It was still there, somewhere deep in his memory, locked away in his body. The body doesn't forget, even if sometimes the mind wills it to. He still knew how to play. The years that had gone by since he gave up didn't mean that everything had been undone: it just meant that he was rusty, and the skills he'd learned were undeveloped. But he hadn't lost everything. There was something there still.

After that he asked round for a teacher. Janice, Laurel and Sonia, between them, probably knew someone who knew just about everyone in Kettlebridge and the villages around it. He was given recommendations, and found someone who lived close by. She was a patient, motherly woman whose approach to teaching him was to be quietly encouraging, and was therefore the precise opposite of what his dad's had been.

And somehow practising and playing helped to see him through the next, awful phase of grief. Janice and Emily shouldered the worst of the business of tying up Callie's affairs – settling Billy with Janice and Ron, sorting through Callie's things, dealing with a solicitor about Billy's inheritance and care given that Callie had died without making a will, and finally, painfully, preparing to sell her flat so that the money could be set aside for Billy when he reached adulthood. When Janice was going through Callie's papers she found the note Reuben had written to her, asking if they could meet, and returned it to him. At first he thought that would break him. But then he realised that he was glad she had kept it, and that meant he had to be grateful to have it back. He was grateful, too, that he had not been the one to find it.

Janice left her job to work through it all and focus on Billy. Ron seemed to struggle a little with her being so preoccupied, but perked up after Emily intervened and had a word with him, and Janice let him go away on a fortnight's golfing holiday to Spain with his friends. Reuben saw how Janice's fondness for her stepdaughter, which Callie had found so difficult to accept, was going to help to steady Billy's new life with his grandparents, and keep Ron in line.

Billy had not really wanted to go back into the flat on Goosegreen Close without Callie there, and Reuben felt the same way. But he forced himself back to say goodbye. The last time he looked around at it, all empty and bare, he was struck both by its slight shabbiness and its atmosphere of having been beloved. The sofa where he and Billy and Callie had sat together, and where Callie had slept for so many years, had already gone. But the tired old living room carpet, the avocado bathroom suite and the ancient white goods in the kitchen were all still there, and there was a butterfly flitting around above the long grass in the garden. The whole place was filled with the sweet, unbearable weight of the past.

But then he pulled himself together and retreated, knowing that he would never go back. He told himself the flat had been a backdrop only, and with neither Callie nor Billy there it had become a husk of a place, its future in the balance, poised between being the refuge it had been for one little family and the potential it still had to be a home for somebody else.

That evening he went to Janice's house and asked Billy to show him what he'd told him he'd seen, the words Callie had written all those years ago underneath the windowsill. There it was: *Callie 4 Reuben 4 ever*. He looked out from Billy's bedroom window and saw the window of his own old room with the tendrils of ivy licking their way across it. It was time to sort the place out. Somehow, he would have to persuade his dad to agree.

Theresa had finally packed her bags and moved out soon after Callie's funeral. As she had said when she told Reuben she was going, there was never going to be a good time. *I've got the rest of my life ahead of me,* she had said. *I can't put all that on hold just because someone I don't love any more happens to be in a bad way.*

She hadn't gone far – she'd got together with someone local, and had moved in with him. Reuben had seen her in the village soon after she'd left his dad, waiting in the queue at the post office, and she'd acknowledged him but rather distantly, as if he belonged to a part of her past that she was quite happy to have put behind her.

At the time, Reuben had been so wrung out by grief he'd been unable to muster much of a reaction to her departure, other than numbness and resignation, and a vague sense of dread about what it meant for the future. With Theresa gone, it had become much more obvious that his dad was struggling to cope, and that his decline was accelerating.

Reuben could see his dad's future, one in which his life would shrink and his capacity to act on his own behalf would be gradually eroded, a future that would be both smaller and more confusing than the present. And sometimes he thought his dad could see that too, and that it frightened him.

Often, when Reuben went round, his dad had the put-upon, plaintive expression of a child who feels hard done by, as if suffering from an unjust punishment inflicted by the grown-ups. Sometimes he talked about Theresa as if he expected her to return. Reuben couldn't help but feel sorry for him, and he carried on calling in on him, even though, on bad days, he still felt coldly and violently angry with him for what he'd done to Callie, and to them all. But even so, he couldn't bring himself to hand his dad over entirely to the professional carers who had started going in.

His dad would still sometimes go and sit at the piano and move his hands over the keys, but the music came out in little fragments and drifts rather than whole pieces, as if it was a language whose words he was beginning to forget. From time to time he would peer at his old sheet music as if it now made no sense to him at all. Then he would turn and notice Reuben watching him, and frown, and ask him what he was doing there, and why he was watching him. He clearly understood that Reuben was not comfortable with him, and once or twice Reuben thought that maybe he remembered why.

Every now and then he asked why Reuben went so often to visit the house across the road, and sometimes he mentioned Callie or Billy, but Reuben made a point of not reacting or explaining. It was easier – maybe for both of them – if he distracted his dad by putting on the radio, or by picking some-thing out of the large collection of classical records in the living room and putting it on the turntable. His dad might have begun to lose his old fluency at the piano, but listening to music still absorbed him in a way that nothing else did.

Finally, in December, Reuben was invited to come with Billy to Emily's wedding, and found himself once again standing on the edge of a celebration, watching the whirl of people drinking and dancing.

Billy, unexpectedly grown-up in his suit, seemed to be enjoying himself. It was good to see him happy – he'd been so quiet for so long. But then, when the evening disco got under way, Reuben spotted him sitting by the dance floor and yawning, and asked if he was ready to go. Billy said he was, so after they'd said a round of the necessary goodbyes they walked out into the cold of the night and found Reuben's car, and Reuben drove them back to his flat.

This was to be the first time Billy had ever stayed overnight with him, and he'd gone overboard on the preparations. His flat only had one bedroom so he'd got that ready for Billy to sleep in, while he was going to sleep on the sofa – which instantly made him think of Callie. So had going to the wedding, though he had not mentioned this to Billy. There were so many things that reminded him of her, but it usually seemed best to keep that to himself.

He'd got a Christmas tree and put it up in the living room and decorated it, which was the first time he'd ever done that. Billy's present was already waiting underneath it – a guitar, which was something Billy had asked for, and which Janice had slightly reluctantly agreed would be OK for Reuben to get. Billy sometimes liked to sit and play on Reuben's keyboard, and Reuben had suggested that he might like his own, along with lessons so he could learn to play it properly, but Billy had preferred the idea of learning the guitar. Reuben couldn't play himself, and found the idea of his son being able to do something he didn't know how to do, but would have secretly liked to learn, strangely satisfying.

Billy went off to take off his suit and hang it up and have a bath, and Reuben got into his jogging bottoms and an old shirt and jumper and slippers, the clothes he wore to work from home when he knew he wasn't going to see anybody. He made them both hot chocolate, and both of them tried not to yawn as they finished it.

'Could we watch some telly?' Billy said hopefully.

'I think it might be bedtime,' Reuben said, although it would have been nice to have Billy's company a little longer. But Billy looked exhausted, and it was obvious he needed to crash out. 'We can watch telly tomorrow.'

Billy got to his feet. 'OK,' he said, as if Reuben's answer was exactly what he had expected, and was the sort of dull, sensible thing a parent was bound to say. 'It was a good day today. I think I quite like weddings.'

'It's a long time since I've been to one,' Reuben said. 'But I agree with you. I like them too. Apart from anything else, it's nice to see people dancing.'

Billy pulled a face. 'I'm not so sure about that,' he said, and then went off to brush his teeth and go to bed.

Right on cue, a message arrived from Janice on his phone to ask if Billy was OK, and Reuben replied to say, *Yes, fine, in bed now. How's the wedding going?* Janice didn't reply immediately, but once Reuben had finished clearing up the kitchen another message came through: *All good. I think Ron and I are going to be the last ones standing.*

Of course Ron, the proud dad, had been in his element all through the day. But Reuben had been sitting next to Janice during the ceremony, and right at the end, he'd turned to her and had seen that she was crying, and had known that she was thinking of Callie, whose wedding she would never see. He'd reached out and held her, and had thought of his mum and all the times he had missed her. How strange it was, the way people you thought you had lost came back to you in other people, years later, at times that you could neither control nor predict.

Alone in his flat with his sleeping son, he felt all the more acutely the particular sense of responsibility that goes with looking after a defenceless child on your own. Callie must have felt like this day in, day out. He could see how it had given her a sense of purpose, how it was both a form of pressure and a kind of drive. He wondered if he would ever get used to it. Perhaps, if he sold his London flat and could find the right place for the right price here, Billy could have his own room and come to him for weekends, if Janice agreed. He could give Billy another home, and be as much of a dad to him as it was possible for him to be, given all that they'd already missed, over the years ahead.

What would it be like to be Billy's parent when he was a teenager? When he was twenty, twenty-five, forty? Callie would never know. And that thought hurt him like someone had just blown a hole through his heart. At the same time it made him absolutely, furiously, rigidly determined, with a mixture of anger and grief and love that was perhaps more powerful than anything he'd ever felt, to stick around.

He went off to find his coat and hat, carefully slid the French doors open and stepped out of the living room onto the little patio.

It wasn't that long since he'd stopped smoking. He'd cut down in those last days that he'd spent with Callie because she didn't like it and didn't want Billy breathing in second-hand smoke. After Callie's death, he'd indulged in the habit as if it was the only thing keeping him going – it seemed marginally safer than turning to drink – but then Billy had commented on the smell and he'd finally been ashamed enough of himself to force himself to quit. Even so, he still liked to follow some of his old rituals, like stepping outside first thing in the morning and last thing at night, even if he didn't have the cigarette to go with it.

There was something to be said for taking a minute, once or twice a day, to stand outside and breathe in the air. It was a way of marking time or perhaps of slowing it down – he wasn't quite sure which.

The grass beyond the small paved area of the patio was already stiff and white with frost. It was very quiet, and even the distant sound of traffic on the nearest main road was subdued. But the windows of the house opposite were glowing behind drawn curtains, and there were shining white bulbs wound round the charcoal-black branches of the leafless tree in its front garden. It looked like a tree from a fairy tale, the kind that might have the power to grant wishes.

Something flitted past – perhaps a bat? – and an owl hooted, startlingly loud. He looked up at the starlit sky and the plume of his milky breath rose towards it.

He imagined Callie coming out, slipping her arm through his, saying something about the wedding – '*It went off well, didn't it? Billy seemed to enjoy himself. And who'd have thought Mum and Ron would dominate the dance floor the way they did?*'

It was so real it was like a hallucination, as vivid as the times she had come to him in dreams. He wondered if he was losing his mind but was grateful to see her anyway. He could almost feel the warmth of her touch and see her breath.

'*What a beautiful night,*' he heard her say, her voice as light and clear as if she really was standing right next to him. '*It's going to be a cold one. It's amazing how the more you look at the stars, the more you see and the brighter they seem.*'

And then she really was gone, and he found himself alone again.

Except he wasn't, because he had Billy.

He turned his back on the cold, starlit night, stepped back inside and closed the French windows. He drew the curtain to keep out the dark, and retreated gratefully back into the warmth and brightness of the living room.

FORTY-ONE

CALLIE

Five months earlier

Summer 2014

On the day of the operation, as Reuben sat next to her in the waiting room, time slowed to the ticking of a clock.

She was famished and thirsty and violently anxious, and at the same time she felt weirdly and completely calm. Everything was surreal. Everything was magical and precious, almost unbearably so – every bit of dust dancing in the sunlight, each look, each breath. Everything mattered. Right there, in the waiting room, and all around them.

Why was it that you only ever understood what you had, and what you'd been given, when it was possible that you might be about to lose it?

She thought of Billy, perhaps reading or watching TV or playing a card game with her mum, trying to be brave. And then she remembered the very first time she'd held him, and going further back, the first time she had felt him move, that fluttering in the womb, and she thought what a privilege it was to have been that close to someone, and to have seen them grow and change before they even knew what change was.

And she thought of Mum, and what she'd said in the hospital – that they couldn't afford to be estranged any more – and of how it had felt to be held by her, after such a long time. She thought of her dad, and of his bright eyes and how pleased he'd looked after listening to her playing the piano he'd given her. And she thought how lucky she had always been, and she was so grateful and glad for all of it that it was like being lit up inside, and it was impossible to worry about the operation any more.

When the nurse came to tell her it was time, and she got up to go with her, she knew Reuben was watching her all the way. She turned back just before she reached the door and smiled at him and gave him a little wave.

'Thank you,' she said, and blew him a kiss. Then, because he looked like a man who needed to be entrusted with a task to keep his mind off things, 'Take care of Billy, OK? Maybe you could take him out for dinner tonight.'

He nodded and tried to smile but looked absolutely forsaken, like someone whose whole world has been stolen away from them. As she walked away she felt much sorrier for him than for herself.

It would be good for him to take Billy out. She hoped he would. It would be good for both of them. Mum wouldn't object, would she? Not if Reuben said she'd suggested it. And after all, she already knew the two of them could get along just fine without her.

All they needed was a bit more time together to get used to each other. Thank goodness, they could have that. It wasn't too late. There was still so much ahead of them. They had all the time in the world.

EPILOGUE

JANICE

2019

Janice wasn't at all sure it was a good idea. You had to keep moving forward, and not allow yourself to go back. Like a shark. Was that really how sharks behaved? In any case, it was what you had to do. Otherwise the past would drown you. She didn't believe in therapy or any of that stuff, which was just a way for people to make money out of other people's misery. You might as well talk to the wall, and then go and buy yourself a nice blouse. That was her approach, anyway. And she had lost a husband and a daughter, so she knew a few things about getting through the kind of losses that made you feel as if the world had ended. And that hurt so much, you wouldn't be capable of caring if it did.

But Reuben, the son-in-law she should have had, took a different view. He sometimes chose to look back. And so did Billy, the light of her life and the apple of her eye, her only grandson. So tall now. And handsome too! 'The girls'll be after him,' she'd said warningly to his father. 'You'd better watch out.'

'I think he can look out for himself, Janice,' Reuben had

said, in that tone of voice which meant that he hadn't made even a token effort to take what she'd said on board.

It was funny how people had selective memories. She wasn't one for contemplating old wounds, but even she remembered how, not that long ago, Billy had fallen victim to a couple of nasty little toe-rags who'd messed around with him near a railway line. Yes, he was bigger and more confident now. But dealing with girls was a whole different ball game, anyway.

Well, she was prepared to look out for him even if his dad wasn't.

Oh, but Billy was a delight! She couldn't help but feel sorry for her friends, sometimes, who had grandchildren who weren't quite as wonderful in every way as Billy was. So charming, so thoughtful. So *nice*. Even as a teenager. Ron had actually had some problems adjusting, in the beginning – didn't like playing second fiddle – and she had been forced to make it clear to him that if it came down to a choice between him and Billy, Billy would win hands down, every time. The trick with Ron was to get him out of the house. The other trick was to make him feel important, but that was difficult sometimes when she was wrapped up in making sure Billy had everything he needed.

Anyway, their marriage had survived, and it had helped when Emily had a baby. A girl, who she had named after Callie, known in the family as Little Callie, for now, though maybe that would change when she got big. Or maybe not. And luckily Little Callie was one of those babies who seems born to charm a family and bring it back together, a round-faced, beaming, genuine bundle of joy. One of her favourite photographs ever was of Billy holding Little Callie, who was smiling up at him.

'He'll make a wonderful dad one day,' she'd said to Reuben. 'You can see it already.'

And Reuben had said, 'Yeah, you're probably right. Don't know where he gets that from.'

She'd said, 'Oh, stop fishing,' but afterwards Reuben's

throwaway comment bothered her. It seemed like he might still be beating himself up for having been absent for most of Billy's childhood, and what was the point of that? She could do the same, if she let herself. She'd missed out too. But what was the point? There was nothing either of them could do about it now.

You couldn't go back. Which was why she wasn't at all sure about going to the beach. She'd heard about this beach before – Billy had mentioned it, once or twice, as a place he remembered going with both his parents, just before they lost Callie. It had been clear to her that Billy wanted to go back, and equally clear that Reuben wasn't ready. And then, all of a sudden, five years had gone by since they'd lost Callie. Which was hard to believe, except it wasn't, because she had so much more white in her hair (and even in her eyebrows, although she tinted them) and Billy had shot up and was almost a young man, and even Reuben was beginning to show the signs of middle age.

He hadn't put on weight, but his hair was thinning just a little, compared to how she remembered it. Plus he'd taken up birdwatching. She'd said to him, half joking, that she wasn't sure whether that would improve his chances of finding a girlfriend, and he'd said to her, not joking at all, that he didn't care.

It was Reuben who had told her he was taking Billy back to the beach, and that Billy had told him he'd like her to come too.

'I think Billy wants to do this as a way to remember her,' he'd said, with that special softness and wistfulness to his voice that he always had when he talked about Callie.

He'd not been involved with anybody else since. Not as far as she knew. Not in all that time. She'd hoped that he might meet someone nice, someone who would remind him that he still had plenty of life left to live, and that it really was possible to keep on living (and loving) after losing someone. After all, he was still young. But he seemed not to be interested. Perhaps, in a way, it made his life more straightforward. Anyway, there was still time.

How could she have said no to the beach, under the circumstances? She didn't really want to go. She knew it would be upsetting. But if Billy wanted her there... She said yes, of course she would join them.

'But if it's pouring with rain, I'm not walking on the beach. You can leave me in the pub,' she told Reuben, and again, she was only half joking.

As it turned out, the day they'd agreed on for the outing was a beautiful one. The only problem was, once they got to the beach and walked out across the sand, she began to think of Callie, and it hurt. It was almost unbearable. She tried to focus on the view of the English Channel stretching towards the horizon, calm and almost unruffled by waves, with one or two big boats in the distance, too far away for it to be easy to make out their shapes. Container ships, maybe. But still she couldn't shake the feeling that if she turned round quickly enough, she might just catch a glimpse of her daughter out of the corner of her eye, briefly and impossibly back among the living, as if she'd never gone away.

Billy went down to the water's edge, took off his socks and trainers and went in for a paddle. She kept her distance from the water – she wasn't all that keen on getting wet, as it always made her hair go wild – and settled on the sand some way back from the shore. Reuben came over and sat next to her, and she dug her hand into the sand and then let it trickle through her fingers as they watched Billy together.

'Nice beach,' she commented. 'Not too crowded.'

'Yeah. It's a good place.'

She sneaked a glimpse at his face in profile. He looked sad, but not on the edge of losing it completely. She decided it would be all right to broach the subject of his dad, who had passed away in a care home a couple of months earlier.

'So how are you? Are you bearing up all right? After losing your dad, I mean.'

'I try not to think about him, to be honest,' Reuben said. 'He wasn't in a good way at the end, as you know. It seemed like a mercy when he went, really.' He kept his eyes on Billy as he said, 'I never knew what to say to him, even when I knew he could understand me. Not once I knew what he'd done to Callie.'

'What he'd done...? What do you mean, what he'd done to her?'

Reuben shot a quick look at her. 'So she never did tell you. I've often wondered. But I didn't want to bring it up.' He turned back towards Billy. 'Made me feel awful, I guess. Still does.'

'Reuben... what are you talking about?'

'He assaulted her,' Reuben said. 'The day after Sonia's wedding. The morning after we... after I spent the night with her, at your house.' He cleared his throat apologetically. 'I left, and she went over the road to see if I was there, and my dad, he...' He swallowed. 'Well,' he said. 'I came back and walked in on them and her lipstick was smudged and her clothes were half undone. I thought it was obvious what had been going on. I was wrong. And she didn't want to tell me. She felt for me losing my mum, and she didn't want me to lose my dad too. But the way it turned out, I lost him then anyway. Or as good as. Perhaps there wasn't all that much to lose. He never liked me much. But that can feel like a kind of closeness, in a way. Anyway, she didn't tell me what had really happened until years later. Until she had that accident, when she got hit by Ethan Byers on his bike. And you called me and I came back. Just goes to show, accidents aren't always disasters.'

'But no,' Janice heard herself say. 'That's not...'

She made an effort to pull herself together. The sun was still shining but it felt as if a thick fog had descended from nowhere, and she could no longer tell what was real and what was not.

'That's not what she told me,' she said, as clearly as she could.

'It's not what she told you? Or it's not what she let you believe?'

She didn't answer. She couldn't. The only sound was the rustle and suck of waves on sand. She stared at the sea and Billy standing in it, looking out at the horizon. It was like looking at a photo from long ago, a collection of abstract shapes, the splash of a red T-shirt and a shock of dark hair against the wash of blues fading into the sky. Then it was Billy again, her beloved grandson, her lost daughter's only child.

Suddenly she found herself able to speak again.

'One of the neighbours told me she'd seen her that morning, coming back from your dad's house. We fought about it when I went over for Billy's first birthday. I said terrible things to her. Harsh things. I'm ashamed of them now. But she never said anything to me about... that. About what you just said. Why would she lie... about something like that? Why wouldn't she have told me? I'm her mum, for heaven's sake. Why would she cover for him?'

Reuben still didn't answer. Janice closed her eyes and covered her face with her hands. She felt the pain of the truth lodge somewhere under her breastbone and begin to spread as if it was being pushed through her blood by each beat of her heart. Then she took her hands away and looked up again.

'How *dare* he,' she said. 'If I'd have known I'd have *killed* him. That dirty old man...' She stopped. 'I'm sorry, Reuben, I know he was your father... but still.'

'Believe me, there have been times when I felt the same myself,' Reuben said. 'I was so angry with him. But I think the part of him that remembered it just wanted to shrug it off. I don't think he ever thought he'd done anything wrong.'

Janice tucked up her knees under her chin and wrapped her arms round them. If only she could go back. If only. But it was too late. The sea seemed to hear the words and whisper them back to her: *too late... too late... too late...*

'I was awful to her,' she said. 'And now I can't even say sorry.'

Reuben reached out and touched her lightly on the arm. 'Don't be too hard on yourself,' he said. 'That's the last thing she would have wanted. Whatever you said, she forgave you. She loved you. And she learned so much from you. Pretty much everything she knew.'

'That's definitely not true,' Janice said. She could feel tears gathering in her eyes, and the pain in her chest still expanding outwards, turning into an ache that was like a hunger that could never be fulfilled.

Too late... too late... too late...

'It *is* true,' Reuben said patiently. 'Where did she learn to be such a good mum from, if not from you?'

Then she wept, and she couldn't stop. He passed her a handkerchief, said soothing words she couldn't hear. She kept on crying. Very gradually she became aware of someone else sitting patiently on her other side, waiting for her to stop.

'Callie,' she said, suddenly filled with hope.

Callie as a baby, smiling, showing off her one tooth. A little girl, delighted with her party dress. Playing that piano. Singing in the morning. Such a happy child. It wasn't possible that she'd gone. It had to be a mistake, this whole business of five years having passed by without her. A terrible mistake. How could she possibly just have disappeared?

'Granny,' she heard Billy say. 'We're here, Granny. We'll look after you.'

She straightened up and wiped her eyes. The image she'd conjured up of Callie dissolved, and there was Billy, sitting close by, watching her with real anxiety in his eyes.

He reached out and she let him and then he was holding her and she was still crying, and the pain inside her began to soften. By and by she was able to breathe calmly and quietly again, and then Billy let her go and she was able to say, 'I'm sorry. I don't normally... I don't like to make an exhibition of myself like that.'

'Don't be silly,' Billy said sternly. 'Of course you're upset. Why wouldn't you be upset? Tell you what, I think we should go find a café and get you a nice cup of tea and something to eat.'

'Or a stiff drink,' Janice said hopefully.

She got to her feet – Reuben offered her a hand, but she didn't need it – and the three of them turned their backs on the sea and set off together towards the promenade that ran along the beach.

She felt as if she was being lifted up, as if the warmth of the sun and the love they all still felt for Callie was combining somehow to console her. And she knew then that Reuben was right, and whatever she'd said or done had been forgiven long ago. She knew this because the sea kept on making the same gentle sound, over and over, but there were no words to it, and no reproach. There was nothing but rhythm, like the sound of a beating heart or the slow breathing of a sleeping child, endlessly repeated and reassuring.

A LETTER FROM ALI

Thank you for choosing to read *A Child's Goodbye*. If you would like to keep up to date with all my newest releases just sign up at the following link. Your email address will never be shared and you can unsubscribe at any time.

www.bookouture.com/ali-mercer

Who's going to look after your child if, for one reason or another, you are unable to? The main theme of *A Child's Goodbye* is a question that is close to my heart. My son, who is now fifteen, is autistic and has a learning disability, and my other half and I have always worried about what will happen to him when we're not around. We have a supportive family and have started to put some practical arrangements in place, but still the dread remains. The job of a parent is to make yourself redundant, but with our son, we're just at the beginning of figuring out how to get there.

I grew up in a family headed by a lone parent, my mum, while my dad lived abroad. I vividly remember – maybe you can recall a similar experience – how appalled I was the day I figured out that eventually my mum was going to die. Perhaps I couldn't quite believe it. I was still quite little, perhaps five or six. I don't know exactly how I phrased the question when I asked her about it, but I do remember her answer. 'Oh, you don't need to worry about that,' she said briskly. 'I'm going to live for years and years yet.' This turned out to be true. It also comforted me straight away, because it seemed to me there was no point getting upset about such an unimaginably distant event, however devastating it might be.

Like Billy in *A Child's Goodbye*, I was an anxious child. I felt that the world around me was unpredictable and unstable, however safe it appeared, and could easily give way to something more threatening. My son is sometimes anxious too, especially when it's difficult for him to process what's happening to him and to understand what's coming next. Since the onset of the pandemic I've heard about numerous children and young people who have struggled with high levels of anxiety, and the toll this has taken on them and their families. If that strikes a chord with you, you have my sympathy and very best wishes for more settled times ahead.

What happens when your mum can't be there for you, and who, or what, can help to fill the gap a loved one leaves? This question is at the heart of *A Child's Goodbye*, and it's also a theme I touched on in *Lost Daughter*, the first of my novels to be published by Bookouture (*A Child's Goodbye* is the sixth). In *Lost Daughter*, Viv worries about her son Aidan, who has a learning disability and is now middle-aged. Who will visit him in his care home when she is no longer able to? As in *A Child's Goodbye*, it turns out that answers to painful questions can sometimes be found in unexpected places. For Viv and Aidan, a newfound friend makes all the difference. For Callie in *A Child's Goodbye*, facing up to the past is the key to her son's future.

One of the things that helps me keep anxiety at bay is reading. There's always a book to turn to in the middle of the night when you can't sleep. Maybe that's true for you, too. I really hope this novel has touched you and taken you out of yourself. If you enjoyed it, I'd be very grateful if you could rate it on Amazon, and if you have time, leave a short review (one line is fine!) It all helps other people to discover the book.

Thank you so much for reading *A Child's Goodbye*. Do get in touch with me on Instagram or Twitter, or via my author Facebook page – I'd love to hear from you!

Love to you and yours,

Ali Mercer

www.alimercerwriter.com

facebook.com/AliMercerwriter

twitter.com/AlisonLMercer

instagram.com/alimercerwriter

ACKNOWLEDGEMENTS

Thank you so much to Kelsie Marsden, my brilliant editor, and to everybody at Bookouture. Thanks to Noelle Holten and the rest of the publicity team: Kim Nash, Sarah Hardy and Jess Readett. And thanks to Laura Gerrard, who has done such a great job of copy-editing this book.

Thank you to Judith Murdoch, my agent, and Rebecca Winfield, who handles my foreign rights.

Thank you to Dr James Grant, Dr Harriett Grant and Dr Candida Borsada, who generously gave their time to answer my questions about emergency medicine. Thank you to Sue Acton for helping with my research request. I'm also very grateful to Jennifer and Roger Lamboll for help with my questions about the police response to accidents. (Any errors are of course my own.)

In the heatwave summer of 2022, I was struggling to find childcare for my son so that I could carry on working on this novel. Two life-changing Oxfordshire charities that run holiday clubs came to the rescue: Yellow Submarine and the Parasol Project. I'm also grateful to the Bodleian Library for granting me a reader's card. It is a magical place for a writer to have access to.

Thanks to my family and friends. It was so good to be able to see more of you in 2022! Thanks to Helen Rumbelow and Nanu and Luli Segal, to whom this book is dedicated. Thank you to Neel Mukherjee. And thank you to my husband (who I first met more than twenty-two years ago! Where has the time gone?) and our children.

And finally, a huge and heartfelt thank you to all my readers. I'm very grateful for all your support.